CHAMPAGNE IN A BROKEN TEACUP

Adventures of a French résistante

CHAMPAGNE IN A BROKEN TEACUP

Adventures of a French résistante

*An historical novel inspired
by my aunt's wartime
activities*

Greg Duncan

Kenebec Media

www.kenebec.com/books

First published in Great Britain by Kenebec Media 2024

First Edition

Available as paperback, hard cover and Kindle e-book

Contents

This book is dedicated to those who in
World War II risked their lives to free
the world of Hitler's Nazi tyranny

ACKNOWLEDGEMENTS

I would like to acknowledge the help and assistance I have received
in producing this novel. On the research side Anic Nandrot of the
Resistance Museum in Nevers (Musée de la Résistance de Varennes-
Vauzelles) was particularly helpful in not only identifying which
buildings the Germans occupied in Nevers, but in supplying me with
pictures of copies of *Le Courrier de l'Air* as dropped by the RAF in
Nevers in March 1941. In this regard I also owe thanks to the Royal
Air Force Museum which was able supply me with scans of leaflets
dropped on Nevers. I would also like to record my appreciation of the
on-line access to historic newspapers provided by the National
Library of France which enabled me to read the actual daily
newspapers which my characters would have been reading in 1940
and 1941.

The *France Libre* pin used on the cover and front page was bought by
my French mother in Britain in 1941 in support of de Gaulle's Free
French Forces.

I have also received assistance, feedback and encouragement from
my friends in the Christchurch Writing Group in Dorset. In particular,
I would like to thank Caz Nolder for her comments on a draft version
of the book.

However, my greatest debt of gratitude is owed to my amazing wife,
Valerie, for her tireless support, extensive editorial contributions and
for her incredible patience and encouragement throughout the whole
project.

PREFACE

HISTORICAL CONTEXT

This fictional saga is set in the Second World War, partially in Paris and partially in the city of Nevers (pronounced *nev-air*). Although with hindsight we have the benefit of knowing what happened, the characters in the narrative obviously do not. I have, therefore, attempted to have the people learn and react as a consequence of what they would have been reading in the newspaper or hearing on French and BBC radio. In this respect, apart from researching through various sources, I have had access to photocopies of all pages of one of the main French daily newspapers (*Le Petit Parisien*) published during the relevant time period. I have also been able to read copies of some of the actual leaflets dropped on Nevers by the Royal Air Force and transcripts of speeches broadcast in French over the BBC.

My aunt, Marie-Thérèse Pellissier, was a document forger in the French resistance in Nevers.

WHAT THEY WOULD HAVE KNOWN IN MAY 1940

The characters in the story would have known that, although France and Britain both declared war on Germany on the 3rd of September 1939, there was very little land-based fighting in Western Europe until the spring of 1940. This period, from the 3rd of September 1939 to the 9th of May 1940 was colloquially referred to as the *'drôle de guerre'* (Phoney War). During this time the French felt they were secure from German invasion, protected by three defensive considerations – the heavily fortified Maginot Defensive Line, the perception that the dense Ardennes Forest was impenetrable and the assessment that, as neutral countries, Belgium and The Netherlands would act as a land barrier against invasion by Germany.

MAP OF FRANCE AFTER GERMAN OCCUPATION

Britain

Netherlands

DUNKERQUE

Belgium

Germany

English Channel

ARRAS

Luxembourg

• REIMS

• PARIS

• NANCY

• CHARTRES   • TROYES

Occupied Zone of France
(Under German control)

• NANTES

BOURGES

• DIJON

• NEVERS

Switzerland

MOULINS •

• VICHY

Atlantic Ocean

Unoccupied Zone
(Under French
Vichy Government)

GRENOBLE

Italy

• TOULOUSE

• MARSEILLE

Spain

Mediterranean Sea

| 0 | 100 | 200 Km |
| 0 | 50 | 100 Miles |

PART 1 - COURAGE

Chapter 1

Monday, 16 December 1940, Nevers, France.

The child's picture and his words have shocked and worried me, reminding me how much we are all at risk now – even innocent young children. If I was back in Paris I would know who to talk to about my concerns. But here? In Nevers?

I'm not saying I don't like being here. I do like being the art teacher in this primary school. I enjoy helping the children with their art. I just wasn't prepared for the answer Philippe gave when I asked if he'd drawn a pile of logs ready to go to the sawmill.

What was it he said? "They are not logs Mademoiselle. They are dead Germans piled in a heap. My uncle says all German soldiers deserve to be killed. So that's what I've drawn. Bang, bang, dead – pile them in a heap."

When he said those words I immediately stopped talking to him in case other children in the class heard our conversation and innocently repeated it to others. What if a Gestapo informant heard Philippe using such language? The consequences could be fatal for both the child, his uncle and his parents.

As soon as the lunch break starts I leave the classroom, go outside and sit on my own in the hope the cold December air will help me focus my thoughts. It still worries me just thinking of his words and how he might repeat them to other people. But should I become involved? Can I really make any difference?

It's only been a couple of months since I escaped from Paris and I still feel quite alone. Although I've grown to like Nevers I

3

would not have chosen to hide in this small provincial town in the occupied part of France, but then I wasn't given much choice. And right now, today, I have no one with whom I can discuss my worries about Philippe. The writing teacher, Françoise Deferre, has become a good friend and I could have talked to her but she's not here today. And there's no one else I feel I can fully trust.

As I look up I realize I may have chosen the wrong place to sit because I see Philippe walking towards me holding his drawing.

"Mademoiselle. You liked my picture. Do you want it?"

If I take the drawing, then no one else will see it or ask him what it is.

"Thank you Philippe. That would be nice. It's an unusual picture. May I ask why you drew it?"

"My uncle says the Germans invaded France and are killing French people. He says we need to resist and fight the German soldiers."

"Oh I see. Is that what your uncle says?"

"Yes. He and his friends speak all the time about fighting the Germans."

"Do you spend much time with your uncle?"

"Yes Mademoiselle. I live with my uncle now since my house in Nancy was bombed."

Tears begin to appear in Philippe's eyes. I put my arm around the boy and pull him close for a hug. "Where are your parents?"

"My father, mother and sister were all killed by the bomb. My uncle is my new Papa. He looks after me but I miss my real Papa." He begins to sob and I try to comfort him. "I'm sure you do. You are very brave and I'm sure your uncle is proud of you."

Our conversation is interrupted by the sound of the school bell indicating the end of the lunch break. I give Philippe a handkerchief to wipe his tears away so the other children will not ask him why he's been crying or make fun of him. He thanks me and after drying his eyes returns the wet handkerchief to me.

I hold the drawing. "I like this picture. You say I can keep it?"

"Yes Mademoiselle."

"Let's keep this picture a secret – just you and me. So please do not draw any more Germans and don't tell anyone what your uncle has been saying. Is that ok?"

"A secret? Oh yes Mademoiselle. I won't tell anyone."

After Philippe goes back to the classroom, I put the drawing carefully in my bag, slipping it in with my other papers. I know it's a risk for me but I feel I must alert Philippe's uncle. His unguarded comments in front of the child could result in someone reporting him to the Germans. And that could lead to arrest and execution. If something happened to his uncle Philippe would be on his own and I could never forgive myself for not acting.

But ever since June, when the Germans defeated and occupied my country, my France, I've become acutely and personally aware of the dangers I could be facing by talking openly to people, especially those I don't know. With all the betrayal I've seen and experienced I know I'm not alone in being suspicious of everyone, but I mustn't let that deter me from talking to Philippe's uncle.

When I arrived here from Paris the uppermost questions in my mind were all to do with survival. Who can I trust? Who is a collaborator? Who is involved in the resistance? I've seen with my own eyes how just a murmur of dissent can result in summary punishment. In November I witnessed Pierre LaFarge, an old veteran of the Great War, being arrested and sent to Fresnes prison for spitting at a German army patrol as it marched down the street.

And as for me? I now have an incriminating picture in my bag. I can't ask Philippe where he lives as he might ask why I want to know. I go into the classroom as if nothing is worrying me.

During the afternoon break I go into the school office to find Philippe's home address. I hope Madame Segal, the secretary, will be out – but no such luck. She looks up from her desk as I walk in. "Hello Mademoiselle Bruneau. Can I help you? Is it important? I was just going to take my break in the staff room."

A little lie is called for. "No. Nothing critical. I was just wanting to check some dates. On you go. I'll lock up as I leave."

"Thanks. I understand Madame Duchamps has brought in some special pastries and I've been looking forward to that. Don't take too long or there might not be any left."

I think of what she's just said. Pastries? Rationing has certainly made such once common delicacies extra special.

"That sounds wonderful. So go and enjoy. I'll be along soon."

Once Madame Segal leaves the office, I search quickly through the pupil register and find Philippe's address, 22 Rue d'Antoine. To avoid potential questions during the frequent Gestapo street searches, I memorize the address rather than write it down. I leave the office, lock the door and join the others in the staff room.

On the table is a plate with some pastries the likes of which I haven't seen for months. Madame Segal looks at me. "You're just in time Mademoiselle Bruneau. There aren't many left."

"Thank you for leaving some for me. I would hate to have missed this."

Between mouthfuls I express my pleasure. "This is delicious. I understand you brought these in Madame Duchamps. How did you get them? Or would that be an inappropriate question?"

She smiles at me and explains. "No, no. That's fine. I've already told the others. My brother, Tomas, runs the bakery, La Bouchée Parfaite, on Rue d'Antoine and the Germans asked him to provide pastries for a visiting dignitary. He told them that due to shortages, they would have to supply the flour and he somehow over estimated the amount he needed. And of course it would be stupid to let it go to waste."

With a broad smile I concur. "Of course, that would be a waste. Let's hope they invite more dignitaries."

As the staff chuckle at my suggestion, I try not to show concern at the incriminating revelations that Madame Duchamps has just made. Does she not realize she has just put her brother in potential jeopardy? I also hope my flippant comment will be sufficient to distract anyone from questioning my lateness. But no. Madame Segal asks me if my hunt was successful. "Did you find the dates you were looking for?"

"Yes, thank you. I could not remember which of the two Navarro children has a birthday this month."

At this point grumpy Monsieur Garnier speaks up. "Why do you want to know birthdays? You're not going to do something for them are you? Pupils need to be disciplined not indulged. Birthdays are not a reason for frivolous celebration."

I feel like telling him to mind his own business but instead just remark, "I am sure you're right Monsieur Garnier. Your subject is a disciplined subject but art is more of a creative subject and it's important that the —"

"Art is not a subject!" he interrupts me scornfully. "It's a waste of time. Teaching them German would be a better thing to do."

I disagree but keep my thoughts to myself rather than antagonize him further. Is Monsieur Garnier a collaborator or sympathizer? I'm certainly not going to ask him about his political views. What has this world come to?

I steer the conversation to a different subject. "It's a pity Mademoiselle Deferre is off sick. I'm sure she'd have enjoyed these pastries. Do we know when she'll be back?"

The secretary replies to my question. "I understand Mademoiselle Deferre will be back later this week. Apparently it has just been flu and she's recovering well."

Thankfully at this point the headmaster makes an announcement. "Break time is over. Back to classes please, but before we go, I think we all need to thank Madame Duchamps for the pastries."

After we all murmur our appreciation we leave the room and return to our classes. I take note that today's exchange with Monsieur Garnier is a stark reminder of the need for caution when expressing any opinions.

The second half of the afternoon feels as if it drags on forever and I'm increasingly concerned about the picture in my bag. How am I going to broach the subject with Philippe's uncle? He's obviously anti-German but I need to find a way to warn him to rein in his comments and not say such things in front of the child.

At the end of classes I grab my coat and hat and leave the school as inconspicuously as possible. I know the bakery, La Bouchée Parfaite, run by Madame Duchamps' brother, which means I don't need to ask where to find Rue d'Antoine. But the route there takes me past the Hotel de France, defiled by long red banners with their brazen Nazi swastikas. As I walk by I dream of ripping them down and burning them, but if I did that I wouldn't see tomorrow. So I just walk by as if nothing bothers me.

As I turn the corner into Rue d'Antoine I think I hear footsteps behind me and my heart begins to race. Have I been followed? I almost turn around to check until I realize to do so could indicate that I had a reason to be followed. No, I must just walk on as normal. The concept of normal, though, has gone out of the window. I'm embarking on a course of action which could lead to my arrest or worse. What's normal about that?

I stop at number 87 Rue d'Antoine on the pretence of looking at a little bird pecking at a bird feeder hanging from a tree. This gives me an opportunity to look back to see if I'm being followed. I cannot see anyone so perhaps I'm being too paranoid.

I begin to doubt my actions. Why should I care what happens to Philippe's uncle? I've never met him. It's the boy I'm more worried about. This uncle obviously holds some strong views and what if he doesn't listen to what I have come to tell him? Why should he listen to a strange woman who has knocked on his door uninvited? Perhaps I should turn back.

But no. I don't turn back. Philippe is just a child and what he said was said with feeling. I may be frightened but so are many others. And what would happen to Philippe if his uncle were to be arrested?

As I approach La Bouchée Parfaite my mouth waters at the memory of the pastries Madame Duchamps' brother baked for us. Unlike times gone by there isn't much on display in the windows these days. I walk on and all too soon I'm there at Number 22.

I reach up to use the heavy door knocker and pause. Am I really doing the right thing? Is this sensible? There's still time to turn around and walk away – no one will know.

As I pause I think back to spring last year, before the Germans invaded my France. Seven months ago I was living in Paris with my dear husband, Emile, and my family and friends. I even had my own married name back then, Madame Marie-Claire Blanchet, but not now. Here I am Mademoiselle Marie Bruneau – a single woman and all alone. Alone in the world.

The reality of my situation takes hold and I experience debilitating self-doubt. What am I just about to do? This is madness. I begin to walk away with the intention of forgetting the whole idea of talking to Philippe's uncle.

As I retrace my steps I recall my friend Katia showing incredible courage and selflessness just before she was caught by the Gestapo near the Avenue des Champs-Elysées in Paris. She told me that what she did was dangerous but that didn't stop her. Katia showed unwavering determination in her fight for France. With a chest-tightening feeling of guilt that I am choosing the easy option of not being brave enough to talk to the uncle, I stop.

I think about what I'm doing and realize that I owe it to Katia, and all of the others who have gone, to display the same level of courage and selflessness myself.

So I turn around, stride up to the house, bang the knocker on the door – and stand back.

Part 2 - Paris

Chapter 2

Thursday, 9 May 1940, Paris. (seven months earlier)

Marie-Claire woke to the soft tones of Emile's voice as he leant over the bed. He gently swept her long dark hair off her face so he could kiss her forehead. "My darling, it's time for me to go to work but I've brought you a coffee so you can lie in bed a bit longer. I'll see you this evening."

"Thanks. And by the way – we're going out for a celebration dinner tonight."

"That's a lovely idea, but almost two months of marriage isn't normally regarded as an outstanding achievement."

"Silly man. I want to celebrate your promotion to assistant manager. Luck seems to follow you and that bookshop is lucky to have you."

"I haven't always been lucky. When I was young I didn't think having tuberculosis was lucky." He paused. "But I suppose I have to admit it did get me out of being conscripted into the army to fight the Nazis."

"Do you think the Germans will invade France? I thought the Maginot line was designed to prevent that. It's there to protect France, isn't it?"

"Yes it is. But my dear, though I would love to stay and discuss world politics with you, if I don't go now I'll be late."

"Don't forget to bring *Le Petit Parisien* back with you. I'm following the serialized novel in the newspaper."

With a laugh he shook his head. "Don't tell me. It's another of those sexy romances you seem addicted to."

In response to his friendly jibe she threw a pillow at him but he was just able to close the door before it hit him. Rather than retrieve her pillow from across the room she merely reached over and propped herself up using his as she cradled the steaming cup of coffee. She knew she was especially lucky to have Emile as her husband and soul mate. Life was turning out to be all she could have hoped for.

As she lay in bed she mulled over the events of the last few months. Just before their wedding they'd found a lovely apartment near the centre of Paris. Although her mother had offered to have Marie-Claire stay on at home with her new husband she knew that would not really have worked out. Although she loved her mother dearly she had not wanted to start married life sharing an apartment with her.

And her darling Emile was wrong. She couldn't stay in bed. She needed to get up to prepare for her students. Although disappointed she'd been unable to obtain a full time teaching position in a school, giving private tutorials in her apartment on just Tuesdays and Thursdays gave her freedom to do her own sketching and painting on the other days. Today was Thursday which meant four students. The attendees were mothers who wanted some creative activity while their children were at school.

As the ladies tidied up at the end of the lesson, Madame Girard asked Marie-Claire, "Have you thought of holding sessions for children? You're such an inspiring teacher, I'm sure my daughter Amélie would benefit from your guidance. Would you consider running a class on Wednesday afternoons? There's no school that day. I'm sure we would all welcome such a class for our children."

Marie-Claire thought for a moment and then nodded her head. "Yes. That would be possible on Wednesdays, but only after two o'clock. Before then I work at the Soup Kitchen on Rue Saint-Denis. I wouldn't want to give that up. There are so many people needing help."

"I wasn't aware you worked at one of those soup kitchen places," remarked the rather pompous Madame Charbonnet, with a pained expression. "Are you sure they're clean and safe?"

"Oh yes. And perhaps I should not have said work. I volunteer on Mondays and Wednesdays at lunch time."

Marie-Claire was pleased when three mothers expressed an immediate interest in the classes. "Fine. We'll start next Wednesday, the 15th of May. You can drop the children off at two o'clock for a two hour session. Shall we say, half the adult rate?"

She knew she could have charged more, but the thought of being able to encourage children to be creative artistically would be fulfilling in itself.

After everyone left she had a quick lunch and wandered out to do one of the things she enjoyed most – drawing in Montmartre. There she sketched people, she sketched artists, she sketched artists sketching people. In fact she sketched anything which caught her eye. Fortunately she was never likely to run out of paper as the bookshop where Emile worked also sold paper.

Back in the apartment following her afternoon of sketching she selected her clothes for the special evening – her favourite floral dress and the little pill box hat her mother had given her. She opened her jewellery box and chose the ruby earrings Emile had given her as a wedding present. She was still applying her make-up when Emile arrived home with a large bouquet of flowers. She saw him in the mirror as he entered the bedroom and jumped up to greet him, almost knocking over her precious bottle of perfume. "These are lovely darling. Thank you. Is there a special reason why you've brought them?"

"I just wanted to say thank you. This dinner tonight – I appreciate the support you show me for what I do."

She gave him a loving hug. "But surely you know you'll always have my support, whatever you do. I love you so much."

She put the flowers in a vase, breathed in their lovely scent and gave him another kiss. "Shall we go?"

Arm in arm they slowly sauntered through the romantic streets of Paris to their favourite bistro, chatting about their day and the new classes she would be running on Wednesdays. During the meal he told her about his new responsibilities as assistant manager. As they finished the delicious chocolate dessert Emile mentioned that he had had a piece of luck at the bookshop. "You know that book I was looking for?"

"My dear, you're a bookseller who loves books. I do try to take in everything you say, but I can't be expected to remember the titles of all the books you want."

Emile smiled as he ignored the remark and continued. "Well, you won't believe it but today somebody came in with a bundle of second-hand books and there it was – *'Voyage au Bout de la Nuit'*. In good condition too."

"What a weird title – *'Voyage to the Edge of the Night'*." She adopted a teasing tone. "Is it a sexy romance? Is that what you've been looking for? I must remember this."

"No, no. Nothing like that. It's an autobiographical novel by Louis-Ferdinand Céline based around his life, especially his time in the trenches of the Great War."

In a voice that showed she didn't really mean it, she said, "Oh, how interesting."

"Yes actually it is. As one of the critics put it – 'It is one of the most negative but realistic novels of this century'. The story's depressing, yes, but full of insight into the human condition. In essence he points out that during war survivors are those who are willing to act like animals fighting for their very existence."

"Let's not talk of war," said Marie-Claire. "You've told me France is quite safe from invasion and this is not supposed to be an evening of melancholy. It's supposed to be a night of celebration. Anyway that bizarre title *'Voyage to the Edge of the Night'* reminds me of that game you and I used to play. Do you remember? Inventing weird titles for books, books we're unlikely ever to write."

"Oh but I do intend to write mine. It may take some time but I still want to write it as a detective novel."

"And are you still thinking of calling yourself Pascal?"

"Of course. Pascal, author of *'Champagne In A Broken Teacup'*, winner of this year's Prix Renaudot. How does that sound?"

"Actually I've always loved that title. You must never mention that title to anyone. I mean that. Promise me."

"If you really think so," responded Emile, "then I promise I'll never mention it to anyone and keep it strictly to myself until I can publish it. Would you use the silly title you came up with?"

"What was wrong with my title? I still like it – '*Oranges Are Just Sunburnt Lemons*'. It would leave the reader wondering what the book is about."

"We're agreed on that. Would you still call yourself Hortense?"

Marie-Claire nodded. "Certainly. As you well know Hortense was my grandmother's name. So yes, I would hide behind that pen name. My book would probably be a fantasy thriller. Perhaps about an artist who paints the future."

"If that's the plot, I would call it '*Angels Have Four Wings*'. That invokes fantasy and mystery."

"I like that. And as I told you when we played this game before your detective novel should really be called '*Hiding Behind A Lamppost*'. Isn't that what detectives do?"

They both laughed and continued to play the game, coming up with ever more ridiculous titles.

At five thirty in the morning Marie-Claire woke up with a fright. She rolled over in bed and whispered to her husband. "Emile. Emile. Wake up. Someone's banging on our door. Who can it be at this hour?"

"Stay here. I'll see who it is." He pulled on his dressing gown as he rose from the bed and tiptoed to the front door. Marie-Claire stayed in bed cowering under the sheets until she heard voices in the living room. Not just Emile's voice but another voice she recognized – her mother's. *What is Maman doing here at this hour? She sounds upset*?

Marie-Claire got up, pulled on her dressing gown and went through to the living room. She saw her mother was shaking and had tears streaming down her face. She immediately rushed over and put her arms around her mother. "What's wrong Maman?"

When she didn't answer immediately Emile explained. "Your mother said your aunt phoned her from Rotterdam to tell her that around four this morning German planes started bombing the

14

Rotterdam airport close to where they live. Apparently your aunt sounded terrified and your mother's extremely worried."

Marie-Claire helped her mother to an armchair. "Oh my God, how frightening. Is Aunt Ghislaine alright? And the rest of the family – are they ok?"

Through her tears her mother tried to answer. "I don't know dear. I can't tell. It was awful. While I was talking to her I could hear bombs exploding in the background. The explosions kept getting louder and louder and then the phone line went dead – completely dead. I don't know why. I tried phoning back but the operator said she couldn't connect me."

Her mother put her hands together as if in prayer. "Oh please God, let my sister still be alive."

Chapter 3

Marie-Claire found it hard to believe what her mother was telling them. *Did Maman really say the Germans have attacked The Netherlands? And Rotterdam is being bombed? And she could hear the bombs before the telephone went dead?* She knelt down beside her mother. "This is so frightening. What can we do?"

"I need to go to Rotterdam," declared her mother. "I need to help my sister."

"No. No Maman you can't. You mustn't do that."

"But I have to help my sister. Ghislaine needs me. I need to go to her today."

"Marie-Claire is right," said Emile. "Even if you could get there, Rotterdam will now be a very dangerous place."

"But my sister is in trouble. She needs me."

Marie-Claire put her arms around her mother's shoulders. "And so do we. We need you here. Think about it. There's nothing you can do there. As Emile said, Rotterdam is now a very dangerous place. We don't know if German soldiers came in immediately after the bombing as they did in Poland."

"But I'm a civilian. Surely the Germans only shoot military people. They won't attack me."

Emile shook his head. "Yes, you are a civilian, but so were thousands of Polish citizens killed in Warsaw when Hitler's forces bombed the residential areas. Hitler and his forces don't respect such ideas as civilians – or international agreements for that matter. The Netherlands is, or at least was, a neutral country but that has obviously not stopped Hitler from attacking it."

"But I feel so helpless."

Marie-Claire tried to console her mother. "I understand. But your brother-in-law Coenraad is a resourceful person. If anything can be done he'll already be doing it."

Emile looked alarmed. "Uncle Coenraad is Jewish, isn't he?"

16

Marie-Claire's eyes opened wide. "Oh my God Emile. I see why you're asking. Maman, you must not go to Rotterdam. You would be asking strangers what has happened to a Jewish Dutchman. You would just be pointing him out to the Germans. You would be putting his life in danger."

"So what can we do?" pleaded her mother.

"I have some Jewish friends here in Paris," replied Marie-Claire. "I can ask one of them to see if they can find out what's happened."

"Please do. Yes please do."

Marie-Claire became aware that her mother was beginning to wilt with the shock and horror of the situation. "Look Maman, you must stay with us right now. I don't want you being on your own. This has been a terrible shock for all of us and you've been awake for hours. Why don't you lie down for a while."

Her mother raised no objection as Marie-Claire led her to the bedroom, helped her to lie down and gently covered her with a blanket. Her mother fell asleep almost immediately. Marie-Claire closed the bedroom door and went into the kitchen where Emile was preparing a warm drink. "Maman has dropped off to sleep. Oh Emile, this dreadful news is so frightening. Do you think there'll be something on the radio?"

"I'm sure there will be." He passed Marie-Claire a cup of coffee before turning on the radio. Although welcoming the drink Marie-Claire put it down for a moment as she collapsed into an armchair. The moment turned into an hour. When she woke she saw that Emile was still listening to the radio with a glum face. "Did you hear any news?"

"Yes I did. And it's the worst possible news. The attack on Rotterdam wasn't an isolated incident. It wasn't a warning shot or some perverse practice skirmish. It was a full scale invasion of The Netherlands, Belgium and Luxembourg. The Germans attacked with planes, parachuted soldiers, land soldiers, tanks – the whole works."

Marie-Claire shook her head in disbelief. "Oh Emile. What does this mean for my family in Rotterdam?"

17

"I don't know, but one thing is for sure. We can't let your mother even think of going to help her sister, if she's even still alive."

"Oh don't say that. I don't want to think like that and we mustn't let Maman know we even have such fears."

They agreed that Marie-Claire would try to keep her mother's spirits up and stop her from doing anything rash. Going to see her sister was certainly not an option.

The following evening her mother insisted that she was perfectly capable of returning home. "I need clean clothes and you two need to live your own lives. Thank you for looking after me but I am not an invalid – tonight I'll sleep in my own bed." Marie-Claire knew there was no arguing with her mother when she spoke with such determination.

Both Marie-Claire and Emile spent every free moment listening to the radio in the vain hope of hearing good news but there was none. On Saturday, just two days after the invasion of The Netherlands, the French Prime Minister made a broadcast voicing his opinion that France would be invaded next and overrun by Germany as foretold in Hitler's book *Mein Kampf*.

This prompted Emile to bring home from the bookshop a copy of *Mein Kampf* which he spent most of the evening reading. He put the book down and sighed, "He was right."

"Who was right?" asked Marie-Claire. "Hitler?"

"No. The Prime Minister was right when he said it was all in *Mein Kampf*. You know that game of silly titles we play? Well, Hitler's book could have been titled '*We Must Destroy France*'. It's obvious Hitler's invasion of The Netherlands and Belgium wasn't prompted by the desire to conquer them. It appears it was a plan he developed years ago as a way to reach the undefended borders of France."

Marie-Claire listened with apprehension. "Are you saying this war will come to France? To Paris? To us here? Are we going to be bombed like Rotterdam?"

"I don't know, but I wish now that I had been able to join up and fight for France."

"Well I for one am pleased you didn't. I don't know what I would do if you went to war and were killed. But Emile, on a serious note, is there anything we can do?"

"Not against bombs and tanks. You saw the picture in *Le Petit Parisien* of the destruction in Rotterdam."

"Yes, and I'm glad you didn't show it to Maman. She's worried enough about her sister without seeing such horrific pictures."

Although Marie-Claire had talked to her Jewish friend about her Dutch relations, the Dagloonder family, she had not told her mother that there was little chance of any news, especially now that the newspapers were reporting that The Netherlands had surrendered to the Germans.

On Wednesday Marie-Claire wasn't sure if any of the children would turn up for the art class. She was right to be anxious. Only one child did, Amélie Girard, the daughter of the lady who had suggested the class.

"Is my Amélie the only one?"

"It looks like it. We'll have a session today, but probably not again. When I was at the soup kitchen at lunch time virtually everybody was talking about leaving Paris. They fear we could get bombed like Rotterdam, but hopefully it won't come to that."

"Hopefully so, but did you see that Nancy was bombed? That's getting too close. My husband is arranging for us to leave Paris to stay with our relatives in Dijon so Amélie wouldn't be here next week anyway."

"Amélie. What would you like to draw to remind you of Paris when you're in Dijon?"

"The Eiffel Tower. With a big French flag at the top."

"We can do that Amélie. I have a small model of the Tower you can work from."

For the rest of the session Marie-Claire taught her young student how to draw a stylized image of the Tower complete with a big flag which Amélie coloured in with crayons.

As Madame Girard prepared to leave she thanked Marie-Claire.

"I hope you and Monsieur Blanchet stay safe. I'm not sure how long we'll stay in Dijon, but if we return I'll come by to see if you're still doing lessons."

"Please do, and bring Amélie with you. I enjoyed teaching her and she shows great promise."

That evening Emile pointed to an article in the newspaper reporting that over 25,000 children had been evacuated from Paris to the countryside.

"But hold on," said Marie-Claire. "Hitler wouldn't attack children. Adults maybe, but not children. Surely."

"Stop for a moment dear and think about it. Bombs don't make such distinctions. And anyway, Hitler has shown his ruthlessness. Don't you remember reading in the paper that he had two of his colonels executed by firing squad? Not for disobeying an order but for merely openly criticizing Hitler. That's how much he values other people's lives – not at all."

Chapter 4

On Saturday Marie-Claire and her mother had their first real life introduction to the reality of war. They were sitting outside a cafe when their conversation was interrupted by the piercing whine of sirens. That was closely followed by the thunderous racket of engines sounding like a hundred cars backfiring.

Marie-Claire looked around her. People in the cafe were abandoning their drinks – some running away, others crawling under tables. "What's that noise?" asked her mother. "What's happening?"

The waiter who was bringing them a coffee refill appeared remarkably unperturbed as he answered. "That, Madame, is an air raid warning siren and a flight of German bombers. Unfortunately we don't have an air raid shelter but I suppose you could hide under a table like my other customers."

Although visibly frightened, her mother replied. "My dear young man, crawling under a table is not something I do at my time in life."

"Perhaps not, but if you don't take cover you may not have a life. Although these tables wouldn't really help much. They're too flimsy." He looked up and added, "Anyway, we should be safe."

"What makes you think that?" asked Marie-Claire.

"Look. The German bombers are heading away from us."

Marie-Claire and her mother looked up and stared in fear. They saw not one, not two, but many bombers all bearing German markings. Then as quickly as they had appeared, the squadron of bombers disappeared behind the buildings.

Her mother grabbed Marie-Claire's arm. "Is that what my sister would have seen and heard in Rotterdam?"

"No. In Rotterdam they attacked at night without warning. All she'd have heard was the sound of bombs exploding."

She immediately knew she should not have answered truthfully as her mother began to cry. "Will we ever hear from them again? I'm so worried, but I keep telling myself they'll be alright. I need to live in hope."

Marie-Claire read that the German bombers flying over Paris did not drop any bombs. It was reckoned the purpose of the flight had been to scare the people of Paris – and in that it was successful.

"Emile have you seen in the paper? Dance halls are being closed, ration cards are being issued and the authorities are telling everyone they must not leave Paris. Everyone must stay at work. Does that apply to you as well? Should we consider leaving?"

"I can't leave my job. My boss, Monsieur Bernier, has already fled to Dijon with his family. I'm effectively the manager now."

"Perhaps we should leave too. What would it matter? Is anybody really buying books right now?"

"Actually, yes. But that's not the real issue for us. We don't have a car, and even if we did there's almost no petrol now in Paris."

"We could go by train."

"Have you not read about the stations in the paper? Apparently they're crammed like a football game and the trains are packed like sardines. Anyway, where would we go? No dear, we just have to stay here and hope – and try to keep your mother's spirits up."

The next day Marie-Claire read the devastating news of the imminent capture of the British and French forces at Dunkerque. She could not decide whether to keep reading or just hold her head in her hands and pretend it was just a bad dream.

She put the paper down but Emile picked it up. "I see that there are now around three million refugees in France from The Netherlands and Belgium. Three million."

"I know there are lots in Paris. At the soup kitchen the queues have become much longer. But three million? Where are they?"

"The Minister of State says that they're being gathered into groups and then transported to other parts of the country."

"What do you mean?"

"Well, the article says many Belgian refugees have turned up at Reims and are now being sent by train to Nevers."

"Nevers – it's near Dijon isn't it?"

"Yes. Have you ever been to Nevers?"

"No. Have you?"

"Many years ago as a child, but it didn't leave a lasting impression. I doubt you'd find much to do there except perhaps sketch the cathedral. It's rather unusual. When part of it collapsed they rebuilt it facing two ways which means it has two altars."

Marie-Claire laughed. "I'm sure it's fascinating and if I ever go there, I'll sketch it. But I'm not thinking of going there. Especially not if it's now full of Belgian refugees."

A few days later Emile looked up from the newspaper and asked, "Does your mother read *Le Petit Parisien*?"

"I don't think so. Why? Is there something she should see?"

Emile shook his head. "Absolutely not. There's an article here by an American reporter who's been to Rotterdam and says the civilian death toll is between ten and fifty thousand, with most sections of the city flattened."

Marie-Claire felt tears welling in her eyes. "Perhaps you shouldn't have told me. We haven't heard from my aunt and that makes me feel we may never. Oh Emile, I'm so worried."

Later that week Emile commented on another article in the newspaper. "It says here that telephone lines in cafes, tobacco shops, restaurants, hotels and garages have been suspended."

"Why? You understand these things. Why have they done that?"

"Unlike your mother few people have a telephone, which means the government could be worried people might be using phones in such places to spread rumours. Or perhaps they just want to keep the lines clear in case of some attack. I don't really know why."

"An attack? I thought you said the Germans were only trying to frighten Parisians, not kill them."

"That's what I've read – but who knows."

The next day, the 3rd of June, Marie-Claire experienced the brutality of war for herself. Early in the afternoon she was travelling by bus to visit her friend Violette when suddenly the

Paris air raid warnings sounded. This was soon followed by the roar of planes overhead. The bus stopped abruptly and the driver yelled for everyone to get off.

As Marie-Claire did as he ordered she looked up and saw a sight she never wanted to see again. The sky was filled not just with German bombers but also with what seemed like hundreds of bombs falling down around her. The sound of the planes was soon drowned out by the noise of bombs exploding and the screams of injured people.

She turned to run but there was no safe place to go. Everywhere she looked she could see bombs falling and flames rising. She cowered beside the bus to try and get some protection from the flying debris from exploding buildings.

As she did so she heard a woman screaming, "Please help me. My husband's trapped and the house is on fire. I can't free him by myself. Help! Please, someone help me!"

Marie-Claire looked around and saw that no one was moving to help. *Why is no one helping? I can't leave them to die.*

Although terrified, she ran across to the woman. She could see that the man's foot was trapped under a fallen timber. She and the woman took hold of the timber and tried to lift it. Initially the two of them were unable to move it. As the flames grew closer they tried again, and with an almost superhuman effort were just able to raise it enough for the man to wriggle free. Although his leg was obviously badly injured he was able to stand up.

The lady turned to Marie-Claire. "Thank you so much. I couldn't have saved my husband without your help." She pointed to a parked van. "We'll take cover behind that van." Marie-Claire wanted to help the injured man but the lady refused. "No you've done enough. Go back to the bus. Hurry – go on."

Marie-Claire ran to the bus. She crouched down beside it and looked back. The couple had nearly reached the van when there was a massive explosion. When the dust cleared all Marie-Claire could see was a hole in the road – no van, no couple. She began to shake violently with shock at the realization of how close she had come to being killed.

In her panic and fear she completely lost track of time. If asked, she would have said the attack lasted for many hours but in fact it was just over one. As suddenly as it started, it stopped. No more planes, no more bombs, no more explosions – just the eerie crackle of burning buildings, the screams of the injured and the wail of approaching sirens.

She stood up and found it hard to believe she had been spared. Her hands were filthy and her muscles ached from lifting the timber but apart from some minor scratches she had no physical injuries. Though shaking from shock and covered in dust and debris, she knew she was not in need of medical care unlike so many others. In a dazed stupor she walked away from the bus and headed home, thankful she was still alive.

For Marie-Claire, 'war' was no longer just a word.

Chapter 5

When Emile came home he found Marie-Claire curled up in a ball on the sofa in her dressing gown, shaking and shivering. She looked up at him with eyes red from crying. "Oh Emile. Thank God you're here. It was awful."

He dropped his bags and rushed over to console his wife. "I know. I heard the air raid sirens as well. But apparently it was just another flyover to frighten us. Why are you so upset?"

"It wasn't a flyover. They dropped bombs on buildings full of people. People were screaming. People were killed."

"What are you saying?" asked Emile. "I was told it was just a flyover with no bombs. Who told you this?"

"Nobody told me. I was there. Bombs were falling all around me. I had nowhere to run. It was terrifying. I was almost killed."

Emile stared at her with a shocked expression. "Almost killed? Thank God you're safe. What happened?"

"I took a bus to visit Violette but before we got there the sirens sounded. The bus stopped and we all got off just before the planes started dropping their bombs. Oh Emile – hold me please."

He put his arms around her and pulled her close. "Were you hurt? Have you been to hospital?"

"No I wasn't hurt, just a few scratches. I hid beside the bus – it shielded me. I came straight home. There was nothing I could do to help the injured people. It was awful. There was blood and bits of —" She did not finish her sentence. She just leant into Emile and started crying again.

Emile held her tightly. Soon she stopped shaking and weeping, her breathing calmed down and within a few minutes the shock of the event took its toll and she fell asleep in his arms.

It was the next morning before she woke, still lying on the sofa. She shuddered as she remembered her experiences of the previous day. She saw Emile was in the kitchen. "Emile. We must leave. We can't stay in Paris with the Germans bombing us. You saw pictures of what happened in Rotterdam. Well I saw and experienced the horror here, in Paris. I know you said something before about no car, no train, but I want to leave. I don't want to die."

"I don't either, but even before the bombing so many people were leaving Paris the roads became and are still impassable."

"Most of my friends have said they are planning to leave."

"Who? How?"

"Simone, Hannah, Juliette, even Stella. They're all intending to leave so why can't we?"

"Ok, so how are they leaving?"

"I don't know. All I know is they are planning to go soon."

"I don't understand how. Public transport is overcrowded if it's running at all. I read that people are even walking out of the city because they can't get a bus or train."

"Walking? Paris is so large I could walk for a day and still be in Paris. What can we do?"

"I don't know but it's probably safer to stay in Paris than risk the roads. If they start bombing Paris again then yes, we will need to think again. And what about your mother? We couldn't leave her behind and could she stand the strain of such a journey? Where would we go? Where would we stay? How would we get food?"

Marie-Claire just shook her head and buried her face back in the sofa cushions. For a few days neither spoke about leaving even though it was obviously on their minds.

Le Petit Parisien newspaper did not help her mood when it reported that the Paris bombing was worse than initially described. It was now known that 254 people were killed and over six hundred injured. And the pictures were not reassuring. They showed the same level of destruction she had seen in the cinema newsreels from Warsaw and Rotterdam.

Emile refrained from commenting but Marie-Claire didn't. "These pictures of Paris show you what I witnessed and you can see they look like the ones from Rotterdam. Are the Germans going to come back? Will Paris be flattened as well?"

"I don't know. I hope not. I sincerely do. But talking of Rotterdam, has your mother heard from her sister?"

"No. She doesn't know if the Dagloonders are safe or dead. For all we know all three of them, Uncle Coenraad, Aunt Ghislaine and cousin Anna may be heading to Paris."

"If they're coming to Paris then they'll expect us and your mother to be here. So that's a very good reason for not leaving."

Marie-Claire grimaced. "Stop being so logical. After Monday's experience I'm still afraid and I want to leave. Have you tried shopping? When I went with Maman we found the shops which were open had empty shelves due to panic buying. Many of the shops were shut, apparently because the shopkeepers have left the city." She paused. "Paris is haemorrhaging. It feels like this is the end of life as we know it."

"I understand what you're saying and I feel the same. But we must remember – we're alive, you and I, and we have each other. Many women in Paris are alone, their husbands conscripted into the army with no idea when or even if they'll return."

With an overwhelming sense of hopelessness she walked over to Emile and wrapped herself around him, sobbing quietly into his shoulder. Her loving words, 'Je t'aime' were said with such emotion he also had tears in his eyes as he whispered back, "I'm here and I'll do everything I can to protect you my love."

No one came to Marie-Claire's art class. She stayed at the apartment in case anyone showed up but no one did. When she felt she'd waited long enough, she went out with her sketch pad and pencils to try and distract her mind. But the city was showing the effect of so many people having left. The streets were devoid of the sounds which made Paris a living dynamic space. She felt the newspapers were not exaggerating when they claimed over two million Parisians had fled.

While out Marie-Claire overheard a piece of news which did nothing to calm her fears. "Emile. Did you know our government has fled? Apparently they have upped and run away to Bordeaux. What does that say about the safety of staying in Paris? If they don't think it's safe then we must go as well."

"Yes I did hear about the government, but I have some news."

"You've found a way for us to leave and take Maman with us?"

"No, not a way to leave. And believe it or not we're now probably safer here in Paris. Apparently retreating French soldiers have been hiding in amongst the crowds fleeing Paris."

"What's that got to do with being safer here in Paris?"

"The Germans are aware the roads are being used by the retreating army so the German airplanes have been bombing the roads and strafing them with machine-gun fire. They don't care who dies and many civilians have been killed."

"Are you saying we're basically doomed no matter what we do? So tell me, what's your news?"

"It's not exactly good news but it means we don't need to leave. Paris has been declared an 'Open City'."

"What does that mean?"

"It means that France has told Hitler that Paris will not be defended. There will be no fighting in the streets. It's as if the fighting aspect of this war will bypass Paris. But most importantly for us there'll be no more bombing of the city."

"But the Germans – what will they be doing?"

"That's the downside. German soldiers will just march unopposed into the city."

"Paris occupied by the Germans? And that's better?"

"Yes, in the sense there'll be no fighting in Paris so we don't need to be afraid for our lives. We are safe here in the city."

"Maybe for you, as a man, it'll be safe. But I fear the women of Paris may have a different view, especially with most French men either away in the army or captured."

A few days later, on the 14th of June, Marie-Claire set out to meet her friend Katia at their favourite cafe just off the Champs-Elysées. She had not put the radio on that morning and had not heard the announcement telling everyone to stay at home. As a consequence, she was not prepared for what happened that day.

When she reached the cafe she was surprised to find it was shut and Katia was nowhere to be seen. There were lots of people milling around with glum faces, whispering in hushed voices. She began heading home when she became aware of an unexpected sound – not bombs, not gunfire, but trumpets and drums.

As it grew louder she realized where it was coming from. There were hundreds of German soldiers marching in formation down the middle of the empty Champs-Elysées, preceded by a marching band and soldiers carrying large Nazi flags. Each company of soldiers had its own set of drums, adding to the ominous noise. No one around her spoke. Everyone was too shocked by the arrogant display of German triumph at the occupation of Paris.

Marie-Claire walked home, feeling stunned and completely demoralized, unable to get the aggressive thump of the German drums out of her mind.

When she left the apartment the following day she hardly recognized the city. German soldiers were everywhere – on the streets, in the few shops that were open, even in the cafes. Long red banners with Nazi swastikas hung from the buildings. Sentry posts with German soldiers brandishing machine-guns had appeared outside many offices and hotels.

Her life and that of all Parisians was immediately constrained by a curfew from ten in the evening until five in the morning. The newspaper reported that those foolhardy enough to flaunt the curfew found themselves in jail for the night. She and Emile had always enjoyed late night meals, evening dances and walks by the Seine but she realized with a feeling of melancholy that these were now a thing of the past.

Four days after the Germans walked into Paris Emile came home with a glum face. "Our government has resigned and Marshal Pétain has been appointed as head of a new government."

"Wasn't he the hero of Verdun?"

"Yes, he was a hero then but not now. Within an hour of his appointment he threw in the towel and asked Hitler for an armistice. Can you believe that? He's thrown France to the wolves, betrayed our Allies and disrespected all the fighting men of France, including those who've died trying to protect France."

"Where did you hear this?"

"The papers are full of articles about it. Most are horrified and find it hard to believe what Pétain has done. Pétain speaks of seeking from Hitler 'an honourable armistice between soldiers'. An honourable armistice with Hitler? A man who violates every treaty and law imaginable? A man who kills off his own countrymen and wrote that he wanted to crush France. It's unbelievable. It won't be an armistice – Hitler will turn it into a humiliating defeat."

"And are we to become part of Germany as happened to Austria when it was annexed by Hitler? Is this the end of France?"

"I don't know, but I've heard that tonight General de Gaulle will broadcast a special rallying message to the French people."

"What can he do? He's just part of the French army isn't he? And you said Pétain has basically surrendered."

"De Gaulle is not in France – he's in Britain. And he's not just part of the army. He is, or at least was, Secretary of State for War."

"Will he be speaking on behalf of the army or the government?"

"Neither, I suspect, since he is under military orders not to do public speeches and he's been sacked by Pétain. He'll be broadcasting tonight on the BBC."

That evening they listened to de Gaulle make a passionate appeal for French people not to lose heart, not to lose hope. Marie-Claire was puzzled. "What did he mean at the end when he said 'Whatever happens, the flame of French resistance must not and will not go out?' Is there some organization he was referring to?"

"Not that I know of. I think he means we shouldn't accept the armistice as the death of France – we must find some way to keep France alive in spite of the German invasion. Pétain may have taken the fight out of the land of France, but de Gaulle is trying to keep it alive in the hearts of the French people. I know who I respect. Pétain is almost a traitor."

When a few days later de Gaulle broadcast yet again to the French people Marie-Claire cheered with Emile when the General said he was setting up a Free French Fighting Force in Britain. And she cheered again when he called on those who were still in France and could not join him to follow his example and fight on.

After the broadcast finished Marie-Claire sat quiet for a few moments absorbing the implications of de Gaulle's words about it being the duty of free French people everywhere to continue the fight for France. She repeated to herself his final inspiring words – 'Vive La France Libre'.

Marie-Claire read in the paper that the armistice was regarded by many as a dishonourable surrender. She also read with dismay that it had been agreed and signed within days and that one of the main aspects was that France was no longer one country but effectively had been divided into two parts. The north and west, including Paris, was now under German occupation with a military government. The other part, referred to as the Unoccupied Zone, was to be governed by Pétain. The border between the two was to be referred to as the Demarcation Line, with controlled checkpoints restricting travel between the two parts.

On the positive side she knew the armistice meant the fighting had ceased – at least the open fighting had ceased. When out for a walk, she had heard German vehicles touring the streets of Paris with loudspeakers. They were demanding people hand over all firearms and ammunition. She mused to herself that if she or Emile had any firearms, they would hide them rather than hand them over. She paused for a moment. *Is this what de Gaulle was meaning by resistance – quietly disobeying German orders? Or did he mean something more?*

She was glad Emile was not a fighting man. She knew he wasn't a pacifist but equally he was not someone to grab a rifle and start shooting. She was, therefore, surprised when a few days later he said, "I have something important to tell you. Some of my friends and I have taken to heart de Gaulle's call to the French people that 'the flame of French resistance must not die'."

"What do you mean?"

He paused before answering. "We feel we cannot stand idly by as France is destroyed. We are going to form a resistance group."

Chapter 6

"Emile – what exactly are you saying?" asked Marie-Claire. "Do you mean you're going to join a resistance group or start one?"

"Start a group. I don't know of one in the area."

Marie-Claire looked at her husband in silence. *Is Emile losing his mind? Or is he being courageous? Should I feel horrified or proud?* "So what are you going to do? Are you going to fight? Is that the idea? Have you ever even held a gun?"

"No I haven't. We're not thinking of taking up arms. We're talking about passive resistance."

He took both her hands in his as he looked intently into her eyes. "I know even passive resistance can be dangerous. I hope you can understand why I want to do this. More importantly, can you accept me doing this?"

Marie-Claire's thoughts were in a whirl. *This could be dangerous. I'd hate to lose him. But he said passive resistance – that should be safer. Would he resent it if I said no? How can I say no when so many women in Paris have already lost their husbands?*

Eventually she said, "I don't think I'd be brave enough to do anything myself, even passive resistance, but I'll support you if this is what you feel you should do and really want to. I love you very much darling."

"Thank you. I feel this is the right thing to be doing. We are hoping to get set up in the next few days."

"You've said we more than once. Who is 'we'?"

"Well there's my —"

"Stop right there. If you're thinking of doing this then you need to do it properly. I said stop because you were just about to violate the most important rule – secrecy. You were about to tell me who the other members of your group are."

"Well yes, you asked."

"And your reply should have been 'It's better that you don't know'. Never tell anyone the names of the others – not even me."

"But I can trust you, can't I?"

"Of course you can, but you don't know how I'd react under interrogation. If I don't know something then I can't reveal it. And never ever write the names down."

He looked at her with a puzzled expression. "Where are these ideas coming from?"

She laughed. "I don't just read romantic novels, I read crime and thriller books as well. They all reveal you should never give out more information than necessary. I don't need to know who's involved so don't tell me."

"You're absolutely right. As a group we must only share information on a need to know basis, but that means I may sometimes not tell you what I'm doing. Can you accept that?"

"Of course I can, I trust you." She knew Emile would tell her if there was ever something he felt she absolutely needed to know.

Although the German governing authorities said that everyone was safe, she never felt safe seeing so many German soldiers on the streets. She also hated the sight of all the Nazi swastikas hanging from buildings. "I'd like to pull those long red Nazi banners down and burn them," she said to Katia on Friday over a drink in their favourite cafe.

"You may think about it," cautioned Katia, "but don't do it. One of our group was arrested and tortured in Fresnes prison for trying to set fire to a swastika banner."

"One of your group?"

"Yes. I belong to a group of like-minded women who do what we can to make the Germans feel unwelcome. We aim to do just subtle things but Gabrielle got carried away with her matches. None of us approved of her burning the banners. Doing things like that is for resistance groups and we're not that. As I said we're for subtle actions, not active aggression. We're a fun bunch, just not towards Germans. You're very welcome to join us if you want."

"Perhaps. But first can you explain what you mean by subtle?"

"Well for example some of the girls work in cafes. They serve the Germans slowly with cold coffee and stale food. Some even add laxatives to the food."

At that moment a German officer approached their table. "I'll show you a good way to discourage attention from German soldiers," whispered Katia.

The officer enquired in German if either of them spoke his language. Katia pouted and shrugged. He tried again in faltering French. "May I you lovely ladies a drink buy? Perhaps Pernod?"

Before Marie-Claire could even refuse Katia faked a prolonged bout of coughing. "Non Merci. I cannot have alcohol with my medication." Pulling a blood-stained handkerchief from her purse she coughed violently into it. "But thank you."

With repulsion written across his face at the sound of coughing and the sight of the blood-stained handkerchief, the officer turned on his heels and marched away.

"That was clever," exclaimed Marie-Claire, "Pretending to have TB frightened him away."

"Apparently the Germans are always very concerned about getting ill. This pre-stained hankie always gets rid of them faster than any words can."

Although Marie-Claire would prefer German soldiers weren't in Paris at all, she very much liked Katia's methods for making them feel uncomfortable.

Now that there was no further danger from bombing, some of the ladies who attended Marie-Claire's art classes returned to Paris. However the numbers had dwindled to the point that she only ran one class per week. One of her former students who fled Paris during what had become known as the Exodus was now in the Unoccupied Zone of France and therefore prohibited from returning. Another lady, who Marie-Claire knew was Jewish, said she would no longer be attending as she and her family had decided it was time to leave France while they still could.

With only one class per week Marie-Claire had more free time so she headed to the soup kitchen. The man in charge was surprised to see her. "Madame Blanchet this is Tuesday, not Wednesday. I'm not expecting you today."

"You're right Monsieur Laroche, but I thought with so many people coming here perhaps you'd appreciate more assistance."

He was quick to accept her offer. "Thank you. It would be great if you could look after the bread table outside."

She'd done that before and had simple answers to the various requests – 'Sorry but it's only one slice per person' – 'No we don't have any butter' – 'I know you are large but small people also get hungry and we only have a limited amount of bread'.

Towards the end of the session a man with a limp approached her table. As she was about to hand him a slice of bread the air was filled with the unmistakable sound of a police siren. Everyone in the queue looked frightened when a police car stopped at the soup kitchen and two policemen got out with pistols drawn. In the resulting commotion the man leant forward and whispered in English, "Can you help me get home to Scotland?"

She pulled back slightly. *How should I respond? Is he a genuine British soldier or a German stooge trying to flush out those involved in the escape lines? But I've never heard any German mention Scotland – only England or Britain.* She decided to help. Trying to remember the English she'd learned in school she whispered back to him, "Say nothing. You smile. I talk."

In French she kept up a flowing one-sided conversation until she saw the police arrest a man near the back of the queue. They bundled that unfortunate person into the police car at gunpoint and drove away, leaving everyone looking shocked.

She resumed talking in French to the man in front of her, repeating certain words. How beautiful the flowers are in Place de la Madeleine. What lovely benches they have in Place de la Madeleine. How people often go to Place de la Madeleine just to sit. As he held out his left hand to receive his slice of bread she noticed a scar across the inside of his palm and almost failed to hear his quiet whisper of 'Place de la Madeleine'. She inclined her head slightly in acknowledgement and turned her attention to the next person in the queue.

However, she fretted for the rest of the session. *Have I done the right thing? Should I have ignored him? What would Emile have done?* When the session ended she caught the first Metro which would take her to the bookshop where Emile worked.

When she arrived at the bookshop he was dealing with a customer. It seemed ages before he was finished and came over to where she was waiting impatiently. "What's wrong? You look worried?"

She grasped his hand and spoke quickly. "I've done something and I don't know if I've been stupid. Can we have a coffee together? Right now, please."

He nodded and arranged for one of the other staff to cover for him. "I know the very place for us, Le Bistro d'Angel."

"Ok, if we can talk quietly there. We've not been there before have we?"

"No, but you'll see why I've chosen it when we get there. Now tell me why you're so upset. What have you done?"

On the way she recounted her experience at the soup kitchen. She described how she had witnessed the police arresting a man in the queue at gunpoint and how during the upheaval another man in the queue unexpectedly whispered to her in English, asking if she could help him escape to Scotland. She explained to Emile that she had suggested the man should go to Place de la Madeleine, but now she was worried he might have been an informant rather than a genuine British soldier.

"I can only imagine how difficult that must have been for you. But please don't say anything else until we're sitting down in the bistro. Trust me on this." No sooner had they sat down, than an elderly waiter appeared. "Hello Emile. Would you be wanting your coffee with sugar as usual?"

"Yes please Reynald. And I would like to introduce you to my wife, Marie-Claire."

"Hello Madame Blanchet. Can I bring you a drink as well?"

"A coffee, please, and no sugar."

Reynald looked quizzically at Emile who explained. "Marie-Claire requires the same service please, and I'll explain it to her."

When the waiter had walked away Marie-Claire looked at her husband with a puzzled frown. "This waiter seems to know you well so why was he asking if you wanted sugar? And why did you say yes? I've never known you to want sugar with your coffee. And what do you mean I'll require the same service?"

Emile chuckled. "If Reynald brings coffee without sugar it's a sign that there are no Germans in the place. But if he brings sugar, or brings some later, it's a sign someone suspicious is in the bistro and to watch what we say. I asked Reynald to do the same for you in case you need a safe place to talk to your friends."

"Thanks. That could be useful."

"And always pay for your drinks here at the table when they arrive, not at the end. Reynald will be expecting you to do that."

"Why? That's not the custom. We always pay when we leave."

"Because if you need to leave quickly, you don't want to hang around waiting for the bill."

"I see what you mean. That makes sense. But what I need right now is to know I did the right thing talking to that man in the soup kitchen and whether something can be done to help him."

"Why have you told me about him? Is it because you're afraid you may have done the wrong thing? Or do you think I can do something? I told you we are not involved in active resistance."

"I know, you told me. But this man needs help and I thought you might know someone who could help him."

"I might do but why did you send him to Place de la Madeleine? I've never mentioned it."

"I needed to mention an address and that's where my parents were living when I was born so that's what came to mind. Is that a problem?"

"No, but how are we, I mean how are they, going to be able to recognize him?"

Marie-Claire smiled at her husband. "Darling, have you forgotten I'm a portrait artist?" She reached into her bag and pulled out a sketch of the man she'd drawn while in the Metro. "You can see here he's got a scar on his left cheek. I also think he's in borrowed clothes. His trousers are those of a farmer but his fingernails are spotless. He has a slight limp in his left leg but that's either recent or false."

"This is amazing. But why do you question his limp?"

"Simple. His shoes are old but his left shoe isn't worn down as it would be if he'd been limping for years."

"Very observant. The reason I questioned Place de la Madeleine is I didn't think I'd ever mentioned it to you. It happens to be one of the places we use for meeting people who are trying to evade being captured by the Germans."

"That's twice you've used 'we' instead of 'they'. Has 'passive resistance' become 'active'?"

"Not 'active' in the sense of destroying things, but 'active' in the sense of helping people who are risking their lives for France. We arrange help for downed British airmen and stranded allied soldiers wanting to escape to Britain."

"Don't tell me any details. I said I'd support you and I still do, but I'm not sure if I'm dreading the thought you could be arrested for helping escapers, or proud of you fighting for France. Does what you've said mean someone will be able to help my man? Will someone find him in Place de la Madeleine?"

"I'll contact someone, and with your description and sketch it should be quite easy to find him. But right now we need to change the subject immediately."

"Ok, but why?"

"You always need to be on the lookout. Look, Reynald is bringing our drinks with sugar. We should drink them quickly and leave."

Chapter 7

A few nights later Marie-Claire was woken by loud noises coming from the hall outside their apartment. Her immediate reaction was one of panic. The unmistakable sound of banging on a door in the middle of the night had become one of the most dreaded sounds in all of Paris. The banging continued, accompanied by a German voice shouting 'Aufmachen, Aufmachen!' which Marie-Claire knew meant 'Open up, open up'.

She began trembling uncontrollably and rolled over in bed against Emile who was lying still and silent. "Wake up Emile. Wake up. What's going on?"

"I'm already awake. Did you think I could sleep through that?" He put his arms around her. "We must be quiet. It's not our door they're banging on. I think it's the Coutreaus' door."

"I haven't told you," whispered Marie-Claire, "but more than once I've heard other voices in their apartment – English voices. Perhaps they've been hiding Allied soldiers. Will the Germans just search the apartment and go away?"

"No, if they have been hiding soldiers they'll take the Coutreaus away and imprison them – or worse."

She began to shake again as the enormity of his words were confirmed by new shouts outside in the hall. "Move, move."

She heard people stumbling along the corridor and the sharp crack of a pistol shot. "Oh my God. Has someone been shot?"

Emile was about to get up to investigate when Marie-Claire pulled him back. "Don't! Don't! There's nothing we can do. If you open our door they might shoot you. Please Emile, don't go."

As he hesitated the noise in the hall grew louder, with more shouting and the clatter of German hob-nailed boots trampling back and forth. Madame Coutreau could be heard protesting their innocence, but her voice stopped abruptly when a German shouted 'shut up'. Marie-Claire heard a dull thud followed by a low groan and she feared Madame Coutreau may have been hit. There were more commands in German, "Downstairs, get going."

Emile lay back in bed, his body tense. She lay against him, holding him tightly. He kept muttering, "Is this what life is now?"

Finally the sounds in the hall receded and silence descended.

In the morning as they drank their coffee substitute Marie-Claire said, "One of us will need to open the door and look in the hall."

Emile rose quickly from his chair. "I'll do it."

He tiptoed to the door and listened for any sound in the hall. He undid the locks and pulled the door open just enough to look down the hallway. "There's no one here and I don't see anything out of the ordinary. Maybe the shot was just to scare them."

He closed the door and put on his coat. "I need to go. I mustn't be late for work. We must pretend nothing happened and not ask anyone about it, not even our concierge."

"But surely Madame Baudry would know what happened and who was arrested and why."

"Yes she may know, but she may be the person who betrayed them. You know the rule – listen but don't talk and don't ask."

After Emile left Marie-Claire cleared away the coffee cups and prepared to go out to meet her friend Katia. Looking in the mirror she was upset to see her face showed signs of strain from the stress and lack of sleep. She knew if there was ever a time to use some of the little makeup she had left it was now. To go out looking so upset would be to invite questions.

The street outside was calm with no evidence of the previous night's commotion. It was the same disheartening atmosphere as every other day. Marie-Claire hated how quickly the Germans had changed Paris. She loathed seeing the replacement of French street signs by ones in German script. It felt to her like a perpetual insult. She knew from the speed with which they were put up that they had been made well ahead of the invasion of France. It reinforced her belief in Emile's words from his reading of *Mein Kampf* when he said the occupation was always going to happen and that France never stood a chance.

Before the occupation she had seldom taken a taxi, preferring to go by Metro, but that did not reduce her anger at having the option removed. Taxi cars were no longer available to be used by Parisians, only Germans. She was amused to see that to counter this some enterprising Parisians had begun to operate horse-drawn taxis. There were even oriental style human rickshaws. She smiled to herself – *at least they're readily available as no self-important German would allow himself to be seen in such a thing.*

She had often commented to Emile that the buzz of Parisian life had been extinguished by restrictions and the curfew. The streets were now filled with Germans in jackboots and long overcoats. She knew that most Germans weren't openly physically abusing people. They didn't need to be physically abusive – their mere presence in the streets, cafes, shops and cinemas meant Parisian social life had been replaced by silence, secrecy and lack of trust.

She knew she could talk to Katia and was looking forward to seeing her. *I can't keep all my thoughts bottled up inside.*

Marie-Claire took the Metro to the Champs-Elysées. From there it was only a short walk up the avenue to the cafe on a side road where she and Katia always met. The Champs-Elysée was no longer the same as it had been in May before the Germans occupied the city. Back then it was crammed with buses and cars and ladies in elegant garments displaying their wealth and status to the world. Now Marie-Claire felt the street was so quiet she could hear her heart beat and beat it did with hatred at the sight of German officers flaunting their possession of her city.

When she reached the cafe Katia was already there, sitting at a table outside. The tables around her were empty. "Hello Marie-Claire. Isn't this a lovely day?"

Marie-Claire was still feeling depressed. "The sun is shining but that's about all that's lovely."

"Come on, think about it. We're both alive and free to meet."

"Yes but for how long? Last night our neighbours were arrested and I have no idea why. It was so frightening just listening. There was even a gunshot. I don't know if anyone was hurt but I was absolutely terrified."

"That must have been horrific. Was it the Germans?"

"They were speaking German so yes. There was nothing we could do, nothing at all. How can we fight against these people?"

Katia lowered her voice. "Actually I have begun doing something. Remember I told you my friends and I were trying to make life uncomfortable for the Germans? Well that's changed – I am now part of an active resistance group."

"You shouldn't be telling me this," whispered Marie-Claire.

"I trust you and I need to tell someone. I've been hiding a British Spitfire pilot who'd been shot down over Dunkerque."

Marie-Claire looked around quickly to check if anyone could have heard such an incriminating statement but fortunately the surrounding tables were still empty. "Katia, you mustn't say such things. Someone might hear."

"There's nobody near us and I've simply got to tell you. It was thrilling and frightening at the same time. I had to go to Place de la Madeleine and find this person I'd never seen before. Can you imagine how I felt? But it wasn't as difficult as I thought it would be. I'd seen a sketch of what he looked like and I'd been given a description of his clothing."

Marie-Claire wasn't concerned with how Katia felt. She was too disturbed by her friend's revelation. *Does she suspect it was my sketch?* "Did you say Place de la Madeleine?"

"Yes. Your mother used to live there, didn't she?"

"Yes. Number 6, above the shop. So what did you do with the person, this airman? Did you take him somewhere safe?"

"He stayed with me for two days."

Marie-Claire found it almost impossible to believe what she had just heard. "Katia. Are you sure you know what you're doing?"

"Oh yes. I feel I'm now doing something useful in this war. His name was William MacDonald and —"

"You shouldn't have told me his real name. I didn't need to know. Oh Katia, what have you done? Why did you have him stay with you for two days?"

"He stayed while we had an ID card forged for him. He gave us all the details saying that way it would be easier for him to remember. After we obtained the new card Rosette came and took him away to another safe house."

"From what you've described I doubt I'll ever join the resistance. That sort of excitement is not for me." She suddenly dropped her voice. "Katia we need to change subject. Someone has sat down at the next table and might hear us."

When Marie-Claire returned home Madame Baudry stopped her in the hall. "I thought I should warn you. You have a new neighbour. The Coutreaus have left Paris and while you were out German soldiers stripped their apartment. It's now occupied by a German officer. Did you know the Coutreaus well?"

"No. We said hello and were polite but nothing more than that. I wouldn't say we knew them at all."

"I see. Well I thought I should warn you."

As Marie-Claire walked away, she was troubled by Madame Baudry's words 'I thought I should warn you' and could not decide if the warning was friendly or threatening.

When Emile returned home in the evening she told him about their new German neighbour and Madame Baudry's warning. She then asked him, "Why didn't you tell me Katia was involved in your resistance group? How could you keep that from me?"

Emile looked askance at his wife. "What are you talking about? She's not part of our group. What made you think she was?"

"Because Katia was the person who collected my airman from Place de la Madeleine. That's why."

"I can assure you my group was not involved. I passed on the details and your sketch to a contact I know in an escape network. You say Katia did the pick-up? That's seriously dangerous work."

"Would she be sent to prison if she was caught?"

Emile sighed and looked at her with a troubled frown. "If only that were all, but I'm afraid it would be much worse. She'd be taken to 84 Avenue Foch."

"Avenue Foch? Wasn't that named after the French general who won the Great War against Germany."

"Yes, ironic but perhaps intentional. The building at 84 Foch is

44

now the Gestapo headquarters. I've heard that is where they torture and execute French prisoners."

"Could Katia be executed for just helping that man?"

"Sadly yes. The Germans follow Hitler's ruthless ideology. I've heard that just over a week into the occupation a German military court in Rouen ordered a Frenchman, Etienne Achavanne, to be executed by firing squad just for cutting a telephone line."

"Death for cutting a telephone line? I didn't see anything about that in the papers."

"No, and you won't. Apparently the Germans were afraid of retaliation if it became widely known, but the news spread like wildfire throughout the various resistance groups."

"Do you think Katia knows? Should I tell her?"

"No, no. You mustn't tell her. She might want to know how you heard about it."

"Are you saying perhaps I should stop seeing her? It's bad enough already. When she told me about her adventure and I didn't tell her it was my sketch it felt as if I was lying to her."

Emile reached over and held her hand as he tried to reassure her. "You weren't lying to her. Not saying it was your sketch was protecting both of you. You did the right thing. If she'd asked if it was your sketch and you had said no that would be lying, but she didn't. So I'm not saying don't see her, just stay away from any resistance related conversations."

She was silent for a moment then gave him a lingering kiss. "Enough talking. The curfew's not for another two hours. Let's pretend the world is as it was and go for a stroll along the Seine."

"Good idea, but before we go, let me just say one more thing. Be careful who you sketch. There aren't many people who draw the way you do or as well as you do which would make it quite easy for the Gestapo to track you down."

Chapter 8

On Saturday the 6th of July Marie-Claire woke early and crept out of bed before Emile was awake. She wanted to surprise him with a special breakfast as it was his birthday and she'd persuaded him to take the day off. On Friday she had purchased some petit fours as a treat. She didn't get a large cake as it would have used up too much of the ration card, leaving them with virtually no bread for the rest of the week.

She covered a tray with a colourful napkin, put the plate of cakes and two cups of coffee on it and took it through to the bedroom. "Happy Birthday my love. Here's a little something to start the day."

"Thank you darling. This looks delicious."

As they were eating the cakes she told him she had plans for the day. They would take a leisurely stroll along the Seine to a small restaurant where she had booked a table for lunch. "You can choose what we do in the afternoon, but in the evening I have a surprise for you. All I'll say is we need to be in the Latin Quarter just after six."

After a lovely and enjoyable afternoon they reached the Latin Quarter at six o'clock. As they passed a small jazz and cabaret club Emile stopped and looked at the poster for the venue. "I see Edith Piaf is playing here for two weeks. She has such a lovely voice, I'll see about getting us tickets for next week."

"Well you could get us tickets for next week – that is if you want to go and listen to her for a second time."

Emile looked at his wife with a broad grin. "Are you saying this is where we're going?"

She leant over and gave him a big kiss. "Happy Birthday dear. The tickets for tonight are in my pocket."

Emile gave her a loving hug. "This has been the best birthday ever. Thank you."

Later that week Marie-Claire arranged to meet her Jewish friend, Simone Milhaut, at Le Bistro d'Angel. Marie-Claire arrived first and chose an outside table next to the bistro wall so no one could sit behind them and overhear their conversation. It also gave her a good view of everyone who came and went.

Fifteen minutes later Simone arrived, slightly breathless. "Hello. Sorry I'm a bit late but I wasn't sure if someone was following me. I took a round about route just in case, but I think I was just being paranoid."

"Better paranoid and alive than careless and dead."

"I see you've finished your coffee. Do you want another?"

"Another of that stuff? Not yet – I can still remember what real coffee tasted like before the Germans hi-jacked it all. But let me get you one."

When the waiter came over he asked Marie-Claire if she wanted a coffee for her friend, with sugar. She remembered this was the coded message asking if Marie-Claire wanted Reynald to keep a watch for undesirable customers.

Marie-Claire smiled. "Yes please Reynald."

"You seem to know this waiter well," commented Simone after Reynald left. "Do you trust him?"

"Completely. Emile told me he's known Reynald for years and they used to work together. Although he's fluent in German he claims not to be. It means the German soldiers talk freely when he's around, not realizing he's listening carefully to what they're saying. Apparently a glass of Pernod helps loosen their tongues."

"Useful. People often forget waiters have ears. But anyway, I had a word with my Rabbi and he said it might be possible to get some information about your family in Rotterdam but it could take a few weeks."

"Any news would be good. Maman is still talking about going there even though I keep telling her it's impossible. She'd have no valid reason for applying for a travel permit."

"You're right. Claiming she wants to check on the whereabouts of her Jewish brother-in-law is hardly going to be received well. Can't you get her to see that?"

Marie-Claire shrugged her shoulders. "Oh I keep trying but you know what mothers are like."

"Talking of mothers, mine asked after you the other day. Come to think of it, are you free on Friday? She is visiting me in the afternoon and I'm sure she'd love to see you."

"Yes I'm free and it would be great to see her."

"Be aware, there's a new concierge in my apartment block."

"What happened to that nice Madame Chenaux?"

"She left during the Exodus and never returned. The new lady is a real dragon and keeps tabs on everybody. I don't trust her one bit. Just to keep her from asking too many questions, why don't you bring a book and say you're just returning it. I'm sure you can find a book somewhere."

"I just might be able to. Emile may have one to spare."

The girls chuckled and then spent the next hour reminiscing about the old times and complaining about the freedoms they no longer had. When Reynald came to their table bringing a bowl of sugar Marie-Claire understood his coded message and decided it was time to leave.

On Friday afternoon Marie-Claire took the Metro to the station closest to Simone's apartment. Although she thought it was totally unnecessary, she was carrying an old book. When she had told Emile about Simone's idea, he'd insisted that she do so and said he'd get her a second-hand book from the shop. The following day they had laughed at Emile's initial mischievous choice of Maupassant's *Boule de Suif* – a collection of short stories about the German occupation of France in 1871. He had however decided this could be misconstrued so had settled for a romantic novel.

Simone's apartment building was an imposing five story block with a single entrance. The loge where the concierge lived had an internal window through which she could see all comings and goings. Marie-Claire had not even reached the window when the concierge opened her door and shouted, "Where are you going?"

In as pleasant a tone as she could muster Marie-Claire replied. "To see Mademoiselle Simone Milhaut in Apartment Seven."

The concierge's response, "No you're not," took Marie-Claire by surprise.

"Excuse me, but why not? Is she out?"

"She's gone. Gone for ever. Arrested along with her mother."

"Arrested? Why? What has she done?"

"She was a dirty Jew and I won't have Jews in this block. I reported her to the Germans last week and they finally came and took her away. I'll have the place fumigated tomorrow. Why were you going to see her?"

Marie-Claire tried to contain her shock at the anti-Semitic tirade. "I was just returning this romantic novel she leant me."

"A waste of time reading that stuff. You should be learning German if you know what's good for you."

Realizing that any form of disagreement could provoke the woman further Marie-Claire responded discreetly. "I'm sure you're right. I guess I can't return the book to her."

"Not here you can't. Try the Drancy prison where they keep all the human vermin before sending them East. But are you Jewish as well? Show me your papers."

Marie-Claire stepped back slightly. "I won't. I don't believe you have any authority to demand to see my papers."

The concierge moved towards Marie-Claire. "Show me your papers now. This is my apartment block and I demand to see your papers. If you refuse I'll call the police. Perhaps you'll learn to do what you're told when they haul you away to Drancy as well. Show me your papers – now!"

Marie-Claire feared that the woman would still call the police whether or not she showed her papers. She knew this would mean her details would be logged in police files and she would be tagged as suspicious. So she turned and rapidly walked away. The woman shouted after her, "I'm calling the police." Marie-Claire believed her and knew she only had a few minutes before the police would arrive.

She was about to head back to the Metro when it dawned on her that they would be likely to look for her there. She quickly turned off the main road into the first side street she came to, spied a small cafe and almost ran to it when she heard the sound of a siren approaching. *Can I hide in plain sight?*

As she reached the cafe she saw a gentleman getting up from his table. Although there were some empty tables, she rushed over and sat down at his table before the waiter could clear away the dirty dishes. She took off her beret, then pulled off her jacket, folded it up as a cushion and sat on it. Obviously sensing something was amiss, the waiter came over quickly. He was about to speak when Marie-Claire blurted out, "I need a hat, a large hat, anything which doesn't look like the beret I was wearing."

Without hesitation he nodded. "Certainly. I'll be right back."

She knew asking the waiter for help was a risk but the sound of the approaching siren had forced her hand – she had to do something to hide. She was in luck. In no time at all the waiter reappeared with a large straw hat. "Will this do Madame?"

She pulled the hat down over her face just before a Gestapo van, siren blaring, sped by heading towards the apartment building she had just left. The waiter stood motionless until the vehicle was out of sight and then leant over and quietly asked if she would like a coffee – on the house. A nod was all she could muster.

He returned shortly with a brimming cup of strong coffee. It was real coffee, black and aromatic – just what she needed to calm her nerves. The waiter appeared to understand her predicament and whispered, "I assume you want me to leave these dirty dishes – perhaps they show you've been here a long time and are obviously not the person they're looking for?"

This time Marie-Claire was able to speak, "Exactly, thank you. I'll wait here for a while if I may."

"Certainly you can. I'm glad to help."

Marie-Claire waited for an hour before she felt she could risk the trip home. She stood up and took off the large hat. As she did so the waiter came rushing over. "No Madame. Don't take it off – keep the hat. And here's a bag for your jacket. Keep the disguise until you are home."

She looked at him with a puzzled expression. "But why? Why are you helping me? You don't know me."

"You're right, I don't know you, but I had a daughter about your age. She was a nurse in a TB sanatorium just outside Arras near the Belgian border. The Germans murdered her and all the patients when they invaded. They even burned the hospital to the ground. Need I say more?"

"No monsieur, I understand. And you have my deepest condolences, and my sincere thanks."

Emile arrived home at six o'clock and found Marie-Claire sitting at the kitchen table. She had opened a bottle of wine and poured herself a glass but had not drunk any of it. She promptly jumped up, threw her arms around him and burst into tears.

"My darling – what's wrong?" asked Emile in a worried voice.

She told him everything about the afternoon and the despair she felt for her friend's safety. When she'd finished, he shook his head then asked. "You said Simone told you this was a new concierge?"

"Yes. The other one left Paris during the Exodus and didn't return. Simone called this new person an untrustworthy dragon, but I guess she didn't listen to her own warning. Emile, is this what Paris is like now? French people betraying other French people?"

He took a deep breath. "In my little group we don't give traitors a second chance. I'll talk to the group and we'll decide what to do but we can't have her continuing to betray French people to the Germans. That apartment may soon need a new concierge."

She sat in silent thought for a long time then turned to Emile. "You know I've always supported you in your resistance activities, right? Originally I thought that was enough. But the behaviour of this lady, a blatant and horrific betrayal, has made me realize I want to do more. I need to do something positive."

She paused and Emile said nothing so she continued. "After everything that's happened and with the arrest of Simone just for being Jewish, I can no longer sit back and watch. I'm choosing to become actively involved. If you are taking risks, then so can I. Please don't try to dissuade me – my mind is made up."

Emile pulled her into a tight embrace. "I won't even try to dissuade you. I think you could be an excellent résistante."

51

Chapter 9

Marie-Claire was excited by the prospect of doing some resistance work. However, after a week had passed and Emile had not asked her to do anything, and had not even mentioned her decision, she felt disheartened. After dinner one evening she broached the subject. "You remember I told you I wanted to become part of your resistance group."

"Yes, and I appreciate you volunteering."

"But you haven't asked me to do anything. Why not?"

He paused before answering. "Sorry, but that was intentional."

"Intentional? What do you mean? Don't you trust me?"

"Of course I trust you. I trust you absolutely, but that night when you said you wanted to become active, you were very upset about your friend Simone and I needed to make sure it wasn't just an emotional reaction to her arrest."

"Are you saying you don't trust I can make a rational decision even when I'm upset?"

"That's not what I mean. It's just that providing silent support to someone is very different from actually doing something. I needed to give you time to consider the dangers involved and make sure this is something you definitely want to do."

"It's something I've been thinking about all week and I can assure you I do want to do something to fight back."

"Actually, there is a job you can do on Friday. We need someone to take a message to a fellow résistant and that would be a good introduction to resistance activity."

"Take a message to someone? Is that all? It seems a rather simple task compared to what others are doing. There's Katia risking her life helping a British airman. She even kept him hidden in her house for two days."

"How do you think Katia knew who to pick up, where to pick that person up and who to pass them on to? The answer is messages. Messages are the backbone of resistance. Obviously we can't use the phone or the post as everything is monitored. The only way to communicate safely is messages and for that we need resourceful messengers, the type who are aware of the dangers and can adapt quickly if circumstances change." He paused. "In my mind you fit the description perfectly. In the soup kitchen you showed you could be resourceful and quick to adapt."

Marie-Claire smiled. "Thank you. But getting back to messages, are you saying without messages, and messengers to take them, the resistance could not operate?"

"Put simply, yes. Without them there can't be any real meaningful resistance. We can't make public announcements about what we're doing. Everything has to be done discreetly and for that we need messengers."

"If I take your message on Friday what would I need to do?"

Emile picked up a book from the coffee table. "You would need to take a book, such as this book, to an address I'll give you, hand it to the concierge and say 'Alberto is returning this book'."

"So the message is inside the book? What if it falls out?"

"There is no message in the book and the actual book is irrelevant. No, the message is the fact a book is being returned from someone called Alberto. The recipient will then know to do a prearranged task. You could call the message a trigger."

"I see, so what will this person do when they get this message?"

"Remember the rules on secrecy? I can't tell you and it's not because I don't trust you, it's because I don't know. I've just been told what needs to be done. A book needs to be handed to someone with the words 'Alberto is returning this book'."

Marie-Claire nodded her head. "I see. If that's all that's involved then I'll do it."

"Thank you. But please remember, the most important thing is do not react if you are challenged. One of my group put it very nicely when he said – 'if you have a secret message, you must not only hide the message but you must also hide the fact you have something to hide'. If you are challenged, try to act normally. I know it's difficult but it's critical."

On Friday Marie-Claire set off on her first resistance activity. She wasn't carrying guns or grenades or ammunition. She didn't have any pieces of paper with messages written in invisible ink. She hadn't memorized a message. And yet she was feeling just as anxious as if she was doing any of those things. All she was doing was carrying a shopping bag with some food and a book. Emile had told her many times to always carry a bag with some food in it to give her a reason for being out if stopped at checkpoints.

As she turned a street corner she saw a military checkpoint and a gruff German voice called out, "Halt! Papers please."

This was a new checkpoint. Marie-Claire had been this way yesterday and it wasn't there. She had experienced checkpoints before but never as a résistante. The officer examined her papers in detail, even sniffing them. He then demanded to see inside her bag. Marie-Claire tried not to show concern. *Will he suspect I'm carrying a message of some sort*?

When he picked up the book her fear grew stronger, even though she knew there was no physical message. The officer appeared to sense her anxiety and staring directly at her he held the book upside down and shook it so any loose pieces of paper would fall out. When she showed no reaction he asked her, "Madame, do you like reading? Is this a good book?"

She recalled telling Emile the cardinal rule of resistance – 'never give out more information than necessary'. "Yes I like reading but I haven't yet started this book."

He did another shake of the book before handing it back to her. "That's all. You can pass. I hope you enjoy the book."

She put the book back in her bag and walked on with her heart pounding. Fortunately it didn't take her long to reach the address. She wondered what action she was triggering by returning the book but also appreciated how important it was that she did not know and would never find out. She was pleased to see the concierge in the hall and passed the book to her saying, "Alberto is returning this book."

The lady nodded and took the book. Marie-Claire left and set off to the nearest Metro station. She had arranged to meet Katia in their favourite cafe. Sitting in the Metro she began to calm down and came to a significant conclusion – *being a messenger is not as easy as I had thought.*

Usually when Marie-Claire arrived at the cafe Katia was already there, but not today. Her nerves were on edge and Katia's absence worried her. *Has Katia been arrested? Has she been betrayed by someone?* She was wondering if it was wise to stay when Katia came bounding up in her usual effervescent mood.

"Hi Marie-Claire. Have you got any more sketches for me?"

Marie-Claire's heart started to race. *How does she know I did the sketch?*

"What's wrong?" Katia smiled. "You've gone quite pale."

"I was just wondering what you meant. I haven't done a sketch for you in years."

"Come on. You know, the sketch of the man I had to meet in Place de la Madeleine."

"What makes you think I did it?"

Katia laughed. "The moment I saw it I knew it was yours. It had your signature all over it."

Marie-Claire was caught off guard. "What? Did I sign it?"

"No, but I sat with you in school art class for many years. I was hopeless at sketching but you were brilliant. I saw it was your style immediately."

"Oh. So why didn't you mention it when we talked last week about your adventure in Place de la Madeleine?"

"I should have but I wasn't sure how you would react, but then I realized we shouldn't be keeping secrets from each other. I have to say, it was a very good likeness."

"Thanks. You didn't show the sketch to him, did you?"

"No, of course not. Actually I burned it before going out to find him. Sorry, perhaps I should have returned it to you."

"No, of course not. And you did the right thing burning it."

"I thought so. And you need to be much more careful. You fell for a simple trap."

"Trap? What trap?"

"I said your signature was all over the sketch and instead of asking what I meant you asked if you had signed it, thereby admitting you had drawn it."

"That was stupid of me wasn't it."

Marie-Claire debated with herself whether or not to tell Katia that she was now involved in resistance work and had just completed her first assignment. Although it seemed as if she was being dishonest, she decided it was safer not to admit her involvement and instead she changed the subject.

"Any news about Hannah? Last I heard she left with her family during the Exodus and was going to stay with relations in Toulouse. Do you know if she made it?"

"Actually I bumped into her a few days ago. Her family went but she stayed in Paris. She's still working, writing under a false name for one of the newspapers."

"I didn't know. I must call on her and see how she's doing."

"Ah, you won't find her at their old apartment. With the Germans hunting down and arresting prominent Jewish families, she felt it was too dangerous to stay there. She's in hiding and I don't even know what name she's using."

"Pity, I would like to have seen her."

"If I see her again, I'll let her know you'd like to see her. But right now I need to be serious. As you know, I'm deeply involved in resistance work now and I'd hate to be responsible for anything happening to you. Sometimes I wonder if I'm being followed and if I am it could be disastrous for you to meet me or even appear to recognize me."

"What are you suggesting? We stop meeting? I'd hate that."

"No of course not, but we could have a sign such as the one we use in our little group. If we're approaching another member and we have our hands clasped together in front it means 'I think I'm being followed – ignore me'."

"That seems simple, but I hardly think it's necessary."

"With the way the Gestapo are operating it's worth having such a sign – but hopefully we'll never have to use it."

Chapter 10

Marie-Claire found her work delivering messages for the resistance very rewarding. No matter how small the task, it gave her a sense of satisfaction doing something to help in the fight against the tyranny of the German occupation. Over the next few weeks she became increasingly confident, but she never lost the sense of anxiety which kept her alert to the dangers involved.

She was now taking a much wider range of messages. Sometimes she had to memorize the message and recite it directly to the recipient. Other times she had to leave a message at a prearranged drop off point such as a hole in a wall. However, she was always more concerned when she had to collect a message from a drop off point in case someone was watching to see who collected the message and follow them. Fortunately she never detected anyone following her.

Although most of the places she was being asked to go to were in areas she would not normally frequent, she had to deliver one message very close to her mother's apartment building. After making the drop off she decided to call in on her mother. Recently her mother had always suggested the two of them meet at some bistro or cafe and Marie-Claire realized it had been a long time since she had visited her mother at her apartment.

When she arrived at the apartment block Marie-Claire stopped to have a friendly chat with the concierge, Madame Mercier. The same lady had been working there ever since Marie-Claire was a small child and she knew her well. After an exchange of good wishes and enquiries after Emile Madame Mercier was called away and Marie-Claire headed up the stairs.

She was about to use her key to open the door to her mother's apartment when she heard voices coming from inside – her mother's and another that sounded like a man's voice. *That's strange. Madame Mercier didn't say anything about Maman having a visitor.* She knocked and waited. The voices inside ceased abruptly and after a few moments silence she heard her mother's voice asking who was there.

"It's me, Marie-Claire. Open the door."

Her mother opened the door just enough for her to step into the hall and pulled it almost closed behind her. However, as she did so Marie-Claire had a clear view into the room and saw a young man she'd never seen before sitting at the table. Before she could say anything her mother asked, "What are you doing here?"

Marie-Claire was taken aback. "Since when have I needed an invitation to visit?"

Concerned about her mother's behaviour and anxious for her safety, she pushed past her mother into the apartment. Seeing the surprise on the man's face she put a protective arm around her mother's shoulders. "Who is this man sitting at your table?"

Her mother hesitated before answering. "This is – Cédric."

The man rose from the table, picked up his coat and hat and left with a curt "I'll see you later" directed towards her mother, followed by a polite "Goodbye Madame" to Marie-Claire.

After he had gone Marie-Claire turned to her mother. "Maman, what's going on? Who is he? Are you safe? Is he threatening you?"

"No, he's no threat. He's a friend."

"Really? It didn't look that way. What sort of friend is he?"

Her mother hesitated, then pulled Marie-Claire down to sit beside her on the sofa. With hands clenched tightly together she spoke in a soft voice Marie-Claire could hardly hear. "I should perhaps have told you but there's a need for secrecy. I know I can trust you and Emile but I was told to tell no one."

"Tell no one what?"

"Don't be worried, but I'm involved with a resistance group. Well not so much a resistance group as an escape line."

Marie-Claire stared at her mother in utter amazement. Finally she spoke. "Are you saying this apartment, the place where I grew up as a child, is now being used as a safe house?"

"Yes. Apparently the Germans don't suspect older people, especially older women – silly fools."

"Have you any idea how dangerous this is? And how did you become involved? Were you forced into it by this Cédric person?"

"No, no. Nothing like that. In fact the exact opposite."

"Maman. Please explain because right now you're not making much sense."

"You remember Betje, Uncle Coenraad's sister?"

"Yes, she was often there when I stayed at the Dagloonder's. But what's she got to do with this? Did she get you involved? Is she running an escape line all the way from Amsterdam?"

"No. Let me explain. A while ago my door bell rang and when I opened the door there was Betje, all alone and very frightened. The Germans were beginning to round up Jews in The Netherlands and she had to escape. You may recall she's a journalist. She was working for a Jewish newspaper and had written many anti-German articles. As a consequence she knew she was high on their hit list. Fortunately, with the help of Dutch friends, she was able to escape through Belgium to France."

"You said she was on her own. Did the Dagloonders not come with her?"

"No. She tried to contact them in Rotterdam, but like me she couldn't get any answer. She knew she couldn't stay in The Netherlands so she came to me, to see if I could help her. And of course I couldn't turn her away – she's family."

"So where is she now? Is she living here with you?"

"No. She wanted to get to England so she could write freely about what was happening in The Netherlands. I agreed to see what I could do to help her escape."

"You agreed to help her? But how? I didn't think you knew anyone in the resistance."

"You're right, I didn't. But I decided to ask our friend Madame – no, I won't tell you who I asked. It's safer for her and for you if you don't know. Let's just say my friend asked her friends and we found someone who knew someone who was involved in helping people escape to Spain."

"A friend of a friend of a friend? And you trusted them?"

"If Betje was to escape we didn't really have much choice."

"So has Betje escaped? Did she get to England?"

"Yes. We've had a coded message that she made it to London."

Marie-Claire breathed a sigh of relief. "That's good news – and we don't get enough of that these days. It's just a pity she wasn't able to contact her brother and take the Dagloonders with her."

"I know, but at least she made it."

Marie-Claire looked at her mother with a puzzled expression. "I understand why you helped her but that doesn't explain why you are now running a safe house."

"Well, after we found out how to smuggle Betje out of Paris to Spain my friend suggested we might be able to help other people. We all find it very rewarding, so that's what we're doing."

"So where does Cédric come into this? Is he someone you are hiding? If so, why did he walk out?"

"Cédric is not an escaper. He's one of the people who brings me someone to hide. That's what we were discussing when you arrived. We help anyone who needs help to escape – Jews, French soldiers, British airmen."

Marie-Claire was taken aback by the confession that hiding people had become a way of life for her mother. As she sat in stunned silence worrying about her mother's involvement in this hair-raising scheme she noticed that the family photographs were missing. "I see you've removed all the photographs. You used to have them everywhere. Is this to hide them from all the strangers coming to the apartment?"

"Yes, all the people in my group have removed all photographs of children and friends. We did it in case we're raided or the person we are hiding is an informant. We don't want the Gestapo thinking you might be involved and coming after you as well."

"I'm sure they wouldn't be fooled by that Maman."

"No, but without a photograph or address they wouldn't know who they were looking for."

"Have you removed all references to our address as well?"

"Yes. I know where you live. I don't need it written down."

Marie-Claire was becoming more and more concerned for her mother's safety. "You said earlier it was rewarding, but have you any idea of the dangers involved – of what they'd do to you if you were caught? This seems an incredibly dangerous thing for you to be doing. Why didn't you talk to me before becoming involved?"

"Why? Because you would have tried to stop me."

"You're right – I would have."

"And that's why I didn't. I know you're worried about your dear old mother but it's what I want to do. It makes me feel I'm doing something for the war effort. After all there's not much else I can do, and it's the same for my friends. As I said, my group's made up of older people – many of them older ladies who appear quite frail. We're the last kind of people the Germans are likely to suspect."

Marie-Claire sat silently wondering what she could say. Eventually her mother broke the silence. "Marie-Claire, please say something. Don't just sit there disapproving of what I'm doing. I want to do something to fight the occupation and it's the most sensible thing for me to be doing at my age. If me and my friends are caught, well we've had good long lives. It's better that we're caught rather than young people. Which is why I'm pleased neither you nor Emile are involved." She paused then asked, "You two are not involved in resistance, are you?"

Marie-Claire realized it would be safer to lie to her mother. "No. I was quiet because I was just thinking over what you've been saying and worrying about your safety. I am, though, proud of what you're doing and I'm sure Papa would also have been proud."

"If your father was still with us I'm sure he would be an active résistant. But I'm pleased you and Emile are not involved in any resistance work. At least I don't need to worry about that."

Although Marie-Claire was upset at lying to her mother she knew it was the best thing to do. However, her mother's next disclosure did nothing to put her mind at rest.

"You said what I'm doing is dangerous. I know it is. And I know if I'm caught or betrayed I'll probably be shot but I'll take at least one of them out with me. I still have your father's pistol and ammunition from the Great War."

Bewildered, Marie-Claire rose to her feet and paced back and forth trying desperately to reconcile this gun-toting elder citizen running an escape line as the mother she had always previously thought of as a rather prim, proper and law-abiding Parisian lady.

Her mother watched for a while. Finally she stood up and put her arms around her daughter. "Please don't worry about us. We are all aware of the dangers and are very careful. And now I think we both need a cup of coffee. And I have a little surprise to share with you. One of my friends gave me some real coffee."

While they were in the kitchen making the coffee her mother asked, "Do you have any news about Ghislaine or Anna or Coenraad? Betje didn't have any."

"Sorry, no news yet Maman, but it can take a long time. Nobody can use the post for such information. It has to be passed person to person and that takes time."

When the time came to leave Marie-Claire gave her mother an extra long hug. *Does Maman really know what she's doing? Does she really understand the risks? This could be the last time I hold her*. She tried hard to hold back her tears but failed.

Her mother noticed, pulled out a handkerchief and wiped her daughter's eyes. "Marie-Claire, I can see you disapprove of what I'm doing but it's my way of fighting back."

"Maman, I understand why you're doing what you're doing but please be extra careful. It's so important to be wary of who you trust these days. Does Madame Mercier know what's going on?"

"Don't worry about her. She's not a problem."

Marie-Claire was not sure what her mother's answer meant but decided not to ask. As she headed off to the Metro she decided that in light of her mother's new activities she must never use her key to access her mother's apartment again – she must always knock. Given the weight of the key, she also decided that since she'd never use it again she might as well remove it from her key-ring.

The more she thought about what her mother had told her, the more bewildered she became. *My mother – a pistol-wielding resistance worker hiding Jews and Allied airmen? It's so unbelievable. I want to tell Emile but I'm not sure if Maman would want me to. But can I really keep such secrets from the man I love?*

Chapter 11

For the next couple of days Marie-Claire struggled to come to terms with what her mother had told her. Although she would have preferred it if her mother was not running a safe house, she knew she could not change her mother's mind and also realized it would be wrong to even try. Apart from the importance of helping the escapers, the whole operation gave her mother and her friends a sense of purpose and achievement in the fight against the Nazis.

When Marie-Claire thought about it that way, her mother's actions inspired her to want to become more involved in Emile's resistance group. On their customary Sunday evening walk she asked him about doing more but he seemed preoccupied and did not respond. She repeated her request. "Did you hear me? I want to become even more involved."

At this point Emile stopped suddenly and hugged her – but with no sense of passion. He appeared to be looking over her shoulder. "Why have we stopped?" she whispered. "What's happening?"

Instead of answering Emile released her from the embrace and ran over to a young blond-haired lady who had fallen and was obviously in pain. Marie-Claire knew he'd been on some first aid courses and would know what to do but the speed of his reaction startled her. She saw he was kneeling down and appeared to be whispering to the lady. He beckoned Marie-Claire to join him and she ran over and crouched down beside the lady.

"Inside her shopping bag is a package," whispered Emile. "Get it out and put it inside your bag. Do it now without making a fuss – quickly."

Marie-Claire was surprised by this request and looked at the lady who whispered, "Yes, quickly."

Marie-Claire transferred the package to her bag and asked Emile, "Why are we doing this? Who is this lady?"

"You wanted to be more involved? Well now you are. That

package contains radio tubes for a resistance radio operator and we were following Sylvie in case anything went wrong."

A crowd was beginning to gather around so Marie-Claire made sure she showed no reaction to this revelation. In a loud voice Emile said. "It appears you may have broken your arm. Can you move it?"

With an almost imperceptible flicker of acknowledgement, Sylvie responded loudly, "No, I can't move it. I'll probably need to be taken to hospital." Then in a soft whisper, "Sorry about this — lucky you were here to help."

A man stepped out of the crowd and offered to call an ambulance. After he left Marie-Claire stood up and looking directly at Emile said, "Darling. We're going to be late for the service and you know how important that is to Père Ronan. You're not medical so there's nothing you can do to help this woman. There are other people here and if we leave now we can still get there in time."

An elderly lady spoke up. "If there's somewhere you two need to be, then go. I'll stay with this woman."

Emile took Marie-Claire's hand and they walked quickly away, turning into the first side street to get away from prying eyes.

Emile stopped and hugged her, this time with passion. "That was brilliant. I was wondering how we were going to get away before the ambulance or police arrived but what you said was perfect. If I have shown any doubts about you and resistance work, I apologize."

"Thanks. I surprised myself, but right now we've got to decide what to do with these radio tubes. Do we deliver them ourselves?"

"Yes and no. Yes we will need to complete the delivery but no we can't do it the same way. Sylvie has met the contact before and was heading to a park to hand over the package. Whereas I know the park, I have no description of the contact. Neither Sylvie nor the contact are part of my resistance group. We're here because they had an emergency and I was asked to stand in and recover the parcel if something happened."

"So what do we do now? Do we return it to this other group?"

"No. As a back-up plan in case something went wrong, I was given the contact's home address in an encoded format which means I will be able to deliver the package tomorrow morning."

"Can't we do that now?"

"Not really. There isn't time to go home, decode the address, make the delivery and return before curfew. No, I'll just have to take time off work and deliver it tomorrow morning."

"You don't need to take time off. I can do it tomorrow."

"Being caught with radio tubes is not the same as carrying a coded message. It's much more dangerous."

"You've said to me in the past that a woman carrying a shopping bag is less suspicious than a man carrying a parcel."

"Yes I did, but the tubes are in a parcel and if they look in your bag they'll see it and ask what's inside."

Marie-Claire thought for a while. "I have an idea. Why don't I hide them inside a hollowed out baguette in my shopping bag? Everybody carries bread in their shopping bags."

Emile stopped walking and looked at his wife. "That's a brilliant idea."

Marie-Claire smiled at his approval. "Early tomorrow you go out and get us a baguette. I'll hollow it out and put the tubes inside. When you go off to work I'll go out with the bread in my bag as if I've just bought it and deliver it to the address."

"Except for the fact it uses up our bread ration, I think it's a great plan. But as for right now, I suggest we head home directly before we're caught with the package."

When they finally reached home Emile started up the stairs ahead of her, two at a time. She walked up more slowly and had only gone up a few steps when she felt a light tap on her shoulder – the shoulder with the bag. She flinched then turned around and found herself face to face with a German in army uniform. She froze. *Who is he? Will he want to look inside my bag?*

"Excuse me Madame. I did not mean to frighten you. I just wanted to introduce myself. I am Major Pfeiffer, your neighbour. Madame Baudry tells me that you are an artist. Is that right?"

Marie-Claire really did not want to have a conversation with a

German officer while Sylvie's parcel was in her bag. *Why did he stop me today of all days. I must follow the golden rule – say as little as possible.* "Yes. I am."

He smiled. "What a coincidence. Before this war started, I ran an art gallery in Dusseldorf. Maybe we can get together sometime and discuss the art scene here in Paris."

"I believe most art galleries have put their pictures in storage so there's not much of a scene here now."

"What a pity."

"I must ask you, please, to excuse me. My husband's not feeling well and I really must be going."

"Certainly. Maybe we can continue this conversation another time? And I hope Monsieur Blanchet recovers soon and this is not a recurrence of his tuberculosis. Please accept my apologies for detaining you. Goodbye Madame."

As she turned and continued up the stairs Marie-Claire was perturbed by his comments. *Why did he want to know from Madame Baudry what I did? And how and why does he know Emile had TB? I don't think even Madame Baudry knew that. I didn't trust him when he moved in and I certainly don't now.* She reached their apartment and closed the door with a sigh of relief.

"Emile. Our German officer neighbour stopped me in the hall and introduced himself as Major Pfeiffer. He not only knew I'm an artist but also the fact that you have had TB. That worries me – why does he know all this about us?"

"Did he ask to see in your bag?"

"No. He said he ran an art gallery and wanted to talk about art. I don't believe that for one moment. He frightens me."

"Are you suggesting he might be with the military intelligence branch of the German army? It's not the same as the Gestapo, the secret police."

"It would fit. I mean why is he billeted here on his own and not with his regiment? He keeps odd hours and often when he goes out during the day he's not in uniform. I think we need to be extra careful and restrict who comes to visit us."

"I agree, but right now I think the most important thing is to hide the radio tubes. If you pass them to me I'll put them under the false bottom of the armoire."

After hiding the tubes he went to the bookshelf, pulled out a book and retrieved a piece of paper which had the encoded delivery information. It took him almost half an hour to decode the details. When he was finished he called Marie-Claire over to show her the address and explain the password exchange.

"This is not like normal simple passwords. This time we have two complete phrases which must be word perfect. Once you've met up with the person you ask them, 'Do you know how to get to Rue Caron'. They are then supposed to reply with 'Yes. That's where Jean-Luc lives with Flavia'. But if instead of 'Flavia' they say 'Josephine' this means they are the contact but there is a problem so don't continue. If what they say is completely different, they are not the contact."

Emile then asked her to repeat the passwords and the address back to him. When he was confident she was word perfect he lit a match and burned all the paper he'd been working on.

Early the next day Emile went out and returned with a fresh baguette. As he handed it to Marie-Claire he apologized for only being able to get a long baguette.

"Actually long is much better," replied Marie-Claire. "I was wondering how to hide the fact I needed to cut the bread in order to hollow it out. But at this length it wouldn't fit in my bag, so breaking it in two to make it fit won't look suspicious." She hollowed out the two halves, inserted the radio tubes and plugged the cut ends with some of the hollowed out bits. She was rather proud of her subterfuge as she placed both parts of the baguette in her shopping bag along with some vegetables.

It should only have been a twenty minute walk to the address Emile had given her, but luck was not on her side. Just before reaching the address she turned a corner and ran into a German checkpoint. However, unlike other checkpoints she had encountered, this particular checkpoint was manned by a young soldier who spoke in a friendly manner.

She handed over her papers which he examined and handed back. He pointed at her bag. "What's in your bag?"

"Vegetables and some bread."

He gave a cursory glance inside and then started a conversation. "Perhaps you can answer a question for me. I'm new to Paris. I was only posted here a few days ago and I'm puzzled. I had been told that France, especially Paris, has the world's best croissant. But no one seems to have any. Do Parisians not like croissant?"

"Oh we do like croissant but I guess you don't know. Our government in Vichy passed a law at the beginning of August prohibiting people in France from making croissant."

"You cannot be serious Madame. A law forbidding French people from making croissant? That is the most ridiculous thing I've ever heard."

"Actually it's true and there is a reason. Croissants are made with lots of butter and our butter, the butter we make here in France, we're not allowed to keep. We are required to send it to Germany. So – no butter – no croissant. That's why."

He smiled wryly as he waved her through the checkpoint. "Maybe I need to go back to Germany to get a French croissant." Marie-Claire nodded her head as she walked away. *Yes, why don't you and all your friends go back to Germany.*

She encountered no more checkpoints and was soon at the address. It was a small building with no in-house concierge so Marie-Claire was able to knock on the apartment door without first having to explain who she was and why she was there.

But as the door opened she discovered to her horror that something appeared to be seriously wrong.

Chapter 12

When the door opened Marie-Claire stared in stunned silence. However, it wasn't entirely evident who was more surprised, Marie-Claire or the person who opened the door – her old school friend Camille. Although they had been close at school they had lost touch when Camille moved away from Paris.

Camille looked puzzled. "Marie-Claire? What a nice surprise."

She ushered Marie-Claire in and, after looking up and down the hall, shut the door and pulled the bolts over. She then gave Marie-Claire a big hug. "It's so good to see you. It's been such a long time since we've seen each other. But what are you doing here?"

Marie-Claire was not sure how to answer so she ignored the question. "You're right. It has been a long time. We haven't seen each other since you moved to Grenoble with your parents."

"Yes. I went to the electrical engineering college there. I see you've got married. Anyone I know?"

"No. I met my husband about two years ago and we were married in the spring. And you? Is there anyone special?"

"There's nobody now. But Marie-Claire, I need to know how you found me. It's very important. I haven't been in touch with any of our old friends since I returned to Paris."

Marie-Claire began to wonder if in fact Camille was the contact, especially since at school she was always interested in electronics. *If she is doing highly sensitive resistance work that would explain why she wants to know how I found her address and why she hasn't contacted any of us.* She decided to try a cryptic comment. "I must have got the address from Sylvie."

Camille did not respond immediately but instead looked at Marie-Claire with a puzzled expression. "Did you say Sylvie? A blond-haired lady about our age?"

Marie-Claire decided to take a risk and spoke the opening password line. "Do you know how to get to Rue Caron?"

Camille stared at Marie-Claire for a moment before responding. "Yes. That's where Jean-Luc lives with —" and she paused again before adding the final word of the response, 'Flavia'.

They looked at each other in total amazement then both burst out laughing. "Talk of unlikely coincidences, is this really why you're here?" asked Camille. "But why isn't Sylvie here? Has something happened to her?"

"Yes. She had an accident. On her way to see you she fell and broke her arm and had to go to hospital. But don't worry, she's going to be alright."

"At least she wasn't caught. I've been really worried about her. I waited in the park until late but had to come back because of the curfew. But why are you here using her handover passwords? Are you acting as her replacement?"

"Yes, you could say that."

"Does that mean you know why Sylvie was coming here?"

"Yes, you could say that as well."

Camille looked at her friend and laughed. "You always did like teasing me. So tell me straight – do you have something for me?"

With a broad grin Marie-Claire pulled the two parts of the baguette out of her bag. "Yes. In here. Hidden in this baguette."

"What a fantastic hiding place. And superb cushioning against breakage. Who's idea was this? Or do I really need to ask – it was yours wasn't it? You always did have a good imagination. But don't tell me this is your bread ration."

"Yes it is, but we have other things to eat and getting the tubes here was important."

"And so is your bread ration. It would be silly to waste it and I have some jam and coffee. Do you have time to stay?"

"I do, and bread and jam sounds just perfect."

Camille carefully removed the radio tubes from the baguette and cut up the bread. As they were enjoying the bread and coffee Marie-Claire asked a potentially awkward question. "You don't need to tell me if you don't want to, or if you can't, but why haven't you contacted any of us? We'd have loved to see you."

Camille didn't answer immediately.

She held her cup firmly in two hands while staring off into the distance. Finally she put down the cup and spoke quietly with a slight tremor of emotion. "I suppose I really shouldn't tell you but it's been so lonely and seeing you has been so wonderful. And I do trust you completely."

"Camille, you have my word that what you say will go no further. If you don't want anyone else to know you're here that's fine, but why are you saying you're lonely?"

"You asked earlier if there was someone and I said 'nobody now'. Well there was. I came here to Paris with Roland, my fiancé. We met in Grenoble and were madly in love. He was studying languages at the university. It was his idea we come to Paris."

"May I ask why?"

Camille hesitated before replying. "I probably shouldn't say but I feel I need to tell someone. Let me ask – did you listen to de Gaulle's broadcasts in June just after France fell?"

Marie-Claire nodded and Camille continued. "Well, a number of us in Grenoble listened to him and decided we'd form a special resistance group. With my training in electronics and Roland's fluency in languages the intention was to establish a radio link between France and de Gaulle's London headquarters which could then be used for sending messages back and forth. Roland felt that Paris would be the centre of resistance activities and we should, therefore, set up our communication base here."

She paused for a moment. "So Roland and I came to Paris, but incognito. For security reasons we use false names. My ID card doesn't even show my name as Camille. We only communicate with other members via messages left at drop off points. Roland was to be the contact person and my job was to become the radio link to London. You may recall I was always fiddling with radios at school, even building my own."

"Yes I remember you did, and we used to listen to short-wave broadcasts from around the world."

"As you know, Grenoble is in the Unoccupied Zone. Since we obviously couldn't bring radios through the checkpoints on the Demarcation Line I've been building my own here."

"So that's why you needed the radio tubes. You're building the radios and Roland will use them to communicate with London. Talking of your fiancé, where is Roland?"

By Camille's reaction to her question Marie-Claire knew something was seriously amiss. With tears in her eyes Camille answered in a soft whisper. "I don't know, I just don't know. He went out one day to deliver a message and never came back. It's been almost two months now and there's no one I can ask. I certainly can't ask the police and I don't even know where he was going. There's no way I can find out if he's been caught or injured. After all this time I fear he's never coming back."

Marie-Claire moved over to where her friend was sitting to console her. They sat still and quiet, locked together in a hug, each caught up in their own thoughts. *I thought yesterday's actions were about securing the radio tubes, but that wasn't half as important as saving Sylvie. I can see our actions saved her life. Had she gone to hospital with the radio tubes and they'd been found, she would have been handed over to the Gestapo. Was Roland captured by the Gestapo when he was out delivering a message? Poor Camille will probably never know. I don't know what I'd do if I lost my Emile like Camille's lost her Roland.*

Camille was the first to speak again. "I think you can see why I couldn't contact any of our friends. I don't know who I can trust. Basically I'm here on my own and to be honest, with Roland gone, it's very lonely. It's been so good to see you."

"It's been good to see you too although I wish it was under better circumstances. If you want I can drop in again or perhaps you can visit me."

"Marie-Claire. I'd really like that but I can't endanger you or your husband. What I'm doing is extremely dangerous. If I'm caught I'll be interrogated and then shot as a spy. I don't even want to know your married name or where you live, and it's far too risky for you to visit me here again."

"I have an idea. Do you know Le Bistro d'Angel? I'm usually there on my own on Wednesday afternoons doing some sketching. It's a safe place."

"Yes, I know it and I'll keep it in mind. But much though I'd like to, I can't promise I'll be able to join you there."

For the next hour they chatted about life in general. As Marie-Claire rose to leave she gave her friend a final hug and reiterated her invitation. "So perhaps some Wednesday afternoon at Le Bistro d'Angel? Just the two of us. Remember it's ok to meet me – after all your cover is blown with me." They both had a chuckle at this unexpected situation.

As she walked home Marie-Claire was frustrated by the realization she couldn't tell Emile that the contact was her school friend Camille. *He obviously doesn't know. How many more secrets must I keep from him?*

On Friday Marie-Claire was due to meet up with Katia for their weekly coffee and chat. Much though she wanted to, she knew she mustn't tell her friend about the dramatic events of the last week and her meeting with their school friend, Camille. *I can't even share secrets with my best friend.*

As usual she took the Metro to Champs-Elysées. It was a pleasant sunny day and Marie-Claire enjoyed the stroll up the avenue. She turned up the side street towards the cafe where they were supposed to meet and was surprised to see Katia walking towards her – away from the cafe. Marie-Claire was about to wave a greeting when she noticed Katia make a definite movement of clasping her hands in front of her. With a feeling of shock Marie-Claire recognized the sign as indicating that Katia thought she was being followed and that Marie-Claire must not acknowledge her.

She walked past Katia without showing any sign of recognition. The dilemma now facing Marie-Claire was how far to walk before turning around to see what Katia was doing. Her concern for Katia's and her own safety meant she continued walking without looking back until she reached the next junction. Before going around the corner she glanced back towards her friend and a wave of horror swept over her. She saw that Katia was now encircled by Gestapo and French police officers and they were all pointing pistols at her and shouting.

Although her instinct was to rush back and somehow help Katia, she knew it would just be a suicide mission. She felt her knees buckle as the shock of what she was seeing took hold and she began to collapse. Just before she hit the ground she felt strong arms grab her. With a rising sense of panic she began to struggle. *Am I being arrested as well? How did they know about me?*

As she continued to struggle a hand covered her mouth and she felt hot breath on the back of her neck. A male voice whispered in her ear, "Don't move! Don't make a sound!"

Marie-Claire still struggled to break free but her attacker was too strong and was able to pull her quickly around the street corner. As he did so, she glimpsed Katia being shoved into the back of a waiting police van.

The man whispered in her ear. "There was nothing you could have done to help your friend Katia. You would only have been arrested or shot. I'm trying to save you. Those bastards who have arrested her also keep watch on the people around to see if anyone is upset and arrest them as well. That's why I dragged you away when I saw you begin to faint. Keep struggling and you'll just draw attention to yourself. Now, I'm going to take my hand off your mouth if you promise to keep quiet. Agreed?"

Marie-Claire nodded. The hand was removed from her mouth but the other hand kept hold of her arm. She was able to swivel around to face her captor. She stopped struggling as she recognized the older man who was restraining her. He was someone she'd often seen in the cafe when she was there with Katia. He spoke again in hushed tones. "By drawing those following her away from the cafe, and by signalling to you to ignore her, your friend just saved your life. You owe it to her not to throw your life away by becoming another target for the Gestapo. You saw Katia was pushed into a van? They'll probably take her to 84 Foch – and I assume you know what that means. I know you two were very close and it pains me to say this, but I doubt we'll ever see her again."

With those words he released his grip on her arm. The emotion of the situation became too much for Marie-Claire and she began sobbing uncontrollably. The man quickly produced a clean handkerchief. "Don't. You mustn't show such emotion here. Do it at home – wherever that is. I already told you the Gestapo scan for people acting as you are, so please stop."

"Who are you?"

In response he merely put his finger across his mouth in a silencing gesture. "Just think of me as a old veteran who wants to see 'La France Libre' again."

He then turned and walked away.

As she watched him disappear around the corner Marie-Claire stood transfixed, her mind filled with unanswerable questions. *Who was that? Who betrayed Katia? Was she deceived into helping a German spy? Will she be tortured? Will I ever see her again?*

Chapter 13

The loss of Katia affected Marie-Claire deeply. They had met in primary school and had been close ever since. After leaving high school the friendship had continued and Katia had even been a witness at her wedding. She had other friends but none so close and none who could replace the bubbly Katia.

She stopped volunteering at the soup kitchen – the place invoked sad memories of Katia's excitement at helping the downed Scottish pilot join an escape route.

She often thought about the man who had pulled her away when Katia was being arrested. *What did he say – Katia saved my life by drawing the Gestapo away from the cafe and by signalling to me to ignore her. Katia – wherever you are – I'll never forget what you did.*

One night she woke from a nightmare about the horrific scene of Katia's arrest to the sound of banging noises and loud German voices. "Aufmachen! Aufmachen!"

She recognized those words as the ones used when her neighbours, the Coutreaus, were arrested. *Oh my God. Are the Gestapo coming to arrest me? Katia knows I did the sketch. Has she said something? Are Emile and I in danger?*

"Aufmachen! Wir wissen, dass du da drin bist." The German shouting continued as Marie-Claire turned to Emile, "Tell me it's not our door – please. Oh God. What are they saying?"

"It is our door and basically they're saying 'Open up – we know you are in there'."

The banging continued with more aggressive shouting. Emile translated for her again. "That last shout was something along the line of 'Open up or we'll break down this door'. I'm going to have to open it."

As Emile began dressing, she whispered, "Should I get up and get dressed as well?"

He nodded. As she pulled on her clothes she asked, "Should I hide in the cupboard?"

He shook his head. "No. I've heard that instead of looking in cupboards they just shoot through them. At least if we're arrested openly we'll still be alive."

"Emile. Do you think someone has betrayed us?"

He turned sharply and rebuked her in a hushed voice. "Don't ever talk about possibly being betrayed. It implies we're doing something which we shouldn't be doing. Anyway, stay here in the bedroom. I'm going to answer the door before they break it down."

"Be careful dear – I love you." She wondered if these would be the last words she would ever speak to him. *Damn – I didn't give him a kiss.*

She crouched down behind the bedroom door, leaving it open just a crack so she could see the front door to the apartment. She watched him slide the bolts back and open the door. Four German soldiers stumbled in, pushing him aside, then stopped. As Emile spoke to the Germans the conversation gradually became less belligerent. Marie-Claire found it hard to believe what was happening when they appeared to apologize and leave. Emile closed the door and bolted it. As he turned around and slumped against the door, she ran over and knelt down beside him. "What was that all about? Who were they?"

He put his arms around her. "Relax, love – there's nothing to be afraid of. It was all a big mistake. They were just four German officers returning from a night out drinking. They were drunk and were in the wrong apartment block. They even apologized for disturbing us."

Marie-Claire let out a long sigh of relief. They both returned to bed but neither of them slept well.

Over the following week it seemed to Marie-Claire that there were even more German soldiers in Paris. When she mentioned this to Emile at dinner one evening he agreed. "I can't go anywhere for lunch without having to sit amongst German soldiers."

"I may have a solution," said Marie-Claire. "I've found a small cafe which the Germans don't use. I'll come by the bookshop tomorrow just before lunch and we can have a quiet meal just as we did before the occupation."

"Sorry, but I can't. I've got a critical job to do tomorrow."

"Is this something to do with the bookshop?"

"No. One of our passeurs is sick and no one else is available so I've got to take her place."

"You said 'passeur'. Is that someone who passes an item rather than a message from one person to another? The same as I did with the radio tubes? But surely it won't take long. Wouldn't we still have time for lunch?"

"No. It could take more than two hours – even if I'm quick."

"But what about the shop? Can someone cover for you?"

"No. Janine's away and Henri is off sick so I'll just have to shut it while I'm out."

"You can't do that – you could lose your job and we need your income. But I'm free tomorrow, so I can be the passeur."

Emile's response was so forceful it almost frightened her. "No. I can't let you – it's far too dangerous."

"Why? How is carrying a package from one place to another dangerous? Are you going to be carrying explosives?"

"Not exactly, but it's almost more dangerous."

"What's in the package? Emile, be honest."

He paused for a moment. "The package, as you put it, is not a thing – it's a person who is escaping from the Germans. And unlike radio tubes you can't hide a person in a baguette."

Marie-Claire hesitated. *I can see why he says it's dangerous. Should I really be volunteering?* "Was Katia being a passeur when she collected that man from Place de la Madeleine?"

"Yes, she was. You say you're willing to do this but first let me explain what's involved. An escape line is made up of different sections and for security reasons the people in the different sections never meet. Usually they don't even know who the other people are, which means if they're caught they cannot reveal the identity of the people in other sections of the line."

"That makes sense, but where does a passeur fit in?"

"As I said, the people in the different sections never meet but the escaper needs to go from one section to the next. For that we use a passeur, someone who acts as a go between, taking the escaper from one section of the line to another. The passeur does not know the people in either section. All the passeur knows is where they are to find the escaper, usually on a park bench or a pew in a church, and where they are to leave them. The escaper then becomes the responsibility of the next section in the line and so on down the route until they reach freedom – usually in Spain."

"Let me get this straight. The role of the passeur is basically to escort the escaper from one safe place to another without ever knowing who runs the safe places. I assume throughout the whole journey the passeur pretends to know this person, perhaps walking arm in arm? Surely that means it's preferable to have a female being the passeur so they can look like a couple?"

"Yes, but —"

"No buts darling. We agreed I would become involved in your resistance group. I've already delivered messages and here's an opportunity for me to do something even more important."

"But all things considered I feel it would be better if you covered for me in the bookshop while I did this job."

"Wait a moment. When you said your passeur was sick you said you'd take 'her' place as a passeur. So this escaper will be expecting a woman, not a man. If you, a man, turn up won't that make him suspicious?"

"Possibly, but I still can't ask you to do this job."

"You didn't ask – I'm volunteering. This escaper is expecting a woman, not a man, so it has to be me."

"I'll explain the details for this particular operation and after I've finished you can tell me if you still want to go ahead."

"Why wouldn't I?"

Emile paused before answering. "If you are caught, the escaper will be sent to a POW camp but you, the passeur, will be shot. That's why it's so dangerous and I really don't want you to do it."

"So, it's ok for you to be shot, but not me? We both take risks and this passeur needs to be a woman, so it has to be me."

Emile reluctantly agreed and explained what she would have to do. She was to find this person on a bench in the park near Saint Jacque's Tower, exchange passwords and then escort him via the Metro to the park at Square Claude de Molinet. There he was to go into this other park and wave goodbye to her, whereupon she was to return home.

"I take it this person doesn't speak French."

"I doubt he does. He'll probably only speak English, but to avoid attracting attention you should always speak in French."

"I'm glad to hear that. As I've told you before, at school I had no trouble reading and listening to English but speaking it was more of a problem."

"That's ok because in order not to look suspicious you need to keep chattering to him in French, even if he doesn't understand."

"Chatter? What about?"

"Perhaps the plot of one of the books you've been reading or that film we saw the other week. Anything just to avoid silence. And he will have a limp."

"You said 'will have a limp'. Don't you mean 'has' a limp? Is he injured?"

"No, he's physically fine. It's just a young man with a limp being helped along by a pretty girl is less likely to attract questions – the limp provides an excuse for him not being in the army."

"What if he forgets to limp – won't that be more suspicious?"

Emile laughed. "That won't happen. He'll have a coin taped inside his shoe under his heel, so every step will be painful."

"Ouch! Do you think that's why the man at the soup kitchen appeared to have a recent limp?"

"Possibly. Fortunately most informants and Gestapo agents are not as observant as you – they're unlikely to notice the lack of wear on the shoe."

"Ok, so you said I just leave him in the park – is that right?"

"Yes. You just wave goodbye, keep on walking and catch the next Metro back home. It's important you do not go into the park with him in case anyone is watching. And please call in at the bookshop afterwards to let me know everything is ok."

"Of course I will. So tell me, what happens to the man after I leave him in the next park?"

"He'll be taken to a green house, as we call it, for the night."

"A greenhouse? Surely you don't mean one of the greenhouses for plants?"

Emile looked uncomfortable as he answered. "No, and before I answer let me say I don't ever do that part of the operations – the term green house refers to a brothel."

Marie-Claire looked at her husband askance. "Did you just say brothel? This escaping soldier is being taken to a brothel? I'm glad you're not asking me to go there. But why a brothel?"

Emile grinned as he replied. "It may seem odd, but because many Germans frequent the Paris brothels they never search or raid them for fear of finding their senior officers there. As a consequence they are used extensively as safe houses. The girls are sympathetic to the resistance cause and often pass on information the Germans inadvertently reveal."

Marie-Claire understood the magnificent irony of using brothels as safe houses. "Ok. I think that's enough information and it's settled. I'll be your passeur tomorrow."

Chapter 14

Marie-Claire woke early the following day and lay in bed thinking about her role as a passeur. Although she knew it was dangerous, she felt inspired by the courage shown by Katia. The memory of her friend being arrested made her even more determined to do whatever she could to fight against the Germans.

At breakfast time Emile asked her to go over all the instructions and passwords again. When she had done this without hesitation or mistake he smiled. "Darling I have no doubt you'll do just fine, but remember – try to behave normally. If you show you are nervous the Germans will think you have something to hide. I don't have any cigarettes, so when you go out you'll need to buy a packet as asking for a light is part of the password exchange. I've got to go to work now and I'll be worrying about you so please don't forget to call in when you're finished."

Marie-Claire was not due to pick up the escaper until the afternoon so rather than spend the morning worrying she decided to do the one thing she knew would distract her – sketching. She went to Montmartre and in a small cafe she found a table with a good view. The street was filled with inspiration, ranging from the street sweeper in his baggy clothes and scruffy beret through to the haughty lady with a hat adorned with feathers. She soon became so absorbed in her sketching she forgot about everything else.

Suddenly she felt a tap on her shoulder. She flinched, looked up and saw a German officer looking over her shoulder at her work. He asked politely in fluent French if she'd do a portrait of him. "I'd like to send it to my wife in Hamburg."

Sketch a German officer in public? That's the last thing I want to do, but I can't refuse. Reluctantly she smiled. "Of course. Please sit down." She completed the portrait as quickly as she could. When it was finished, he smiled and said, "You are remarkably talented. My wife will appreciate this picture."

When he offered to pay her for the portrait Marie-Claire refused. "I teach art to students – I'm not a street artist, but thank you for the offer." *Given the number of Germans in Paris I could probably earn a lot doing street portraits but if I did that I might appear to be a collaborator.*

As he got up he asked if she would at least accept a packet of cigarettes as a small token of his appreciation. Marie-Claire nodded but was surprised when he passed her a pack of Gauloises – a brand known to be associated with resistance fighters. She did not react but detected a slight nod of his head, a glimmer of a smile and a raising of his eyebrows as if to indicate he knew exactly the implications of what he was doing.

After he left she kept sketching. At noon she packed up and asked the waiter for the bill. "It's already been paid Madame. Your friend the German Major has covered it."

She was about to respond with annoyance that the officer was no friend but just in time remembered Emile's warning that she must not do anything to attract attention. Instead she just thanked the waiter and vowed to herself never to return to this cafe.

With conflicting feelings of fear and excitement she set off on her mission as a passeur. She took the Metro to the Square of Saint Jacque's Tower. In the adjacent park she was to find someone dressed in a brown jacket sitting on a bench reading a newspaper. She soon spotted a man who seemed to fit the description. *I think that's him, but what if I approach the wrong person?*

She walked over as calmly as she could, took a cigarette out of the packet and asked in French if he had a light. She was relieved when he looked up with an expressionless face and mumbled the correct French response, "Pas aujourd'hui." She then asked his name and he answered 'Gustave' – the correct second password.

She put her cigarette away and sat down on the bench feeling slightly vulnerable. The man turned to her and whispered in English, "And you?" Marie-Claire suddenly recalled she needed to give him a password. When she said her fictitious name, 'Danielle', his slight nod confirmed to her that this was her escaper.

83

She wondered who he was but knew she must not ask and would never know. She leant over and whispered in her broken English. "No more English speaking and I call you Gustave. You listen, I make the talking. We walking arm around arm. Ready?"

They both stood up, she took his arm and they began walking to the Metro. She already had tickets so they did not need to face the scrutiny of the ticket seller. The Metro was crowded in the 2nd class carriage which meant they blended in easily and did not stand out. She clung to him as if her life, not his, depended on it – which in a sense she knew it did.

Marie-Claire was aware that ID papers were often checked as people entered or left a Metro station. Although the Porte de Vanves Metro station was the closest to their destination it was the terminus of the line and she felt it would have ID checks. Thinking it would be safer she planned to get off one stop earlier at Plaisance and take a longer walk.

As the Metro train approached Plaisance she overheard two ladies complaining. "Would you believe it Paulette. This is the third time this week they've been checking ID papers at Plaisance. It's as if they're looking for someone."

Marie-Claire tried not to show any reaction to what she'd heard and decided they must carry on to the end of the line and hope there wouldn't be any ID checks there. Her companion must have sensed her concern and he whispered, "Do we have a problem?"

She put her hand in her bag and partially withdrew her identity card. He understood, pulled out his card and slipped it into her hand. As she looked at it she felt as if her whole world was collapsing around her. His card had the wrong kind of stamp on it. She knew that anyone inspecting the card would immediately see it and arrest both of them.

A shudder went through her whole body and all sorts of thoughts went through her head, *There's nothing I can do to correct this card. Emile's instructions didn't allow for this catastrophe. What can I do? I don't want to abandon him, but my life is at risk if I stay with him. He would just be sent to a POW camp, but I would be shot!*

The man must have sensed there was a problem and looked at her quizzically. She gave him back his card and whispered, "Gustave, your card, wrong stamp. That stamp travel document – not ID card. You need new card. We could be arrested."

He leaned towards her and whispered back, "Danielle. I won't let you risk being arrested. We will leave separately and meet outside the station."

"Are you sure?"

"Absolutely. If we are arrested you would be shot, not me. So I will walk out on my own. We were taught if your plane's on fire – you trust your parachute."

So this man is an airman who flew over France risking his life for my country. She understood his expression 'you trust your parachute' to mean that he would trust her to find a solution to their dilemma. She whispered, "If anyone wants to check your card, I'll see if I can distract them."

She sat back and rummaged in her bag, looking for anything that might help. In her purse she found some coins and tipped them out of the purse to lie loose in her bag.

At the terminus the airman left the carriage first and she followed a few paces behind. Keeping their distance from each other, they walked up the steps towards the concourse at the street level. At the top she glanced around and spotted the station guard deep in conversation with two women. *Perhaps we'll get by without him stopping us to check our cards.*

The airman limped slowly forward and Marie-Claire followed. She looked towards the guard and her heart almost stopped as he said goodbye to the women and turned towards the airman. *I've got to stop the guard before he asks to see Gustave's ID.*

She walked rapidly forward until she was between the guard and the airman. She then pretended to trip, falling almost at the feet of the guard. At the same time she dropped her bag so the coins spilled out onto the floor.

The guard immediately bent over and tried to help her stand up. *I must put on a good show here or it's game over.*

She grimaced and let out a small cry, as if in pain.

85

"That was a nasty fall. Are you alright?" the guard asked her with a concerned expression.

"I think I might have twisted my ankle."

Out of the corner of her eye she could see the airman limping away. *A few more steps and he'll reach the exit to the street.* "My money," she said to the guard as she tried to pick up her coins. "Can you help me?"

The guard knelt down, gathered up the remaining coins and passed them to her. Marie-Claire could see that the airman had now left the station, so she thanked the guard and hobbled towards the exit.

The airman was waiting outside and she linked arms with him. She whispered softly. "Our parachute worked."

He smiled and nodded as they began walking away from the station on their way to the park. "That was very quick thinking. Thank you. Your action saved the day. I hope you didn't actually hurt yourself."

"No. It was just an act. I'm fine." Not entirely believing their good fortune, Marie-Claire started talking to him in French about the film *Gone With The Wind*, not caring if he had seen the film or understood anything she was saying.

When they finally reached their destination, Square Claude de Molinet, she leant forward and whispered in her limited English, "This your park. Sit, someone come for you."

He looked into her eyes, gave her hand a tight squeeze and whispered, "Merci. Merci beaucoup Danielle." He then did something which surprised her – he gave her a kiss on the cheek before turning and walking away.

She hoped he understood her comment about the problem with his identity card. *His forged card could put not only his life in danger but also the life of anyone helping him. If I ever act as a passeur again, I will check the cards at the start of the journey not halfway through. Since Emile might know who made the cards he could inform them of their error. I don't know how the forger could make such a stupid error.*

She stood stock still.

Error? Perhaps the wrong stamp is not an error. Perhaps the maker is actually a German agent producing invalid forged cards in order to have the escaper and their helper arrested and executed. Marie-Claire shivered at the thought of the close shave she and Gustave just had. She knew she had to warn Emile to check out the forger immediately.

When Marie-Claire reached the bookshop she looked around for Emile and was dumfounded to see he was serving the same German major she had sketched that very morning. Not wanting to be seen by him, she hid behind some bookshelves and tried to hear what they were saying. Unfortunately, they were speaking in German so she only understood the odd word. She saw Emile pass the Major a package – and it didn't look like books.

Their friendliness concerned Marie-Claire. *How can Emile be so sociable with the enemy*? She waited impatiently but it wasn't long before the Major left with a cheery goodbye. There being no other customers in the shop Marie-Claire approached Emile and fired a salvo of questions at him. "What did that Major want? What have you sold him? And where did my airman get his false papers? Who made them for him? Can you trust the maker?"

Emile raised his hands in a gesture of surrender. "Just a moment – hold on. I've been worried all day and it's a great relief to see you're ok. Did everything go according to plan?"

"No it didn't, and your forger may be a German agent."

"What are you saying? Was there a problem with his papers?"

"Most certainly," she replied in an agitated manner. "And it almost had both of us arrested. His ID card had a travel stamp not an ID card stamp. Fortunately we weren't stopped. I told him he needs to get a new card immediately. I don't know if it was a mistake or an intentional error to get us caught."

"Thank God you weren't stopped. You can see why I said it's dangerous. And well done for noticing the problem with the card. The Germans are trying to infiltrate resistance networks and our new forger could be a spy – if so it's a clever move on their part."

"You better check out all other documents he's done. But right now I want to know – what were you selling that German Major?"

Emile pointed to a narrow door near the back of the shop. "That doorway leads downstairs to our basement. Just before the Germans invaded, the owners of the bookshop installed a large printing press down there. The Germans haven't confiscated it because they find it convenient to have us do small print jobs for them – posters, flyers, announcements and such things."

"A large printing press? How did the owners get it down to the basement through that narrow doorway?"

"They didn't. The basement has a loading bay from the courtyard at the back. I'd take you down there to show you the press but I can't leave the shop unattended."

"Are you saying you work for the Germans? Selling the Major a book is one thing but doing a print job for him? How is that different from being a collaborator?"

He smiled. "Me? A collaborator? No, no – I'm exploiting them. The magnificent irony is that the Germans are paying for our resistance work. You see for their jobs they supply us with ink and paper and we always seem to request too much and use the excess for printing resistance documents."

"I see. But tell me, are you always that friendly when you're selling stuff to Germans?"

"I can see how it might have looked but my chatty banter with Major Kaufmann is part of the act. He's my contact for their jobs and for providing both paper and ink. Tell me – why did you hide when you came in and saw me talking to him?"

"I met your Major Kaufmann this morning in Montmartre. I was sketching and he asked me to do his portrait so he could send it to his wife in Hamburg. Instead of payment he persuaded me to accept a pack of cigarettes – Gauloises cigarettes. And he appeared to be fully aware of the resistance implication."

Emile was shocked. "I'm glad he didn't see you here – and I hope he never works out what else we print using his paper."

Chapter 15

Later that week Marie-Claire met up with Juliette, one of her old school friends who had left Paris during the Exodus. She had only recently returned and was still looking for a job. After an enjoyable morning with her at a favourite cafe, Marie-Claire was in a cheerful mood as she walked back home.

However, her mood changed abruptly when Madame Baudry came out of her loge and asked to have a quiet word in private. The invitation put Marie-Claire on guard. Although they often had a chat, the request for a 'quiet word in private' was rather unusual.

Her concern intensified when Madame Baudry closed the door behind them and locked it. "I don't want anyone walking in on our conversation or overhearing us. I've heard that you and Emile are not entirely pleased with the German invasion. Is that right?"

Marie-Claire was immediately overwhelmed with a sense of panic. *What has Madame Baudry heard? Is this a trap? Is that why she locked the door – to prevent me escaping? Was she the person who betrayed the Coutreau family*? "I'm not sure many people are pleased with the German occupation, but at least we're not being bombed or shot at. Life goes on."

"Yes, but there's more to it, isn't there."

Marie-Claire could not hold back. "What have you heard?"

Madame Baudry looked intently at her then asked, "Do you know Jamel Guyon?"

Of course Marie-Claire knew of Jamel. Emile had mentioned his name as one of the people who helped recruit and vet new members of his resistance group. But she knew now was not a good time to admit to anything which could be incriminating. "Why do you ask?"

"Don't look so worried. Jamel is my nephew and I know he and Emile work together on resistance activities. That doesn't worry me, in fact I approve of what he's doing. No. What worries me is I don't like what is happening and what I've been seeing here – in this street."

"Sorry, but I don't understand."

"Haven't you noticed? All your mail is being read before you get it – and that's by the Germans, not me. The German officer upstairs has been having an increasing number of military visitors recently. And then there's the man outside."

"I suspected the mail was being examined ever since the Germans took over the postal system. But what man outside?"

"Don't pull the curtain back but go to the window and look over to your right. See the man leaning against the wall?"

Marie-Claire walked over to the window and looked through the curtain. She turned back to Madame Baudry and in a trembling voice asked, "Who is he?"

"It's not always the same man but there's nearly always someone there."

"Who are they? What do they do?"

"They pretend to be reading a newspaper but instead they keep watching the street."

"I've seen a man there before but thought he was just someone reading the paper. You're saying he's not?"

"Oh no. Often before he leaves someone comes and takes his place. It's like a shift system. I don't know if he's a Gestapo agent watching our building or doing some other surveillance. It may be nothing at all to do with you and Emile and your resistance work. However, since we don't know why he's there, I think for your safety we should have some kind of simple signal to warn you not to enter the building. It could be dangerous for you or Emile if the Gestapo were in the building when you entered, even if they were not looking for you. We can't be too careful."

"What kind of signal are you suggesting? Surely if Emile and I can see it, so can other people."

"I'm thinking we could do the same as the concierge has arranged where Jamel lives. It's all to do with the flowerpot in my window. Before you come into the building look at my window. If the flowerpot is in the middle, this means everything is normal.

However, if the flowerpot is missing or is over to the side this means – 'Do not enter'. Just walk on by and go to the mustard shop around the corner."

"Why there? What have they got to do with this?"

"That's where Jamel works. He's the manager there. If there's a problem, go to the shop and ask if they have any *Moutarde Baudelaire*. Jamel will understand and pass you any message I've left explaining the problem."

"That's so simple but effective. I'll tell Emile about the arrangement as soon as he returns. Thank you for thinking of us."

"These days we need to do what we can to protect each other."

"So it wasn't you who betrayed the Coutreau family." As soon as she uttered the comment Marie-Claire felt guilty. *What have I just said?*

"No dear, it wasn't me but there was nothing I could do about it. The Gestapo just burst in without warning."

"I'm sorry for thinking it might have been you but these days one can't be sure of where people's allegiances lie."

"You're right to be cautious and suspicious which is why I wanted to let you know that we're on the same side."

Marie-Claire found it comforting to know that Madame Baudry was not just anti-German but was willing to take an active step to protect both her and Emile. She gave her a warm hug. "Thanks again. What you're doing means a lot to me, but let's hope it's never needed."

Late the following morning when Marie-Claire returned from doing her daily shopping Madame Baudry stopped her as she was about to go upstairs. "While you were out I had a visit from a young lady, about your age with lovely red hair. She said she couldn't wait for you but instead wrote you a short note. Wait here. I put it in my desk."

Madame Baudry returned with a small envelope. Marie-Claire thanked her, put it in her bag and headed up to her apartment. She opened the envelope, withdrew a small note and immediately recognized the handwriting. It was from her friend Hannah.

*Just heard about K   would love to see you
before I leave to join my parents Come here
if you can   Han*

me your artist at your sport our poet

Marie-Claire recalled Katia saying that Hannah was now living at a secret address while writing for a Jewish newspaper under a false name. She was amused by the final eight words. The clues to Hannah's false name and address reminded her of the fun they used to have racing to see who could be the first to solve the crossword puzzle in *Le Petit Parisien*.

I love you Hannah dear. You should be in the resistance – those clues wouldn't mean anything to anyone else except me. My favourite artist – Berthe Morisot. The number on my handball shirt – 12. Our favourite poet – the 19th century romantic Alphonse de Lamartine. So Hannah, dear, I guess you're living as Mademoiselle Morisot at 12 Rue Lamartine.

Since the note did not mention when Hannah would be leaving and the address was within walking distance Marie-Claire decided to go immediately. She packed her bag with sketch book and pencils and left the apartment.

Her heart skipped a beat as she looked towards the 'watcher' and saw he was looking directly back at her. *Don't react – ignore him.* She glanced away and walked on as if he was not even there. At the end of the street she looked back and was relieved to see he was ignoring her and no one appeared to be following her.

As she turned the final corner into the road where Hannah lived she became aware of a disturbance at the far end of the road. The Gestapo were dragging a struggling woman out of a building to a waiting van. Her heart rate soared as she saw the woman's red hair and realized it was Hannah.

She felt almost sick at the sight. Memories of seeing Katia arrested flooded her mind. Although her initial instinct was to run and help defend her friend, she didn't. She knew she'd be arrested as well if she did anything at all to help or to draw attention to herself. She was reminded of the words the man had said when they watched Katia being arrested. 'They look for anyone reacting and arrest them as well.' She was overcome with a feeling of helplessness. *Another of my friends arrested? What will they do to her? Will I ever see her again?*

As Marie-Claire watched in horror Hannah broke free and started running in her direction. It didn't appear as if Hannah had seen her – she was just running down the middle of the road. Marie-Claire then saw a Gestapo officer pull out his luger and aim at Hannah. A single pistol shot echoed through the street.

Hannah had gone no more than ten paces before she collapsed with her head now oozing a red stain on the road.

Marie-Claire went into shock at the realization her friend had just been murdered right in front of her. *Why did Hannah run? Surely she knew what would happen. Did she really think she could escape? Or was it her way of avoiding torture and ending it quickly, knowing they would execute her anyway?*

A German soldier who had been walking along the street just ahead of Marie-Claire, stopped when he saw the commotion. He had stood back when Hannah broke free and she was virtually next to him when she was shot. He took one look at her corpse lying on the street, turned around and began running towards where Marie-Claire stood. He almost knocked her over in his haste to get around the corner of the building. Stumbling to keep her balance she heard his footsteps stop, followed by the unmistakeable sound of him being sick.

In a fit of rage she followed the German soldier around the corner and found him kneeling down, holding his head in his hands as he continued to retch. Her anger at the murder of her friend overtook her common sense and without thinking of the possible consequences she went up to him and pushed him over so he almost fell into his own vomit.

Overwhelmed with anger and grief and with tears streaming down her face she flung her bag on the ground and began punching and kicking him, again and again.

Eventually she paused. *Why isn't he fighting back? Why isn't he arresting me?* She looked down at him. He was huddled against the wall mumbling to himself. She leant forward to hear what he was saying. He was repeating the name Greta over and over.

"That wasn't Greta. That was my friend Hannah you just killed. Do you hear me? My friend." She began punching and kicking his body again, with a hatred she'd never experienced before.

Finally he reacted, "Stop! It wasn't me. It wasn't us. Stop!"

She stopped attacking him and realized what a dangerous thing she had been doing. "What do you mean 'it wasn't you'? You're a loathsome German soldier occupying my country and killing my friends. Hannah is dead because of you – do you understand – dead. You vile German soldiers just killed her."

He answered in perfect French. "It was not us, army soldiers, who killed your friend. It was a Gestapo officer. Blame Hitler and Himmler. Not me. Not us. That was the secret police – the Gestapo. They have a distinctive uniform with SS on their collars, we don't. They are not soldiers. They even have skulls as their hat badges and that should tell you something about them. They are Hitler's paramilitary thugs. We are the German army. We're soldiers not thugs. We're as frightened of them as you are. And I never wanted to occupy your country. I don't want to be here. Believe me, I hate being here as much as you hate me being here. I didn't volunteer – I was conscripted into this army."

Marie-Claire could see he was having trouble keeping emotions in check. He stopped talking and buried his face in his hands and whispered Greta again. At the same time, she found her legs and body were beginning to shake. Fearing she might fall, she sat down beside him. She pulled a handkerchief from her pocket and started to wipe the tears from her eyes. In a soft voice she asked him, "Who is Greta? You keep saying her name."

With a sad face he looked at her and answered slowly. "Greta was my fiancée. We met at university. She was studying art, I was studying French. She was so beautiful. With red hair just like your friend Hannah. I miss her so much."

"What happened to her?"

An agonized look came over his face. "Are you aware of the anti-Jewish riots which took place in Germany in November '38, the Crystal Night riots? Well that night my Greta was shot by Hitler's thugs – just like your friend. And like your friend she was left to die in the street."

He stopped talking and his eyes filled with tears. She waited a moment before asking, "Why? Why was she shot?"

He had trouble responding. "Why? Because she was Jewish. There was nothing I could do to stop them. I had to watch her die. Today, seeing your friend Hannah being shot, it was just like seeing my Greta die all over again."

Marie-Claire was surprised to find herself feeling sorry for a German soldier. She could see he was struggling to keep his emotions in check. She began to see him not as a despicable German enemy but rather as a person who had feelings and who had also suffered a loss at the hands of the Gestapo. "You must have loved her dearly."

"I did – and I still think of her every day. And from now on when I think of Greta I will also have memories of your friend Hannah being shot the same way by the same set of thugs."

They both sat in silence. Marie-Claire's eyes were beginning to fill with tears again so she wiped them before asking, "You said she was Jewish. Does that mean you're Jewish as well? Surely not since you're in the German army?"

"No, I'm not. Greta was, not me."

"You said you were studying French. Is that why you're here?"

"Yes. Because of my fluency in French I've been forced to be a translator at the German headquarters. But as you've just seen I'm as horrified as you by what my country is doing."

Marie-Claire felt an odd connection to this man. She found it hard to see this tormented soul as the enemy. With the murder of her Jewish friend Hannah she felt she shared his sense of loss. She found it hard to envisage the anguish she would feel if she were to lose her Emile.

They heard noises from around the corner and scrambled to their feet. When he began to hunt in his pockets for something with which to wipe his face, she instinctively offered him her handkerchief.

He took it and was about to wipe his face when he stopped and tried to hand it back. "I see it's embroidered with your initials – O T. Thank you but I can't accept it."

Marie-Claire had forgotten this was one of a pack she had bought on sale in a market and the monogram had no significance. She did not wish to hurt his feelings so she responded with a name she'd read in one of the novels serialized in the *Le Petit Parisien*.

"Please do accept it. You really need to wipe your face before anyone sees you. And O T? In your memories of today think of me as Olivia – Olivia Tardieu."

"Your initials are close to mine, O V. Otto Voigt, Corporal Otto Voigt. And in spite of my uniform know this – I am not your enemy. But please always be aware of, and be afraid of, the SS and the Gestapo. They are psychopathic thugs."

The noises around the corner grew louder. He wiped his face quickly and helped her gather up the things which had fallen out of her bag when she flung it down. He held on to the sketch pad for a moment as his eyes began to fill with tears again. "Greta had one just like this. You would have liked her. But listen, you must leave quickly before they come around the corner. Take care, Olivia."

"And you too, Otto."

She turned and walked away.

Chapter 16

Marie-Claire walked home in an emotional daze. Putting her head down, she tried to hide her swollen eyes and tear-stained face. It was late afternoon before she reached her apartment block. There was no 'watcher' and the red flowerpot was in the middle of the window. She entered the building and collapsed on the stairs with her head in her hands.

Madame Baudry came out of the loge, took one look at Marie-Claire and sat down beside her. "What's wrong? Are you hurt?"

With tears streaming down her face Marie-Claire confided, "No, far worse than that. I was just about to meet my friend, the one who was here earlier, when I saw her being shot by the Gestapo – right in front of me."

Madame Baudry gasped. She put her arms around Marie-Claire and helped her to her feet. "I can't imagine how awful that was for you. You shouldn't be on your own right now. Come inside dear. You can wait with me for Emile to come home."

When they were inside Marie-Claire told Madame Baudry about the letter, about going to see Hannah, about seeing her being arrested and about seeing her being shot. "And then, and then —" She stopped. She did not tell Madame Baudry about attacking the German soldier. She was not even sure she would tell Emile.

Madame Baudry brought her a warm drink and a blanket. Marie-Claire lay down on the sofa and soon fell into a deep sleep. A few hours later she woke to the sound of voices. Madame Baudry was talking to Emile. Seeing Marie-Claire was now awake he rushed over to her.

"My darling, Madame Baudry was just telling me about your horrific experience. How awful." After thanking Madame Baudry, he helped Marie-Claire upstairs to their apartment and held her lovingly as they sat on the sofa. "Please, tell me exactly what happened. I'm here for you and there's no rush."

Between repeated efforts to wipe her eyes Marie-Claire tried to describe the events in detail, but found it almost impossible to put into words seeing her friend being shot and killed in front of her. After a long pause during which she began shaking she described her ill-advised attack on the German soldier.

He held her tightly until her sobbing subsided. He then spoke quietly. "I'm so sorry to hear about Hannah. I remember her at our wedding. How awful for you to lose another friend." He paused. "I don't suppose I need to tell you how dangerously stupid it was to attack that soldier. I can understand your rage and fury at what you saw, but taking it out on a passing soldier could have resulted in you being shot as well. You are very lucky this man, Otto, was so upset by what he witnessed."

She looked at him and sighed. "I know I should never have attacked Otto and I'm sorry for being such an idiot – are you mad at me?"

As he pulled her close he reassured her. "No, I'm not mad at you. I'm alarmed that I came so close to losing you. I don't know how I'd carry on without you."

The trauma of seeing her friend Hannah executed in front of her affected Marie-Claire. She experienced moments of vivid memory often followed by periods when her mind went blank. Sometimes she felt as if somehow she was a contributing factor to the demise of her friends. First there was Violette – killed by the German bombs as Marie-Claire went to see her. Then there was Simone – arrested for being Jewish just before Marie-Claire arrived at her apartment. Then there was the dramatic scene of Katia being arrested as they were supposed to meet for coffee. And now Hannah being murdered just as she was about to call on her.

In order to stop her mind dwelling on these thoughts she kept herself busy. On Wednesday she made sure she was at Le Bistro d'Angel early. Since Camille had said she was trying to remain incognito Marie-Claire had not really expected her to appear. It was, therefore, a pleasant surprise when she showed up and sat down beside her.

Marie-Claire smiled. "Hello stranger. I was hoping you would come by. Can I get you a coffee? It's not the best but I've tasted worse recently."

"You're not selling it well, but yes please."

Marie-Claire motioned to Reynald who came over and took the order. "A coffee for my friend, with sugar please." She turned to Camille. "You look excited. Has something good happened?"

"Yes. You recall why we met recently?"

"Are you saying the radio transmission worked well?"

Camille looked worried. "Hush. You mustn't say such things. I wouldn't have come if I thought you would talk that way. What if the waiter heard you."

Marie-Claire smiled. "You mean Reynald? Let me put your mind at rest. Reynald is one of us. In fact he's my lookout here. Anyway, can I assume from your excitement the transmission did work?"

"Absolutely, and that's why I came today – to celebrate with the only person in Paris who actually knows who I am. Before coming to Paris I arranged with one of our group a specific day and time and radio frequency for a test. We tried it out at the weekend and I received confirmation from my contact in Chartres."

"Chartres? Do you need radio for that short a distance? Can't a messenger take any messages directly?"

"Well actually we're not transmitting any real messages. We're just trying it out. Next time it'll be Marseille, and if we can do that then we know we'll be able to contact London and de Gaulle's group."

"So what are you transmitting?"

"Just a few words in Morse code. We keep the messages very short to avoid detection."

Marie-Claire wanted to know more, but Reynald appeared with a bowl of sugar which she knew was the warning sign.

"Camille – Reynald has just indicated to me that it's not safe for us to talk about such things."

Camille did not need a second warning. With a nod of her head she began chatting about the serialized novel in *Le Petit Parisien*.

Marie-Claire was more than willing to discuss the novel as she was also reading it. Later, when Camille got up to leave, she gave Marie-Claire a hug. "It's been so good to have someone to talk to – it's been just like old times. I'll try and come back next week."

Marie-Claire watched carefully as Camille left to see if anyone followed her but no one did.

The following Wednesday Marie-Claire made sure she was at the bistro early in case her friend turned up. She had almost finished her second cup of coffee when a very worried looking Camille arrived. "Camille, what's wrong? You look frightened. Come and sit down and I'll order you a drink."

Reynald came over quickly, took the order and returned with a steaming brew.

After looking around quickly Camille whispered, "Is it safe to talk right now?"

"Yes. So what's happened?"

Camille whispered in an agitated tone. "I've been raided. Well, not me but my apartment. I was coming back from shopping when my neighbour stopped me in the street. The Gestapo raided while I was out and apparently they are still there – lying in wait for me."

"Oh my God, how terrifying. Does the neighbour know anything about what you do?"

"No she doesn't. It was just pure luck that I was out and we met as I was coming back. I've heard they will tear a place apart if they are looking for something. I'm sure they'll find both my receiver and the transmitter I built. It means I can never go back – never."

Camille tried to pick up her drink but her hands were trembling so much she spilt much of it on the table. Ignoring the mess, she asked. "What can I do? I can't go back."

Marie-Claire looked at her frightened friend. "I wish you could stay with us but we have a German officer living in the adjoining apartment and we think he might be in counter-espionage. That could be far too dangerous."

"I need to disappear and I don't know how."

"When you say disappear what do you mean?"

"I can't stay in Paris. I want to go to Grenoble. It's in the Unoccupied Zone, but the Gestapo may have already circulated my details which would make it impossible for me to cross the Demarcation Line. I just don't know what to do."

Marie-Claire thought for a moment before replying. Reaching over she took Camille's trembling hands and spoke quietly. "I may have a solution, but I can't tell you what it is until I check. Right now I need you to compose yourself and we need to hide you while I check out my plan." She called Reynald who came straight over. "My friend needs somewhere to sit quietly out of sight for an hour or so. Is there —"

She did not finish her sentence before he nodded his head. He then indicated Camille should follow him and led her into the bistro. He reappeared a few minutes later and nodded discreetly to Marie-Claire. She then promptly left the bistro and headed to her mother's apartment.

When she knocked on the door her mother opened it and welcomed her with open arms. "Oh Marie-Claire what a nice surprise. Come in – I was just about to make some coffee."

Marie-Claire shut the door behind her. "I can't stay Maman. I've just come to ask if you still operate an escape line?"

"Yes dear we do, and no – I'm not going to stop doing that."

"I'm not here to try and stop you, in fact the opposite. I know someone who needs to escape."

"You are bringing me an escaper? I thought you disapproved of what I'm doing."

"No Maman. I didn't and don't disapprove. I just wanted to make sure you fully understood the dangers."

"So are you no longer worried about the dangers?"

"I am still worried about the dangers but you're the only person I know involved in an escape line."

"This man must be very important to you. It's not Emile, is it?"
"No, it's not Emile."

"Thank heavens. But this man – can you trust him?"

"It's not a man Maman, it's a woman. And actually you know her – it's my friend Camille."

"Camille? Camille Devaux? Your school friend? I thought she moved away."

"She did but she's back under a false name. And now she needs to escape from the Gestapo. She needs to get to Grenoble using a different false name. Can you help?"

"Of course. Bring her here and we'll get her new ID cards and send her on down our line. So what's happened? Why does she need to escape?"

"The Gestapo raided her apartment while she was out."

"If she's escaping the Gestapo, I assume you mean she needs to go right now. Is she waiting outside?"

"No, she's in hiding. If you can help I'll go and bring her here."

"Of course I will help. Don't bring her all the way here yourself. When you get close, say just around the corner, tell her which apartment to go to. I'll tell Madame Mercier to watch out for her."

"Madame Mercier? Are you sure?"

"You didn't think I could do this without her help did you? So, what is Camille wearing?"

"A bright floral dress with a little green jacket."

"We should be able to recognize her. And thank you."

"Why are you thanking me? I should be thanking you not the other way around."

"No dear. I'm saying thank you for trusting me with your friend's life. Now off you go and get her. Go on."

The journey back to the bistro seemed to take forever. When she arrived Reynald took her through to a back room where Camille was hiding. The wait had not done her nerves any good and she still looked very frightened.

"Have you got a plan? Can you help me?"

"Yes, and we need to leave now. Thank you Reynald."

When they were out in the street Camille asked again. "What's your plan?"

"I've arranged for you to join an escape line and they can push you through to Grenoble. You may be surprised by where I'm taking you. The contact's not the sort of person you might expect."

"Don't tell me – you're taking me to see your mother."

Marie-Claire stopped abruptly. "Why did you say that? What do you know?"

Camille looked puzzled. "I was joking. You said it would be a surprise and your mother being involved seemed the most unlikely thing I could think of. Surely it's not her."

"Actually it is. Maman is waiting for you. She can arrange new ID cards and send you on down her escape line."

"And I thought having the radio tubes brought to me by you was unbelievable but – your mother? Running an escape line? That's even more unbelievable."

When they were just around the corner from her mother's apartment block Marie-Claire repeated the instructions her mother had given her. It was then time to say goodbye. They clung to each other in silence.

Marie-Claire was the first to speak. "I know Maman will do everything she can to help. I'll be with you all the way – not in body but in spirit. Unfortunately you won't be able to let me know you've made it. That could compromise the line."

"I'll find a way, and there are no words of thanks that come even close to how I feel. And it's not goodbye – we'll meet again." Camille wiped a tear from her eye, turned away and walked on around the corner.

Before heading back to her own apartment Marie-Claire stood still for a minute or two, lost in thought. She doubted she'd ever see her friend again – but at least it would be for all the right reasons.

Although she wanted to tell Emile about how she'd been able to help one of her friends escape she knew she couldn't. He had never mentioned the radio tubes again and to tell him would raise all sorts of questions.

Instead she just felt an inner glow at having been able to rescue at least one of her friends from the clutches of the Gestapo.

Chapter 17

A few days after Camille's escape Marie-Claire arranged to meet her mother at a local cafe. She wanted to know if her mother had any news about Camille. She thought about her friend every day and wondered if she had escaped successfully.

The cafe she had chosen was quite small with only a few outdoor tables but it did have one major attraction – very few Germans ever went there. Amongst the Germans this cafe had developed a reputation for slow surly service, cold coffee and high prices. Oddly enough the genuine Parisians never seemed to have such problems.

Marie-Claire arrived first. Although it was mid-September, the weather was pleasantly warm and she sat down at a table outside. She was about to order when her mother turned up with an anxious look on her face. Marie-Claire gave her mother a hug and kiss. "What's happened Maman? You look upset. Is it Camille?"

"Don't worry about her, she's well on her way. No – it's Madame Mercier."

"What? What can she have done that's so bad? We've known her for years and you two have been very close friends. I thought you said she helped you."

"Yes she did and I relied on her completely and I can't do that anymore."

Marie-Claire was puzzled. "I hope you're not going to tell me that she's betrayed you or turned traitor in some way. I just can't believe that."

"No, no, dear. This morning Madame Mercier has been – how did they put it – 'replaced'. She was told she no longer had a job and had to leave the loge."

The news stunned Marie-Claire. "But she's been there for years. Why does she have to go? And who told her she had to go?"

"The new concierge was the one who told her – a nasty arrogant little woman called Madame Lemoine. She had an official letter and was accompanied by a policeman who confirmed the arrangement. I don't know what Madame Mercier's going to do now but I think she has an older brother who still lives in Paris. It's all so sudden. And it really upsets me."

"It upsets me too. I've known her most of my life and she's always been good to me." Marie-Claire shook her head in disbelief. "How do you know all this? Were you there?"

"Yes, I was talking to Madame Mercier at the time. The policeman and this weasel of a woman interrupted our conversation to tell Madame Mercier she had to vacate her apartment by the end of tomorrow. Can you imagine that – just two days to pack up and leave."

"Can we help her?"

"I offered to help but she said no, it could draw attention to me. She said she'll do it herself. Oh it makes me so mad that they gave her just two days notice after all her years of service. I'm going to miss her so much. And this nasty woman then demanded to know who I was, where I lived and if anyone else lived with me."

"Was Madame Mercier told why they were dismissing her?"

"The policeman said they had been watching the building and they felt she had not been doing her job properly and she was not checking the identity of people entering."

Marie-Claire almost dropped her drink at the mention of someone watching the building. She felt that perhaps having a 'watcher' outside her own apartment was even more sinister than she had thought. "Have you ever seen anyone watching your building?"

"There was a man who often leant against the wall reading a newspaper, but I thought he was just an older man who liked to be outside. How wrong I was."

"Did you say Madame Mercier had to leave because she was not checking ID cards of people entering the building?"

"Yes. From now on everyone who enters will have to show their ID card. If you meet the new concierge don't admit to being my daughter."

"So do you think she's definitely a collaborator?"

"Absolutely. When I leave here I will have to tell my friends we can no longer use my apartment as a safe house. I suppose we'll need to shut down the whole escape route, at least temporarily. And we were helping people. It just makes me so angry."

"You're right, you must stop your line immediately – and by that I mean right now. Not tomorrow, not later today, but right now. Is there anything I can do to help?"

Her mother smiled at her. "Thanks for the offer but no, I need to do this on my own. Involving you could raise all sorts of questions. And you're probably right, I should go now."

They stood up and hugged each other. Marie-Claire spoke quietly. "When you see Madame Mercier please let her know how much this news has upset me and how I wish I could help her."

Marie-Claire sat down to finish her drink and watched her mother walk away. She had rarely seen her so distraught.

Later that week Emile came home from work with some more upsetting news. "Do you remember Major Kaufmann?"

"The officer I sketched? Isn't he your contact in the bookshop?"

"Yes. I've been doing a lot of work for him recently. I've just heard he's been taken away."

"What do you mean been 'taken away'?"

"I have some friends who work in Le Bourget airport. They told me they'd seen Major Kaufmann in handcuffs being escorted under Gestapo guard to a plane bound for Berlin."

"Oh my God. Do you know why?"

"Hard to say. My contacts have suggested he might have been helping resistance groups and has been discovered."

"Does he know anything about our group?"

Emile shrugged his shoulders. "I don't think so, but given the number of times he's visited the bookshop I think we should lie low for a while."

"Have you told the others?"

"Not yet. We need to send everyone a message first thing tomorrow. Can you do that?"

"Of course. How and how many?"

Emile pulled four books from his satchel. "Remember your first message – returning a book? Well, receiving a book 'from Gilbert' is a prearranged 'stop everything' sign. I'll give you the addresses in the morning."

The following day straight after breakfast Marie-Claire set off to distribute the warning messages. In her shopping bag she had four small books. The addresses were far apart and it was late morning before she finished.

The last address was near her mother's place so she decided to call in, even if it meant running the risk of meeting the dreaded Madame Lemoine.

As she approached her mother's apartment building she passed a grim looking priest who was just leaving. She entered the building and was relieved to find the new concierge was nowhere to be seen. When Marie-Claire reached her mother's apartment she knocked, hoping her mother would be in a happier mood than she had been last time they met. She was, however, not expecting the exuberant reaction she received when the door opened.

"Oh my dear, come inside quickly." After she closed the door her mother almost danced with excitement. "They're alive. I can hardly believe it after all this time. They're alive."

"So no one here has died?"

"Of course not. Why do you ask?"

"I met a grim looking priest leaving the building."

"No, no. He was just delivering an envelope to me. Inside was a picture of two children playing with a rabbit and a note on the back from my sister. They're alive. Here – look."

Marie-Claire looked at the picture and the words on the back.

Jeu de Snoepje Lapin Rouge

"It's a rather odd note so what makes you sure it is from her? 'Snoepje's game Red Rabbit' is hardly much to go on."

"It's Ghislaine's style of drawing and her handwriting, and when she was young we always referred to her as 'Red Rabbit' after her favourite toy. What I don't understand though is what she means by 'Snoepje's game'. Perhaps you do."

Marie-Claire read the message again and to her it made perfect sense. "Maman, remember when I was young you often sent me to Rotterdam to spend time with your sister and my cousin Anna? Well, Anna's parents often called her by a Dutch nickname, Snoepje, which means little sweetie." She paused. "Maman, the message is that they are alive but they are in hiding. That's why they have not said where they are. At least not directly."

"What do you mean?"

"One of Anna's favourite games was one where something was hidden and we were then given a cryptic clue. I think the message means your sister and her family are the things which are hidden and they've probably sent their address to me using a clue only I can understand."

"If you really think so can you please go and see if they've sent you the address and put my mind at ease."

Marie-Claire rose to leave. "I'll go right now."

"Wait a moment. In my excitement about the Dagloonders I almost forgot to tell you Camille reached Grenoble safely."

"Oh that's such a relief. I've been worried about her. But how do you know she got there? Surely she wouldn't have written to you here."

"Don't worry. She didn't send me a letter. I know you like reading the *Le Petit Parisien*. Do you also read *Le Matin*?"

"That Nazi collaborationist newspaper? No I don't. And I'm surprised you even ask. Don't tell me you do."

"Oh I don't buy it for the articles but the Germans don't know that. They think me buying it shows where my sympathies lie – silly fools. They don't seem to realize that the Classified Advertisements section is full of secret resistance messages. That's how I know about Camille."

"Using the newspaper that way is brilliant. I must tell Emile. And thank you again for helping her."

"That's why we ran this escape line, to help people like Camille. But as I told you in the cafe I can never be part of an escape route again. I'll never trust Madame Lemoine. And be aware, she is now keeping a register of everyone who enters the building."

"Not that good a register. She didn't see me come in."

"Good. The less she knows the better. But right now please go and see if Ghislaine has sent a letter to you."

Marie-Claire gave her mother a large hug with the reassuring words, "Of course – I'll be right back."

As Marie-Claire hurried back to her own apartment she kept thinking about Camille and the Dagloonders. She was excited to have received some good news after all her horrific experiences of the last few months.

When she turned into the street where she lived she was initially pleased to see there was no 'watcher' leaning against the wall. After what happened to Madame Mercier at her mother's place Marie-Claire had become very conscious of the watchers. Although pleased, she was at the same time slightly perturbed as the absence of a watcher was unusual.

Then, as she walked towards the front door of the apartment building, she noticed just in time that Madame Baudry's flowerpot was at the side of the window – not the centre.

Chapter 18

Trying not to show any emotion Marie-Claire walked past her apartment building and with her head down walked towards the mustard shop. She knew Madame Baudry would not have made a mistake and that the position of the flowerpot was definitely a warning signal. She heard footsteps, looked up and was relieved to see Madame Baudry approaching from the direction of the mustard shop.

"I'm so glad you saw the flowerpot and didn't go in," said Madame Baudry. "The Gestapo raided the building this morning looking in all the apartments for a person called Tarik. They even searched the German officer's apartment. I told them there was no one in the building with that name but they've stayed upstairs so it's not safe for you to go in. Before they came someone brought a letter for you and I've left it with Jamel. Right now I had better get back and see what's happening. I'll put the flowerpot in the centre again once they've gone. Goodbye and good luck."

Marie-Claire did not even have time to reply before Madame Baudry walked quickly away. *Was she afraid she might have been followed? If that's the case, will anyone follow me now? I'll have to be extra vigilant when I go to Maman's apartment – I don't want to draw attention to her.*

When Marie-Claire entered the mustard shop she saw Jamel was serving another customer. She waited until the shop was clear and then asked if he had any *Moutarde Baudelaire*. He nodded, went into the back of the shop and returned with an envelope. "My aunt brought this just now. She put a note inside. I hope it's not bad news."

Marie-Claire opened the envelope. Inside was Madame Baudry's note and another envelope. The note explained what she already knew, the Gestapo were searching all the apartments for someone and were still in the building.

I'm so glad Madame Baudry set up the warning system. I really don't know how I'd have coped with being interrogated by the Gestapo. I don't think we have left anything incriminating in the apartment but I certainly need to warn Emile.

She was aware how dangerous it would be if she was found with the note in her possession. It would implicate both her and Madame Baudry. "Jamel, can you destroy this note?"

"I can take it out back and burn it."

"Yes please. Your aunt wouldn't want anyone to see it."

"I'll do it right now and please wait as I've got another package for you."

He took the note and returned with a small paper bag. "May I suggest you take this bag of mustard powder which is, of course, the only reason you came into this shop, isn't it?"

Marie-Claire understood what he meant, "Of course it is."

With a slight smile he added, "I don't want payment but if you are stopped and searched, it's a sample of a new blend and cost three francs."

Marie-Claire smiled back. "Emile said you were thorough and I can see why. Thank you Jamel."

Marie-Claire decided not to open the other envelope until she had made sure no one was tailing her. After walking for ten minutes she felt confident no one was following her so she opened the envelope. Inside was a drawing of two girls in a small boat. On the back, in her aunt's handwriting, was a simple message.

Snoepje et amie dans un bateau

When Marie-Claire read 'Snoepje and friend in a boat' she instantly recalled the happy holiday she had enjoyed many years ago with cousin Anna. That summer the Dagloonders had rented a charming riverside house for a couple of weeks near the small Dutch village of Ammerstol. She and Anna had spent much of the holiday messing about together in a boat on the Lek River. She knew that as a prominent Jewish businessman Uncle Coenraad would need to hide and from her memories of that summer she could see that rural Ammerstol was a perfect hiding place.

111

As she walked back to her mother's apartment building Marie-Claire couldn't stop worrying about the Gestapo raid on her own building. *I remember Camille saying she could never return to her apartment after the Gestapo raided it, but then she had illegal radios there. At least we don't have anything like that. I do hope they've gone by the time we get home. If not – where can we go? I'm sure Emile will have made some contingency plans. He's never mentioned any but I'm sure he will have. I must go and see him as soon as I can. But right now I need to tell Maman the good news about her sister.*

As she approached her mother's building, she wondered what she should do if she was stopped by the new concierge. *If Maman doesn't trust this woman is it sensible for me to tell her I'm visiting my mother? I'd have to give her my details, including where I live. That could be dangerous since the Gestapo are currently searching my apartment building.*

However, since her mother was waiting for the news about her sister Marie-Claire decided to take the risk and go in. The main door to the building was open and she stepped quietly into the hall hoping to slip by undetected as she had done earlier that morning. She had only gone two steps in when she became aware of loud shouting coming from behind the closed door to the concierge's loge. Although she could not quite make out all the words, it was obvious that Madame Lemoine was angry with someone and was telling them they could not leave.

Marie-Claire tiptoed by and headed up the stairs to the top floor where her mother lived. At her mother's door she knocked.

No answer. She knocked again and still there was no answer. She cursed herself for having taken the key to her mother's door off her key-ring. It was a bulky key and with her mother running a safe house, she had decided she should never again just walk in unannounced. *Stupid mistake.*

She knocked again and spoke in a loud whisper. "Open up – it's me, Marie-Claire."

She heard the door open on the other side of the hall where the Guillons lived. They had moved in a few years ago and were close friends of her mother. Madame Guillon gestured to Marie-Claire and whispered, "Shush – stop knocking and come in here quickly. I mean it – quickly."

The urgency in her voice alarmed Marie-Claire and she crossed the hall rapidly and quietly. Madame Guillon closed the door behind her and bolted it shut. She then explained in an agitated tone. "Your mother's downstairs with our new concierge. Madame Lemoine came up about fifteen minutes ago and insisted your mother go back downstairs with her, apparently to sort out some paper work – but I don't believe that for one minute. Initially your mother refused but Madame Lemoine turned quite nasty and said if your mother didn't go with her she'd have to call the police."

Marie-Claire frowned. "Are you saying Maman is still down there? I heard Madame Lemoine shouting at someone in her loge as I came by but it never occurred to me that it could be Maman. I need to go downstairs to help her."

"Are you sure? Have you met Madame Lemoine?"

"No I haven't, but from the little I heard as I came by it seems Madame Lemoine is almost imprisoning Maman. I heard her shouting at someone that they could not leave and had to remain in the loge. I really must go and help and —"

"Don't go!" interrupted Monsieur Guillon. He was standing at the window looking out into the street. "Come here and look outside. You can't go. You're too late. They're here now."

Marie-Claire rushed to the window, "Who's here? Why? What are you —"

She didn't finish her own question as she looked down into the street and saw men in Gestapo uniforms emerging from a van with pistols drawn. Marie-Claire stayed at the window, transfixed by the scene developing in the street below. Madame Lemoine emerged into the street and spoke harshly to one of the Gestapo officers. The window beside Marie-Claire was slightly open so she and the Guillons were able to hear the conversation.

"Why have you taken so long to get here? I called you ages ago. I almost had to let her go but I've locked her in my rooms. Here's the key."

Marie-Claire realized with horror that Madame Lemoine was referring to her mother – locked in the loge awaiting the arrival of the Gestapo. Marie-Claire also realized it would be futile to attempt to intervene and she began to tremble. Madame Guillon came over and stood at the window beside her holding her hand tightly. As they looked at the scene below they saw Marie-Claire's mother being marched out of the house by the Gestapo.

The officer in charge began shouting at her. "It has been reported that you've been running an escape line for enemy soldiers and Jews."

"No I haven't – you have the wrong person."

"No we don't. We have evidence from your concierge. But you can't have been doing this on your own. Your concierge says you have a daughter who is a résistante. Where is she? Was she helping you? Where is your daughter?"

Her mother's response was loud and clear. "I don't have a daughter – you have the wrong person."

The officer shouted back. "No we don't have the wrong person and we know you have a daughter. So where is your daughter?"

Her mother repeated firmly, "I don't have a daughter – you have the wrong person."

The officer yelled menacingly at her. "You can tell me now – or we'll take you to 84 Foch where you will tell me. I repeat – where is your daughter?"

Marie-Claire knew her mother would be aware that the officer was threatening to take her to the torture chambers at the Gestapo headquarters. She did not want to let that happen to her mother and was just about to scream and knock on the window to reveal her presence when Madame Guillon pulled her back.

"There's nothing you can do to help your mother. Absolutely nothing. The Gestapo want both of you and giving yourself up won't stop them arresting and interrogating your mother. You heard them. Your mother has been betrayed by Madame Lemoine. They know that your mother was running a safe house on an escape line."

"Are you saying you knew what Maman was doing?"

Madame Guillon nodded. "Yes, and she helped my nephew escape for which we will always be grateful. And we sometimes helped her. If, like us, you think what your mother was doing was right, then continue her work – something you can only do if you are alive and free. You mustn't let them catch you. And right now all you can do is hope that after they interrogate your mother they send her to the Fresnes prison rather than execute her."

Marie-Claire nodded her reluctant acceptance of what Madame Guillon was saying and they both went back to the window. Marie-Claire's breathing was now erratic and her hands clutched the window-sill. As she watched the scene below unfold she gasped with fear when she saw her mother reach inside her bag.

Marie-Claire recalled with horror the promise her mother had made – 'I know if I'm caught or betrayed I'll probably be shot but I'll take at least one of them out with me'.

Marie-Claire wanted to yell to her mother to stop but all she could manage was a croaking, "No, no."

In one quick movement her mother withdrew Papa's pistol from her bag, pointed it at the Gestapo officer's chest and fired.

As the officer fell the air was shattered again by the sound of two other pistols firing almost simultaneously, followed by what seemed an eternity of silence.

Marie-Claire watched in disbelief as her mother sank to the ground, her head and body bloodied and disfigured.

As Marie-Claire began to faint Madame Guillon pulled her back from the window and lowered her gently to the floor.

Chapter 19

Madame Guillon's smelling salts did their trick and a few minutes after fainting Marie-Claire regained consciousness and became aware she was lying on the floor in the Guillon's living room. As she tried to stand up Monsieur Guillon took her arm and slowly helped her to the sofa where she slumped back, her face ashen white. After a few moments she looked up, her face devoid of any expression. "What happened – did I faint?"

With tears in her eyes Madame Guillon sat down beside Marie-Claire, put her arms around her and held her tightly in a motherly embrace. "Yes you fainted at what you saw in the street. Nobody should ever witness what you saw."

Marie-Claire began shaking uncontrollably. "Did I really see Maman being shot? Please tell me I'm wrong – please. It must have been a dream, a terrible dream. This can't be real."

Madame Guillon struggled to reply through her own tears, "I can hardly believe it myself, but it wasn't a dream."

With a great effort Marie-Claire stood up and stumbled over to the window. As she looked down at the scene below and saw her mother's bloodied body lying in the road her knees began to buckle and she started to collapse again. Monsieur Guillon rushed over and gently guided her back to the sofa.

"How did your mother have a pistol?" he asked, his voice wavering with emotion.

Marie-Claire wiped the tears from her eyes. "It's my father's pistol from the Great War. Oh Maman – what have you done?"

Madame Guillon looked puzzled. "But why did she fire at the officer? Surely she would have known they would fire back."

Marie-Claire trembled as she replied. "Oh she knew alright – and that's why she did it. A few months ago when she started running her safe house she told me that's what she would do. I thought she wasn't being serious but obviously I was wrong."

"What do you mean? What did she say?"

"She said if she was caught or betrayed she knew she would be shot but she would take one of them out using Papa's Great War pistol. I think she shot the officer on purpose knowing exactly what they would do. I think she chose not to be interrogated – not to be tortured – not to wait for a firing squad."

Madame Guillon pulled Marie-Claire close in a comforting embrace. "From what you've just said, I can believe that your mother knew exactly what she was doing. And by denying she had a daughter she was trying to protect the most precious thing she had – you. If you want to honour your mother's memory, continue her fight for France when you are able."

Marie-Claire began sobbing uncontrollably again. "But why were the Gestapo even here?"

Madame Guillon responded softly. "From what Madame Lemoine said in the street and the fact she locked your mother in the loge, it looks like our new concierge is a traitor working with the Gestapo. And that puts you and us in extreme danger. She will know you're up here and direct the Gestapo to your mother's apartment. I'm surprised they're not here already."

Monsieur Guillon looked out of the window. "Right now they're standing around the dead officer. Why didn't Madame Lemoine say you were up here when the officer was asking where you were?"

"Because she doesn't know I'm here," said Marie-Claire. "When I came in she was arguing with Maman behind a closed door and she wouldn't have seen me enter."

Madame Guillon put her hands on Marie-Claire's shoulders and looked directly into her eyes. "I know this is dreadful. I can't imagine how you are feeling, but you can't stay here. They'll soon start searching all the apartments. Somehow you've got to get away before they do."

"If they haven't started searching, perhaps I can sneak downstairs and go out through the back door."

Monsieur Guillon shook his head. "No you can't. They or Madame Lemoine would be sure to see you. Even though she doesn't know you're in the building, there is no way you could slip by unnoticed. It's too risky."

"So what can I do? I can't even hide in my mother's apartment – I don't have a key. And I can't hide here, it would be too dangerous for you. It's the only thing I can do – try to escape downstairs. Oh my God. I absolutely must get out and go to Emile."

"You're right," said Monsieur Guillon. "You can't hide here and there's no way you can escape downstairs. Perhaps you could hide upstairs in the attic. We have a key to the attic and the last time I looked there were loads of boxes you could hide behind."

Marie-Claire suddenly sat bolt upright. "But of course – the attic. Did you say you have a key to the attic? I won't hide up there – I can escape through the attic."

Madame Guillon looked puzzled. "How would you do that?"

"All the buildings in this street have a common attic space," replied Marie-Claire. "It's not divided into different units. If I go up here I can go along the attic and come down into another set of apartment units and go out the back way. When I was young I had a friend, Charlotte, who lived two doors down the street in this same building. We used to play in the attic. I can go up here and go down in what used to be her block and escape out through the courtyard into another street."

"But how would you get out of the attic into that block?" asked Monsieur Guillon. "Although I have a key to the attic from this set of apartments, you'll need a different key to unlock the attic door in the other unit. It's highly unlikely to be the same key."

"You're right, it isn't the same key. Charlotte and I had duplicate keys – one for each door and they are in a red candy box hidden under a floorboard in the attic. We did that so we could call on each other without going outside. Please get your attic key."

As Monsieur Guillon went to retrieve the attic key Marie-Claire headed towards the door. Madame Guillon held her back. "You've just suffered an unimaginable shock and you fainted. I agree you need to go to Emile but I can't let you go on your own. I'm coming with you."

"I can't ask you to do that."

"You didn't ask. Your mother was a dear friend and helped my nephew when he needed help. Now you need help. It's the least I can do given what your mother did for us."

Monsieur Guillon reappeared with the key and asked, "Should I come as well?"

Madame Guillon grabbed her coat. "No. With your heart condition it's probably best if you stay behind. If they ask where I am tell them I went out earlier to do some shopping. Now come on. We have no time to waste."

She slid the bolts back, opened the apartment door and listened. All was quiet. The three of them hurried along the passageway to the attic door as quietly as possible. Monsieur Guillon turned the key in the lock and the door swung open with a loud creak. They looked at each other in alarm. When they didn't hear any sound from downstairs Marie-Claire slipped through the doorway and started up the attic stairs.

As Madame Guillon was about to do the same Monsieur Guillon embraced her and whispered, "Darling, here's the key. Lock the door behind you. You'll need the key to get back out if you can't find the candy box. Good luck and take care."

Madame Guillon leant over and kissed him on the cheek. "I'll be careful my love." She closed the door, locked it and followed Marie-Claire up into the attic. "I thought it would be dark up here. I didn't realize the top row of windows were for the attic. Now where is this candy box?"

"It's been many years since I've been up here. We hid the box beneath a loose floorboard under a rafter which has a big red spot on it. We painted it red with Maman's nail polish. I never told her – and now I can't." She paused as the reality of her words struck home, "I can never say anything to her again – never." Her eyes filled with tears and she sat down sobbing.

Madame Guillon came over to her. "This is why I'm here with you. I know it's hard for you, but you need to keep going." As she helped Marie-Claire get back to her feet, she whispered. "Is that the red spot you mean – on the rafter to our left?"

Marie-Claire wiped her eyes, looked up and scrambled over to the rafter. The floor was piled high with large boxes. The ones on top were easy to move but at the bottom of the heap was a large suitcase. Marie-Claire's first attempt to shift it made no impact. "It's too heavy for me to move – we'll need to try together."

As they began to push the case it made a loud scraping sound on the floorboards. "Stop," whispered Madame Guillon. "That sound will be heard in the apartment below."

"But we need to move it." Marie-Claire tried the lock. "It's not locked. Perhaps if we pull out enough of whatever is in it we will be able to move it." She opened the case and stared in astonishment before sinking to her knees.

Madame Guillon looked at her. "What's wrong? You look as if you've seen a ghost. What's in the case?" She looked inside. "I don't understand – these are just books."

Marie-Claire's eyes were watering again. "These are not just books. They're special books. They are my books from when I was a child." She picked up a well-worn picture book and tried to suppress a sniffle. "See the inscription – 'To Marie-Claire from Maman, Christmas 1921'. That was just before my brother, Lucien, died from pneumonia."

Madame Guillon knelt down beside her. "Marie-Claire. I know discovering this treasure trove of your books is very emotional for you, but right now what is critically important is getting you out of here. We need to take enough books out of this case so we can move it and get at the keys."

"You're right. I just didn't know Maman had kept all these."

"Look – you take the books out, pass them to me and I'll pile them up neatly. When this is all over I'll come back and put them back in the case."

"Thank you – that means a lot to me."

When the case was half empty they were able to move it away quietly. It did not take Marie-Claire long to find the loose board which lifted easily revealing a small red candy box. "It's still here," she whispered excitedly. Brushing aside many years worth of cobwebs she retrieved the box, opened it and smiled. "I think we'll ignore these old sweets but look – two keys." She took both keys out of the box, closed it, put it back amongst the cobwebs and replaced the floorboard. "Ok – let's get out of here."

Holding the keys tightly in her hand, she stood up and led the way to the attic staircase leading down to Charlotte's old apartment. They crept down the stairs and tried the door. As expected, it was locked. The first key Marie-Claire tried failed to turn. With trembling hands she tried the second key. It turned easily and she opened the door. They stepped out into the hall and closed the door behind them. Marie-Claire locked it again and passed both keys to Madame Guillon. "You can put these back in the red box. You never know – you might need them some day."

They tiptoed down the main staircase listening for any sounds. As they reached the ground floor and turned towards the back door a voice called out Marie-Claire's name. She spun around and found herself face to face with Madame Verdier, the concierge she had known when Charlotte lived in this block. They stared at each other for a moment then Madame Verdier flung her arms around Marie-Claire. "Oh you poor girl. I saw what happened in the street. I'm so sorry about your mother, but I'm so pleased you haven't been captured. Are you alright?"

At that moment they heard German voices outside and Marie-Claire asked anxiously, "Is the back door open? We need to get out of here now before the Gestapo find me. Is it open?"

"Yes," replied Madame Verdier, "and if you go across the courtyard, the coach door at Number 20 is always open at this hour. If the Germans knock on my door I'll try and stall them."

Marie-Claire thanked Madame Verdier then she and Madame Guillon ran out of the back door and across the courtyard. Even though Marie-Claire knew the coach door opened onto a different street, they both paused at the entrance and listened for any German voices. There was silence. Madame Guillon took Marie-Claire's arm and they headed down the street as if nothing was troubling them. After a few minutes they felt confident that no one was following them and Madame Guillon asked, "How far is it to Emile's bookshop?"

"From here I would normally take the Metro."

"I'm not sure that's a good idea. You still look very distressed and that could lead to awkward questions."

"I suppose we could walk but it's a long way."

"Given your state I think we should take a horse-drawn taxi. There's a cab stand around the next corner."

"I've seen them but I've never been in one. Can we trust the drivers? Won't they ask questions?"

"Many of them are veterans of the Great War so they have no love for the Germans. I know one of the drivers well and he won't ask any questions. Let's hope he's there."

As they approached the long line of waiting cabs, one of the drivers waved at Madame Guillon. "We're in luck – my friend Bruno is available."

When they reached Bruno's cab Marie-Claire gave directions to the bookshop. Bruno looked at her face and turned to Madame Guillon. "Your companion looks upset. I don't want to know why, but a short while ago we all heard some gunshots. Are we to take a fast route to this bookshop or a safe one avoiding checkpoints?"

"A safe one please Bruno." As they climbed into the carriage Madame Guillon whispered to Marie-Claire. "It make take longer but Bruno knows how to avoid the checkpoints. You said you've never ridden in one of these? Well, you need to sit back and hold on. The ride is rather bumpy but it's better then walking."

The clatter of the horse's hooves on the road made conversation difficult so they sat in silence as Bruno drove through the back streets. When they were only a street away from the bookshop Marie-Claire asked Bruno to stop. "I can easily walk from here."

Madame Guillon took her hand. "Are you sure?"

"Yes, I'm feeling much better now. I greatly appreciate what you've done, but the bookshop is literally just around the corner and I can walk from here on my own. Please have Bruno take you back home. I'll never forget what you and Monsieur Guillon have done to help me."

"If you are sure, then yes, I'll head back. And with respect to Madame Lemoine – my husband has friends who know exactly what to do with traitors. She won't know what hit her. And as for you, take care Marie-Claire and may God be with you."

Marie-Claire watched as the cab drove away. She then turned around to head towards the bookshop. As she did so she heard the unmistakeable sound of machine-gun fire. In alarm, she looked around and was horrified to see a cloud of smoke rising above the buildings.

Fearing the worst, she ran around the corner and stopped at the sight of a large crowd watching flames pouring out of the bookshop. In front of the bookshop she saw Gestapo officers with machine-guns pointed at the crowd. She also saw a team of firemen standing around apparently doing nothing to put out the flames.

As Marie-Claire scanned the crowd for any sign of Emile she heard a woman shout.

"There she is. Put her in the back."

Almost instantly arms grabbed Marie-Claire from behind. Although she struggled she was no match for the strength of her captor who pushed her into the back of a waiting van. As the driver climbed in he spoke in a gruff tone. "Lie still and don't make a sound and you'll come to no harm."

From her position on the floor of the van she was acutely and painfully aware of the vehicle driving off at speed.

Chapter 20

Marie-Claire lay on the floor of the van feeling terrified and alone. She had no idea who had kidnapped her and feared no one would be coming to rescue her. Emile would not know she had been kidnapped. She had not seen him anywhere – not in the crowd and not standing outside with the firemen. *He won't even know I'm missing until he gets home. Oh my God – will the Gestapo still be at the apartment?*

Slowly she raised herself to a sitting position and took stock of her surroundings. It appeared she had not been taken by the police or Gestapo. She was in the back of a baker's van and had not been restrained – her arms and legs were free. She saw two people in the front of the van. They were speaking in such low tones she could not make out what they were saying. One was a woman, the other a man. She did not recognize either of them.

In a shaky voice Marie-Claire called out, "Who are you? Where are you taking me? Why have you kidnapped me?"

The man responded in a gruff voice. "Tarik told us what to do. And you've not been kidnapped. We've just saved your life and we're taking you to a safe place."

Marie-Claire found it hard to believe his words given how roughly she had been forced into the back of the van. *This is the second time today someone has mentioned Tarik – first the Gestapo and now these kidnappers. Who do they think I am?*

It dawned on her that in the commotion they had kidnapped the wrong person. She was a victim of mistaken identity and as a consequence her life could be in danger. "Who is this Tarik and why should he care? I don't know anyone called Tarik."

There was silence. She watched as the man and woman glanced at each other. This time it was the lady who answered in a soft voice. "Actually you do – you were married to him."

"Married to Tarik? You've kidnapped the wrong person. I'm

married to Emile, not some person called Tarik. Let me out! I said you've kidnapped the wrong person – let me out!"

There was another moment of silence before the man responded. "Tarik was Emile's resistance identity."

"He never used that name with me." Her mouth began to quiver. "Oh no, the Gestapo raided my apartment this morning looking for a person called Tarik – so they were actually looking for Emile. But why did you say I *was* married to him?"

The lady turned around and Marie-Claire now recognized her. "You're Nadine, aren't you? Part of Emile's resistance group."

"Yes I am, and that's why we're helping you. But in answer to your question, we had just left the bookshop after talking to Tarik when the Gestapo, police and fire engine all arrived together. Gestapo officers kicked opened the door to the shop and sprayed the whole of the shop with machine-gun fire. They were firing indiscriminately, mowing everyone down."

Marie-Claire was hardly able to ask, "Everyone?"

"Yes, everyone – shop workers and customers. It's obvious they were after Tarik and they wanted to make sure they got him."

Marie-Claire gasped at the implication of the words she'd just heard. She began shaking and found it hard to breathe. *First Maman and now Emile. The two most important people in my life both gone, both shot today by the Gestapo. But no – they must be wrong about Emile. I can't have lost him as well, I can't!*

"Could anyone have escaped?"

"No. Not with the fire."

"But the fire – how did it start? You said the fire department arrived with the police."

"The firemen weren't there to put out the fire. They started it. Perhaps to make sure even the injured didn't survive."

Horrified by what she had just been told Marie-Claire struggled to speak. "If you say the Gestapo, the police and the firemen all arrived together they must have been tipped off. Did someone in the group betray him?"

"Tarik said his contact, Major Kaufmann, had been arrested. Perhaps Kaufmann talked to save his own life. We don't know."

Marie-Claire was still puzzled. "But why were they so anxious to kill Emile, or Tarik as you call him?"

"But surely you know. He was the leader of a powerful resistance group and would have been high on their hit list."

"He never said anything about that."

"I suspect he didn't tell you for your own safety. However the Gestapo won't know that. They'll think you were working with him. That's why Tarik told us to save you if he was caught."

Marie-Claire lay back on the floor, curled up into a ball and began shivering uncontrollably. "You have not saved me," she moaned. "It would have been kinder to let the Gestapo shoot me. I have now lost everyone I loved. With Emile dead my world is gone. I have nothing left to live for. Stop and let me out."

"Tarik wanted you to live," replied Nadine. "He loved you so much. That's why he asked us to look after you if something happened to him. It's fortunate we saw you. I'm sorry we treated you roughly but we had to act quickly."

"But how can I carry on? I've got nobody left. Nobody at all."

Nadine seemed puzzled. "What do you mean nobody left? Tarik told us to take you to your mother's house."

Marie-Claire moaned again. "But she's gone too." Her voice broke. "I saw her, my mother, being gunned down earlier today in a Gestapo raid at her apartment."

Nadine gasped. "Oh my God. How awful."

"They said they were looking for me," groaned Marie-Claire.

The man spoke quietly to Nadine but not quietly enough. "That changes everything. Tarik told us not to take her home and now we can't take her to her mother's. We'll have to hide her."

After a moment Nadine suggested, "How about Chantal's greenhouse? We've never used it."

"What?" yelled Marie-Claire. "You're taking me to a brothel?"

"If you know the term then you'll know it's the safest place for you to hide. We never told anybody about Chantal's and we've never used her place before. We kept it in reserve in case of emergencies. We'll take you there, but don't worry you'll be safe. I trust her completely. She's part of my family."

"How long will I be there?" asked Marie-Claire.

"Probably a couple of days," replied Nadine. "The Gestapo will be hunting for you so you can't go out and certainly you can't go home. At some point you'll have to leave Paris and —"

The man interrupted her. "After we take you to Chantal's you won't see us again. We don't know how wide or deep the betrayal has been, so we need to disappear. Once we drop you off we're leaving Paris immediately."

"If I have to leave Paris as well why can't I go with you? Why are you taking me to Chantal's?"

"This van is often stopped and searched," explained Nadine. "If they found you hiding in the back we'd all be arrested and probably shot. Anyway, do you have ID papers in a false name?"

"No."

"That would be essential. Without papers all we can do is take you to Chantal's. To bring you with us would be far too dangerous for all of us. I wish we could but I hope you understand."

The man spoke firmly to Nadine. "Stop making excuses. Taking her with us is just not an option. Tarik asked us to do something and we're doing it. So just tell her no and be done with it."

Nadine looked at Marie-Claire. "Sorry, but Chantal's is the best we can do. As I said you'll be safe there."

Traumatized by seeing her mother gunned down and by the realization that Emile was dead Marie-Claire fell back on the floor of the van sobbing quietly. Eventually the van stopped and Marie-Claire heard Nadine talking to someone she assumed was Chantal. Nadine was explaining the circumstances and that Marie-Claire needed to be hidden and provided with a new identity prior to being evacuated from Paris. A few minutes later Nadine opened the back of the van and helped Marie-Claire out. She then wished her good luck and before Marie-Claire could even respond, Nadine climbed back into the van which then drove off at speed.

Chantal took Marie-Claire's arm and helped her into the house and into the kitchen. There she was greeted by some of the working girls who instantly formed the wrong impression. To a chortle from the others, one girl commented. "Take it from me love, you need to cheer up. No trick's going to choose you looking so glum – not even a German."

Chantal hushed the girls before any more comments could be made. "Yvonne isn't coming here to work. The Gestapo have just killed her husband and earlier today she witnessed her mother being gunned down by the Germans. She's here because she needs somewhere to rest and recover." All the girls gasped and in a faltering voice the girl who made the comment apologized.

Marie-Claire was about to explain her name was not Yvonne but Chantal cut her off. "I don't know and don't want to know your real name – none of us do. So here you're Yvonne. That way we can deny ever knowing you."

The word 'deny' reminded Marie-Claire of her mother saying 'I don't have a daughter' and she started weeping again for the loss of her mother. Chantal took her to a small bedroom and gave her a comforting hug. She left only to return a few minutes later with a warm drink. "Drink this dear – it will help you sleep."

When Marie-Claire woke up and discovered it was now afternoon, she deduced she must have been drugged. At first she was annoyed but then appreciated it was probably the best thing. She rose groggily from the bed and noticed a neat stack of clothes on the chair with a note – 'I know you came with nothing. The girls and I hope these will fit'.

When she appeared in the kitchen she was greeted with genuine warmth by the girls. No questions were asked. Marie-Claire was just accepted as Yvonne who hated the Germans as much as they did. She was, however, slightly embarrassed when Rosa, one of the girls laughed. "That skirt looks better on you than it ever did on me." Although Marie-Claire knew that none of the girls would expect payment for the clothes, she was very concerned to find she only had a few francs she had found in her jacket – there was no sign of her bag.

"Has anyone seen my bag? I'm sure I had my bag with me."

"No dear," answered Chantal. "When they brought you here you didn't have a bag. You must have left it in the van."

Marie-Claire was about to disagree – she never went anywhere without her bag. It contained everything she needed – her money, her sketch book, her pencils, her identity cards. She panicked. *Oh no – no cards! Without cards I don't exist. I certainly can't go out. Oh my God – what can I do now?*

She recalled Emile telling her, 'Even if a situation looks hopeless, if you want to survive then you must never give up'. Now completely dependent on Chantal, Marie-Claire decided that since she wanted to survive she needed to make herself useful. "Chantal, I appreciate your help, truly I do. Is there something I can do in return? I used to assist with food preparation at one of the soup kitchens. Perhaps I can help in the kitchen."

One of the girls picked up on the conversation. "That's where I've seen you before. I always liked being served by you. You were never rude and never looked down on anyone. If there's anything you need Yvonne, let me know. I'm Armel."

Marie-Claire thanked her. There was something but she decided not to ask immediately. *Tomorrow I'll give Armel the few francs I have and ask her to get me a sketch book and some pencils.*

Although the sketch pad Armel obtained for her was not of the quality she normally used Marie-Claire was grateful. It gave her something to occupy her mind. The first picture she drew was a portrait of a young man with dark hair, a round face, laughing eyes and an engaging smile. When Armel saw the picture she raised her eyebrows and grinned. "Wow – I'd like to meet him."

As Marie-Claire stared at the portrait she'd just drawn of her beloved Emile, tears welled up in her eyes, "So would I – so would I – but that's now not possible."

"I'm sorry," said Armel. "Is that a picture of your husband?"

"Yes. The Gestapo killed him which is why I'm here."

Armel moved her hand onto Marie-Claire's and gave it a squeeze. "Maybe not right now, but would you do a sketch of me? You draw so well."

The sketch she did of Armel produced a clamour from the others for their portraits, which she did over the next week. Doing the sketches and assisting in the kitchen helped pass the time.

If only I had a real life and I was free, I suppose I could earn a living doing portraits. But I don't – so I can't. A life? What life? My mother's been shot, my Emile has been murdered, and now I have to carry on without them. My life has been destroyed. I don't even have my own name and I have to hide. And of all places I could be – I'm hiding in a brothel.

Time passed slowly. The days were made bearable by the friendship of the girls but every night Marie-Claire cried herself to sleep. She slept fitfully, and frequently had nightmares about the horrors she had witnessed. Near the end of September, a week after Marie-Claire arrived at the brothel, Chantal came into the kitchen and said, "Yvonne, you have a visitor – a man."

The horrified look on Marie-Claire's face made Chantal laugh. "There's nothing to worry about. Your visitor is not a client, he's here to help you escape."

Marie-Claire was initially puzzled when Chantal ushered a priest carrying a suitcase into the kitchen and introduced him as Père Miguel. Her concern must have been evident to Chantal who reassured her that she'd known Père Miguel for years and that he was, 'One of us'.

Feeling relieved, Marie-Claire sat down with him to hear what he had to say.

"My child I understand life has dealt you some terrible cards. I am here to help you."

"Yes it has, but, Father – I'm not of your faith. I am Huguenot protestant, not Catholic."

"My child, in my eyes and those of God, you are nevertheless someone in need of help. We need to move you to a safer place. I'm taking you to a convent while we arrange for a different life."

"Are you suggesting I become a Catholic nun? Really?"

He smiled. "No, of course not. Perhaps I expressed myself badly. I'm suggesting we move you to a convent because the Germans don't search convents. While you're there we will give you a new name and a new identity card. We will also find you a job and place to live somewhere outside of Paris."

"I can't let you risk escorting me to this convent. What if we're stopped? I have no identity card. It was lost on the way here. I can't let you put your life at risk just to help me."

He smiled. "I already have a card for you in the name of Sister Yvonne, a nun at Convent St Josephine. And I've brought a nun's habit for you to wear. We'll leave once you've changed."

"A new ID card? How? You don't have a photo of me."

"The one we've used will be close enough once we put the bandages on your face and pull the wimple tightly around."

"Bandages?"

He chuckled, "Don't you remember? The bandages are needed to cover the bruises you received when you were attacked by a German soldier a few days ago."

Marie-Claire smiled. "You've done this before, haven't you?"

The priest smiled and shrugged his shoulders. "And remember, as a nun you are sworn to silence, so if questioned let me do all the talking. We need to go now. The nun's habit is in this case. Once you've changed put whatever you need in the case and I'll carry it. We need to something about your wedding ring. If you don't want to take it off we'll have to put a bandage on your hand to hide it."

Marie-Claire changed into the nun's habit. Chantal then helped her with the fake bandages and the wimple. "Good luck with your new life Yvonne. We're going to miss you. Although we'd love to know what happens to you, please don't attempt to get in touch. All our mail is monitored and it could be dangerous for us." With these words, Chantal gave her a big kiss on the cheek.

"I'll be forever grateful for the help and friendship you and the girls have shown me," said Marie-Claire. "Please tell them all. I'm going to miss all of you."

She gave Chantal a big hug and handed her case to Père Miguel. In the doorway she paused, worrying what kind of life lay ahead for her.

She took a deep breath, stepped outside and followed Père Miguel into the street.

Chapter 21

With a feeling of trepidation Marie-Claire set off with Père Miguel on the journey from Chantal's greenhouse to the convent. The precautions they had taken were put to the test almost immediately. As they approached the Metro they encountered a German military officer conducting identity checks. When asked for their papers Père Miguel handed both ID cards to the officer who took a cursory glance at them, handing them back without comment. However in passable French he directed a question at Marie-Claire. "Sister, how did you come by your injuries?"

Père Miguel responded. "Sister Yvonne is sworn to silence so let me reply for her – although you may not like the answer. Do I need to remind you of the conditions of the Armistice. I believe German soldiers are required to respect the people of France. I think you would agree that what you see here is not the result of respect for a nun. Does something like this really demonstrate respectful behaviour by a civilized occupying force?"

The officer looked suitably embarrassed as Père Miguel waited for an answer. Marie-Claire began trembling with fear that she'd be discovered. Père Miguel used her trembling to advantage. "You see how the presence of another German soldier is causing intense distress for poor Sister Yvonne after all she's been subjected to."

"Where are you going?" asked the officer. "Is it within Paris?" When he was told they were heading to the Convent St Josephine in the southern part of Paris, he thought for a moment then said. "I am truly ashamed of such behaviour by our soldiers. I am not permitted to leave this checkpoint but my staff car is parked over the road. As an expression of my feeling of horror at such an event, please let me have my driver take you there."

The two were escorted to the German staff car and the officer gave the driver instructions. He then turned to Marie-Claire and spoke softly to her. "Sister Yvonne – may God have mercy on your soul and help you recover from such an appalling ordeal."

During the journey they encountered frequent roadblocks and checkpoints but with the German army staff flag fluttering at the front of the car they were waved through without being stopped. At the convent the driver even carried Marie-Claire's case to the door. Both Père Miguel and Marie-Claire refrained from showing any emotion until the convent door was firmly closed behind them.

The nun who had answered the door asked them to wait while she fetched the Abbess. Marie-Claire collapsed on a bench, not knowing whether to laugh or cry. Even Père Miguel looked visibly affected by the strain of the journey. Marie-Claire smiled at him. "Father, I thought as a man of God you are not supposed to tell lies. Will you need to confess to such transgressions?"

He laughed. "Yvonne. Think back. I told no lies. I merely asked questions and let him draw the wrong conclusions. And there's nothing in the Armistice about Germans needing to respect French people but I was banking on the fact he wouldn't know that."

The Abbess joined them in the hall and Marie-Claire was surprised to see her and Père Miguel embrace warmly. He smiled at Marie-Claire's reaction. "My child. I've known the Abbess since we were young – she's my cousin. You can trust her completely."

The Abbess turned to Marie-Claire with warm eyes and a gentle smile. "My cousin has explained your recent circumstances. You have my heartfelt condolences on your losses, but please don't tell me anything more about yourself. Although I don't expect you to live as a nun, we have some strict rules. Tell no one about your life. I'll tell everyone you are here as a person in need of rest. You can dress as you would outside. And with the exception of prayers I would like you to merge in with our daily routine. Until Père Miguel has arranged an escape plan you must not leave this convent. To do so would risk not only your life but that of everyone here. I understand you can help in the kitchens?"

"Yes. I'm happy to do that."

"That would be appreciated. I've also been told you draw. You are welcome to do that but I must insist your drawings do not violate our senses or beliefs."

"I am grateful for your refuge and will do whatever you ask."

Père Miguel looked at Marie-Claire. "With respect to your drawing, is this more than just a hobby?"

"Yes. I studied art at college and trained as a school teacher."

"That's most interesting. It gives me an idea. I need to check but I might just know of a place for you to live and work outside of Paris. While I'm gone, stay here and stay safe."

He left and the heavy door closed behind him with an echoing thud. The Abbess then asked one of the nuns to show Marie-Claire to her room. Marie-Claire suspected it would be Spartan and it was – a bed, a desk with a chair, a wardrobe and a chest of drawers. No rugs, and except for a simple crucifix the grey walls were bare. As she unpacked her clothes she uncovered the drawing she had done of Emile. *Sorry my love, but you'll have to stay hidden.* She gave it a quick kiss before putting it back in the case. She then changed out of the nun's habit and went downstairs to find the kitchen and make herself useful.

Although grateful to the Abbess for giving her refuge, Marie-Claire strongly disliked life within the convent – up far too early, a never changing pattern of activities, protracted periods of silence and a monotonous menu. She found it hard to imagine a greater contrast of living styles between Chantal's place and the convent. Each was a community of women but with different approaches to life. However, both, in their own ways, could provide people like Marie-Claire with a safe refuge from the Gestapo.

She still cried herself to sleep each night but the nightmares were fewer. Without the company she'd had at Chantal's, each day was just as unexciting as the day before and she found the time dragged. Père Miguel returned the following week. "With respect to getting you out of Paris, I have a plan but first we need to produce a false ID card and for that we need to make some changes. Let's start with your name. Obviously we can't use your real name as the Gestapo may well have that on their wanted list. However, it's best if your new names start with the same letters as your real names. So, what's your new name going to be?"

A new name? I suppose I have to. My personal name is easy – I can remove the Claire part and become just Marie. But a new family name beginning with B? I don't want to use any of the names of people I know – that could be too painful. After a moment's reflection she answered. "My given name will be Marie and as for my surname, I like Bruneau. I think it means 'the dark haired one' which seems most appropriate."

"Marie Bruneau it is then. That reminds me – you need to change your hair style. I suggest short. It will change the shape of your face."

"My hair? You want to cut my hair? Please no – it's taken me years to grow it and Emile won't like it if it's short."

Realizing what she had just said, she let out a soft moan and she buried her face in her hands. Père Miguel said nothing for a minute or two, allowing Marie-Claire to regain her composure. "I assume Emile was your husband?" She nodded.

"It's alright to be sad my child. Do you want to stop for a rest?"

"No – please go on. I want to leave here as soon as possible."

He then pointed out she could not use her real place of birth or even date of birth. With respect to a place of birth Père Miguel explained that in May during the evacuation of the British soldiers, the Germans bombed Dunkerque so heavily it conveniently destroyed all birth records. This meant no one could check anything so it was safe to claim she was born in Dunkerque instead of Paris. When he suggested she pick a new birth date she chose Katia's – it was easy to remember as they had always celebrated it together since childhood.

Père Miguel pointed to her hand. "Remember when you came here we had to hide your wedding ring? Well I'm sorry but you can't continue to wear a wedding ring. If you say you are or were married, people will ask questions about your husband."

"Really? I have to pretend I've never been married?"

"It's safer that way. It's something you'll have to be very aware of at all times. A few minutes ago you mentioned Emile and you mustn't do that. It could lead people to ask awkward questions. It's

135

much easier to say you were never married."

"I see what you mean. If I take my ring off where can I put it? If I'm searched at any time and they find it, wouldn't that be worse? It would show I'm lying."

"Yes it would. I suggest you leave it here in the convent with the Abbess. She'll look after it as she does with all the personal possessions the nuns have when they come here. When the war is over you can come back for it. It will be safe here."

Marie-Claire gazed at her hand. She then slowly removed the ring, gave it a lingering kiss and gently placed it on the table. *I'm not forgetting you Emile – you'll always be in my heart. I don't need a ring to remind me of you.*

With long sigh she asked. "Ok, so what is this plan?"

"I've found you a job as an art teacher in a primary school in Nevers. Have you ever been there?"

She recalled Emile asking her the same question just before the fall of France. It seemed like years ago – not a few months. "No, I've not been there. Is that a problem?"

"No, the exact opposite. No one is likely to recognize you."

"Is Nevers in the zone occupied by the Germans?"

"I'm afraid so but you should be safe there as Mademoiselle Bruneau. With this war, being single is not unusual."

"So who in Nevers knows who I am and my situation?"

"No one. A local priest asked me if I knew anyone who could fill a teaching post mid-term. Even he does not know your situation. And that reminds me. We need to create a convincing backstory for those times when people ask you about your past."

"I thought you might be saying that and I've done some thinking about it. After all, I have had some spare time."

For her backstory Marie-Claire had decided to draw on events which had not actually been part of her life but which she knew about. Emile had often talked to her about his experiences living in a TB sanatorium. She also recalled the helpful waiter who had given her a hat when the Gestapo were chasing her. She remembered him saying his daughter had been working at a TB hospital in Arras which the Germans had totally destroyed meaning there were no records which could be checked.

"Ok," said Père Miguel. "Let's test your backstory. 'Hello Marie – I understand you've just moved to Nevers. Where were you before you came here?' And your answer is?"

"As a youngster I had TB quite badly and was sent to a sanatorium in Arras. By the time I recovered my mother had passed away and my father was in the merchant navy. So I stayed on and joined the staff. I had learned to draw and paint and so I spent my time teaching the patients. Just before the fall of France my father came back from sea with a serious heart condition so I went to live with him. He had been gassed in the Great War and in September the distress of seeing Germans everywhere became too much for him and he took his own life. It's still very raw for me so I'd rather not talk about it if you don't mind."

He nodded his head. "I like it. There's some nice detail in there. But tell me, have you ever been to a TB hospital? And for that matter is there one in Arras?"

"No, I've never been to a TB hospital but my husband spent much of his youth in one and often spoke about his experiences. And as for Arras, there was one there but it was completely destroyed by the Germans and everyone was killed by them."

"Your backstory sounds convincing. Is any of it actually true?"

"No. Before he died my father was an electrical engineer managing part of the Maginot line. In fact he told me that one day he discovered that for a major section of the line the critical electricity was coming indirectly from Germany. Can you imagine what that would have meant if he hadn't detected it?"

"Unfortunately I can – what a mistake. But to return to your backstory, you should keep going over it in your mind so it becomes second nature. And as for me, I need to go and make preparations for your arrival in Nevers."

Over the next few days her life underwent a complete transformation – new hairstyle, new clothes, new hat, new forged ID card with her new name. However no one in the convent, not even the Abbess, was told her new name. Since she would no longer be hiding from the Paris police she felt it was safe to keep her sketch of Emile. After pulling it out of her sketchpad, she stared at his face for a long time before giving it a silent kiss and tucking it into the bottom of her new case.

When Père Miguel came to accompany her to the Gare de Lyon train station she knew she had to accept that her life was changing. There was no going back. Saturday the 12th of October would forever stick in her mind as the day she became a different person.

As she stood on the platform at the station she reflected on her situation. *I'm on my own now. As a child I relied on Maman to guide me. Then I fell in love with Emile and I relied heavily on his guidance. But both of them have gone. From today I must make my own decisions, take my own risks and have confidence in what I do. What was it Madame Guillon said? 'If you want to honour your mother's memory, continue her fight for France when you are able.' But How? And will I be able?*

"Am I just running away Père Miguel? Am I being disloyal to those who loved me?"

He held her hand to comfort her. "No my child, exactly the opposite. Your mother and your dear husband were killed fighting to rid France of the invaders and provide a safe life for others – others such as you. If you don't live the life they died to protect – then you would be being disloyal. These are troubled times and if you are going to survive you need to live for the future and not in the past. I know that will be hard but I have every confidence you can. You are much stronger than you realize."

With his words ringing in her head, she boarded the train and waved goodbye. Goodbye to Père Miguel. Goodbye to Paris. Goodbye to everything she had lived for. Goodbye to being able to share her memories with anyone. That last goodbye was the hardest of all.

As of today I have to rebuild my life without the help of any of my friends or family. I'm now entirely on my own.

PART 3 - NEVERS

Chapter 22

Saturday, 12 October 1940, Nevers.

On the train journey south to Nevers Marie-Claire sat quietly, trying to hide her tears. In spite of Père Miguel's words of encouragement she did not feel confident. With each click of the train wheels on the tracks she felt like she was being ripped apart piece by piece. She pulled out her bag and looked again at her ID card in the name of Marie Bruneau to convince herself this was reality and not some nightmare.

As she looked, reality became a nightmare.

How could I not have seen the error in this forged card? Her immediate feeling of panic reminded her of her first job as a passeur when Gustave, the airman, had the wrong stamp on his card. But this time it was her own card which had the error. There was a misspelling of REPUBLIC in the forged red stamp. The B was missing the lower part and looked like a P – REPULIC.

There's no way this card will pass inspection. With this card I can't get off the train, but I'm at risk if I stay on it.

With shaking hands she put the card back in her bag. She tried to control her racing heart but her nerves were on edge for the rest of the journey. Every time the train stopped at a station she felt a sense of panic. *Will somebody come through the train checking ID cards?* Fortunately no one did.

When the train arrived in Nevers she saw that ID cards were being checked at the exit of the station. She knew this was not an immediate problem as she had been told that she would be met in the station waiting room by Madame Segal, the school secretary.

139

Perhaps if I leave with her, they won't check my ID.

When she reached the waiting room she saw that it was empty – there was nobody waiting for her. She felt an increasing sense of panic. *I've got to get out of here now.*

While the stationmaster was busy checking the ID cards of other passengers she walked away along the platform looking for another way out. She found another gate but it was padlocked. She slowly walked back to the waiting room and sat down, her nerves at breaking point.

In despair she put her head in her hands. *What on earth can I do? I don't know anybody in this town and I have a badly forged ID card.*

Her thoughts were interrupted by approaching footsteps. She looked up, expecting to see Madame Segal. Instead she was confronted by the stationmaster. He looked at her for a moment then extended his hand. "Papers please."

Reluctantly Marie-Claire handed him her identity card and travel papers. *With no one else in the station he'll have time to examine them in detail and find the flaw. Have I done all this only to be caught before I even start my new life?*

As he studied the papers for a disconcertingly long time she tried to hide her fear by concentrating on his name badge – Monsieur Gost, Stationmaster. Finally he looked at her with a frown, which she took to mean he'd found the error.

"Mademoiselle Bruneau, what brings you to Nevers?"

Although Marie-Claire knew her cover story was solid, she also knew that she must not give out more information than necessary. "I'm starting a new job here in Nevers."

"A job? And what would that job be?"

"I'm taking up a position as the art teacher at a school."

"Oh yes? At what school? Remember, I can easily check."

"Ecole Napoleon Bonaparte."

She thought his faced appeared to relax slightly. "Really? And who are you waiting for?"

"Madame Segal, who should have been here by now."

"It's unusual for her to be late. And by the way, I'm very glad you have come to Nevers." When she looked puzzled he smiled. "My son goes to that school and has been missing his art classes ever since Mademoiselle Monnier left."

Marie-Claire thought he hadn't detected the error in her card until he stooped over and said in a low voice, "Mademoiselle Bruneau. I assume in your art classes you will be using various inks – perhaps Watermans red ink, the kind we use in the station for stamping cards. I suggest you use that ink to correct the second P in *REPUPLIC* to a B. In all other respects this is a good forgery. I'll not ask if you did it or where you got it from, but make that correction as soon as you can."

Marie-Claire was about to respond when he straightened up. "Oh look, here's Madame Segal now. Allow me to introduce you." He handed back her papers. "Madame Segal, if you're looking for your new art teacher here she is, Mademoiselle Bruneau."

"Hello. I'm sorry I'm late – a small family crisis. Monsieur Gost, I hope you've been looking after Mademoiselle Bruneau."

"I have," he said, "and we had an interesting chat, didn't we?"

"Yes we did," replied Marie-Claire. "Monsieur Gost told me he has a child at the school."

Madame Segal smiled. "Yes, and a very bright boy he is too."

The stationmaster beamed a proud father's smile. "Thank you. But don't let me detain you two ladies. I have a station to run."

Once he was out of earshot Madame Segal spoke in a hushed voice. "I suppose I don't need to tell you, but you need to be very careful what you say to people these days. I'm not sure about Monsieur Gost, so you should be on your guard."

"Thanks for the warning. Do we have far to go?"

"No, it's not far to the boarding house where I've booked you a room. Madame Favier runs a very respectable house and I'm sure you'll like it."

As they walked to the boarding house Madame Segal kept up a steady stream of conversation, pointing out various buildings in Nevers. "I'm sure you'll enjoy sketching our cathedral. It is unusual for a French cathedral as it's actually two buildings joined together and has two altars."

Marie-Claire remembered Emile telling her many months ago that the only thing she might find of interest in Nevers was the cathedral. She also recalled having replied that she had no intention of ever going to Nevers. *And yet here I am, not visiting but hiding and starting a new life here – without you my love.*

When they walked past the Hotel de France Marie-Claire observed with disgust the red Nazi banners hanging across the front of the building, each with a daunting swastika – a blatant sign of the German occupation. She almost commented on the ubiquitous banners until she realized that without knowing Madame Segal's views expressing an opinion could be dangerous.

When they reached the boarding house the secretary introduced Marie-Claire to the landlady, Madame Favier, who greeted them with a welcoming smile and offered them a drink. Madame Segal declined. "Thank you but we're running a bit late and I still need to show Mademoiselle Bruneau the route to the school."

On the way to the school Madame Segal reminded Marie-Claire that she would need a new ID card showing her Nevers address and job. When she suggested doing this on Wednesday Marie-Claire realized she only had four days in which to correct the problem with her existing card. "I'm sure that will be fine," she said, "but don't we teach on Wednesday?"

"No. Only on Mondays, Tuesdays, Thursdays and Fridays. Some other schools do half day on Wednesday and even Saturday, but not us."

When they arrived at the school gates Marie-Claire saw that they were closed and locked. "Will you be showing me inside today? I was wanting to see what art supplies there are. You know paper, pencils, paints and inks."

"No, we can do that on Monday. And the children don't use inks in art. We found ink was too messy. We use it in the writing classes run by Mademoiselle Deferre but not in the art classes."

Marie-Claire made a mental note of the need to cultivate a friendship quickly with this Mademoiselle Deferre person and obtain some red ink with which to amend her ID card.

As they stood in front of the locked school Madame Segal

apologized again. "I'm sorry I was late at the station but I really need to be heading home now. Can you find your own way back?"

"Yes I can, thank you."

After Madame Segal left, Marie-Claire stared at the school. *So this is my life now. I wanted a teaching post – but not like this. It was supposed to be in Paris and I was supposed to be living with Emile. They say I'll get over his loss but I don't see how I ever can.*

At bedtime she took her sketch of Emile out of her suitcase and sat staring at it. *My love. I can't put you on the wall but you'll always be in my heart.* After putting the picture back in it's hiding place she cried herself to sleep.

Chapter 23

The following day was Sunday and Marie-Claire spent the day at the boarding house, too afraid to venture out in case she had to show her ID card. She would like to have been able to wander around the town looking for an art shop, but she knew that even if she found one, it would be closed. She realized her only hope was that Madame Segal was right and that Mademoiselle Deferre's class did use Watermans ink – red Watermans ink.

But how can I ask her without sounding suspicious?

On Monday she arrived at the school early and was introduced to the other teachers. There was a grumpy Monsieur Garnier who barely even acknowledged the introduction, a bubbly Madame Duchamps who Marie-Claire decided was best avoided as she looked as if she would ask too many questions. And of course there was the headmaster, Monsieur Thibault, who seemed genuinely pleased to see her.

"Mademoiselle Bruneau, I am so glad you have been able to join us. In these troubled times I feel art is such an important aspect of life for the children. It gives them a way of expressing their feelings without having to hunt for words. If there's anything I can do to help, you only need to ask. My door is always open. But for all administrative matters, such as a new identity card, Madame Segal is the person."

"Oh yes. Madame Segal mentioned something about doing that on Wednesday." *I must correct my card before then – but where is Mademoiselle Deferre? I can't ask about her or about ink.* As each female teacher was introduced Marie-Claire hoped it would be Mademoiselle Deferre, but no. However just as the school bell rang to indicate the commencement of classes Marie-Claire saw a lady about her own age running into the school.

After the bell rang Monsieur Thibault took Marie-Claire along to her classroom and introduced her to the class of smiling young students. She immediately felt a warmth in their welcome. She started her lesson by asking the children to draw their favourite thing. As she walked around the classroom talking to the children about their drawings she was pleasantly surprised at the quality of their work. Before she knew it the lesson was over. She repeated the exercise with the next group of students. She said a silent thank you to Père Miguel – *I think this job is going to work out better than I thought possible.*

At lunch time in the staff room Marie-Claire was about to seek out Mademoiselle Deferre when she came over and introduced herself. "Hello. I'm Françoise Deferre. I'm sorry I wasn't here when Monsieur Thibault was making the introductions but I was running a bit late this morning." She paused for a moment then added. "Please don't misunderstand me but it's so nice to see you're a younger person. You've probably noticed most of the teachers here are quite a bit older than me. Not that I'm against older people but ever since she left I've been concerned Sarah's replacement would be an older person."

"Sarah? Was she the art teacher before me?"

"Yes, Sarah Monnier. She was a close friend and I miss her."

"Actually, if you knew her well, you might know where she got her art supplies."

"Yes I do. Is there anything in particular you're looking for? Sarah worked mostly in pen and ink which I got for her. We use ink in the writing classes. Do you work in pencil or ink?"

"Both, but I had to leave all my inks behind. If any of the bottles had broken in my suitcase it would have ruined all my clothes."

"I can give you some if you want. We only use Watermans. Red, black and blue. I hope that's alright."

Hallelujah – Watermans red ink. "If it's not too much trouble, all three please."

That evening, behind a locked door at the boarding house, Marie-Claire corrected the problem with her ID card, filling in the lower portion of the B. She was surprised at how easy it was to amend an ID card.

On Wednesday her forgery was put under scrutiny when she and Madame Segal went to the town hall to have a new card issued showing her Nevers address and occupation as a school teacher. She need not have worried. The clerk took only a cursory glance before issuing a brand new card and sealing it with a red stamp.

For the next couple of months Marie-Claire kept a low profile. She spent most of her free time sketching, walking around Nevers and trying to teach herself German. She wished she had listened to Emile when he had offered to teach her. Although she thought about her beloved Emile and her mother every day, she knew she could not mention either of them to anyone. To avoid awkward questions she kept mostly to herself, with the exception of Françoise Deferre with whom she became close friends. The two women often went out together for meals and walks in the parks. Although they never discussed politics Marie-Claire formed the opinion that while Françoise was certainly not a collaborator, she did not appear to be involved in resistance.

This quiet and non-eventful life suited Marie-Claire as she needed time to come to terms with her losses and adapt to her new life. However in mid-December she faced a major challenge to her decision to keep a low profile. Philippe, a small boy in one of her art classes, had drawn a picture of what appeared to be a pile of logs ready to go to a sawmill. When she commented on his drawing, the boy told her they weren't logs.

"They are dead Germans piled in a heap."

Initially horrified by his response, she asked him why he'd drawn the picture.

"My uncle says the Germans invaded France and are killing French people. He says we should resist and fight the German soldiers. Bang, bang, dead – pile them in a heap."

Marie-Claire looked around, fearful the other children might have heard Philippe, but no one appeared to react. She doubted Philippe knew the significance of his words and the peril he was creating for himself, his parents and his uncle if somebody reported what he was saying.

"Do you spend much time with your uncle?"

"Yes Mademoiselle. I live with my uncle now since my house in Nancy was bombed and everyone in my family was killed." Philippe began to cry at the mention of the loss of his family. She put her arms around him to console the young lad.

The mention of bombs and killing brought back dreadful memories of her own experiences and the loss of Violette, Katia, Hannah, her mother and Emile. All sorts of thoughts ran through her mind. *If the Gestapo or an informant or even just a Nazi sympathizer hears Philippe, his uncle will be arrested and probably executed. And then what will happen to Philippe? Somehow I should warn this uncle. But after all the trouble I've taken to keep a low profile should I even think of becoming involved? But I can't just sit back – I must act.*

That afternoon she obtained the address where Philippe was living. When classes ended she left the school and headed towards 22 Rue d'Antoine.

When she reached the house, the reality of her situation took hold and she experienced debilitating self-doubt. *What am I just about to do? What if Philippe's uncle doesn't understand the seriousness of the issue? This is madness.* She turned and walked away, intending to abandon the whole idea.

As she retraced her steps she recalled her friend Katia showing incredible courage and selflessness just before she was caught by the Gestapo. She had told Marie-Claire that what she did was dangerous but that didn't stop her. Katia had shown unwavering determination in her fight for France. With a chest-tightening feeling of guilt that she was choosing the easy option of not being brave enough to talk to the uncle Marie-Claire stopped. She thought about what she was doing and realized that she owed it to Katia, and all of the others she had lost, to display the same level of courage and selflessness herself.

So she turned around, strode up to the house, banged the knocker on the door – and stood back.

Chapter 24

When the door to 22 Rue d'Antoine opened Marie-Claire's heart almost stopped. The person standing in the doorway was a German officer. *What am I going to do now?* The officer looked at her and spoke in perfect French. "I'm sorry but if you've come to see Monsieur Dupont you are too late. He'll be working for us now."

What does he mean I'm too late? Why say 'he'll be working for us'? Does that mean Philippe's uncle has become a collaborator? Marie-Claire knew she had to respond but all she managed was a simple, "Oh I see."

"Yes. However if what you're wanting is something simple like putting up a shelf, I'm sure we can arrange for him to have time to accommodate a young lady like you. I'm not surprised you want his help. We chose him to do our office renovations because we were told he's the best carpenter in this town."

What was it Emile said about me being 'resourceful' and 'quick to adapt'? I need to explain why I'm here. "His reputation is the reason I came as well – to ask Monsieur Dupont if he can make me a bookcase. I hope it won't interfere with the important work he'll be doing for you."

"I'm sure that will be fine. I'll leave you to discuss your requirements with him. Goodbye Mademoiselle." He bowed and walked away down the street.

When Monsieur Dupont appeared at the door Marie-Claire introduced herself as Mademoiselle Bruneau and was about to explain why she was there when he interrupted her. "Please come in quickly Mademoiselle. I want to close the door against this bitter cold weather."

She stepped inside and his tone of voice changed. "Bookcase? Really? You're saying you came here to talk about a bookcase?"

Marie-Claire did not like his tone and decided to stick to her story. "Yes, I do need some shelves. I'm the new art —"

"Oh I know who you are," he interrupted. "Bernard told me about you."

Marie-Claire was puzzled. "Who is Bernard?"

"Bernard Gost, the stationmaster. I'm surprised and very upset you came here, to my home. Sarah would never have done that. Coming here so openly could compromise our whole operation."

"I'm not part of any operation."

"So why are you here? Who told you to come here?"

"No one told me. I came to warn you."

"Warn me? Warn me about what?"

Startled by his interrogative attitude Marie-Claire quickly took Philippe's drawing out of her bag and handed it to him. "What do you see here Monsieur Dupont?"

He studied the picture. "Is this something Philippe drew? I see logs piled up."

"That's what I saw. Do you know what Philippe said it was?"

"No. How would I? What are you trying to say?"

"Philippe told me it wasn't logs. He said it was dead Germans piled in a heap. He then told me you and your friends always talk about fighting Germans so he drew a pile of dead Germans. 'Bang, bang, dead – pile them in a heap' were the words he used."

Philippe's uncle looked shaken and his attitude changed completely. "Are you serious? Is that what he said? In class?"

"I am serious and yes, that's what he said. Fortunately I don't think any of the other children heard him. I don't suppose I need to tell you how dangerous this could be if the wrong person should hear him. I don't know what you can do Monsieur Dupont, but you need to do something."

"Thank you Marie for telling me. I think I know what I'll do."

"You called me Marie. I don't recall telling you my name."

"You didn't. Bernard told me and here we call each other by our given name – I'm André. But to get back to Philippe, I'm not his only relation. I have a sister who lives on a farm in Ardèche. I'll take him there."

"But Ardèche is in the Unoccupied Zone, isn't it?" asked Marie-Claire. "How will you cross the Demarcation Line?"

"I told Major Richter, the officer who was here, that I needed to travel across the Line to get supplies for his work so he obligingly gave me a Ausweis pass authorizing me to cross the Line in my van. He's nicely trusting and gullible. We'll leave first thing in the morning before Philippe can talk to anyone else. Can you please tell Stephane, your headmaster, that Philippe will no longer be attending school."

"No, I can't. He might ask why or how I know. That could raise all sorts of awkward questions. So you'll have to tell Monsieur Thibault yourself."

"I suppose you're right. I should be back by the end of the week and I'll tell him then. Thank you so much for telling me what Philippe has been saying. I'm sorry for being so abrupt when you came but I thought you were a new member of our group." He paused, folded his arms and looked at her with interest. "Since you're not, and it's obvious where your sympathies lie, might you be interested in joining our group? Sarah's sudden departure has been a significant loss. We no longer have a skilled artist to do our forgeries."

"No thank you. Although I have no objection to what you appear to be doing, it's not something I want to become involved with. And André, don't forget I need a bookcase."

"I thought that was just a cover story."

"It was, but your nice major may ask you about it or even check you are making me a bookcase. So please make it about a metre high and a metre wide with two small drawers in the middle."

André grudgingly agreed and promised to deliver it by the start of the next school term.

Later that week Madame Segal approached Marie-Claire. "Have you heard from Philippe? He's not been here since Monday and I would have expected Monsieur Dupont to have told me if there was a problem."

"No, I haven't. I didn't think Dupont was his family name."

"It isn't. He's living with his uncle. The reason I thought you might know is I saw you consoling Philippe on Monday."

I'm glad I refused to be the one to tell Monsieur Thibault that

Philippe would be going away. But I must give some response. "He was telling me about his parents being killed in Nancy and began crying so of course I consoled the poor boy. Perhaps he's come down with flu along with his uncle."

"Oh I suppose that could be the case." And on that note Madame Segal turned and walked off.

On the last day of term after all the children had left, Marie-Claire sat at her desk feeling sorry for herself. She and Emile had made special plans for this Christmas – what would have been their first Christmas as a married couple. Eventually she tidied up her things and was about to leave the classroom when Françoise came in. "Oh good. I'm glad you haven't left yet Marie. What are you doing over the holidays?"

It pained Marie-Claire to tell the truth. "Actually I have no plans. I thought I might help Madame Favier at the boarding house but I believe most of the other residents will be away."

"I can't have you spending Christmas on your own. Look, tomorrow I'm going to our family farm just outside Nevers for the holidays and I'm sure you'd be more than welcome to join us." With a glint in her eye she added, "It's a mixed farm which means lots of – shall we say – food the Germans don't know we have. So, would you like to join us?"

"That sounds fantastic but what will your parents feel about you bringing an unannounced guest?"

"I can assure you that won't be a problem. There's a spare bedroom and my parents always like company."

"If you're certain, then yes that would be lovely. Is there anything I should bring? And how do we get there?"

"Just bring your sketch pad and pencils. I'm sure they'd love you to do some portraits for them – you do those so well. And we can cycle there. It's not far."

The following day the two of them then set off on their bicycles to the Deferre farm. The roads had been cleared of snow and the sun was shining but the air was bitterly cold. They had dressed up well against the cold with thick gloves, warm coats and with

151

scarves wrapped around their faces. When they arrived Marie-Claire was made to feel most welcome by both Madame and Monsieur Deferre. The farm was a rambling place with barns, outbuildings and a large old-fashioned farmhouse. The enticing smells coming from the kitchen made it hard to believe there was a war on with food rationing.

After the best meal Marie-Claire had had in a very long time and an evening of friendly chatter, she had no trouble falling asleep.

In the morning as she lay in bed curled up under a warm duvet she became aware of an animated conversation coming from downstairs. It sounded as if Françoise was having a disagreement with her mother. The voices became louder and she could not help but overhear.

"No Maman, I don't think she's a spy. Marie has been with us at the school for over two months and I haven't heard her say anything to make me suspicious. In fact the exact opposite."

"Yes, but you should have told me you were bringing someone new. How can we trust her? If I'd known you were bringing someone I would not have agreed to have an escaper here over Christmas. You know the rules – no contact with an unknown person while hiding someone."

Marie-Claire was surprised by Françoise's response.

"You don't need to tell me the rules – I told you what the rules needed to be when you said you and your friends wanted to be part of an escape line. And Marie is not unknown to me. And with respect to bringing her here, on the last day of term when I saw she would be on her own, I made a spur of the moment decision. But equally how do you know the person in the barn is a genuine British airman? Just because he said so? Just because he said he wanted to get home to Scotland?"

The words 'get home to Scotland' brought back memories to Marie-Claire. *The man in the soup kitchen also said 'get home to Scotland' – a strange coincidence.*

"How long before he can be moved on?" Françoise asked her mother.

"There's a problem. His ID card needs fixing. It's a pity Sarah isn't here. She'd have been able to fix it."

"Fix his ID card? What's wrong with it?"

"It obviously wasn't well made. I took him a pitcher of buttermilk with his meal last night and some spilled on the card. Part of the wording and red stamp have been destroyed – here look at it. He'll be caught if he has to show this card and so will we unless we can fix it – but how? I've kept the inks Sarah stored here for that purpose but she's not here. My hands are not steady enough to do that kind of work. Can you do it?"

"I can't Maman. Sarah tried to teach me once and I was hopeless. But that's Marie's world – she's an artist. I wonder if she'd be willing to help?"

Although Marie-Claire knew she could do it, she wasn't sure she wanted to get involved and wondered what she would say if Françoise were to ask her.

"I know she's an artist," said Madame Deferre. "She told us yesterday evening, but how can we ask her? Are you sure we can trust her?"

Marie-Claire was startled by the strength of her friend's reply. "I'd bet my life on it."

"That's exactly what you would be doing – and ours as well."

There was a short period of silence then Marie-Claire heard Françoise say in a resigned tone. "Look at this ID card. If he is stopped at a checkpoint, with these blank bits it will be obvious the card has been forged and we risk being arrested. I know asking Marie is a risk but I think it's the lesser risk."

There was another moment of silence then Marie-Claire heard Madame Deferre agree. "I suppose you're right. I don't like asking her one bit but perhaps it is the lesser risk. Ok, you go upstairs and ask Marie, but please be careful. I won't get any of Sarah's inks out unless Marie is willing. My God, what a mess."

"Maman, we really have no choice. A bad job correcting this ID card could be a death sentence for all of us and I'm sure Marie will be willing to help. You go and get the inks – I'll go and ask Marie."

Marie-Claire realized the moment of truth was only a minute or two away. *I have the skills – I corrected my own ID card. And Madame Guillon put it clearly when she said 'If you want to honour your mother's memory then continue her fight for France.' Perhaps the time has come for me to do something positive. But if I'm going to be a résistante then I'll be an active one and good at it – no half measures.*

With that resolve in her mind she rose quickly and pulled on some clothes. At the polite knock on her door she opened it. "Françoise, you don't need to ask. Your voices were very loud and I couldn't help overhearing your conversation. If Sarah's inks are here I might be able to fix the ID card. Shall we see?"

Françoise looked relieved. "Thank you. I didn't know how to ask you. There's such a big difference between having anti-German views and actively fighting against the Germans." Her look of relief changed to surprise but she said nothing when Marie-Claire replied. "Oh you don't need to tell me about the difference. Now let's look at this ID card."

By the time they reached the kitchen the man's ID card was on the table along with an array of Watermans inks, brushes and pens.

Marie-Claire looked down at the card and gasped. Her hands gripped the table so tightly her knuckles went white. She turned to Madame Deferre. "Is this photograph a good likeness? Where is this man? Could he have seen me arrive yesterday?"

Chapter 25

Madame Deferre and Françoise looked shocked at Marie-Claire's reaction to the ID card. "What's the problem?" asked Françoise.

Marie-Claire repeated her questions with an authority she didn't know she had. "Madame Deferre, is this a good photograph of the escaper? And could he have seen me arrive yesterday?"

"He looks just like the photograph, including the scar on his cheek. He's hiding in the barn and could not have seen you arrive. And anyway you had a scarf around your face."

"What has he told you? What kind of plane was he flying?"

"He said he was a navigator on a bombing mission to Dijon."

"Not the pilot?"

"No. He explicitly said all the others including the pilot were killed. He said quite clearly he was the navigator."

Marie-Claire frowned. "And he said he wanted to 'get home to Scotland'. Is that right?"

"Yes. He said 'home to Scotland' and that he lives in Berwick."

Marie-Claire looked puzzled. "Are you sure he said Berwick and 'home to Scotland'?"

"Yes, that's what he said."

"Interesting. And does he have a limp?"

"No. He had no sign of a limp. He walked normally."

So I was right. Back then he was faking a limp as part of his cover story. "Can you tell me, is he left or right handed?"

Madame Deferre looked anxious, "Left handed and —"

"Don't tell me," interrupted Marie-Claire. "He has a scar across the inside of his left palm. Am I right?"

"Yes, I saw it this morning." Madame Deferre now looked even more anxious. "Do you know this man?"

"I've encountered him before. The scars on his cheek and his left palm confirm it's the same person." She remembered vividly her previous encounter with this same man in the soup kitchen in

155

Paris. *I even drew a sketch of him that Katia studied before picking him up from Place de la Madeleine. My friend Katia who was betrayed by someone – and now I know who betrayed her.*

She found it hard to contain her anger. "I'm sure he's not what he says he is. His story is completely different from what he said in July when I met him and he was looking for an escape line."

"Are you saying he has used an escape line before?" asked Françoise.

"Yes. Back then he said he was William MacDonald, not William Stewart, and that he was a Spitfire pilot. And he's made a bad error in his cover story. If he's actually from Berwick, he'd know it's part of England not Scotland."

"Are you sure about that?"

"Berwick is on the border between England and Scotland and in the past has sometimes even part of Scotland. Although it's been officially part of England for ages, this man may have looked at a German map of Britain and thought it's in Scotland."

"What have German maps got to do with this British airman?" asked Monsieur Deferre who had just entered the kitchen.

"That's the thing," replied Marie-Claire. "I'm absolutely sure he's not British. When I met him in July he had a totally different backstory. He said he was a Spitfire pilot, not a bomber navigator. No Spitfire pilot would become a navigator on a bomber. He's also made a mistake saying Berwick is in Scotland, not something anyone from Berwick would do. And the escape line he joined in July was subsequently betrayed and everyone arrested."

She paused while she calmed her breathing. "I believe he's a German counter-espionage agent pretending to be British so he can infiltrate and destroy escape lines. And that means betraying everyone associated with them including, therefore, all of you."

When Madame Deferre looked horrified Marie-Claire added, "Fortunately, at this point we have the upper hand because he won't suspect he's been uncovered."

"I can see why you might think he's a German agent Marie," said Monsieur Deferre, "but there is one important factor which I think works against your conclusion. He has two very visible scars and as a consequence would never have been selected as an agent. Agents need to blend in and not be easily identified."

"Exactly. But he's not being a spy in a foreign land where he needs to blend in. He's pretending to be British. And what better person to pick for that role than someone who is so easy to identify he couldn't possibly be a German agent. Using him as an infiltrator is brilliant because those very scars which you say would prevent him being an agent lend credibility to his claim that he's British."

"Yes. But that deception would only work once."

"Not if he betrays that escape line and then moves to a different part of the country before trying the same ruse again. Which is why it's critical that he doesn't see me. If he sees me he'll know his cover's blown and that could make him very dangerous."

"What do you mean 'dangerous'?" asked Madame Deferre.

"I suspect if you searched him you'd find he's carrying a concealed weapon, a pistol of some sort."

"I have a shotgun," said Monsieur Deferre, "and if we prove he's a German infiltrator, I'd be willing to use it."

"Owning a farm gun and being willing to shoot someone are two very different things," said Marie-Claire. "Are you sure you could do that?"

"If this man is planning to betray my family and my friends, then it's the only option. Marie, this is your first war. For me, unfortunately, it's my second. In the Great War I learned very rapidly that when the enemy is attacking you, you need to make a quick decision – kill or be killed. If it fits with your plan I'll get my gun and load it. And if necessary, I'll fire. He wouldn't be the first German I have killed in war and I doubt he'll be the last. That's the reality of war – kill or be killed. So, do you have a plan?"

"Yes, but there's a problem. In order to prove to ourselves that he's a German agent we need to ask him some specific questions and see if he lies to us not realizing we know the real answers. Since he might remember me I can't do the questioning, and because of the danger I don't feel I can ask any of you to do it."

"Marie," said Françoise. "Maman, Papa and I are already taking serious risks by just running an escape line. If we're caught, or if this man betrays us, we will pay with our lives. So if you have a plan, tell us what it is and we'll do it. If he needs to be questioned use me – I speak both English and German."

Marie-Claire paused for a moment then took a deep breath. "Alright, here's my plan. Madame Deferre, when we're ready I want you to bring him out from the barn into the middle of the courtyard where Françoise will question him. Monsieur Deferre, I'd like you to be hiding somewhere which enables you to keep your gun pointed at him at all times, ready to fire if needed."

"I'll get my gun, load up and position myself. I'll be in the tool store and I'll leave the door open when I'm ready." Monsieur Deferre put on his coat and left.

Marie-Claire turned to Françoise. "I want you to question him in English. Ask him where he crashed his Spitfire. As I said, when I met him before he claimed to be a Spitfire pilot. He said he'd been shot down over Dunkerque during the troop evacuation."

Françoise nodded. "After he answers I'll ask him where he's from, but I won't comment or react if he says Berwick in Scotland. Anything else?"

"Yes. I know he was in Paris when he joined the other escape line, the one he betrayed. So ask him how long he spent in Paris."

"Paris? Ok. Any more questions you want me to ask?"

Marie-Claire suddenly recalled something Emile had told her that he had learned from a genuine British airman. "Yes. Ask him the name of his pigeon."

Françoise laughed. "Did you say pigeon? Ask him the name of his pigeon? I don't understand."

"He might not recognize it as a trick question. All British bombers carry homing pigeons. If the bomber is shot down the bird is released with a message which details their position in the hope they can be rescued. And everyone on board would know the name of their rescue pigeon."

"You cannot be serious. How do you know that?"

"Sorry, I can't tell you – at least not right now. But I suspect not many Germans know about the pigeons."

"I'll enjoy asking that one. Anything else?"

"Yes. What we need to do is make him reveal his true identity. So suddenly speak to him in German and accuse him of being a British spy. Perhaps threaten to arrest him. That should put him off his guard. If he thinks you are also in German counter-espionage, he may then admit who he really is."

"Let's hope it works." Françoise looked out of the window. "I see Papa is ready in the tool store."

Marie-Claire turned to Madame Deferre. "I think we're ready now. Can you go and get this man please."

"I'll tell him the next contact has some questions," said Madame Deferre. "You want him standing in the middle of the courtyard where Rémi can see him from the tool shed. Is that right?"

"Yes. Away from any buildings so he can be seen easily by Monsieur Deferre. And don't get close to him. If he becomes suspicious he might try to take you hostage. When Françoise goes out to talk to him come back into the house. I'll keep out of sight in case he recognizes me."

Madame Deferre put on her coat and left. Marie-Claire turned to Françoise. "If we do uncover him as a German agent and deal with him accordingly, it will be retribution for Katia."

"Who is Katia?"

Marie-Claire bit her lip before answering, trying unsuccessfully to hold back her tears. "She was my oldest and closest friend. She was part of the escape line which helped this man before, and she was subsequently betrayed by someone and arrested by the Gestapo. Betrayed after this man stayed in her apartment for two days. I'm convinced he's the person who betrayed her."

Françoise touched Marie-Claire's arm gently. "I'll do my best to uncover him. And afterwards I would like you to answer my question. Up until now I've seen you as just an art teacher. But watching you this morning, I have to ask – who the hell are you?"

At this point Marie-Claire was not sure herself.

Madame Deferre brought the apparent escaper into the cold courtyard. As Françoise went out and stood a few metres away from him Madame Deferre returned to the house. She stood in the open doorway with Marie-Claire beside her but just out of sight. The escaper spoke to Françoise in English. "Is my ID card fixed? When do I move on?"

She replied in English. "We're working on it but first I have some questions. Where did you crash your Spitfire?"

He hesitated. "I'm not a pilot. I've never flown a Spitfire. I'm a navigator in a bomber. Why do you ask? Who are you?"

Françoise ignored his questions and asked. "When were you last in Paris?"

Again he hesitated, as if considering his answer. "Paris? I've never been to Paris. This was my first time over France and we were heading to Dijon, but my plane didn't make it."

"Which part of Scotland are you from?"

"I'm from Berwick in Scotland. I don't know why you're asking me these questions. I've already given these answers to the people who live on this farm."

"I was just checking that you give the same answers. And I have another question. What was the name of your pigeon?"

The man shook his head and laughed. "Did you just ask me for the name of my pigeon? I don't keep pigeons. Stupid question."

Françoise stared directly at the man. She then spoke rapidly and loudly in German in a commanding tone. Marie-Claire could not understand what Françoise had said but she saw the escaper's face contort into a snarl as he immediately responded back assertively and rapidly in German. Marie-Claire was stunned by the aggressive tone in the exchange of words and whispered to Madame Deferre. "My German is not good. He spoke too quickly for me to understand but you speak German – what was said?"

"She accused him of being a British spy and called a corporal to take him behind the barn and shoot him. He replied that he's a Lieutenant in the German Military Intelligence and that she was interfering in an important counter-espionage operation. It must have infuriated his male ego to have a woman order a lowly corporal to shoot him."

After staring at the man for a few seconds Françoise spoke to him in English. "I still believe you are a British spy. However, if you are the person you claim to be then I have a further question to ask that no British spy would be able to answer. But be aware – we know the answer so it is essential for you to tell the truth. How long did you stay in the girl's apartment in Paris in July?"

He paused then replied in English. "Two days. And the girl was stupid. She believed everything I said. But she didn't tell us anything – even under torture. Her death was no loss."

Françoise baited him, this time in French. "Oh, you mean just like your imminent death will be no loss?"

With a startled look of realization he glared at Françoise, reached into his pocket and pulled out a pistol. But before he could even raise it to fire he fell to the ground, his body punctured with shot from both barrels of Monsieur Deferre's shotgun.

When the echoing noise of the shotgun died down Françoise turned towards the doorway where Marie-Claire was now standing. "May your friend Katia now rest in peace."

With tears streaming down her face Marie-Claire rushed over to hug Françoise. "Thank you from Katia and all the others who were betrayed by this man. We can't help them, but today you and your father have saved many other French lives."

Monsieur Deferre came out of the tool store. "I use this gun for shooting vermin. I guess today was no different."

Françoise looked at the body lying in the snow. "What are we going to do with him? If someone comes here and finds him we'll be arrested."

Monsieur Deferre sighed. "On this farm I'm used to doing slaughtering and butchering. I can dispose of him."

Marie-Claire looked at him. "What do you mean?"

"If my pigs are hungry enough they'll eat anything, including flesh and bone."

Suppressing a feeling of revulsion, Marie-Claire did not ask any more questions. Instead she helped Françoise pour water over the blood-stained snow so it would melt and soak into the mud of the courtyard. With every bucket of water she felt a justifiable sense of retribution for the death of Katia.

That evening Monsieur Deferre opened a bottle of cognac. They raised their glasses to the memory of all those who had been betrayed by that man. Marie-Claire wiped a tear from her face.

Françoise turned to her. "Marie, remember just before I went out to question him, I said I would ask you a question? So, exactly who are you? And don't say just an art teacher."

Marie-Claire wanted to tell them her story but she knew it would not be wise. Finally she answered. "I know it may sound odd but the answer is – I am just an art teacher at the school."

"Come on. I've known you for what – over two months? And you have never acted the way you did today – taking charge, giving out orders and knowing exactly how to trap and catch him. So I don't believe 'just an art teacher'. You're among friends here. So who exactly are you?"

Marie-Claire felt cornered and must have shown it. She was surprised when Monsieur Deferre came to her rescue. "Françoise, in the Great War I wasn't just a trench soldier. I was in military intelligence, in counter-espionage. From what I've seen today there may be more to Marie than she's told us. But if she wants to say she is just an art teacher take that as the answer to your question. If and when she feels you need to know more, then she will tell you. It's probably safer for all of us that she doesn't divulge more of her background than she feels is appropriate. So rather than ask more questions, let's just be thankful she was here today. I think we owe our lives to Marie."

"I suppose you're right Papa," said Françoise. "Marie, the reason I asked is that you surprised me and I was curious. If at any time you want to talk, you know I'll be there."

As she lay in bed that night Marie-Claire thought about her answer to Françoise's question. *The truth is that at the moment all I am is an art teacher. After my decision this morning to get involved and my actions today, I suppose I have to ask myself – where do I go from here?*

Chapter 26

The following morning Marie-Claire woke early and lay in bed imagining what this Christmas was supposed to have been like – her first Christmas married to Emile. She should have been preparing a special Christmas dinner and exchanging presents with her mother and Emile. But the Nazi occupation of France had changed everything. *Every time I look at my ID card and see the name 'Marie Bruneau' I'm reminded of everything and everybody I've lost.* She longed to talk about Emile, how wonderful he was and how much she missed him. However she knew that talking to anyone, even Françoise, could jeopardize her safety. She knew life would never return to how it was before the war came to France.

Yesterday I resolved to become an active résistante again but what will I do? Although I never did any forgery with Emile's group, I was able to fix my own ID card and I was willing to try to fix that man's card. As she thought about the missing parts on the dead man's card she realized she could not recollect seeing any damage to the card. This brought back a memory of Emile saying that they had great trouble amending ID cards because they couldn't remove Watermans ink without damaging the card.

Madame Deferre thought the man's card was badly made but since he was a German officer it must be a genuine card made with Watermans ink. She said some buttermilk spilt on the card. So perhaps something in the buttermilk dissolved the Watermans ink but didn't damage the card. I'll take a look after breakfast.

Over breakfast she turned to Madame Deferre. "It's odd to think yesterday's events all started because his ID card needed fixing. Obviously that's no longer necessary but I'd like to see how well I could have fixed it."

After breakfast was cleared away Madame Deferre fetched Sarah's inks and the escaper's ID card. Marie-Claire found it hard to conceal her excitement as her detailed examination of the card confirmed what she thought. Part of the red stamp and some of the blue lettering was missing but in those places the underlying texture and colour of the card had not been affected.

"Do you think you can restore it completely?" asked Françoise.

"I think so. But it will take some time. I'll let you know when I'm finished and you can tell me what you think."

They left Marie-Claire alone to work in peace. She looked for a part of the man's name where the buttermilk had split and the name was missing a letter. As a test she carefully recreated the letter with blue Watermans ink. *Will this new ink also disappear or has the erasing power of whatever was in the buttermilk worn off?* She waited five seconds, ten seconds, thirty seconds – the new ink did not disappear. *What a discovery! It means I could amend ID cards and all manner of documents. Is this what I should do – become a resistance forger?*

After she finished amending the card she called them back. "Can you tell which parts of the card I've restored?"

Françoise studied the card carefully and then passed it to her parents. "That's just as good as Sarah would have done. And you say you've never done this kind of work before?"

"No, never. But now we must burn the card. More than that, we need to remove all evidence our dead escaper was ever here, or for that matter that any escaper could be here."

"What exactly are you saying?" asked Madame Deferre. "When we became part of the escape line we arranged a hiding place in the barn. Are you saying we should dismantle it?"

"Yes I think you should at least for the time being, in case the Germans search the farm. That man infiltrated your escape line in order to betray it and we don't know if he contacted anyone."

Monsieur Deferre nodded his head. "I know what you mean, which is why I warned my up line contact that we cannot take any escapers right now."

When Marie-Claire looked concerned he reassured her. "Don't worry. All I've done is left a message telling them that because my hens are suffering in the cold I could not supply them with any eggs. It's a message we arranged a long time ago."

164

"Talking of farm animals, although gruesome, your way of disposing of the body should leave no evidence."

"It doesn't. And my pigs have already finished their meal."

Marie-Claire shuddered slightly. "I don't think I want to know any more thanks. But your escaper – did he have anything else with him? Where are his things?"

"They're in the barn. I'm going to deal with them next by burning everything."

"What about his pistol?" asked Françoise.

Marie-Claire sighed. "Oh my God. Thank you for mentioning that. Since he had a pistol, he'll have had spare ammunition. We need to find that before we burn it with his belongings and blow ourselves up. And the pistol and ammunition need to be hidden somewhere safe."

Monsieur Deferre smiled. "I have the perfect place for them. You've never lived on a farm, have you Marie?" When she shook her head he continued. "I'll put them in a sealed waterproof box and drop them into the slurry pit. I doubt any German will fish around in that."

By late afternoon there were no signs the escaper had ever been there. The pistol and ammunition were at the bottom of the slurry pit, the barn had been rearranged so it had no hiding places and all the man's possessions had been burned.

That evening Marie-Claire decided to ask Françoise about Sarah. "You said she was a close friend but you never told me what happened to her. Did she just leave or was she arrested?"

Françoise took a moment to answer. "She wasn't arrested – she escaped. Sarah is Jewish and at the beginning of October the Vichy government passed laws which prohibited Jews from being involved in teaching. So she had to stop teaching and she decided to leave the Occupied Zone."

"As a Jew she was worried about openly crossing the Demarcation Line," added Madame Deferre. "So the truth is – Sarah went down our escape line."

Marie-Claire smiled. "Since it involved your escape line I can understand why you kept that from me."

Monsieur Deferre leant forward in his chair. "I don't want this escaper episode to take over our lives. We've dealt with him. Now we need to put it behind us and make sure we never mention it to anyone. So let's stop talking about him and enjoy the festive season. Agreed?"

Everyone agreed and Monsieur Deferre poured out another round of cognac.

On Christmas morning Marie-Claire woke to the tantalizing smells of fresh baking which brought back memories of baking with her mother as a child. As she thought about the Gestapo shooting her mother she realized the memory was beginning to have a different effect on her. Whereas before she would have dissolved into tears at the mere thought of the event she had witnessed, now that same memory was hardening her resolve to avenge her death.

When she went downstairs she discovered the source of the enticing baking smells. On the table she saw a large platter piled high with fresh croissant. "But I thought it was illegal to make —"

"Are you forgetting this is a farm?" laughed Madame Deferre. "We produce our own butter which means we can bake whatever we like. If it bothers you that I've made croissant you can, of course, just sit and watch us eat them."

Marie-Claire burst into a broad grin. "Oh no, that would be impolite of me. Wow – it's been almost five months since I had one and this is a perfect start to Christmas."

After a sumptuous Christmas lunch the afternoon was spent playing Monopoly. However the pre-war French version produced by the Miro Company had been slightly modified by Monsieur Deferre. Due to its current abhorrent associations with the Gestapo headquarters, the title of the green property *Ave Foch* had been taped over and was now *Rue de Harlay* – the centre of the French justice system. Marie-Claire smiled inwardly at the change but decided not to comment.

As a thank you for their hospitality Marie-Claire drew portraits of everyone, which were much admired. While Françoise helped her father with the farm chores Marie-Claire helped Madame

Deferre prepare the meals. She was helping in the kitchen on New Year's Day when Madame Deferre asked, "What's wrong Marie? You look upset today."

Marie-Claire tried hard to hold back her emotions. "Today would have been my mother's birthday. She died during the summer and this is the first time I've not been able to celebrate it with her."

Madame Deferre put her arms around Marie-Claire and pulled her close. "It's alright to be sad. I lost my mother about your age and I know how hard it is." Marie-Claire felt safe in her arms the way she had felt with her mother. *Maman would have been happy that I've found such good friends.* "Shall we bake a cake in your mother's memory?" asked Madame Deferre. "My favourite is buttermilk cake. Have you ever made that?"

Buttermilk? "No I haven't. Let's do that."

By the time Françoise and Monsieur Deferre came in from the farm the cake was ready. As they sat down to eat it Marie-Claire turned to Madame Deferre. "This cake is delicious. If I want to make it myself is there somewhere in Nevers where I can get buttermilk?"

"I'll give you a small bottle you can take back with you and if you want more I'm sure you could ask Tomas Vidal at La Bouchée Parfaite. He's one of our best customers. Do you know the shop? It's on Rue d'Antoine."

Marie-Claire nodded. It had been only a few weeks since she had walked by the bakery on her way to warn Philippe's uncle and she remembered it well. *Now I know I can get buttermilk I'll be able to amend and forge documents. I wish Emile was here so I could share my discovery about buttermilk with him.*

Chapter 27

The day before they were due to return to Nevers Marie-Claire was woken early by the sound of motor vehicles approaching the farm. As she lay in bed wondering who it was she heard a loud banging on the front door followed by shouts in German, "Aufmachen, Aufmachen!"

Marie-Claire's blood ran cold. *Have the Germans found out about the escape line*? As the banging on the door continued she jumped out of bed and pulled on some clothes. She could hear the others in the house also getting dressed as the shouting grew louder. They all ran downstairs and Monsieur Deferre opened the front door.

Four soldiers carrying machine-guns burst in. They positioned themselves around the room as a sergeant marched in. He looked around then addressed Monsieur Deferre in French. "Is this everybody? Just the four of you?"

Monsieur Deferre answered in a calm voice although it was evident he was trembling. "Yes – me, my wife, my daughter and a friend here for Christmas. That's all."

The sergeant studied Monsieur Deferre carefully before speaking again. "I should warn you, our soldiers are searching your barns as we speak. If you have lied to me and they find the British airman we're looking for all of you will be shot."

Madame Deferre began to faint and Françoise caught her just in time and helped her to a chair. The soldier stepped forward and shouted directly at Madame Deferre. "I see you are frightened. Is this out of fear we will find the British airman?"

Françoise turned to him in anger. "My mother is not afraid you'll find someone because there is no one here to find. She has a heart condition and is frightened by these soldiers pointing guns at her. You said you're looking for a British airman?"

"Yes. His bomber was heading towards Dijon when it was shot

down. One person was seen to parachute out – we found the bodies of all the others in the crash. We're looking for the parachutist. We believe he was the navigator."

The front door opened and a German officer entered and spoke to Monsieur Deferre in French. "My men have searched all of the outbuildings and found nothing so now they will search this house. Stay here while they do that."

He then gestured to the sergeant to take two men and search the house. They were gone for at least fifteen minutes during which time there were loud sounds of trampling boots, cupboards being searched and doors being slammed. When they finally returned, having found nothing, the officer turned to Monsieur Deferre. "If you see any strangers it's essential you contact us immediately. I hope I don't need to remind you that the penalty for hiding or helping the enemy is death."

Marie-Claire, Françoise and her parents watched in silence as the officer, the sergeant and the four soldiers left the house, joined the other soldiers outside and drove away. Madame Deferre was the first to break the silence. "That was terrifying. I think we owe thanks to Marie for suggesting we dismantle the hiding place. If they had found it they would certainly have arrested us. So thank you Marie. You've saved us yet again. And right now I need a coffee, a good strong coffee."

They all sat down at the table as Madame Deferre prepared a large jug of coffee. "The details about the airmen they were looking for were eerily similar to those of our German agent," said Françoise thoughtfully. "A British bomber going to Dijon, shot down before it gets there, with everyone killed in the crash except for the navigator."

Marie-Claire suddenly exclaimed. "But of course. It all fits. How brilliant."

"What fits? What do you mean?"

"I think you'll find that just before Christmas there really was a British bomber shot down before it could get to Dijon. When the Germans got to the crash they counted the bodies and found one person was missing."

"I'm not following why you think that's brilliant."

"Catching the enemy is the responsibility of German soldiers. That's why they came here. They were genuinely looking for the real missing airman. But at the same time their military intelligence took advantage of the situation to infiltrate a local escape line, which unfortunately happened to be yours."

"You're right Maries," said Monsieur Deferre, "It's brilliant."

Marie-Claire smiled. "With your counter-espionage experience in the Great War, I thought you might see it." She turned to Françoise. "Whenever military intelligence learns there is a missing airman they use a military officer, like our man, to impersonate the airman. He then goes and finds someone in the area to help him 'get home'. And guess what? Our obliging resistance workers also know a bomber has been shot down and, thinking the agent is the escaping airman, they unsuspectingly send the agent down the escape route."

"I think in future we'll need to interrogate our escapers in detail," said Madame Deferre. "I particularly like the question about pigeons. That should flush out fake airmen."

During the day the snow began falling faster and thicker than normal. The Deferres had commented throughout the holiday that this winter of 1941 was the coldest and harshest they could remember. Looking out of the window Françoise said to her father. "We cycled here but with all this snow we can't cycle back. Can you take us in your van Papa?"

He shook his head. "The van's not here. I'm having it converted to run on charcoal and I won't get it back for another week. But I can take you back on the farm cart wrapped up in blankets against the cold. The Germans haven't yet confiscated my horse."

"Thanks Papa. It's been a while since I rode on the cart."

The next day the bicycles were strapped to the cart along with a big crate for the girls to sit on. Wrapped up well against the cold, Monsieur Deferre, Françoise and Marie-Claire set off for the journey back to Nevers, singing songs, sipping cognac and enjoying the countryside scenes through the gently falling snow.

At her boarding house Marie-Claire thanked Monsieur Deferre and Françoise for the wonderful Christmas and waved as they drove away. Inside the house she was warmly welcomed by Madame Favier. "Did you have a good Christmas?"

"Yes thank you. Madame and Monsieur Deferre made me feel very welcome. We exchanged a few presents and I did some portraits for them and helped in the kitchen. It was just a nice relaxing time away from the Germans."

"Monsieur Dupont came by a few days ago with a piece of furniture for you. I let him put it directly in your room. He does a lovely job."

"He's delivered it already? I must go and see."

Marie-Claire went up to her room and when she opened the door she saw a beautiful bookcase standing in the middle of the room. *Philippe's uncle has done a magnificent job. I can see why his services have been requisitioned by the Germans.* As she studied the bookcase, admiring the craftsmanship, she realized she had not agreed a price for the work. She became very concerned he may be expecting more than she could easily afford.

She looked at her watch and decided there was plenty of time to go to his house, thank him and find out how much he was going to charge her. She took the small bottle of buttermilk out of her bag, put her coat back on and set out to André's house.

As she trudged through the snow she tried to decide exactly what to say. *Obviously I have to thank him for the bookcase and ask about the price. And I'll ask about Philippe. I wonder if he'll ask me again about joining his resistance group. And if he doesn't, do I volunteer?*

With all these thoughts running through her mind it seemed like no time at all had passed before she was standing in front of the door at 22 Rue d'Antoine staring yet again at the knocker. She paused, thinking of her previous visit and the fright she had when the door was opened by a German officer.

With more confidence this time she raised the knocker and let it bang against the door.

Chapter 28

The door to 22 Rue d'Antoine was opened a few centimetres and an attractive young woman peered out. She stared at Marie-Claire, eyeing her up and down before asking in an unfriendly manner, "What do you want?"

Although taken aback by her attitude Marie-Claire replied politely. "I came to see André. Is he in?"

"I'm not sure. Who are you?"

The unwelcoming tone upset Marie-Claire and she wondered if she should just leave. But she did need to see André, so she answered, "I'm Marie Bruneau and I've come to see him about the bookcase he delivered."

The name had an astonishing effect on the young woman who suddenly smiled and opened the door wide. "Oh, please come in. I've heard a lot about you. André is in his workshop at the back of the house. I'll fetch him for you."

It was not long before André appeared in clothes covered in sawdust which made Marie-Claire smile. "I came to ask about Philippe and to say thank you for the bookcase."

André smiled back. "Philippe is fine. He's now with his aunt at a farm in Ardèche. Apparently the whole community is strongly anti-German so he should be safe there."

"I'm glad to hear that. I also came to thank you for the bookcase. You've done a wonderful job. However, when I asked you to make it I forgot to ask how much it would cost."

"Marie, it is I who need to be saying thank you. What you did in December by coming here and warning me about Philippe probably saved our lives. And you didn't even know us. So please accept the bookcase as a token of our thanks."

"It's not just André who owes you thanks," said the young woman. "Had an informant heard Philippe the Gestapo would have had a field day destroying our network."

André put an arm around the woman. "Sorry, I should have introduced you. This is my fiancée, Nicole. We're planning to marry in the spring. As I said, we owe you our lives and according to an old proverb that means there's a special bond between us. Nicole and I would be honoured if you'd come to our wedding."

The mention of a spring wedding reminded Marie-Claire of her own wedding less than a year ago to Emile. Struggling to hold back any display of the emotion she was feeling, she replied with grace. "Thank you. I'd like that."

"André told me you are the new art teacher at the school where Sarah worked and that you have replaced her. Is that right?"

"Yes, I'm now the art teacher at that school."

"Have you ever thought of using your skills outside of school hours? Perhaps doing portraits – or things like that?"

Marie-Claire smiled. "If you're trying to ask me in a round about way if I would be interested in helping your group André asked me back in December and —"

"Nicole," interrupted André. "I told you. Marie said no and she's already done enough for us."

Marie-Claire looked at them for a moment. "I was about to say that back then I wasn't ready to become involved, but since then I've had time to think. So if you're still looking for someone with art skills, then perhaps I can help."

"If you're sure," said Nicole. "We actually have a problem right now with an ID card. You've probably guessed we're part of an escape route, but only for French people. Although we'd like to help foreign soldiers, many of our friends have been caught doing that. British airmen don't blend in – they stand out like sore thumbs. They walk too straight, they stand with their hands in their pockets and their hair is too short. And Americans chew gum."

"So who do you help?"

"Resistance workers who have been compromised, Jews trying to avoid being arrested, French soldiers trying to join de Gaulle in England. The main thing is they must blend in."

"I can understand what you mean. You said you have a problem with an ID card?"

"When Sarah was helping us she was able to obtain blank ID cards which she just filled in and painted on the stamps. But she couldn't get any more blank cards after the person who supplied them was arrested. Sarah said she had trouble amending real cards because she couldn't remove the ink. She said it appeared to be indelible. This means our escapers can't use their own cards because they have their real names and birth dates."

"You just said 'escapers'. Is there more than one?"

"Yes," replied André. "We have a few in hiding, but at the moment one person needs to get out as soon as possible."

"Is he genuine?"

"Oh yes. I've known him since childhood and he's genuine."

"I'm not sure I can help but I'm willing to give it a try. Rather than risk damaging that person's card, do you have any old cards I could practise on?"

André rose from the table, went into a back room and returned with what looked like a heap of old rags. He untangled them and extracted a well worn French ID card. "Would this do? Our friend Malik escaped last summer using one of the new cards Sarah created and I kept his old one."

Marie-Claire took the card and examined it closely. "Yes. I can practise on this. I'll see if I can change the name from Malik into something else." She opened her bag and put the card in a secret pocket in the side of her bag.

"I see you have a secret place in your bag," commented André. "Would I be correct in thinking you didn't find the secret compartments in the drawers of the bookcase."

"What do you mean? I didn't see anything like that."

André smiled. "They wouldn't be secret if you could see them. I thought they might be useful, and given what you've just agreed to do I think they will be." He then explained to her how to open the hidden compartments.

"Thank you. I can hide the card you've just given me in there until I have an opportunity to try and change the name."

"If you can change the name, that would be fantastic," said Nicole, "but according to Sarah, it's not possible."

"I can't make any promises, but I'll give it a try." She turned to André. "When I first met you, you were annoyed that I came here. If I'm not supposed to call here, where can I contact you?"

"At the bookshop."

"There's more than one. Which bookshop do you mean and how do I contact you there?"

"We use the Beaucoup de Mots bookshop run by Odile Joubert," replied André. "She's the daughter of your landlady, Madame Favier. Nicole works there most afternoons. If she's not there and the shop has no customers, ask Odile if you can see her second-hand art books. She'll take you into the office where you can leave things or pick them up."

"Thank you. I know the shop you mean. I'm not sure how long this will take me but I'll get back to you via the bookshop as soon as I can. Talking of time, I should be going. I don't want to walk home in the dark."

She walked down Rue d'Antoine past the bakery, La Bouchée Parfaite, and was about to turn into Avenue Gelleton when she noticed Monsieur Garnier, the pro-Nazi teacher at the school. He was marching quickly in the opposite direction on the other side of the street. She was surprised when he rushed over and grabbed her arm. "Don't say anything. Just turn around, link arms with me and walk this way."

Marie-Claire struggled to release herself from his grip. His response was to grip her arm more tightly. "Marie, don't be stupid. Do what I'm telling you – right now."

There was something in his unexpected use of her first name and the intense look in his eyes that made her decide to comply. She stopped struggling, linked arms and began walking with him back the way she had come. "Monsieur Garnier, what —"

"My name's Gerhard and before you say any more, I've just saved your life."

Marie-Claire tensed. Those words 'just saved your life' reminded her of being kidnapped outside Emile's burning bookshop. *Is this another kidnapping?* As this thought rolled through her mind she unconsciously began to walk more slowly.

Monsieur Garnier spoke forcefully. "You've go to walk faster. There is no time to waste. Come on."

She was trying desperately to imagine what sort of misfortune he was dragging her away from when she had a frightening thought. *Is he actually dragging me into danger, not away from it? And I have someone else's ID card in my bag.*

He suddenly jerked her arm and pulled her down a small alley running along the side of the La Bouchée Parfaite. She had never thought of him as a sexual predator but his actions were beginning to panic her. She became even more concerned when he stopped abruptly at the back door of the bakery. He rapped on the door, two quick knocks, a pause then four more. The door was immediately opened, whereupon Monsieur Garnier pulled Marie-Claire into the bakery, and the baker, covered in flour, shut the door rapidly behind them.

"What's up Gerhard?" he asked. "You said you'd only call here in an extreme emergency. And who is this you've brought with you? What's going on?"

"Tomas. Sorry for the intrusion – but this is an emergency."

The baker motioned to Monsieur Garnier and Marie-Claire to sit down at a table. "Emergency? What's happened?"

"The Gestapo are doing a roundup of hostages on Avenue Gelleton. They are arresting everybody they can see and forcing them into a truck. I was at the other end of the avenue when I saw what was happening and I was able to get away before they saw me. And fortunately I saw Marie walking towards the avenue and grabbed her before the Gestapo could see her. This was the closest safe place so that's why we're here. Thank goodness you opened up so quickly."

Tomas looked at Marie-Claire. "Marie? Are you the Marie Bruneau who replaced Sarah, the art teacher?"

"Yes. I am."

"Sorry, where are my manners?" said Monsieur Garnier. "I should have introduced you. This is my close friend Tomas Vidal. You know Madame Duchamps at school? This is her brother. And out of school I'm Gerhard and this is Tomas."

Tomas looked at Marie-Claire. "I wish we could have met under better circumstances but at least you're safe. Excuse me calling you Marie, but we never use formal names."

That is what Emile said about his resistance group. What have I just tumbled into?

Marie-Claire turned to Monsieur Garnier. "Thank you so much for saving me from the roundup. I have heard that the Gestapo do what they jokingly refer to as 'hostage harvesting' but I never thought they would do that here in Nevers. I apologize for not trusting you but when you grabbed me it worried me."

Monsieur Garnier laughed. "So it's worked – my cover of being apparently pro-Nazi. I knew why you were struggling but there was no time to explain. And now I can hardly maintain my false pro-Nazi stance with you. At least not out of school."

Tomas shook his head. "You two may need to stay here for a while until we can be sure they've stopped, as you put it, 'harvesting'. Gerhard – would you and Marie like a hot drink? As you might guess, I have some cakes you can have with it."

Both Marie-Claire and Monsieur Garnier answered with one voice. "Yes please."

As Tomas prepared the drinks Marie-Claire turned to Monsieur Garnier. "You mentioned your apparent pro-Nazi attitude as being a facade. It worked, but why did you think you could be honest with me?"

"I think I'm a reasonable judge of character and anyway André told me why he was making a bookcase for you."

Marie-Claire looked surprised. "Is nothing secret in this town?"

As Tomas returned with the drinks and some fresh raisin buns, he smiled. "In this town? Not if we can help it."

"I'll have to remember that. And thanks."

Two hours later Tomas felt it would be safe for Monsieur Garnier and Marie-Claire to leave the bakery. The said their goodbyes and headed off in their separate directions. Fortunately the streets were empty as she hurried home, eager to start working on the ID card.

Chapter 29

When Marie-Claire got back to her boarding house she was immediately greeted by an anxious looking Madame Favier. "Thank goodness you're safe. I heard from my neighbours that the Germans have been arresting hostages today in town and with you being away so long I've been – I've been ever so worried. Come here." She gave Marie-Claire a long hug. "I'm so glad you weren't caught. I've heard the Germans never release their hostages."

"I'm fine thanks. It seems it was fortunate I stayed so long chatting with André and his fiancée."

When Marie-Claire reached her room she locked her door and set out the items for her test – the old ID card André had given her, a collection of small brushes and pens, her bottle of buttermilk and a bottle of blue Watermans ink. She dipped her smallest brush into the buttermilk and dabbed a bit onto the 'M' of the name Malik on the card.

She felt a growing sense of disappointment and frustration as nothing happened. The 'M' stayed just as visible with no change. *Damn! Sarah was right – it can't be done.*

In annoyance, she stood up and walked around the room contemplating what to do next. When she came back to the table she could hardly believe her eyes – the 'M' had completely disappeared. She shook her head and looked again closely. There was now no evidence of the 'M' and the underlying card was not affected. She dabbed buttermilk over the rest of the letters in the name and waited. After a short time, the name Malik had been completely removed.

She waited impatiently for the card to dry. When she was sure it was completely dry, she scribed an 'A' in new ink over where previously there had been an 'M'. Would it also disappear?

It didn't. The test appeared to be working. To be sure the 'A' did not disappear, she decided to leave it alone and not touch the card for a while. When she looked again an hour later, she was excited to see the 'A' had not been affected. Carefully mimicking the writing style used in other parts of the card she wrote in a new name – *André*. With a great sense of achievement and excitement, she put away all her tools and bottles and left the card on the table.

In the morning she woke early and immediately picked up the card. With a sigh of relief she saw that the card was just as she had left it the night before, with the name André showing as clearly as the name Malik had previously.

It was the first day of the new school term and Marie-Claire knew she could not tell the other members of staff the truth about her Christmas break. She had agreed with Françoise that no mention would be made of the raid at the farm so when asked about her holiday she simply said, "I had a nice quiet time at the Deferre's farm."

She also had secrets she had to keep from Françoise. Since she had not mentioned anything about Philippe's drawing she couldn't tell her about André or Nicole. Nor could she say she was now part of his resistance group. And she couldn't recount how Monsieur Garnier had saved her from being arrested. Or that he was a résistant, not a collaborator. She knew such information was not hers to share but still she found it hard to keep it secret.

What was it I read – the tyranny of secrets is not keeping the secret but keeping secret the fact you are keeping secrets.

When the teaching day ended Marie-Claire hurried into town to the Beaucoup de Mots bookshop. She kept her head down so she didn't have to look at the intimidating Nazi banners hanging from the buildings. She had avoided bookshops ever since the day Emile was killed in his bookshop but now she had no choice. It was the place where she was due to meet Nicole and show her the amended ID card. Her heart was racing as she pushed open the door and walked in.

Nicole was nowhere to be seen so, as instructed, Marie-Claire went to the counter and asked to see the collection of second-hand art books. The sales assistant did not respond immediately. Instead she eyed Marie-Claire up and down a few times as if deciding exactly what to do. Only then did she take Marie-Claire through to the office where Nicole was sitting at a desk.

When Nicole saw Marie-Claire she jumped up and rushed over. "Can you do it Marie? Were you able to change it?"

Marie-Claire was horrified by the openness of the questions in the presence of the shop assistant. Nicole must have noticed Marie-Claire's reaction and quickly put her mind at rest. "Don't worry. This is Odile Joubert. She's part of our network. Odile, this is Marie, the art teacher who lives at your mother's house. She was doing a test for us." Turning back to Marie-Claire she asked again. "Were you able to make the change?"

"Let me show you what I've done." She took the ID card out of her bag and passed it to Nicole.

Nicole examined it closely and then without saying anything passed the card to Odile. Odile looked at it, turned it over and looked again before asking, "What am I supposed to see?"

"Pretend you're a suspicious Gestapo officer," replied Nicole.

Odile studied the card again, more closely this time. She held it up to the light and looked at it from different angles. "It all seems perfect to me, so has anything actually been changed?"

Before Nicole could say anything Marie-Claire spoke. "Let's just say it was a test and it was successful. If you can't see what was done, knowing something was done, then we're in business."

"That's fantastic," said Nicole. "We can start with that important card André was talking about yesterday."

"Yes we can, but I must insist on certain rules," said Marie-Claire. "You, André, and now Odile here, know that I am willing to do some forgeries. But you three must not tell anyone else – absolutely no one. If asked by others in the group why I've joined, perhaps you can say you intend to use me as a messenger."

"That's not a problem," said Odile. "However, we will need some secure way of getting documents to you and back again. We could use this bookshop as a transfer point."

Marie-Claire was not convinced. "Surely it will be far too dangerous for me to keep coming here carrying ID cards and I can't do my work here."

Odile smiled. "You're right. We must ensure that if you are searched they never find anything incriminating. Nicole will bring the documents to me here and then take them back to André when they're done. I in turn will courier them back and forth to my mother's house. She can then pass them to you and you can give them back to her when you're finished. This means you never carry any cards or documents yourself. How does that sound?"

Marie-Claire nodded. "That sounds workable." Marie-Claire turned to Nicole. "I suspect you've brought something for me?"

As Nicole reached for her bag Marie-Claire shook her head. "Not here. Let's start the way we intend to go on. Give it to Odile and I'll see what can be done when I get home this evening."

"Thank you Marie. André will be pleased. And since you're now part of our group why don't you join us on Thursday evenings. We meet at the Café du Monde. Do you know it?"

"Yes I do. I haven't been in but it looks nice. But isn't it dangerous to meet together in such a public place?"

"No, it's exactly the opposite," said Nicole. "We meet there so we're seen as just a group of friends playing card games and dominoes. Being a group of friends gives us a reason for meeting."

"I see what you mean. I'd like that, but right now I should be going. I suppose to avoid suspicion, I should leave with a book."

Odile reached down behind the counter and brought out a small book on modern French art. "Keep it in your bag. I'll change it if they search your bag."

That evening Madame Favier knocked on Marie-Claire's bedroom door and passed her an envelope. It contained an ID card and a letter from a Maurice Chartier to a company based in Dijon. The letter was supposedly a reply to their request for his details including his date and place of birth and the address he was now living at.

Marie-Claire smiled at the secure way of telling her what details to change and she promptly set about making the necessary amendments. To her surprise, the buttermilk worked more quickly today and the old information disappeared with only a small application of the magic fluid. On a scrap piece of paper she practised the handwriting as it appeared in the untouched parts of the ID card. She did this until she felt confident enough to write Maurice Chartier and all the other particulars in a way which matched the original handwriting.

It was eleven o'clock before she finished. She sat back admiring her work – her first real forgery. *I wonder what my art teachers would think of me now. But then maybe they are doing the same, especially my calligraphy teacher.* In the morning she handed the envelope back to Madame Favier without comment.

Before going to the Café du Monde on a Thursday evening she went on her own on a Saturday morning to see what it was like. She was not impressed. The proprietor seemed surly, the coffee was lukewarm and there was nothing to have with the coffee. She mentioned this to Nicole on her next visit to the bookshop.

Nicole laughed. "I said come on a Thursday evening. If Marcel does not know somebody, he will try and discourage them from coming back. He does that very successfully with the Germans and as a result the Café has a really bad reputation with them and they rarely visit. If you can, come this Thursday and I'll introduce you. Meanwhile, if you're free on Wednesday why don't you come by the shop and we can go for lunch together?"

Nicole's bubbly enthusiasm was hard to resist. It reminded Marie-Claire of Katia. "Yes thank you. I'd like that." Although she'd only known Nicole for a short while, she felt there was an immediate bond between them.

With only light snow falling on Thursday evening Marie-Claire decided to go to the Café. When she arrived she saw André, Nicole, Tomas and Gerhard deeply involved in a game of dominoes. Nicole looked up and beckoned her over. "I think you know everyone, don't you, but let me introduce you to Marcel Sanchez, the proprietor."

When Marcel came over and introductions were made, he smiled at Marie-Claire. "You were here on Saturday weren't you. I must apologize. I didn't know you were friends with this group and I served you our standard cup of coffee for strangers. It's designed to discourage them from returning. Warm and insipid with slow service. Would you like a proper cup right now – on me?"

Marie-Claire smiled. "Yes, please, I'd appreciate a cup. With sugar please."

"Sugar?" queried Gerhard. "In school you never have sugar with your coffee, so why now?"

Marie-Claire cursed herself for falling back into automatic sugar code mode. Marcel added to her unease by remarking that she had not asked for sugar on Saturday. *Gerhard and Marcel are far too observant. I'll have to give them a plausible explanation.*

"A friend told me about a cafe he often went to which sometimes had German clients. He said he always ordered coffee with sugar, even though he didn't actually want it. He said it was a code asking the waiter if it was safe to talk freely. Apparently, if the waiter actually brought sugar, it meant no, not safe. If he brought the coffee without sugar, it meant safe. However if at some later time he brought sugar it meant 'no longer safe'. I guess you don't do that here."

"No we don't," commented Marcel. "But perhaps I should say we didn't. It's easy and I like it. Shall we do that?"

Before the others could say anything Gerhard asked, "Did you use it often? This sugar code."

Marie-Claire saw through his trap. "Me? No, never. I just thought what Jean-Luc told me was used by resistance groups."

"Who is Jean-Luc?" asked Gerhard. "How do you know him?"

André stopped him. "Gerhard. Marie is one of us. She hasn't come here to be interrogated."

Marie-Claire spoke up. "No, it's alright André. Gerhard is right to question me. I met Jean-Luc at the TB clinic where I worked before the Germans destroyed the clinic. I met him again after the invasion but one night he disappeared without trace."

With a sniff Marie-Claire turned away and pulled out a handkerchief to appear to wipe her eyes. Gerhard softened his tone. "Sorry. I remember what you told us when you first arrived and I just wanted to see if you were consistent in what you say about yourself."

She felt she should appear to be insulted so she rounded on him. "The truth is easy to remember – it's lies which can become inconsistent."

Nicole rebuked the lot of them. "Enough. Marie is one of us."

Marie-Claire joined in the next game of dominoes. The coffee Marcel brought was piping hot. He did not bring any sugar.

Over the next few weeks Marie-Claire's life fell into a fairly regular pattern of dealing with forgery requests, visits to the bookshop and drinks at the Café du Monde on most Thursday evenings. She frequently had lunch with Nicole whose vivacious personality kept reminding her of Katia, and they soon became close friends. She also spent a lot of time with Françoise who was helping her improve her German.

In order not to reveal her involvement with André's group Marie-Claire never went to the Café du Monde with Françoise. Instead they met at the Le Bistro Pour Tous in a different part of town. However, when she was on her own Marie-Claire often went to the Café du Monde. Most cafes were full of German soldiers, but Marcel's policy of discouraging them was very effective and there were rarely any Germans in his cafe.

Late on a Wednesday afternoon in early February Marie-Claire decided to go to the Café before heading back to the boarding house. The Café was busy when she arrived but fortunately someone was just leaving and she gratefully sat down at their table. A waiter she did not know brought her drink. She pulled her book on modern French art out of her bag and soon became so absorbed in her reading that she didn't notice that most of the customers had left.

She almost jumped up out of her chair when she felt a hand on her shoulder and a voice whispered in her ear, "*Marie-Claire!* You're here in Nevers. No wonder I couldn't find you in Paris."

Chapter 30

Marie-Claire froze. *Who knows my real name? How have they found me?* Trying to hide her fear, she started to turn around to see who had spoken. As she did so the person pulled out a chair at Marie-Claire's table and sat down.

At first Marie-Claire recoiled in fright but then the fear which had gripped her changed to total disbelief. The person now sitting beside her was none other than cousin Anna, who she had thought was in The Netherlands.

Marie-Claire was about to speak when Anna looked her in the eyes and said, "Hello. My name is Mieke."

Marie-Claire immediately understood the need for deception. "Hello. I'm Mademoiselle *Marie* Bruneau."

Anna spoke quietly. "You've changed your hairstyle and at first I wondered if it was actually you."

Both girls fell silent as Marcel came to their table. "Marie. Is everything alright?" He leant forward and whispered to her, "When this lady first arrived I thought it was you for a moment, you look so much alike. I was worried when she sat here all afternoon just staring into her drink."

Marie-Claire replied quickly. "There's nothing to worry about Marcel. Everything's fine. She's a long lost relation who I thought had been lost forever."

Marcel's tone softened as he turned to Anna. "If you're staying here, would you like a hot cup of coffee?"

"Hot? That would be nice, thanks. Not wanting to be insulting, but none of the others have been hot."

As he smiled and walked away Marie-Claire chuckled. "I think Marcel must have served you one of his 'special' lukewarm drinks, the kind he serves when he's not sure about the person."

"I'm so glad to see you." Anna looked around the room. "Is there somewhere we can talk? I feel quite vulnerable here."

185

"You don't need to worry about talking here. Marcel will warn us if there's a problem. So, what are you doing here?"

"I was supposed to be picked up early this morning in the cathedral but by lunch time no one had turned up. I came here to warm up while I tried to figure out what to do. I didn't know you were in Nevers. Seeing you was quite a shock."

"Picked up? Are you escaping?"

"Yes. I'm trying to get to England. I joined an escape line back in Paris but something has gone wrong."

"Are you alone? Has something happened to your parents?"

"Oh no. They're fine and hiding in a good place."

"Are they still in Ammerstol?"

Anna smiled. "So you understood our cryptic Snoepje note – two girls in a boat. Yes, they're still there."

"So why are you escaping?"

"Ever since we went into hiding I've been wondering if I should escape rather than just wait in fear. The tipping point came when Seyss-Inquart signed an order in January requiring all Jews and partial Jews to register with the police and SS."

"Seyss-Inquart? Who's he?"

"The SS chief in charge of The Netherlands. A horrid man. I knew registering was just a prelude to persecution so I decided to leave. My parents understood but felt too old to join me. But my escape plan has collapsed, and to make it worse my ID card is faulty. I just don't know what to do."

Marie-Claire motioned Marcel to come over. "Have there been any problems today? Anyone arrested?"

"Yes. Apparently an escape line has been compromised and many people have been arrested. That's why I was worried about this lady."

As he was speaking Marie-Claire glanced out of the window and saw two German officers approaching. She turned to Marcel. "We need to leave quickly. Is there a back door we can use?"

"Yes, grab your coats and follow me."

Both girls followed him out into the hallway at the back of the cafe. "You were right to leave," said Marcel. "Those officers like to show their authority by requesting to see everybody's ID cards every time they come in." He opened the back door. "I don't think they saw you but you should get away quickly."

Marie-Claire thanked him and she and Anna stepped into the alley behind the cafe. Marcel bolted the door behind them. The alley was desolate and poorly lit. An icy wind was blowing against their faces. Marie-Claire linked arms with her cousin as they started to walk away. She could hear the desperation in Anna's voice when she asked. "Where are you taking me?"

Marie-Claire squeezed her arm. "Right now we'll walk to my boarding house. You can stay there while we sort things out."

Anna pulled back. "Didn't you understand what I said? My ID card is faulty. I can't show it to anybody, let alone some nosey landlady. Marie-Claire, we can't go —"

"Please! My name's now just Marie. No Claire. That's critical. And don't worry. I know what I'm doing and Madame Favier, my landlady, is part of the plan. So what's wrong with your card?"

"It got wet when I accidentally dropped it in the snow and some of the ink has run."

"That certainly shouldn't have happened. Whoever made it for you used the wrong kind of ink."

"Wrong kind of ink? Why would they do that?"

"Perhaps the person who made your card is actually a German agent. I've heard they deliberately make defective cards to expose the escape lines. From the sound of it, you were lucky today that your contact didn't pick you up. We'll get a new card for you."

Anna stopped walking and stared at Marie-Claire. "A new card? Are you and Emile part of a resistance group here in Nevers?"

Marie-Claire's eyes filled with tears as she took a moment to answer. "No. Emile is not here. In September he was —" She struggled to get the words out. "In September he was murdered in Paris by the Gestapo. On the same day they gunned down my mother outside her apartment. They were also looking for me which is why I had to escape and become a different person."

Anna put her arms around Marie-Claire and held her close. "How unbelievably awful. It explains why I couldn't find you in

Paris. I went to your apartment but there was a new name on the door. At your mother's apartment, the concierge said if I wanted to visit your mother I'd have to go to hell. I didn't ask her what she meant but now I understand. Oh Marie, I'm so sorry."

Arm in arm they walked on in silence to Madame Favier's. At the house Marie-Claire went straight through to the kitchen where Madame Favier was cooking. Anna appeared horrified when Marie-Claire made no attempt to hide her. "Madame Favier. Do you have a spare pillow and bedding you could put in my room?"

Madame Favier didn't look up from her cooking. "You know the rules Mademoiselle Bruneau. No overnight guests."

Marie-Claire took a risk. "Angélique. Look at us. Can't you see the likeness? She's more than a friend, and I wouldn't ask if it wasn't critical."

This was the first time Marie-Claire had used Madame Favier's first name and it had an immediate effect. Madame Favier stopped and stared at the two young faces. Her stern look melted. "I see what you mean. I'll bring some bedding up right away. But please don't draw attention to yourselves, which means absolute silence after ten o'clock. Will your friend be leaving tomorrow?"

"This is an unexpected emergency and she'll need to stay for a day or two if possible."

"That will be fine. Does your friend have a name?"

Without hesitation Marie-Claire replied. "Aletta Duval."

Madame Favier turned to Anna. "Aletta. In the morning, after my boarders have gone off to work, I'll knock on your door and you can come downstairs for breakfast. And don't be concerned. I'll ask no questions and tell no one about you being here. If Marie says it's an emergency, that's enough for me. Now off you two go upstairs before anyone sees you."

When they were in Marie-Claire's room Anna asked, "What's with all these different names? You're now just Marie and I'm no longer Anna or even Mieke but Aletta Duval? What have I stumbled into?"

"You've stumbled into a group who'll save your life. But please don't ask questions – I'm not at liberty to tell the truth. And as for

Aletta, you needed a new name. You can't use Mieke. They might be looking out for that person."

After Madame Favier had brought the bedding Marie-Claire examined Anna's ID card. The ink had run in several places confirming Marie-Claire's fears this was an intentionally defective card. "At least the photograph's not affected. I can use that when I make your new card."

"You? How can you make me a new card?"

"I decided to put my artistic skills to good use. I needed to do something positive after all that's happened."

"So what did happen? Can you tell me? It's been worrying enough not knowing what happened to Aunt Betje."

"I've got good news about her. She escaped safely to England."

Anna looked puzzled. "How do you know that?"

"Maman received a message from her."

"Why would she tell your mother?"

"Because she used the escape line my mother was running."

Anna gasped. "Your mother was *what*?"

Over a glass of cognac Marie-Claire told Anna about her mother's activities and the day Emile and her mother were killed. Anna then told Marie-Claire about her family's terrifying experience during the bombing of Rotterdam and their escape to Ammerstol. The bottle of cognac Marie-Claire had been given at Christmas was empty by the time they went to sleep.

The following morning at breakfast Madame Favier had a quiet word with Marie-Claire before the other boarders appeared. "I don't want to know but I could see Aletta is either your sister or a close relative. And don't worry, I won't tell anyone about her."

"Thank you. I appreciate your discretion. I hope she'll be able to move out by the weekend. Are you sure you don't mind her staying here in the meantime?"

"Of course she can stay. If anybody should see her, I'll say she's helping me with the cleaning."

After lunch at the school Marie-Claire suggested to Françoise that they go for a walk. When they were away from the school

Françoise asked, "What's up? You look seriously concerned."

"I am, and I have two questions. Firstly, have your parents re-opened their escape line? And secondly, do you know where Sarah obtained blank ID cards for your escapers?"

"Is something wrong? You're not thinking of leaving, are you?"

"No, no. It's not me, but there's somebody I need to help."

"I'm glad you're not thinking of leaving. In answer to your questions, yes – my parents have restarted their line. And with respect to cards, Papa was able to get some blank cards before Sarah left and I believe he still has them. But why do you look so worried? Are you just helping someone or is there more to this?"

Marie-Claire realized there was no point in trying to disguise the situation. *Since Madame Favier was able to deduce that Anna is a relation then surely the Deferres will as well.*

"Did you hear about the arrests yesterday which broke up one of the escape lines running through Nevers?"

Françoise looked worried. "Monsieur Garnier mentioned something about it yesterday. Oh no. Were you part of that line?"

"No. I didn't even know it existed. But yesterday I met someone who had just avoided being arrested along with the others."

"Were they part of the line? Is that why they need help?"

"The person I'm concerned about was the escaper and she was supposed to be picked up in the cathedral but the passeur never appeared."

Françoise looked puzzled. "I know you like to help people but I don't understand why you're so concerned about some escaper you don't know." Her expression changed. "Oh my God – it's just dawned on me. This escaper isn't somebody you *don't* know – it's somebody you *do* know. Is it a friend from your past life?"

Marie-Claire turned to Françoise with tears welling in her eyes. *I've got to tell Françoise the truth if I'm asking her to help Anna.*

"It's not a friend – it's my cousin. We've been close since we were children."

Françoise looked astonished. "Your cousin?"

"Yes. I thought she was living safely in The Netherlands. But no, I bumped into her by chance yesterday."

"Is your cousin the escaper who avoided being arrested?"

"Yes. The passeur was arrested before reaching the cathedral. A few minutes later and my cousin would also have been arrested and I would never have known."

Françoise immediately pulled Marie-Claire into her arms for a hug. "Marie, you don't need to say anymore. Of course we'll do everything we can to help. I was going to see Maman and Papa this weekend. Papa's picking me up late Friday afternoon in his van. I suggest you and your cousin come to the farm with me for the weekend and we can see about sending her on down our line. You asked about ID cards. Does your cousin need a new one?"

"Yes, the card she has was made either by a total incompetent or, more likely, by a traitor hoping the person would be arrested for having a forged ID card."

"What makes you say that?"

"They used the wrong ink and some of it ran the moment the card got wet. I need to make a totally new card for her."

"As you know, we still have Sarah's inks and pens at the farm." She looked at her watch. "But right now we need to get back for afternoon classes."

That evening, when Marie-Claire brought a bottle of red wine back to the boarding house, Anna's eyes lit up. But her expression turned to horror as Marie-Claire carefully pour some of the wine onto Anna's ID card. "What are you doing? It's making it worse."

"I'm giving a reason for the ink to have run. The checkpoints are manned by young German soldiers who will think the problem is the wine not the ink. I'm keeping it off the photograph. There. I'm done. We'll just leave it out to dry."

"That's a clever idea," said Anna, "but let's not waste the rest of the wine." Marie-Claire got out two glasses and they spent the evening reminiscing about their childhood holidays in Ammerstol.

After school on Friday Marie-Claire hurried back to the boarding house. When Madame Favier passed her an envelope Marie-Claire apologized. "I won't be able to deal with this until I get back on Sunday evening. I'm going away with Aletta for the weekend."

191

"That's not a problem. Odile won't be back to collect the envelope until Monday. Have a good weekend."

On the way to Françoise's apartment Marie-Claire raised the issue of names. "My friend Françoise, the person we're going to see, knows you're my cousin but doesn't know any of your names – Anna, Mieke or Aletta. Since your ID card says Mieke Devos, I suggest we call you Mieke."

"After the mess you made of my card it hardly seems relevant, but I'll remain Mieke until you tell me otherwise."

When they arrived at Françoise's apartment Monsieur Deferre was already there and gave Marie-Claire a quick hug. "It's good to see you again Marie. Françoise has told me you have a friend who needs to escape and I'm pleased you feel you can ask us." He looked at Anna with a puzzled expression. "Am I seeing double?"

"No you're not Monsieur Deferre. This is my cousin Mieke."

He took Anna's hand. "I am pleased to meet you. Marie is a special friend and we'll do everything we can to help you."

He turned to Françoise. "I think we should leave as soon as possible. I don't fully trust this new charcoal engine and if something goes wrong I don't want to try fixing it in the dark."

They climbed into the van, Françoise in the front with her father and Marie-Claire and Anna in the back sitting on some boxes. They hadn't gone far when Monsieur Deferre uttered a loud, "Merde Alors!" and the vehicle slowed down.

"Is something wrong with the engine?" asked Françoise.

"It's not the engine. Look. They've put up a new roadblock which means they'll be checking ID cards."

Anna started trembling and Marie-Claire asked. "Can we turn around or at least can Mieke and I get out?"

"No, it's too late," sighed. Monsieur Deferre. "They've seen us."

Marie-Claire turned to Anna. "Let's just hope that the red wine does the trick."

Chapter 31

"Let me do all the talking," said Monsieur Deferre as they approached the checkpoint. "Mieke, what's your last name?"

"On my ID card it says Devos, but there's a problem with my card – some of the ink has smudged and it's covered in red wine."

"That's not good, but as I said let me do all the talking."

Monsieur Deferre stopped at the checkpoint and a French policeman approached the van. Before the policeman could even say a word Monsieur Deferre smiled and spoke in a manner which caused Anna to grip Marie-Claire's hand tightly. "Well you old ugly scumbag, why have you set up a roadblock? If you wanted some more pork chops all you had to do was ask."

"Rémi, I thought it might be you when I saw this smoke-belching wreck of a van. And I see you think you can bribe a policeman with pork chops. What have you got to say to that?"

"How about lunch tomorrow at the farm, you and Yasmine? We haven't seen Yasmine since you got back. Mind, I don't know why she puts up with you."

"Well at least I didn't marry someone I won in a fight." He lowered his voice. "Quick, Rémi, pass me your card, I have to look as if I'm checking something."

Monsieur Deferre pulled his ID card out of his jacket and the policeman made a show of examining it. "Amazing – this seems in order. And who are these lovely girls in this junk of a van?"

"This is Françoise, my daughter and in the back are two of her friends, Mieke and Marie."

"I feel sorry for you Françoise, having Rémi as your father. Anyway, enough chatting Rémi. We can continue this over lunch tomorrow. Yasmine and I will be along, if only to see Tiffany. I still don't know why she married you instead of me." He motioned to the guards to raise the barrier.

With a shuddering jolt the van started up and they drove slowly down the road. Françoise was the first to speak. "Papa. Who was that and what did he mean about you marrying someone you won in a fight?"

Monsieur Deferre chuckled. "I've known Jerome Fleury for years. We were at school together and I fought a duel with him over who would marry your mother."

Françoise appeared horrified. "A duel? You fought a duel with him over who would marry Maman? You cannot be serious."

"Oh yes I am. We were seven at the time and we duelled with pencils. I won so I married Tiffany. He moved away soon after you were born and he's only recently been assigned to the Nevers police force. We've met up a couple of times and we were lucky he recognized this van. As you might have guessed, Jerome is no lover of the German invaders. He might be useful in the future."

When they arrived at the farm Anna whispered to Marie-Claire. "What name do I have here? Am I still Mieke?"

"Yes. And remember I'm Marie and they don't know about my previous life – so no mention of Paris."

"How do you keep track of all these lies?"

"It's quite easy – my life depends on it."

Madame Deferre came out of the house and gave Marie-Claire a motherly hug. "It's lovely to see you again Marie. You're always welcome here." She looked at Anna then back at Marie-Claire. "And who is this you've brought with you?"

"This is Mieke," replied Marie-Claire.

"Pleased to meet you Madame Deferre," said Anna. "Marie told me how much she enjoyed Christmas. I hope my unexpected visit won't be a problem."

Madame Deferre smiled with genuine warmth. "As a friend of Marie you are most welcome here." She studied Anna's face and chuckled. "Marie, either my eyesight is failing or Mieke is more than just a friend. You never told us you had a sister."

Marie-Claire laughed. "I can see there's not much point in hiding things from you. Your eyesight isn't failing, but Mieke isn't my sister, she's my cousin."

Madame Deferre put an arm around Mieke's shoulder as they

walked into the house. "We won't ask about you. Being Marie's cousin is all we need to know, and if you're in need of anything you only need to ask."

"Thank you. It's so good to feel safe and welcome."

Madame Deferre turned to Marie-Claire. "Marie, there are two beds in the room you used at Christmas. I suggest you show Mieke upstairs now, and when you come down we can all have a drink before the meal."

When they were upstairs in the spare room Anna spoke quietly to Marie-Claire. "This is the most relaxed I've felt since I left Ammerstol. Am I right in thinking these are the people running the escape line you mentioned?"

"Yes. I don't know how much Françoise will have already told them, but this evening we'll plan your escape."

During the evening meal Marie-Claire explained the reason for their visit. After Madame Deferre's deduction that Anna was a relation Marie-Claire decided not to try and hide too much. "On Wednesday I was sitting in a cafe when Mieke appeared and sat down beside me. You can imagine my surprise as I thought she was in The Netherlands. It turned out she was on an escape line to England but the line was compromised and the people involved were arrested. Mieke only avoided being arrested because the passeur was captured before making contact. When I asked Françoise if you were running your escape line again she —"

"Marie." Monsieur Deferre interrupted her. "Even if we weren't yet running the line again, we would have done so if that's what your cousin needs. It's the least we can do for you after all you did for us at Christmas."

Anna looked at Marie-Claire with a puzzled look.

Monsieur Deferre turned to Anna. "Without going into any explanations, let me just say your cousin Marie was instrumental in solving a critical problem so we're happy to help you. Where are you trying to get to?"

"I'm trying to get to England, but as Marie has told you the line I was in was compromised. I still find it almost impossible to believe how lucky I was that Marie came into the cafe."

"When we were stopped at the checkpoint you said your ID card is damaged," said Monsieur Deferre. "Can it be fixed or does it need to be replaced?"

"I think Marie needs to answer that question," replied Anna.

"It can't be fixed, it's defective," said Marie-Claire. "When the ink got wet it smudged making it obvious it's a forgery. I poured wine on it to make it look like the wine caused the smudging. Françoise said you might have some blank ID cards. Do you?"

"Yes we do," replied Madame Deferre, "and we still have Sarah's inks. I suggest you deal with the card issue tomorrow. Right now I need some help to clear the plates away while I bring out a little dessert."

Anna smile broadly, "This is such a treat to have so much good food after all the awful rations I've had to put up with."

On Saturday morning Marie-Claire set herself up at a table in Monsieur Deferre's office. Creating a brand new ID card was a delicate job which required peace and quiet. She copied Anna's details from the existing card and attached the undamaged photograph to the new card. The next step concerned her. She had never needed to replicate the official stamps before and felt the pressure. This card was not for some unknown escaper – her cousin's life depended upon the accuracy of her artwork. Later that morning she showed the card to the Deferre family.

"It looks perfect to me," commented Monsieur Deferre. "I see you are now Aletta Duval and not Mieke Devos. Assuming neither of these are even your real name, how do you remember who you are at any one time?"

Anna smiled at Marie-Claire before replying. "It's easy – my life depends on it."

Monsieur Deferre laughed. "Good answer, and I have some news for you. This morning I paid a visit to a friend and tomorrow you will be on your way with your new ID. It's best that you leave this area as soon as possible. We don't know what the passeur who was supposed to meet you might have said under interrogation."

"I see what you mean. How will I be passed on to the next person? Where will I be waiting?"

"Don't worry. We operate our line in a different way. It is based on contacts with trusted friends who we know personally. You will be escorted the whole way and you will never be left waiting for some passeur."

Anna appeared to be overcome with emotion. "But why do you do this when you don't know the escapers? It's so dangerous."

"Every escaper is someone's special person," replied Madame Deferre. "A husband, a son, a daughter. If Françoise was escaping we would want to know that the best help was being given to her, so we do that for the people who pass down our line."

Anna wiped tears from her eyes. "I'll never forget what you are doing for me."

"Well at the moment you can do something to help me. As you know, Jerome and Yasmine Fleury are coming for lunch and I could do with some help in the kitchen."

"Can Jerome be trusted?" asked Marie-Claire.

Monsieur Deferre chuckled. "Absolutely. He's almost a fully fledged résistant."

Lunch was a cheerful occasion with lots of food and friendly banter. After plenty of coffee and cognac it was late afternoon before the Fleurys said their goodbyes.

After they had gone Anna raised her cognac glass. "I know I'll say it again tomorrow but I want to thank all of you for what you are doing for me." She took a sip and put her glass back down. "Understanding the risks you are all taking, and being seen here as a person rather than merely a 'package' to be passed on down a line, has made me decide to change my plans."

Marie-Claire looked askance. "What are you saying? Are you no longer wanting to escape?"

Anna shook her head. "Originally I was escaping just to avoid persecution. I now see how selfish that was. I realize that other people are risking their lives just so I can escape. Last Wednesday I survived but the people helping me were arrested."

"It's our way of fighting the Germans," said Madame Deferre.

"I see that now, and I've decided my escape must be more than just a selfish desire to survive. When I get to England I want to train to do something positive for the war effort. With my language skills in French, German, Dutch and English, I might even be able to train as an agent. On Tuesday, if you had asked me, I would have said the last thing I wanted to do was return. But now I've changed my mind. I want to get proper training and return to fight the Germans. I see it as my way of repaying all the people who are risking their lives to help me."

Monsieur Deferre raised his glass. For a long moment he held it aloft in silence and then spoke with a tremor in his voice. "May your God go with you."

The following morning, soon after breakfast, Monsieur Deferre fired up his charcoal-burning van. "Aletta, it's time to go. My friend will be waiting for us."

With tears in her eyes Anna hugged Madame Deferre, Françoise and finally Marie-Claire. "I owe immeasurable thanks to all of you. Last week I thought everything was lost but I see now that finding Marie in the cafe and meeting all of you here was a sign. I meant what I said last night. I don't know how or when, but I aim to return to avenge the deaths of those fighting for our freedoms."

Wiping away the tears in her eyes, Anna climbed into the van and it slowly chugged away.

Madame Deferre put her arm around Marie-Claire's shoulders. "Don't worry. I'm sure your cousin will survive." Marie-Claire leant against her and made no attempt to hide her own tears. She felt both pride in what her cousin was now planning to do and sadness at the very real prospect of never seeing or even hearing from her again.

Chapter 32

After Anna left Marie-Claire found it hard to hold her emotions in check so she kept herself busy helping Françoise with farming chores. It was late morning when Monsieur Deferre returned and told them that Anna had been passed on to the next contact. "You might be interested to know, we encountered one checkpoint and your new ID card was accepted without question."

"That's a relief. It was the most important card I've ever done."

"If you hear from her let us know," said Madame Deferre.

"I will, but it could be many months. Apparently it can take longer going from Spain to England than escaping to Spain."

After lunch Monsieur Deferre drove Françoise and Marie-Claire back to Nevers. When they reached the boarding house Monsieur Deferre gave Marie-Claire a hug. "It was good to see you again Marie. Come and see us whenever you want. You're always welcome."

Marie-Claire thanked him and waved as the van drove off, spewing smoke from its charcoal engine. She hurried up to her room and began working on the ID cards which Madame Favier had given her on Friday.

She was busy working on the second card when she suddenly heard German voices in the hall outside her room. Her heart started racing. *Has Anna been caught?* She quickly hid the ID cards in the secret compartment in the bookcase. *Thank you André.*

She sat back down and opened her sketch book at an unfinished pen and ink drawing. The voices in the hall sounded as if they were now directly outside her door which caused Marie-Claire to tremble so much she could not even pick up her pen.

After a few minutes the voices stopped, but she stayed in her chair still shaking. Her heart rate shot up again at the sound of a knock on her door. *Is that the Germans? Do they know about Anna and the forged ID card? Will they want to search the room?*

Cautiously she opened the door and was relieved to see it was just Madame Favier. "Don't worry Marie. May I come in?"

"Of course you can."

"This weekend when you were away a senior German officer came and informed me that I was required to provide rooms for two German officers. When I said I was full they said it made no difference – I must supply two rooms. He said if I didn't do so then they would just requisition the whole house and evict everyone, including me."

"Oh how awful. So what have you done? Do I need to find a different place to stay?"

"No. I asked the two workers from Marseille, Paul and Tristan, to leave. I was told the two German officers would come today so Paul and Tristan packed up and left yesterday. They said they understood but nevertheless I felt awful. I expect you heard the German officers in the hall just before I knocked on your door. They will be moving in tomorrow."

Marie-Claire's heart sank. "If German officers are going to be living on the same floor as me perhaps I should move out and find a safer place."

Madame Favier smiled. "Actually, here might be the safest place. Unless our German officers become suspicious, working directly under their noses may be the best place for you. After all, who would be so stupid as to do that? Also, moving away may cause them to wonder why. I think it's safer if you stay."

Marie-Claire relaxed a little. "So who are they?"

"Lieutenant Engel and Lieutenant Schwarz. They actually seemed quite polite and slightly embarrassed by the situation."

"That's not what I meant. Were they in uniform?"

"Green military uniforms. Why do you ask?"

"Did they have SS on the collars?"

"No. They looked like normal German soldiers."

Marie-Claire breathed a sigh of relief. "I was afraid they might be Gestapo and that could have been far more dangerous."

When Madame Favier left Marie-Claire sank back into her chair and tried to relax but she was still trembling. It was more than an hour before she felt her hands were steady enough to complete the ID cards.

On Tuesday morning as Marie-Claire approached the dining room for breakfast she could hear two German voices. As she composed herself before entering her thoughts went back to when she was a child. As an aspiring socialite, her mother had always insisted that a well-mannered child should have a demure face when being introduced to a stranger. Marie-Claire laughed to herself as she recalled the technique. Before entering a room she had to say four words to shape her lips into a tight squeeze – papa, pomme, poule, prune – 'Bonjour Madame'. She chuckled as she recalled such old fashioned rules of etiquette and decided that today she would simply greet the enemy with a smile.

As she walked in she was quite surprised when both officers showed unexpected manners by standing up and bowing slightly towards her. "Guten Morgen, fräulein."

She responded with equal civility. "Bonjour messieurs."

After they sat back down, one of the officers spoke to her in fractured French. "Landlady say you are teacher?"

Reluctantly Marie-Claire felt she couldn't avoid having a conversation. "Yes. I teach art."

"In Berlin my wife also teacher. I worry about her – all the bombing by British. Lieutenant Engel lucky – he not married."

The other officer laughed and spoke in German. The first officer then corrected his statement. "Should say Lieutenant Engel lucky – no one to worry about."

The other officer then smiled at Marie-Claire in a way which she found rather disconcerting. "I see you not married. You have someone you worry about? Yes?"

Marie-Claire wanted to discourage that kind of interest from a German. "Yes. I do." *I don't want to become involved with any Germans no matter how polite they try to be.*

The two officers soon finished their breakfast and rose to leave. "Guten Tag, fräulein. We see you tomorrow morning. We eat dinner with other officers."

After they had gone Marie-Claire relaxed. *If I'm only going to be seeing them once a day, then having two German officers in the house is not going to be as bad as I thought it would be.*

After school Marie-Claire went to the bookshop to talk to Odile and Nicole about the two German officers. As she expected, Odile already knew about the situation and expressed the same opinion as her mother. "Actually, it may be better for you. The Germans are less likely to raid a house where they have officers staying. Have you met them?"

"Yes. One is married, but the other isn't and I'm concerned he might want to ask me out."

Nicole laughed. "You? Going out with a German? Perhaps you could become a spy and find out what they're doing. After all, with no man in your life you wouldn't be cheating. Some of our best informants get their information by dating Germans."

Marie-Claire frowned. "Never. I don't wish to be labelled a collaborator."

They stopped talking when the bell above the door announced the arrival of a customer, but they all relaxed when it turned out to be André. When he was told about the German officers in Marie-Claire's boarding house, he smiled and asked if either of them had asked her out.

Marie-Claire scowled at him. "Not you as well. I will be having nothing to do with either of them, and anyway if I did go out with either of them I'd have to stop forging ID cards for you. Is that what you want?"

André held up his hands. "Absolutely not. In fact, that's why I came here right now. A friend of mine in Guérigny has an escaper hiding with him and his card needs to be amended. Will you be able to do it tonight?"

"I'll process it this evening and you can have it back tomorrow."

André smiled. "That would be great. Right now I can't stay and chat. I need to get back to work."

When he had gone Nicole turned to Marie-Claire. "I'm glad you came by. I want to talk to you about some plans for the wedding.

Not right now but can we meet on Saturday?"

Marie-Claire replied with a smile. "I'd love to help and Saturday's fine. Where shall we meet?"

"How about Le Bistro d'Anjou. André never goes there so we won't be disturbed by him."

"You're not supposed to hide from your future husband." Marie-Claire laughed. "I know where the bistro is. Shall we say two o'clock."

That evening Madame Favier passed Marie-Claire an envelope containing the ID card which needed amendment. She was making the changes when she heard the two German officers talking as they returned to their rooms. She paused until she heard them close their doors. With no more sounds coming from the hall she picked up her pen and continued working on the card.

As usual on Thursday evening Marie-Claire headed out to the Café du Monde. As she pushed open the Café door it struck her how much she enjoyed these evenings with her new friends. It helped her forget, if only for a few hours, how much she missed her life in Paris. Nicole waved to her and Marie-Claire made her way across the room to join her friends who were engrossed in a game of dominoes.

André was sitting this game out and when he saw her he stood up and beckoned her to follow him outside. He checked to see there was nobody nearby, then spoke in a quiet voice. "I didn't want to say anything inside but I have to tell you. Remember that ID card you just did for me? Well it turns out it wasn't needed."

"Did the escaper change his mind?"

"His mind was changed for him. Apparently my friend's brother turned up at the safe house and recognized the escaper. He had encountered him in Dijon and knew he was actually a paid Gestapo informant. Apparently recognition was mutual and the escaper immediately pulled a knife on the brother. Unfortunately for him, he was no a match for the two brothers."

"So what happened to him?"

André paused before answering. "I was told his body was

stripped, mutilated and put in a box. And with Bernard's help the box was put in a train carriage along with boxes of food requisitioned by the Germans."

Marie-Claire suppressed her desire to be sick. "That's gruesome but I suppose he deserved it. It's fortunate he was caught in time. That was close."

"Yes very close, especially since my friend is the head of our escape group."

"I thought it was your group."

"No it isn't. Although I do a lot for the group my friend is in charge. But right now I think we should join the others."

On Saturday, after lunch, Marie-Claire packed her sketch book and pencils in her bag and headed to Le Bistro d'Anjou. When she arrived Nicole was not yet there so Marie-Claire sat at a table and ordered a drink.

When Nicole arrived she looked around the room and whispered to Marie-Claire. "I can see why André doesn't like this place. It has an odd feel to it. And the clientele don't look French if you know what I mean. Shall we go somewhere else?"

"Unless you've got something secret to tell me we might as well stay. At least it's warm and this drink is not too bad. So. What are these plans you want to talk about?"

"We've set the wedding date – the 31st of May – and you've become such a good friend to André and me, and we owe you so much, we'd love you to be one of our witnesses."

Marie-Claire felt flattered. "One of your witnesses? If you really want me to be, I would be honoured to do so."

"There is one other thing." Nicole looked slightly embarrassed. "I'm thinking of my wedding present for André. Do you think he'd like a portrait of me, and if so would you do one for me?"

"I'm sure he would and I'd love to do that for you. First, though, I need to do some sketches of you in different poses to see which you like best. When can we do that?"

Nicole looked around. "Is there enough light for you to do that here? Now?"

Marie-Claire reached for her bag which contained her sketch pad and pencils. "Why not? At least we won't get disturbed here."

Nicole relaxed. "Thank you so much. I was hoping you'd agree as you do such wonderful portraits."

Marie-Claire became so absorbed in sketching Nicole she paid little attention to the comings and goings in the Bistro. She was aware of the fact two people had sat down at the table behind her, but thought no more about it. However, a few minutes later Nicole looked pointedly at the table behind Marie-Claire and said, "I should have ordered sugar with my coffee."

Marie-Claire acknowledged the warning signal with a slight nod and continued sketching. She had nearly finished her sixth sketch when she noticed a look of alarm on Nicole's face.

At the same time Marie-Claire felt a tap on her shoulder and a German voice spoke to her in French, "My friend and I have been watching you."

Marie-Claire turned to face the man and almost stopped breathing when she saw he was dressed in the unmistakeable uniform of the Gestapo.

Chapter 33

Marie-Claire looked up at the Gestapo officer. Trying to control her voice, she asked him, "Is something wrong?"

"No. We're just interested in why you have been doing so many sketches of the same person. Do you have an explanation?"

Marie-Claire was relieved that she could actually tell the truth. "My friend is getting married and she asked me to make a portrait of her as a wedding present for her husband."

The officer held out his hand in an expectant manner. Assuming he wished to see her papers, she picked up her bag to get her ID card. "Mademoiselle. I do not want to see your papers, at least not right now. I would like to look at your sketches."

Surprised by the request Marie-Claire passed him the sketch pad. The officer gestured to his companion to join him and together they looked through it, studying each page closely. Eventually the officer spoke. "If I may say so – these are very good. Are you an artist by profession?"

"I am an art teacher."

"In which school?" he asked brusquely.

Marie-Claire did not like the change in his tone. "Ecole Napoleon Bonaparte. It's a primary school here in Nevers."

He nodded. "I am aware of the school and what they teach. I didn't realize what an accomplished artist they have on their staff."

Marie-Claire blushed. "Thank you. You are very kind."

"Your sketches are excellent. May I ask if you would do a portrait of me? I would like to send it to my wife in Marburg – she has a birthday in a couple of months."

Marie-Claire knew she couldn't refuse so she replied politely. "Of course. Please sit down."

She started drawing and after about half an hour she was finished and handed him the portrait. He studied it carefully then commented, "It's perfect except for one thing."

Marie-Claire was taken aback. "Is something wrong?"

"Oh there's nothing wrong with the picture. I like it. But you have not signed it. How can I hang this if it doesn't have the artist's signature?"

Inwardly Marie-Claire was upset. She did not want her signature hanging on a Nazi's wall. But knowing she had no choice she signed the portrait with a flourish.

He examined the signed portrait with a smile then suddenly his expression changed. He looked at Marie-Claire. "Show me your ID card please."

Reluctantly she pulled her card out of her bag and handed it to the officer. *Why is he demanding to see it now?*

He looked at the card and then at the sketch. "Excuse me Mademoiselle Bruneau – but the signature on this sketch does not match that on your identity card."

Thinking quickly she replied. "The portrait has my signature as an artist. I thought what you wanted was a piece of art, not a piece of administrative documentation."

He bowed his head slightly. "I understand. I thank you sincerely for doing this for me. It is so much easier for all of us when we are not at each other's throats, if you know what I mean."

"It has been my pleasure."

"It would have been nicer to have met under different circumstances but I can assure you Mademoiselle Bruneau, that my wife, Frau Meyer, will appreciate what you have done." He turned to Nicole. "And may you have many years of happy marriage."

The officer bowed politely, put the picture in a briefcase, handed it to the other soldier and the two men walked out of the bistro.

After a few minutes the girls put on their coats and left. Nicole laughed. "We can't even tell anyone about you sketching a Gestapo officer – they might ask what we were doing."

On Sunday Marie-Claire met Françoise for a walk in Parc Roger Salengro. As they strolled along arm in arm Françoise asked about

207

the Germans at the boarding house. "Actually they seem very polite," replied Marie-Claire. "If all Germans were like them we probably wouldn't be at war with Germany."

"Has your Lieutenant Engel invited you out?"

Marie-Claire was indignant. "Why does everybody refer to him as my lieutenant? He's not my lieutenant and never will be. Apart from the fact he's German, right now I am not interested in a relationship with anyone. During a war relationships usually result in loss and heartbreak."

"That was said with strong emotion. You've never told me – was there someone in your life?"

"Let's just say it did not work out the way I planned." *Some day I'll tell her the full story but not right now.* "And you?"

"There was. But he seemed to think having two girlfriends was better than one and I didn't want to play that game."

"That seems to be the way many men think. And talking of such things, I don't like the number of young German soldiers who wander around the town eyeing every girl. Why don't they just go to the brothels the German army has provided."

"I agree," said Françoise. "Normally I would not approve of the increase in the number of brothels, but if they keep the Germans away from us then I'm not objecting."

"And from what I've heard, the girls are frequently able to get the soldiers to tell them military secrets. I suppose you could almost think of them as part of the resistance."

"Not a part I'm interested in joining," said Françoise. "I would never even want to go near one of those places, but at least the girls volunteer for the job and get paid."

Marie-Claire chose not to tell her friend about the horrific stories she'd heard about concentration camp inmates being forced into being sex slaves.

Late on Wednesday afternoon Marie-Claire went to the bookshop to tell Nicole that her portrait would be ready by the end of the week. As she entered the shop she saw that Nicole was comforting Odile who looked as if she'd been crying. "What's wrong Odile?"

Nicole answered. "You know Suzette? Suzette Gaudin. I think you've met her here in the shop."

"Yes. Has something happened to her?"

Odile began sobbing so Nicole continued. "Yesterday evening Suzette was attacked by a German soldier. Apparently he dragged her down an alley and beat her up when she rejected his advances. He raped her and left her so injured she was almost unable to walk."

Marie-Claire was horrified. "How awful. Where is she now? Will she be alright?"

Between sobs Odile answered. "She's in hospital. And it's all my fault. My fault."

"What do you mean?" asked Marie-Claire. "You can't be to blame for what happened. The German soldier is the one responsible. Why do you think you're to blame?"

"I was supposed to meet her but I got held up here in the shop. Oh why didn't I close the shop before that customer came in? Why? Why? Why?"

Marie-Claire put her arms around Odile. "You mustn't blame yourself. You weren't the one who attacked her. It was a deranged German soldier – not you."

"But if I'd been with her he might not have attacked her."

Nicole spoke quietly. "I've tried to point out to Odile that she might have been attacked as well."

Marie-Claire turned to Nicole. "Do we have any information about the soldier? What he looks like? Anything at all?"

"Suzette doesn't remember," said Nicole. "The doctors think she might have suffered some concussion. It makes me worried about walking around alone."

"The soldiers eat their evening meal at six in the Pitié Barracks," said Odile. "If I close earlier, just before six, we should all be able to get home while they're in the barracks."

"That's a good plan," said Marie-Claire, "but you shouldn't be on your own tonight. Does your mother know what's happened?"

"No. I only heard about an hour ago."

"I think you should close the shop right now and come back

with me to the boarding house. Nicole, it's still light outside. Can you get home safely?"

"Yes. I can ask Bastien who works next door to come with me."

When Marie-Claire and Odile reached the boarding house Marie-Claire explained the situation to Madame Favier. Odile fell into her mother's arms and Madame Favier nodded to Marie-Claire. "Thanks for bringing her here. I'll look after her."

Marie-Claire went up to her room and collapsed into her chair. *And it was just a few days ago Françoise and I were talking about our fears about the behaviour of the German soldiers in town.*

The following morning at breakfast when Marie-Claire was greeted by the Germans with their customary 'Guten Morgen, fräulein' she did not reply. Instead she just glared at them.

Lieutenant Schwartz looked puzzled. "Have we upset you, fräulein?"

"Not you personally, but it was a German soldier."

In his fractured French he asked, "What German soldier do?"

"On Tuesday evening a friend of mine was attacked, beaten and raped by a German soldier."

Lieutenant Schwarz looked visibly shaken. "That shocking. Where she now?"

"In hospital."

"I go hospital. We be occupying force but under strict orders respect French people. After see her I speak camp commandant. We need find soldier before people make revenge."

Oh my God. What have I done? If they find and punish this soldier then the other soldiers could become even more aggressive and dangerous. I should not have said anything. We've got to deal with these people ourselves. Have I just made it worse?

Marie-Claire was amazed at how quickly bad news can travel. By the time she reached school that morning everyone in the staff room was talking about Suzette. Nobody other than Marie-Claire knew Suzette, but from the anger being displayed one would think she was everybody's close friend. Except that is, for the new deputy headmaster Monsieur Lefevre. "I don't know this Suzette person, but I'm not surprised. Young girls should be more careful these days. They take far too many chances. I suspect she's partially to blame."

Monsieur Lefevre's comment made Marie-Claire livid. She had already formed a negative opinion about the new deputy headmaster and his comment did nothing to alter it. Fearing she might say something she could later regret, she decided to remain silent.

Monsieur Garnier, however, did not. "I completely disagree. The attacker, this German soldier, is entirely to blame. I'm shocked to hear you think otherwise."

Monsieur Lefevre's next comments showed his upbringing. "In my day girls would never venture out without a chaperone. They would always be accompanied by a man, even if it was only just one of the servants. But now they even go out in the evening alone. How old is this Suzette? Sixteen? Seventeen?"

Marie-Claire was about to say that Suzette was in her mid-twenties but decided it was best not to become involved with the discussion.

During the lunch break Françoise took Marie-Claire aside. "You were very quiet this morning with respect to the Suzette situation. Do you know something you're not telling us?"

"I've met Suzette. She's not a child and from what I've seen she would not have been flirting with a German."

"They're saying she's in hospital. Will she be able to describe her attacker?"

Marie-Claire shrugged. "I doubt it. At least not well enough to identify anyone."

"Because the man is a German soldier the police won't be allowed to investigate and the army won't do anything about it." The frustration in Françoise's voice was evident.

Marie-Claire agreed and they walked back into the school.

Just after two that afternoon Marie-Claire became aware of a loud argument taking place in the hall outside her classroom. The fact it was in German, not French, worried her.

The door to her classroom burst open and a Gestapo sergeant marched in followed by Monsieur Thibault, who spoke in German. "Can't this wait until after the classes are finished? Why do you need to take her away now?"

The sergeant glared at Monsieur Thibault. "I've been told to fetch Fräulein Bruneau immediately. I don't care if she's teaching a class." He turned to Marie-Claire and spoke in German. "You are coming with me now."

Trying not to show her fear in front of the children Marie-Claire quickly decided she would pretend not to understand German. She looked at Monsieur Thibault and spoke in French. "What is this man saying? Why has he barged into my class? He's frightening the children."

"This Gestapo sergeant says you must go with him right now."

"Am I being arrested?"

"I don't know. He hasn't said so, but you can't refuse to go with him." He turned to the man and spoke in German. "Fräulein Bruneau will go with you. May I ask where you are taking her?"

"To L'Hotel de Paris."

In the full view of the children and the other teachers the sergeant escorted her out of the school to a waiting German military car.

As she climbed into the back seat Marie-Claire had a feeling of impending doom. The sergeant had said L'Hotel de Paris which she knew was the Gestapo headquarters in Nevers. Although it used to be a luxurious hotel she knew it was now where the Gestapo interrogated resistance workers – and reputedly tortured them.

212

Chapter 34

The drive to L'Hotel de Paris only took fifteen minutes but to Marie-Claire it seemed like an eternity. She sat hunched in the back seat of the car, head down, trembling at the thought of what might happen to her.

Why is he taking me to their interrogation centre? Have they heard about my forgeries? Has Anna been captured? Has someone betrayed André's group? Or the Deferres? What will they do to me? She tried to reassure herself. *Although the sergeant was insistent that I go with him he didn't appear to be arresting me. I haven't even been handcuffed. So what is it they want with me?*

When they arrived at L'Hotel de Paris Marie-Claire was even more puzzled by the sergeant's manner. He politely opened the door for her and indicated that she should follow him.

Inside the building they walked through what appeared to Marie-Claire to be an office. At one desk a soldier in Gestapo uniform was taking down notes while talking to a young woman. They were speaking in French but she could not make out the words. They stopped talking as Marie-Claire and the sergeant walked by. The woman turned her head away as if she was worried about being recognized by Marie-Claire.

The sergeant stopped at a closed door and knocked. From inside a German voice shouted, "Enter." The sergeant opened the door, saluted someone she could not see and announced in German, "Fräulein Marie Bruneau is here, sir." He then ushered Marie-Claire into the room. An important looking officer who was sitting behind a desk promptly stood up and greeted her in German. "Welcome fräulein. Please have a seat. I am so pleased you could make the time to come and see me."

Although Marie-Claire had learned a lot of German over the last few months, she decided she would continue to pretend that she did not understand German and she adopted a puzzled expression. Internally she was fuming. *Make time to come and see you? Apart from the fact I have no idea who you are, I wasn't given much damn choice.*

The sergeant was still in the room. "I don't believe she speaks German, sir."

The officer spoke brusquely to him. "Well get me a translator. What's the point of having requisitioned a skilled translator if we don't use him. Don't just stand there – get him now."

The sergeant left the room and she heard him bellow in German. "Where's the translator? Get in here now."

Marie-Claire turned towards the door and stared in amazement – the translator was Corporal Otto Voigt, the soldier she had attacked in Paris on the day her friend Hannah was shot. She was relieved she had her back to the officer and that the sergeant had not returned. It meant only Otto would have seen her reaction.

As he walked in the Corporal displayed no obvious sign that he recognized her. The officer spoke immediately to him in German. "Corporal. This is Fräulein Marie Bruneau who does not understand German and I want you to translate for me. Please tell her not to be worried and to please sit down."

Corporal Voigt then turned to Marie-Claire and spoke to her in French, and as he did so he smiled. To the officer it could be perceived as merely a friendly gesture but she felt it was otherwise, especially when he raised his eyebrows slightly as he said her name, "Marie Bruneau? On behalf of Colonel Zeigler I am to welcome you here and say you have nothing to fear – which I can personally confirm. Would you please have a seat."

Marie-Claire nodded and sat down. *Was Otto passing me a message by saying 'I can personally confirm'? Was he saying he recognizes me and he won't reveal that we know each other? And he referred to the officer as a Colonel. Why does a Gestapo Colonel want to talk to me?*

The Colonel then spoke in German which Otto translated as he stared directly into Marie-Claire's eyes. "The Colonel said that he saw a portrait you did last week of Major Meyer and he would like you to do one of him to take home to Germany."

Marie-Claire felt an overwhelming sense of relief. *So they didn't bring me here to interrogate me. This is nothing at all to do with resistance work. This man just wants me to do his portrait.*

Knowing she could not refuse Marie-Claire responded. "Please tell the Colonel that of course I'd be pleased to do so. I don't have my sketch book and pencils with me, so we need to arrange a suitable time. To do the portrait I will need at least an hour."

After a short discussion with the Colonel, Otto turned back to Marie-Claire. "The Colonel is catching a train back to Paris on Saturday afternoon and would like to suggest Saturday morning around nine. He wants to know if that would be acceptable?"

This is getting more unbelievable by the minute. Rather than ordering me about, this Gestapo Colonel is asking me if meeting him on Saturday is acceptable!

"Please tell the Colonel Saturday morning will be fine. Where does he want the portrait done? Will it be here?"

After a few more exchanges with the Colonel, Otto told Marie-Claire. "Yes. It will be here. You will be collected on Saturday. Do you have any more questions for the Colonel?"

She asked if she could now be taken back to her school as her students would still be in class. When Otto translated her request the Colonel yelled for the sergeant in a furious voice. Marie-Claire was surprised by the anger shown by the Colonel as he shouted at the sergeant. "Did you take Fräulein Bruneau out of her classroom? Did you disrupt her teaching?"

Although she was enjoying seeing the sergeant being reprimanded, she knew that since she was not supposed to understand German she must not show any reaction. The sergeant stood rigidly to attention as he replied to the Colonel. "Yes, sir. You said to bring her here so that's what I did."

"And you think marching into school classes and taking teachers out of the lessons will build good relationships between us and the French people? Is that what you think?"

"I thought we don't care what the French think about us, sir."

An expression of exasperation crossed the Colonel's face. "I'm finding it hard to believe you were ever promoted to sergeant.

Don't you understand that we often need French co-operation? In that respect, you certainly have not helped. Corporal Voigt will escort Fräulein Bruneau back to the school, not you. You are dismissed and I'll talk to you later."

The sergeant saluted, turned around and left. The Colonel then turned to Otto. "Corporal Voigt. Please express to Fräulein Bruneau my sincere apologies for my sergeant taking her out of her class. He made a stupid mistake. I would like you to escort her back to her school and apologize to the headmaster on my behalf. You can use my staff car and driver."

After Otto translated the message Marie-Claire smiled and said to Otto, "Please tell the Colonel I accept his apology and that I'll see him on Saturday."

When the staff car arrived at the school with its German swastika flags fluttering in the wind, the driver jumped out and opened the car door for Marie-Claire as if she was royalty.

As she and Otto walked towards the school she noticed astonished faces at all of the windows. Almost immediately Monsieur Thibault came out to meet them. Before he could say anything Marie-Claire turned to Otto. "Corporal Voigt, may I introduce Monsieur Thibault, our headmaster."

In perfect French Otto explained to the headmaster that a Gestapo Colonel who was visiting Nevers wanted Marie-Claire to do a portrait of him and had wanted to meet her to arrange a suitable time. "The Colonel has also asked me to express his apologies for the actions of his sergeant. The sergeant should not have removed Mademoiselle Bruneau from her class. He should have waited until the end of classes. The Colonel hopes the sergeant's inappropriate actions have not caused too much disruption."

"As you might imagine we were concerned when Mademoiselle Bruneau was taken away," said Monsieur Thibault. "Can you please tell the Colonel his apology is accepted." He turned to Marie-Claire. "I'm sure the whole experience must have been a bit – overwhelming? Do you want to take the rest of the afternoon off? I can continue to cover your class."

Marie-Claire declined. "Thank you, but no. I need to go back into class and reassure the children it was all just about drawing a portrait and that I'm fine. I'll come inside in a moment but first I have to arrange a pick up time for Saturday."

Monsieur Thibault took the hint and returned to the school building. Marie-Claire turned to Otto. "I know you said you would be picking me up on Saturday but I notice you have not asked me where I live. Is that because you or the Gestapo already know?"

He laughed. "No, I have no idea where you live, but I saw no need for the Gestapo to know your address which is why I did not ask you before. So tell me now and I'll be there just after 8:30 on Saturday." He smiled. "I'll be on my own."

Marie-Claire gave him Madame Favier's address. With a smile on his face Otto bowed goodbye, returned to the car and was driven away.

Marie-Claire went back into the school and both she and Monsieur Thibault went to her classroom. As they entered the room the children jumped up and gathered around her. "Are you alright Mademoiselle?" Monsieur Thibault explained to the children that their teacher was such a talented artist that an important German officer wanted her to do a portrait of him. "You are lucky to have such a good teacher." Marie-Claire then suggested the children should all draw portraits for the rest of the class.

When school finished for the day Françoise took Marie-Claire aside. "Come on Marie. Does a Gestapo Colonel seriously want you to do a portrait of him? Is that what actually happened?"

"Actually that is all it was and I'm to do the portrait on Saturday morning. To begin with I was really frightened. They took me to their headquarters and interrogation centre at L'Hotel de Paris and I was sure someone had betrayed me. But no, the Colonel was very polite and I was treated with courtesy."

Françoise hesitated a moment. "As you can imagine, we were all concerned for your safety. I have to tell you, though, that the person who seemed most concerned was Monsieur Garnier. He looked positively scared. Soon after you left he hurried away and I followed him. He went into the office and made a private phone call which I overheard. Although the conversation made no sense I wondered if he was talking to other collaborators."

"Originally we both thought he might be a collaborator but I can assure you, he's not. You don't need to worry about Monsieur Garnier. I'll go back inside and talk to him."

Back in the staff room Marie-Claire caught Monsieur Garnier's eye and indicated she wanted to talk to him. He followed her outside. "Gerhard, I suspect you were frightened. I certainly was, but I can assure you there's nothing to worry about. It was all just to ask me to do a portrait of a visiting Gestapo Colonel."

He looked very relieved. "I'm so pleased. I telephoned André to warn him but I can call him back now and tell him not to worry. Will you be able to come to the Café du Monde tonight and tell us all about it?"

"I'll be there."

As Marie-Claire walked into the Café du Monde that evening André saw her enter and beckoned to her. Nicole pulled an extra chair over to the table. "We're all anxious to hear about today. André told me you were arrested, but they released you."

Everyone around the table listened intently as Marie-Claire explained that although she had been taken to L'Hotel de Paris it was not a problem. It was just to ask her if she would draw a portrait of a visiting Gestapo Colonel. She added that she had been treated well and that she would be going back there on Saturday morning to do the portrait.

"I've heard L'Hotel de Paris is where the Gestapo interrogate French people," commented Gerhard. "Apparently they've tortured quite a few résistants there. I don't suppose you saw any evidence of that."

Marie-Claire shook her head. "No I didn't see or hear anything like that, but I did notice something suspicious. At one of the desks a man in Gestapo uniform was taking notes while talking to a French woman. She stopped talking and turned her face away from me as the sergeant and I walked through the office."

"That sounds like something you would do if you were an informant and didn't want to risk being recognized," said Gerhard.

At this point a group of people they did not know entered the Café. When Marcel pointedly brought over a bowl of sugar they ordered another round of drinks and resumed playing dominoes.

With the memory of Suzette's attack still fresh in everyone's mind, it was agreed at the end of the evening that the men, André, Gerhard and Bernard, would each walk one of the women home to make sure they were not walking in the dark on their own.

On Friday morning Marie-Claire was not sure what she would say to the two German officers in her boarding house. She still felt she'd done the wrong thing the day before telling them about Suzette. As usual, she was greeted with a polite, "Guten Morgen, fräulein." and replied politely.

Lieutenant Schwarz then added. "We go end March. We assigned new post Netherlands. I see your friend hospital and talk commandant. He old friend. He say nothing he can do. He also say not good I ask many questions. Sorry. I tried."

"Thank you for trying. I hope asking questions is not the reason you are leaving."

"I think it be. Asking questions not good. So now we sent Netherlands and train other soldiers."

They finished their breakfast in silence and the two officers bowed a goodbye as they left the dining room, leaving Marie-Claire sitting on her own. *He said they were being sent away because they were asking too many awkward questions. I never thought I'd be sorry to see these two Germans go but now I'm worried about who might take their place.*

Chapter 35

On Saturday morning Madame Favier knocked on Marie-Claire's door. "There's a German corporal at the front door saying he's here to pick you up. Are you in some sort of trouble? Shall I say you're not here?"

"No, I'm expecting him. This morning I'm doing a portrait of a German officer and the soldier is here to drive me there."

"Are you serious?"

"Yes. I couldn't refuse and so far I've been treated very well. I should be back by lunch time."

Marie-Claire picked up her bag containing her art materials and met Otto outside. As promised, he was the only person in the car so she sat beside him. She smiled. "Good morning Corporal Voigt, or can I call you Otto?"

He smiled back. "Otto is fine. And good morning to you Marie, or should I be calling you Olivia?"

She laughed. "Marie is the name. The other day when I saw you walk into the Colonel's office it gave me quite a shock. I'm glad I had my back to the Colonel when I saw you so he couldn't see my reaction. I don't think anyone noticed me staring at you."

"And how do you think I felt? When you were introduced to me as Marie Bruneau, not Olivia, I knew it meant something was very different. I had to find some way of letting you know I wasn't going to say anything."

"I thought I saw a flicker of recognition in your eyes but it was only a flicker and I wasn't sure. But when you added that bit about 'personally confirming' that I had nothing to fear, I took that to mean you would not be saying anything."

"I was hoping you would understand and perhaps remember my comment back in Paris about my hatred of the Gestapo. And don't worry, it hasn't changed."

"Oh I do remember what you said in Paris, but if you still hate them, what are you doing here? Being a translator for the Gestapo of all people."

Otto smiled. "Did you have much choice when you were asked by the Colonel to do his portrait? No – neither did I when I was assigned to work for the Gestapo. But rest assured, your past is safe with me."

"How long have you been here?"

"Since Christmas, but it looks as if my secondment will last for many months. May I ask what brought you to Nevers?" When she didn't reply immediately, he added. "Of course you don't need to tell me if you don't want to."

How much can I tell him? Can I trust him? I suppose unlike anybody else here, he already knows one of my important secrets – that I lived in Paris.

"My friend Hannah wasn't the only person the Gestapo took from me. They also killed other friends and family. I came to Nevers to start a new life away from all the pain."

"I'm sorry to hear that, and I know how you feel. Do you remember me talking about Greta?"

"You're fiancée shot by the Gestapo? Yes I remember and I still recollect your pain at seeing my friend being shot."

Otto swallowed hard before continuing. "Well she wasn't the only one. Her parents, Jewish people, went into hiding last summer. They were being hidden by a Catholic family in Düsseldorf but in November somebody betrayed them to the Gestapo. They were captured and sent to the Gross-Rosen concentration camp. They have not been heard of since."

"That's so tragic. I've heard about these concentration camps. What happened to the Catholic family?"

He sighed. "They were executed for 'hiding an enemy of the Reich'. Just because Greta's parents were Jewish did not make them an enemy of the Reich. But I can assure you when the people who had helped them were executed it turned me into an 'enemy of the Reich'. I have no loyalty to Hitler or his thugs or to what has become of my Germany."

He paused and looked at her carefully before speaking. "I

remember in the summer you had a strong sense of injustice and fight in you and from what you have just told me I doubt that has gone away."

Marie-Claire took a moment before replying. "In the past, wars were fought army against army, soldier against soldier. But Hitler has changed all that. He is now pitting soldiers and thugs against the people. And the people will fight back."

After a short pause Otto responded. "I won't ask, and I don't want to know if you are doing anything, but let me just say that in my job I quite often see or hear confidential information and I often translate for some of the informants."

Marie-Claire studied his face before answering. "Really?"

"I have seen documents the German military would not want the Allies to know about. And I know the identity of some of the French informants." He paused. "To put it bluntly – I may at times have information you may find of interest."

She thought for a moment before replying. "You know my name. You know where I work. You know where I live. If you ever want to tell me something, I'm sure there are people who would gladly learn whatever you have to say."

Otto merely nodded his head as he drew up outside L'Hotel de Paris. "We are here now which means you are no longer Olivia or Marie but Fräulein Bruneau. Please be aware, Colonel Zeigler is an important person if you understand my meaning."

She smiled. "I most certainly do – Corporal Voigt."

Otto opened the car door for Marie-Claire and then politely ushered her into the building, through to the Colonel's office and knocked on the door. When they entered, the Colonel immediately stood up and spoke in German, giving Otto time to translate. "Thank you for coming back. I really admired the picture you did of Major Meyer. I've known him a long time and you completely captured the essence of the man."

"Please tell the Colonel thank you," said Marie-Claire. "Could you ask him how formal he wants this portrait. I notice he has unbuttoned his jacket."

Otto's face showed alarm but he still translated accurately. The

Colonel laughed and Otto translated his reply. "The Colonel says it's refreshing to be in the presence of someone who doesn't feel they need to scrape the floor in front of him. He said he laughed because no one here would have dared comment on his clothing. But in answer to your question, he thinks informal. He also asked if you would be offended if he removed his jacket?"

Is this conversation really happening? A Gestapo Colonel is asking me if I might be offended if he took off his jacket.

"Of course not. May I suggest, if he wants it informal, perhaps he might loosen his tie. Or perhaps even take it off?" When Otto translated her question the Colonel laughed again. He then nodded, removed his tie and unbuttoned the top of his shirt.

Marie-Claire smiled. "Please tell the Colonel that he now looks perfectly informal. Can you ask him, please, if he could shift slightly left to get better light on his face. Also, because he'll need to hold the same pose throughout the whole session, could you ask him to make sure he's comfortable before I begin."

Once the Colonel was comfortable Marie-Claire began drawing the portrait. It was obvious the Colonel was not accustomed to being quiet for such an extended period. It was not long before he began a conversation, asking about Marie-Claire's background. A conversation she did not want to have.

She turned to Otto. "I'm finding it hard to draw while he's asking questions."

Otto smiled. "I understand. I'll just say you prefer silence while you work."

It was just over an hour before she felt she had completed the portrait. Praying the Colonel would like it, she tentatively turned the portrait around and showed it to him.

There was a protracted silence. *Oh no. He doesn't seem to like it. I can do another if he wants.*

Finally the Colonel spoke, interrupting her thoughts. Otto translated. "He says it's magnificent. He says he's had photographs done before but they've all been flat and devoid of emotion. He feels this portrait has life and somehow you've been able to show him as a person not as a military officer."

Marie-Claire felt so relieved. She signed the portrait, removed it from her pad and presented it to the Colonel. He opened a drawer in his desk, pulled out an envelope and spoke to Otto. "Please ask Fräulein Bruneau to accept this as a token of my appreciation."

When Otto translated Marie-Claire initially felt she could not accept it. "No, no. Please tell him it has been my pleasure to do this for him."

On being told her response, the Colonel smiled. "If I was having this done in Berlin I would expect to pay the artist, and I see no reason why it should not be the same here. Works of this calibre should be rewarded. I don't want her to feel I have in anyway exploited my position. Please. Tell her."

After Otto translated the message Marie-Claire graciously accepted the envelope. Although she wanted to look inside, she knew that would not be appropriate. Instead she thanked him and put the envelope in her bag. She and Otto then left the office and went back to the car. It was only when they were driving away that Marie-Claire felt she could finally relax.

Otto was the first to speak. "If you felt that was odd, how do you think I felt? I was petrified when you began talking as you did, suggesting the Colonel take off his tie. No one ever speaks like that to a Colonel. Especially not a Gestapo Colonel. What were you thinking?"

"What was I thinking? I was trying to show him that I had nothing to hide."

Otto laughed. "You've got to be more careful with your words. Saying that you were 'trying' to show you had nothing to hide, could be interpreted as implying that you 'do' have something to hide – which of course I'm sure you don't."

"Actually, I think we both do. It would not have been good for either of us if I had admitted that you and I had met under strange circumstances many months ago."

Otto chuckled. "Yes, you're right. We were introduced just a few days ago in Colonel Zeigler's office weren't we. At least that's our official line."

He then said nothing for almost a minute. "If I am ever to pass information to you we might as well make use of the fact we met officially when Colonel Zeigler wanted you to do his portrait. May I suggest that sometime in the future you give me drawing lessons in a bistro. Passing a drawing back and forth would not be seen as odd or out of place."

"Are you suggesting effectively hiding in plain sight? We can do that, but are you any good at sketching?"

The length of time Otto took to answer made her feel she had touched a nerve. Finally he answered. "Greta said I had potential. Doing it this way, I can openly approach and talk to you with a perfectly good reason. I'll contact you when I have some free time for a lesson – and something to tell you."

On Sunday Marie-Claire met up with Françoise in Parc Roger Salengro as usual. Françoise was eager to hear what had happened on Saturday when Marie-Claire drew the Colonel's portrait. After recounting the events of the morning Marie-Claire felt it was a good time to mention Otto, but not by name.

"Oh there is one more thing. The corporal who translated for the Colonel has asked me if I could give him drawing lessons."

"I hope you said no."

"Actually I didn't. It would have been difficult to say no. And no, before you ask, he was not making a pass at me. Quite the opposite. He was very open about it, suggesting we have our classes in a cafe so that it doesn't look as if we've anything to hide or that I'm being a collaborator."

She thought about the Reichsmarks the Colonel had given her and invented a little lie. "Also he is willing to pay for the classes. Not much, but having lawfully earned Reichsmarks could be useful in the future."

Françoise smiled. "I like the way you think around problems and see how to use them to our advantage. So when do you begin teaching this man?"

"We haven't set a date yet but he'll let me know when he's going to be free."

When Marie-Claire visited the bookshop on Wednesday, she found Nicole in a bubbly mood. "I've found the perfect dress for the wedding. It's not traditional but then neither am I. With all the shortages I wanted something I could wear afterwards. You know, something to remind me of the day. When you get married you'll feel the same."

Marie-Claire bit her lip. She wanted to tell Nicole the truth but knew she mustn't. *Oh I know how you feel. It's not even a year since Emile and I were married and yet now I can't even mention his name. But I mustn't let my sadness destroy Nicole's happiness.*

"What colour is your dress? Have you got a matching hat?"

"The dress is a beautiful pale blue. They didn't have a hat, and I couldn't afford one anyway."

"Let me buy one for you," said Marie-Claire. "On Saturday afternoon, you and I will go shopping for the perfect hat. It will be my present to you."

Nicole flung her arms around Marie-Claire. "If you really mean that, it would be wonderful. On Saturday if you come by my apartment first, I can show you the dress and the colour."

When Marie-Claire arrived at Nicole's apartment on Saturday, the dress had been draped carefully over the back of the sofa. As Nicole held it up in front of her Marie-Claire exclaimed. "That's really beautiful. Has André seen it?"

"Not yet. He knows I have the dress and he knows we're going out this afternoon to find a matching hat."

Marie-Claire smiled at her friend. "And so we are. So get your coat and let's go."

Chapter 36

It took Marie-Claire and Nicole a long time to find a hat that complemented Nicole's wedding dress. The shortage of material and the changes in fashion had reduced the number of places selling suitable hats. Finally, late in the afternoon, they found one which they both agreed was perfect.

Marie-Claire bought it and handed the bag to Nicole. "Usually I would wrap your present up and give it to you later but since you'll need to be wearing it on your wedding day, please accept this now with all my blessings."

Nicole's smiled. "Thank you. I'll think of you every time I wear it. I'm so glad you came into our lives, André's and mine. It would never be appropriate to thank Philippe for his picture of the dead Germans piled in a heap, but if he hadn't done that drawing we might never have met."

"Perhaps not. We'll never know."

Nicole put her arms around Marie-Claire and gave her a long hug. "You'll find someone some day Marie. I'm sure you will. Someone as wonderful as my André."

"I'm sure I will – and you're right. André is a wonderful man. But right now my feet are killing me and I need a hot drink."

Nicole linked arms with Marie-Claire. "I know the perfect place. It's a small bistro down by the riverside and it's my treat."

They set off and almost immediately Nicole turned into an alley. It lead to Rue du Calvaire which isn't really a road but rather four flights of stone steps interspersed with flat landings.

"I didn't know this passageway was here," said Marie-Claire. "The way it's nestled between the buildings this must be a very old part of the town."

"It's definitely old and it's a useful shortcut to the road beside the river."

They soon reached the road and turned left to walk along to the bistro. Inside they collapsed into some chairs and ordered hot drinks. Although it had been a tiring afternoon Marie-Claire felt the day had been worth it. Nicole seemed genuinely pleased with the hat and was soon chatting happily. She talked about the wedding and the bookshop and the customers who come into the shop and the kinds of books they buy – or try to steal. Marie-Claire enjoyed just listening to Nicole's enthusiasm for life. She understood completely how André had become captivated by this bundle of energy.

After a while Marie-Claire became alarmingly aware of a pair of German soldiers staring at them. They were speaking loudly and their slurred voices indicated they had already drunk too much. They tottered over to Marie-Claire and Nicole and started making lewd suggestions. They reeked of alcohol and this time Marie-Claire made no attempt to hide her knowledge of German. "We are not interested in your propositions. Please leave us alone."

The waiter came over and very pointedly asked the girls if everything was alright. The tall German tried to confront the waiter but found it hard to stand up straight. The other German, who was only slightly less drunk, pulled his friend away. "Come on Heinrich. Time to go to Madame du Nuit and talk to real girls. The girls in that brothel know what's good for them, unlike these stuck-up ones." The waiter held the door open for the two drunks as they staggered out.

He then came over to Nicole and Marie-Claire. "I'm sorry. I must apologize for that. Those two are really nasty and could have become violent if I stopped serving them or told them to leave. They often come here just after seven and get drunk before going to the Madame du Nuit brothel just down the road. I saw them heading that way when they left. But just in case they come back, I suggest you two leave soon and go the other way."

"Can't the police deal with them?" asked Marie-Claire.

"There's no point in calling the French police as they can never arrest German soldiers. That's only done by the *Feldgendarmerie*, the German military police – and around here they don't see attacking French woman as a crime."

228

Nicole looked very upset. "And we were having such a nice day. Only to have it spoiled by these damn Germans."

"Come on, Nicole," said Marie-Claire. "It's been a good day. Let's finish our drinks and do as he suggests."

"I don't want to leave but you're right, it's probably best we do."

They quickly finished their drinks and the waiter opened the door for them. He looked out. "I can't see those Germans so you should be ok if you go quickly. Sorry to suggest you leave, but it's really for your own safety. I hope you'll come back here another day – perhaps earlier in the day."

The two girls walked briskly back the way they had come. They had just reached the first set of steps in Rue du Calvaire when Marie-Claire heard a German voice behind her. "Madame du Nuit may be too busy tonight, but these girls won't refuse us Heinrich. Not this time. I told you we'd find them again."

Terrified, Marie-Claire yelled at Nicole. "Run. We can go faster than they can. They're drunk, we're not. Come on. Run! Run!"

The girls ran up the steps but even in their drunken stupor the soldiers ran faster. Nicole and Marie-Claire had only reached the first landing when the two soldiers caught up with them.

Heinrich grabbed Nicole and pushed her violently against the wall of the passage. At the same time the other soldier pushed Marie-Claire against the other wall and ran his hands up and down her body. He then began to rip off her coat. Marie-Claire tried to fight back, clawing at his face in an attempt to reach his eyes. The soldier leant his head to the side to avoid her fingernails as she clawed at him. As he did so Marie-Claire was able to see Heinrich on the other side of the passage strike Nicole with a vicious backhand across the side of her head.

The blow was so strong it almost lifted Nicole off her feet. She tumbled over and fell head first down the steps. There was a sickening sound as the side of her head hit a stone step. It was the unmistakeable sound of bones cracking.

Before Marie-Claire could react her attacker looked down the passageway and hollered. "Heinrich, you idiot. What have you done? We've got to get out of here now."

Heinrich looked down the steps, turned and ran quickly up the steps closely followed by Marie-Claire's attacker.

Marie-Claire looked down and saw Nicole's crumpled body lying at the bottom of the steps. She charged down towards Nicole, screaming as she did so. "Help! I need help. Someone. Help."

When she reached Nicole it was evident the stone step had cracked Nicole's skull and blood was spurting out from a ruptured artery on the side of her head. At first Nicole appeared to be lifeless but when Marie-Claire saw a flicker of motion in her eyes she screamed again, louder than she had ever screamed before. "Help! Help!" She bent over Nicole's body and tried to stop the bleeding but with little success. Marie-Claire spoke gently. "It'll be ok Nicole. Stay with me. Please. Please."

She was suddenly aware of a man kneeling beside her. "What's happened? Oh my God. It's Nicole."

Marie-Claire turned and recognized Bernard, the stationmaster. "I was on my way home when I heard your screams." He stood up, "I'll run and phone for an ambulance and the police. Stay with her Marie. I'll be back as soon as I can."

Marie-Claire cradled Nicole's head in her left arm while she tried to staunch the bleeding with her right hand. The spurts of blood were now covering Marie-Claire's coat, hands and face. She spoke with desperation in her voice. "Nicole, stay with me – don't sleep – come on – help is on its way – you'll be alright – please."

Bernard returned a few minutes later. "I've phoned for an ambulance and police and they should be here soon. This is awful. What happened?"

With tears streaming down her blood-covered face Marie-Claire answered. "We were attacked by two soldiers and one of them struck Nicole so hard she fell down the steps head first." She turned back to her friend, "Please Nicole, stay with us. I can hear a siren. Help will be here soon."

It was not, however, an ambulance but a police car. It stopped and a policeman came running over. He took one look at the scene and dropped to his knees. "You're doing the right thing trying to stop the bleeding but I'm not sure it'll be enough." He looked more closely at Marie-Claire. "I know you. You're Marie, aren't you? I'm Jerome. We met at the Deferre's farm." Pointing to Nicole he asked, "Who is this?"

Bernard answered. "It's Nicole, one of our friends. These girls were attacked by two German soldiers."

Jerome uttered a quiet, "Merde. Not Germans." In a louder voice he explained. "Even if I could have caught them, I couldn't have arrested them. I cannot arrest German soldiers. I can only—"

"Where is the ambulance?" Marie-Claire cut into his explanation. "We need an ambulance. We need it now."

Jerome shook his head. "Some of our ambulances have been requisitioned by the Germans. We don't have many now."

"We need an ambulance now. Nicole's losing too much blood. I can't stop it." She turned back to her semi-conscious friend. "Oh no. Nicole, stay with us."

Bernard looked as if he was about to speak when Marie-Claire noticed Nicole's eyes flutter and her mouth move. "Quiet. I think Nicole's trying to say something."

With eyes only half open Nicole looked at Marie-Claire and in a very weak voice she whispered, "Tell André I love him."

She appeared to sigh and her body went limp.

Blood stopped flowing from the gash in her head.

Marie-Claire moaned. "No – no – no. You can't. You can't." Her moan turned into a protracted wail as she withdrew her bloodied hand from the side of Nicole's head.

Bernard reached out and pulled Marie-Claire up into his arms as Jerome held Nicole's wrist and felt for a pulse. Jerome slowly shook his head. "I'm sorry. She's gone."

Marie-Claire's body began to shake with uncontrollable sobs. Bernard held her tightly and turned towards Jerome. "We'll need to tell André, her fiancé."

Jerome sighed deeply. "As the policeman on the scene, it falls to me to do that."

Marie-Claire struggled to speak through her tears. "We'll all tell him, you, me and Bernard." Her voice changed and she muttered.

"I'll kill those two soldiers. I swear, I'll kill them myself. I will personally kill Heinrich."

Bernard looked at her with consternation. "You can't say that. You mustn't say such things in front of a policeman. What if they were found dead. He'd come after you." He turned to Jerome. "Please, take no notice of what she's saying. The shock of Nicole's death has so upset Marie she doesn't know what she's saying."

Jerome replied quietly. "I know Marie and I also know she means exactly what she said." He turned to Marie-Claire. "Marie. I agree those two need to be removed but it cannot be done openly and you cannot do it yourself. If the Germans were to find out what you did, there would be serious repercussions. The German policy is that you would be shot along with fifty hostages. Fifty innocent people will die if you are seen to kill those two German soldiers. Would your friend have wanted that? Would your friend have wanted them to die as well?"

Marie-Claire sobbed again. "But I need to avenge her death."

Jerome waited for a moment before speaking. "Again I agree, but we need to plan it very carefully so that it cannot be pinned back on us."

Bernard looked at Jerome with a puzzled expression. "Are you suggesting? As a policeman, are you suggesting that —"

"As a French policeman, I have to work under the domination of the German invaders," interrupted Jerome, "but that does not mean they control my heart. My heart is French, through and through. So here is my plan. We record her death as an accidental fall – she slipped on the steps. Tragic, yes, but that means there'll be no subsequent official follow-up. However, we will find out who those two soldiers are and deal with them ourselves. It'll be hard to identify them but I'm sure we can do it somehow."

"That won't be difficult," said Marie-Claire between sobs. "The image of their faces is burned into my memory and I can easily produce sketches of them."

Jerome shook his head. "Under the circumstances how can you trust your memory?"

"Have you forgotten? I'm a portrait artist and those two bastards

232

had already pestered us when Nicole and I were in a bistro earlier today. Trust me, I know exactly what they look like."

Bernard spoke quietly. "I'm concerned about what André might do when we tell him. What if he's so distraught he decides to seek immediate revenge. We need to be careful how we tell him and one of us should stay with him tonight to make sure he doesn't do anything stupid."

"I agree," said Marie-Claire. "Someone should stay with him but obviously it can't be me."

Jerome shook his head. "Nor me. If I'm to report this as just an accident, I must not appear to have any personal connection with this André person."

Bernard nodded. "I guess that leaves me and that's fine. I've known him for years, we're close friends. What do we tell him?"

Jerome answered. "You can tell him that the official line is she slipped. You can also tell him the truth that she and Marie were attacked by two unknown German soldiers, one of whom pushed her down the steps. However, we need to impress on him that for all of our sakes he must not tell anyone else what actually happened. Even if you don't end up seeking revenge, no one else can ever know the truth. The Gestapo could easily decide the fact we might seek revenge is sufficient to arrest all of us."

They could hear the sound of an ambulance in the distance. Jerome spoke quickly. "Are we all agreed, then? Officially she just tripped and fell. But we tell André the truth, and finally we will avenge her death – all of us, me included."

Bernard spoke. "Yes, without question."

Jerome turned to Marie-Claire. "Do I have your agreement?"

She wipe her eyes. "Yes. I can see you're right. I hope André sees it that way as well."

The ambulance arrived and the crew ran over. Jerome spoke to them and said it was an accidental fall and he would file the official report. Bernard guided Marie-Claire away from the scene as Nicole's body was transported on a stretcher to the waiting ambulance.

After the ambulance had gone Marie-Claire turned back and

began crying uncontrollably again as she looked at Nicole's blood seeping slowly away between the cobblestones. Suddenly she spoke. "Our bags. Our bags are on the first landing. I had just bought Nicole a hat for her wedding. Oh no. I can't believe what's happened." Bernard comforted her as Jerome retrieved the bags.

"We need to go to André's house now and tell him before he hears from anyone else," said Jerome. "But Marie, you need to clean up first. You have blood all over your face, your hands, your clothes."

Marie-Claire showed her stubborn streak. "I'll wipe my face, I'll wipe my hands, but André needs to know what's happened as soon as possible. And he needs to hear it from us, his friends. I'll not waste time getting changed."

"You could clean up at the bistro," suggested Bernard.

"No. I can't go back there. Certainly not like this. The waiter might guess what's happened and we can't risk him saying something to the Germans. I'll go as I am. So let's go."

On the way Jerome stopped the police car at the police station, went in and returned with a wet towel. "You really do need to clean your face and hands before André sees you."

As Jerome drove Marie-Claire took the towel and started crying again as she wiped her friend's blood from her hands. *We will get our revenge Nicole dear –we will!*

Soon the three of them were standing in front of the door to André's house. With a memory of the day in December when she knocked on this door for the first time Marie-Claire stepped forward, tears streaming down her face. "I'll knock."

She lifted the heavy knocker and let it bang against the door.

Chapter 37

As they waited for André to open the door Marie-Claire started shaking again. "Why isn't he answering?" she asked impatiently. She was just about to knock again when André opened the door. "Marie – Oh my God! What's happened? You're covered in blood. Come in."

When Bernard followed Marie-Claire into the house André looked puzzled. His face then took on a frightened look when he saw Jerome. "What is a policeman doing here? What's going on? Oh no!" Tears began to fill his eyes. "Where is Nicole? She was meeting you today Marie. Where is she?"

Marie-Claire found it hard to reply. "She fell down the steps at Rue du Calvaire."

"Is she badly hurt? Is she in hospital?"

Jerome was about to answer when Bernard spoke quietly. "I'm so sorry, André. It's bad news." As André's knees began to buckle, Bernard took his arm and helped him to a sofa. Marie-Claire sat beside him. "She hit her head on a stone step. She died in my arms. There was nothing I could do to save her."

André shook his head. "No! She can't be dead. She can't be."

Jerome knelt in front of him. "André. She didn't slip and fall. Apparently she was pushed down the steps and cracked her skull. Marie tried everything she could to save Nicole but her injuries were too severe."

André's whole body tightened as he asked in an anguished voice, "You said pushed. Who pushed her? Why? What haven't you told me?"

Marie-Claire tried to control her voice. "We were attacked by two German soldiers. One of them hit Nicole so violently she fell down the steps head first." Marie-Claire began crying again. "I'm so sorry. I tried but I couldn't stop the bleeding."

André put his head in his hands, "No – no – no!"

Marie-Claire spoke softly to him. "Just before she passed away she asked me to tell you she loved you."

Through his tears André whispered, "And I loved her."

It was a few minutes before anyone said anything. Finally André gritted his teeth. "Two German soldiers you say. I'll kill them. If they think they can attack us and get away with it, they're wrong. Where are they now?" He looked at Jerome. "You're the policeman. Are they in custody? Let me at them. I don't care what happens to me. Those two will die for what they did."

"It's not as easy as that, André," replied Jerome. "They're not in custody. They ran away before I got there. And even if I had been there, French police do not have the authority to arrest German soldiers – even if they commit murder."

André's lips quivered, "If we don't know who they are how can I avenge Nicole's death?"

He buried his head in his hands again and began shaking. Marie-Claire put an arm around his shoulders. "André. We don't know who they are but I know what they look like and we can find them. But you can't just go out and shoot them. In reprisal the Germans would execute fifty French citizens. You don't want that to be Nicole's legacy – the death of fifty innocent people."

André was finding it hard to speak. "So how do I get my revenge? We can't let them get away with this."

"I can assure you they won't. As a policeman I can't do anything to help," said Jerome. "But as a Frenchman I can and I will. Marie and I will find out who they are and where to find them."

"We need to plan our revenge carefully," said Bernard, "and now is not the time. Look, I'll stay here with André tonight. There's nothing more either of you can do now. Jerome, can you take Marie back to her house?"

Jerome stood up. "Of course I can. Tonight at the station I will write out an official report stating this was purely the result of an accidental slip on the stairs with no mention of any attackers." He turned to André. "You have my heartfelt condolences."

"My heart goes out to you," said Marie-Claire. "I know exactly how you feel."

As Jerome drove Marie-Claire to the boarding house he asked, "How accurately can you draw those two Germans? The reason I ask is you said the two Germans left the bistro to go to a brothel. The closest to that bistro is Madame du Nuit and —"

"That's the one they mentioned," interrupted Marie-Claire.

"I know Ingrid who runs it. She's one of my trusted informants. If I pick you up on Friday evening we can show her the sketches and see if she can give us any useful information."

"Thank you Jerome. I'll do the sketches tonight."

Madame Favier was in the hall when Marie-Claire walked in still wearing her blood-stained coat. "My God. Have you been injured? Are you ok?"

"It's not me. It's not my blood." Marie-Claire started weeping again. "It's Nicole's."

"What do you mean? What's happened?"

Although Marie-Claire desperately wanted to tell the truth she knew she had to stick to the agreed story. "Nicole fell down the stone steps at Rue du Calvaire and hit her head."

Madame Favier gasped, "Is she alright?"

Marie-Claire found it hard to reply. "No. She died in my arms."

"Oh no. I can't believe it. Does André know?"

"Yes. I've just come back from his house." Marie-Claire began shaking again. Madame Favier put an arm around her quivering shoulders. "Don't go upstairs. You shouldn't be alone right now. Come through to my room."

It was a long time before Marie-Claire felt she could go up to her own room. She was still deeply affected by the day's events and all she wanted to do was sleep, but instead she pulled out her sketch book and made detailed sketches of the two Germans. *Rest in peace, Nicole. We will avenge your death.*

On Monday morning she knew she had to put on a brave face and go into school. During the mid-morning break Monsieur Garnier took Marie-Claire aside. "I saw André yesterday. Although he says he's coping, I've known him long enough to know it's just a front. He's hurting very deeply but is trying not to show it."

"Any word on the funeral for Nicole?"

"Yes. It'll be tomorrow in Varzy, Nicole's home village. André insists it must be a private funeral with none of us there. He said the Gestapo monitor funerals and he doesn't want them recording us." He sighed deeply. "I still can't believe she's gone. André said you were there when she fell. He knows you tried to save her."

Usually Marie-Claire looked forward to a relaxing day on Wednesdays but this Wednesday she knew she needed to go and see André. She was worried he would not be looking after himself properly. Marie-Claire was not sure he would even answer her tentative knock on his door but he did and welcomed her in. As she suspected, he was looking tired and dishevelled. He motioned for her to sit down. "I'm just brewing some coffee, or what I call coffee. Would you like some?"

"Yes please. I came to see how you are."

"Thank you." He paused. "I still can't believe that she's gone and I'll never see her again."

Marie-Claire looked into his eyes which were red from crying. "She's not entirely gone, André. She lives on in your memory and no one can take that away from you. Cherish her memory."

He looked at her and bit his lip before sighing. "I do. But that doesn't stop me from missing her so much."

"I miss her too," said Marie-Claire softly.

"I know you miss her as a friend but you can't imagine the pain I'm in." He paused. "We were due to be married in a few weeks."

"Actually I do know exactly how you feel."

André looked puzzled. "That's the second time you've said you know exactly how I feel. I don't see how you could know unless, unless – what haven't you told me Marie?"

Have I said too much? But I do understand how he feels. Do I dare tell him the truth? Or at least part of it?

Marie-Claire hesitated. "What I'm about to say you must never repeat to anyone. Absolutely nobody. My life depends on it. Not even my friend Françoise knows what I'm about to tell you."

André nodded his head. "You have my word."

Marie-Claire took a deep breath. "You, and everyone in Nevers,

238

know me as Mademoiselle Bruneau, but that's not who I was. Last summer I had a different life and a dear wonderful husband."

She stopped talking as tears rolled down her cheeks. He reached out and took her hand. "And you're going to tell me he was killed by the Germans."

She bit her lip. "By the Gestapo – last summer. That's why I'm here in Nevers with a different identity. Oh André. I do know the rage burning inside you. It burned inside me. It still does."

André looked at her in stunned silence. Then in a shaky voice he said. "Oh Marie. I had no idea. None of us did. You really do know exactly how I feel, don't you." He wiped his eyes. "How have you been able to deal with such heartbreak all alone without telling anyone? I don't know how I would have survived these last few days without the support of my friends."

He shook his head as if in disbelief. "I am so, so sorry that you had to live with your grief without anyone to comfort you. I can't begin to imagine how difficult that must have been. But you know you can always talk to me at any time. I mean it. Any time at all."

Marie-Claire looked at him gratefully. "Thank you, André. You have no idea what a comfort that is."

He took her into his arms and they clung to each other, both sobbing quietly.

Eventually Marie-Claire pulled away and wiped the tears from her face. "When they killed my husband there was nothing I could do. I had to run and hide. But in your case something can be done. We know those two Germans were responsible and they'll pay."

"Oh they will. Bernard is coming here on Saturday morning so we can plan our revenge."

"I'll bring sketches of those two Germans," said Marie-Claire.

On Friday evening Jerome picked Marie-Claire up in his official car and drove straight to the Madame du Nuit brothel. When they arrived it was obvious to Marie-Claire that Ingrid knew him well by the jovial manner in which she teased him.

However when he showed her the sketches and asked if she knew the two men her mood changed. "Heinrich and his deviant friend, Jurgen? Unfortunately yes, I know them. They're here every Tuesday evening around eight after binge drinking at the bistro down the road. They're a nasty pair, especially Jurgen. A couple of weeks ago he asked me if one of my girls could put up a bit of a fight as he had enjoyed a bit of rough fun earlier that evening with a street girl he called Suzette. You're welcome to them. I'd be happy if I never saw them again."

Marie-Claire found it very hard to remain silent. *Two weeks ago? So Jurgen is the German who attacked and raped Suzette and attacked me. And they're here every Tuesday evening around eight, are they? That's exactly what we needed to know.*

After the meeting with Ingrid, Jerome drove Marie-Claire back to her boarding house. When they stopped outside her house he asked Marie-Claire a question which surprised her. "Has André decided how he'll seek his revenge?"

"I don't think so. He's having a meeting at his house tomorrow morning with Bernard. I'll tell them about Heinrich and Jurgen."

"I don't want any of you to be caught. Perhaps I should drop by tomorrow as well to check they don't plan something which could backfire and implicate them."

"I'm sure they'd appreciate that."

When Marie-Claire reached André's house on Saturday Bernard was already there. When they were sitting around the kitchen table she said she knew the names of the two men. She put the sketches on the table. "The Madame at the brothel had no hesitation in identifying them as regular clients – every Tuesday evening."

André looked sternly at her. "You went to a brothel? Oh Marie, I said you mustn't take stupid risks."

"It wasn't a risk. I was with Jerome, the policeman."

André threw up his hands in frustration. "Oh Great! Well that's done it. We can't do anything now if the police are already aware we plan to do something."

Marie-Claire smiled. "It was Jerome's idea that you plan their death to look like an accident. He should be here soon. Not to arrest you, but to check over your plan. He wants you to succeed."

At that moment there was a knock on the front door. André went to answer it and returned with Jerome. "Officially, I'm here to see how you are, André. I can see you've got friends supporting you, so that's the official part done. Now, on a different subject, I understand you're planning your revenge. But before you tell me anything, let me just say I have some good news for you. You don't need to include Jurgen in your plans."

Marie-Claire glared at him. "But he's the one who raped Suzette and attacked me."

"I know, but the reason I say you don't need to kill him is he's already dead. His body was pulled out of the river this morning."

"We didn't do it," claimed André quickly.

"I know you didn't," said Jerome. "According to witnesses Jurgen got into a drunken brawl with some other German soldiers over a girl. He was knocked out and fell into the river. It flows quickly at that point and no one was able to save him."

"That's how we do it," said Bernard thoughtfully. "Heinrich will have an accident and fall into the river. Marie, you said he and Jurgen visit this brothel every Tuesday evening which means —"

"Stop right there Bernard," interrupted André. "By identifying Heinrich and his habits Marie has done more than I could ever have asked for. I do not want her involved in anything more."

Marie-Claire was about to object when André held up his hand. "I'm serious. Bernard and I will plan this and be solely responsible. What we're planning is risky and I don't want you implicated in any way. In fact, we won't say any more until you leave."

Jerome nodded. "André is right. I'll stay for a while to help them plan but you should leave."

"Heinrich was responsible for Nicole's death," said André, "and I don't want to be responsible for anything happening to you Marie. So please go now. And take those sketches with you. I won't forget his face."

"I'm sure you won't," said Marie-Claire, "I won't ask what you're planning to do, but let me just say, I'll be in the Café du Monde on Tuesday evening. If you and Bernard feel like a strong drink – I'll be there."

Marie-Claire found the following days extremely difficult. She kept wondering what André and Bernard would do. On Tuesday evening she sat in the Café worrying. She didn't even notice that the cup of coffee she was sipping was now cold.

She did not know how to react when late in the evening André and Bernard entered the Café and sat down beside her. To begin with nobody said anything. André merely nodded his head which she took to mean Heinrich was no longer a problem. Finally she broke the silence. "I know last Thursday we drank a farewell to Nicole but I feel it might be right to do something like that again tonight. I'll order a round of cognac."

Tears began forming in André's eyes. "Cognac? Tonight? Yes. I think that would be —" He did not finish his sentence. He lowered his head and began sobbing loudly.

Bernard looked at Marie-Claire. "Perhaps coming here tonight was not a good idea. Forget the cognacs, I think we should leave. I'll stay with André tonight. We can drop you off on the way."

"You're probably right," said Marie-Claire. "André, I don't have school tomorrow so I'll come by in the morning."

André stood up and put on his coat. As Marcel held the door open for them, he put his hand on André's shoulder. "There is no shame in showing your loss. We all miss Nicole."

In silence they drove Marie-Claire home. When she got to her room she lit the logs in the fireplace and sat staring at the flames. After a while she stood up and removed the sketches of the two Germans from the hidden compartment in the bookcase. She crumpled up each sketch and flung it onto the burning logs.

Heinrich. Jurgen. I hope you burn in hell !

Chapter 38

On Wednesday morning Marie-Claire went to André's house as promised. Bernard had already left and André was pleased to see her. "You said you wanted to help me? Well I could certainly do with your help today. Up to now I've avoided clearing out Nicole's apartment but I can't postpone it any longer."

"Of course I'll help. Have you been back to her place since the funeral?"

André shook his head. "No. I couldn't face it. Part of me says I want to keep everything but I know that won't bring her back. I'm not sure I can sort it out alone. Thank you for saying you'll help."

"Is there much to sort?"

"Far too much. I got some boxes last week. I didn't have the heart to do anything then, but it has to be done. The rent is only paid up to this weekend so I can't put it off any longer."

Nicole's apartment was cold and damp. Marie-Claire found it hard not to cry at the sight of little things which reminded her of Nicole – a scarf she often wore, her green knitted sweater draped across a chair and a small bottle of her favourite perfume. Some of the sorting was easy. There were some obvious things to throw away such as old newspapers and food. André said the pots, pans and dishes came with the apartment and just needed to be washed. Marie-Claire set about doing that while André started looking through a stack of papers. "What did you do with important documents after your husband was killed?"

That question was too much for Marie-Claire. In a trembling voice she answered. "Nothing. Nothing at all. When he was killed I couldn't go back to our apartment – the Gestapo were waiting for me there. So I have nothing at all from our life together. It was the same at my mother's apartment."

André stopped what he was doing and looked at her. "What do you mean, the same at your mother's apartment?"

Damn. I shouldn't have said that, but I might as well tell him.

"The Gestapo were looking for me and I saw them shoot her when she wouldn't say where I was."

André put down the papers he was sorting, came over to Marie-Claire and put his arms around her. "Oh my God. How awful. Was that before or after they killed your husband?"

Marie-Claire broke down. This was the first time she had spoken about that day to anyone and could not hold back her tears. "It was the same day. That day I lost both of them – and the life I had been living." She paused. "You have no idea what a relief it is to be able to tell someone. You're the only person who knows, and it must remain that way."

"And I thought losing Nicole was as bad as it could get," said André, with tears rolling down his cheeks. "I just don't know how you have coped, keeping it bottled up inside you all this time. But don't worry, I'll never tell anyone. Since you've been able to handle such devastating losses it gives me hope I can eventually learn to handle my own loss."

They sat quietly on the sofa each lost in their own private thoughts. Eventually Marie-Claire stood up. "Come on. We've still got a lot of clearing up to do."

André put Nicole's papers in a box to take back to his house along with her pictures and books. Her clothes were put in a different box to take to the local church, with the exception of the wedding dress. André took it out of its box and held it up. "I never saw her wearing it but I can't give it away. She chose it to please me and I need to keep it. It will remind me of her." He folded it carefully and put it back in its box.

Marie-Claire knew leaving Nicole's apartment for the last time was obviously going to be an emotional experience for André. After they finished loading the van she turned to him. "Take as long as you want upstairs. I'll wait here."

Marie-Claire sat in the van, lost in her own thoughts. She missed her mother and her beloved Emile so much. It would have been their first wedding anniversary on Saturday and she didn't know how she was going to get through that day. She pulled out a hankie to wipe her eyes. *These Germans have taken so much from me, from all of us. We need to stop them.*

Her thoughts were interrupted by André returning to the van. With his hands clenching the steering wheel he muttered. "We're not doing enough to fight back against these damn Germans."

"I was just thinking the same," said Marie-Claire.

"If we want France to be free again we need to become more active and take the fight to the Germans. But what are we doing? You, me and the group? We are helping people escape. Not fight – escape. Although that's important it's not going to get rid of the Germans. We need to do more."

Marie-Claire was pleased to hear such fire in André's words.

"What Pétain signed wasn't an armistice," he continued. "It was total capitulation. It was total surrender. We are literally becoming slaves to the Germans and I, for one, want to fight back."

"I agree. I want to do more as well. We should ask if any of the others in our group also want to do more. We can discuss this at the Café du Monde tomorrow. Depending on what they say it may even mean setting up a different resistance group."

When she arrived at the Café the following evening she was surprised not to see any of the group. Marcel beckoned to her. "They are in the private room at the back. I'll take you through."

When she entered the room, André took her to one side. "Earlier today I sounded out each of our group individually on their feelings about becoming a more active group. I didn't think we should discuss our plans with people who didn't want to participate."

Marie-Claire looked around the room. "But everyone is here, even people who don't normally come on Thursday. I see Tomas and even Madame Favier."

"Yes," said André. "I was quite surprised by the strength of feeling. Everyone seems to want to fight back against the occupation."

Marie-Claire sat down and André addressed the group. "We all know why we are here. We've all agreed we want to do more to stand up against the German occupation of our country. They have destroyed our way of life and hurt so many of our friends and family. The British are fighting from the outside – we need to begin fighting from within. We cannot leave it to the British to defeat the Germans."

"I agree with you," said Tomas, "but what can we do and how are we going to do it? We don't have any weapons or ammunition and the Germans aren't going to give them to us."

"No, you're right," said Gerhard, "but we could steal them from the Germans. And before you ask where from the answer is simple. They ship their armaments and ammunition by train. Derail such a train and we could have a lot of equipment."

"Yes, but if we take too much," cautioned André, "the German army will scour the area to recover it and that could put innocent people at risk. If we do derail such a train we should only steal a few items." He turned to Bernard. "Would you know when such trains are coming?"

He smiled. "Yes. I would. But, and this is a big but, derailing a train could result in killing the engine drivers. I don't think we should do that unless we know the drivers are either collaborators or Germans."

"If we were to derail a train, wouldn't we need a bigger group?" asked Tomas. "While some of us are doing the actual sabotage we'll need lookouts to warn of any approaching Germans. And we'll need places to hide the armaments."

"We need to plan our actions first and then decide if we need new members," said André. "I'm not saying we shouldn't expand, it's just the larger the group the greater the chance of being caught or betrayed. We don't want to introduce new people unless we are sure we can trust them with our lives."

"This is not the same as running the escape line," said Bernard. "It needs to be kept separate from that. Which means we need to have someone new in charge, someone who can plan and take action and who we trust completely. I would like to propose André as the leader."

When everyone nodded agreement André looked around at the

group, took in a deep breath and let it out slowly. "Ok. But if I'm to be leader I want very tight security and all actions must be approved by me before we do anything. It also means, in the interest of security, I might not discuss everything with everybody. That won't mean I don't trust you. It just means I might limit the number of people involved. It will be safer for everyone that way. If you can agree to that, then I'll accept the role."

Nobody raised any objections.

"If our activities are to be successful," said André, "they need to be planned very carefully. Although I like the idea of derailing a German train, it's not something we can rush into. But that said, I'll begin to look at it in detail with Bernard. Meanwhile I'd like you all to give some thought to what we could do and I'll speak to you individually later. Now let's all go back into the main room and have a drink."

At the end of the evening André offered to walk Marie-Claire home. "I didn't ask you in front of the others in case you didn't want to, but I would appreciate if you would be my deputy in this new group. I need someone I can trust to discuss my plans with."

She took a moment to answer. "Yes, if that's what you want, I'm willing."

"Are you free on Sunday morning?" he asked. "I think we need to talk about this new group as soon as possible."

"Yes, I can come to your house, and afterwards I'll take you out for lunch."

The next day Marie-Claire had a quiet chat with Françoise. "Are you available for lunch on Sunday? There's someone I'd like you to meet."

Françoise's eyes lit up. "Is it a man? Is there something brewing that you've kept quiet?"

Marie-Claire shook her head. "Yes the person is a man, but there is nothing brewing as you put it. Remember I told you about Nicole?"

"Your friend who died falling down the stairs? Is this the man she was engaged to? So why are you inviting me?"

"I promised to take him out for lunch and I think it would be better if it wasn't just him and me. And don't worry, I'm not trying to set you up – just cheer him up."

"Of course I'll come. It's typical you though – thinking of others that way."

Saturday was a day Marie-Claire had been dreading for a long time. It would have been the first anniversary of her wedding to her wonderful Emile. She had not been able to tell Françoise because Françoise didn't know about Emile. Only André knew about Emile but she felt to tell him it was her anniversary would be insensitive given Nicole died before they were even married.

Thinking of André and weddings made her realize she hadn't yet given him the portrait of Nicole which she had drawn. She knew it would be very emotional and she had to make sure the moment was right.

After breakfast she went up to her room and sat staring at the portrait she had drawn of Emile soon after he was killed. She was feeling sorry for herself and found it hard to hold back her tears when Madame Favier knocked on the door. She hid the picture quickly and wiped the tears from her face. "Come in."

"That German soldier is here again saying he wants to talk to you. He said something about art. Are you doing another portrait for the Germans?"

"Not that I know of."

Otto? Here today? Of all possible days he had to pick today, when I'm feeling at my lowest. But if he's saying he wants an art lesson then perhaps he has something important to tell me.

Marie-Claire picked up her coat and met Otto outside. Before Madame Favier had time to close the door behind them he asked in a loud voice. "You said you could give me art lessons. Are you free today?"

"Yes. I don't have anything planned for this afternoon." *But if I had, it certainly wouldn't be this. I would never have expected to spend my first wedding anniversary with a German soldier.*

"I thought it might be a good idea to establish our connection," explained Otto. "You know – art teacher and student."

Marie-Claire relaxed. "I see what you mean. A good idea. Can I suggest two o'clock at Le Bistro d'Anjou?"

"Yes. I know the place."

That afternoon at the bistro Marie-Claire chose a seat which was in plain view. Otto arrived on time, and after a short conversation she handed him a sketch pad and pencils. She was pleased to see that Greta's comment that he had potential was quite correct and she actually enjoyed teaching him. At the end of the lesson she gave him an exercise to complete for the next session.

As they left the bistro Otto guided her gently away from the door and out of earshot of any customers. "I have some information for you. I didn't tell you before the lesson for fear it might distract you. Yesterday evening I was translating for a new Gestapo informant who doesn't speak German, and I thought you should know."

Marie-Claire blurted out, "Has someone said something?"

"Don't worry, the informant said nothing you should be concerned about – right now. He gave me details of a safe house in Saint-Eloi and a list of people in the neighbourhood who have shown they are anti-German."

Marie-Claire found it hard not to react. *Fortunately I don't know anyone in Saint-Eloi, but what did Otto mean by 'right now'?*

"He also told me children there made anti-German comments in the street which he said meant their parents were anti-German."

Children making anti-German comments? That's what I was worried about with Philippe saying 'Bang, Bang, Dead. Pile them in a heap.' I'm so glad André took Philippe away.

"I don't quite understand why you're telling me," said Marie-Claire. "You must hear from informants all the time."

"Yes we do. Usually by anonymous notes sent to us at L'Hotel de Paris. However this volunteer informant came in person."

Marie-Claire became wary, "Is this someone I know?"

"When I tell you who it is you must not show any reaction." He paused. "This informant is your school's new deputy headmaster – Monsieur Lefevre."

Chapter 39

Marie-Claire tried desperately not to look alarmed by Otto's revelation that there was a traitor at her school. "I thought you might want to know," he said quietly. Then before turning and walking away he added in a louder voice, "I look forward to our next art lesson."

Marie-Claire was stunned. *Did Otto really just tell me that Monsieur Lefevre is a Gestapo informant? We can't have a spy in our midst, but how can we dispose of a newly appointed deputy headmaster? Tomorrow's meeting with Françoise and André now has a very serious agenda.*

The following morning Marie-Claire went to André's house as planned, but she decided not to say anything about Monsieur Lefevre until after they had met up with Françoise. André did however have some news for her. "I thought you might want to know Jerome came by this morning. He told me that yesterday a body had been found in the river – a German soldier's body."

"Really? Another body. Did he say anything else?"

"Yes. The Germans know that this soldier was a drunk and have accepted that he must have accidentally fallen into the river." André looked at the floor for a long time before adding. "I'm not proud of what we did, but he deserved what happened to him. May Nicole now rest in peace."

He turned away and walked through to the kitchen. Marie-Claire did not follow him as she wanted to give him time on his own. A few minutes later he returned with two cups of coffee. "Let's talk about ways of sabotaging the Germans."

For the next couple of hours they discussed all sorts of options from sabotaging vehicles to blowing up fuel dumps and even blowing up the Pittié Barracks. When André suggested they could start with something simple like cutting telephone lines Marie-Claire remembered something Emile had told her.

"Actually that's not a good idea – especially if we get caught. In July last year Etienne Achavanne, a résistant, was shot on the orders of the German Military Court for doing what you're suggesting – cutting a telephone line."

"Was this person someone you knew?"

"No. It was something my husband told me."

André hesitated before asking, "How long were you married?"

"Not long," she said, stifling a sob. "In fact yesterday would have been our first anniversary."

"Oh, I'm so sorry. I shouldn't have asked."

"Oddly enough, I appreciate you doing so. You're the only person who knows my true situation and somehow being able to mention him makes it easier to bear."

"I know what you mean. You said the other day you lost everything. I know I haven't lost as much as you but Nicole meant everything to me and I don't even have a picture of her."

"Actually – you do. She asked me to do a portrait of her as her wedding present to you. I've never been sure when to tell you."

"A portrait of Nicole? Where is it? I don't suppose you have it with you."

She reached over for her bag, pulled out a parcel and handed it to him. He unwrapped it slowly and carefully. As André sat staring at the picture with tears streaming down his face Marie-Claire began to wonder if she'd done the right thing. She sat quietly, not wanting to interrupt his private moment. Finally he looked up. "Thank you so much. I'll treasure it always."

He stood up and she felt a pang of pain herself as she watched him gently kiss the picture before putting it on the mantelpiece. He stood looking out of the window with his back to Marie-Claire. "It's been a long morning. You said you were taking me out to lunch but I'm not sure I'll be good company."

"I wasn't sure I would be either which is why I've invited my friend Françoise to join us for lunch. I hope you don't mind. In fact, looking at the time, we should be on our way."

"You invited someone else to join us? Am I such bad company?"

251

"Of course not, you silly old fool. I was just thinking of the need to expand the group, and as well as being a good friend I think Françoise is just the sort of person we need."

André's brows furrowed. "Bernard did suggest expanding the group, but we need to be sure we can trust anyone new."

"I trust her absolutely – but just meet her socially first and see what you think. Now get your coat. We don't want to be late."

Françoise was already at the restaurant when Marie-Claire and André arrived. As Marie-Claire had anticipated, André and Françoise got on well and the conversation flowed easily. When Françoise excused herself from the table, André whispered to Marie-Claire, "If you trust her, then yes. We can do with people like her."

When Françoise returned Marie-Claire proposed that instead of coffee at the bistro, they go to André's house. "There's something we need to talk about, but not in public."

Back at André's house Marie-Claire got straight to the point. "Françoise, we are starting a new resistance group. One which is aimed at hurting the Germans and ultimately helping to drive them out. It's early days yet but we need more members." She paused waiting to see what Françoise's reaction would be. She broke into a broad grin when Françoise enthusiastically responded that she would like to join and asked, "So what is this group doing?"

"As we are new," replied André, "it may be a while before —"

"Maybe not that long," interrupted Marie-Claire. "I discovered yesterday that our school has a spy. Our deputy headmaster, Monsieur Lefevre, is actually a Gestapo informant. He has already betrayed a safe house in Saint-Eloi."

André looked shocked and Françoise's face showed real fear. "How do you know?" she asked.

Before Marie-Claire could answer André held up his hand to stop her. "In this group we do not reveal our sources unless absolutely necessary. If Marie says he's a spy that's good enough for me. What we've got to do now is figure out how to nullify the threat he poses."

Marie-Claire shook her head. "Hold on – I'm not thinking we

should kill him. Killing is a bad idea. The Gestapo may want to investigate why their informant died."

She tried not to smile as both Françoise and André agreed that killing a German would not be a good option. She appreciated the fact they were both keeping their individual dark secrets.

"We need to find some way to get him dismissed," said Françoise.

"That wouldn't be enough," countered Marie-Claire. "He might try to seek revenge for his dismissal."

"I see what you mean," said André. "So – any ideas?"

After a short period of silence Françoise exclaimed. "I have it! The one thing the Germans probably hate more than résistants is duplicitous informants. If they find out Monsieur Lefevre is just masquerading as an informant, but is really a dangerous résistant, they'll get rid of him for us."

Marie-Claire smiled, "Yes – that's excellent. All we need to do is have the Gestapo find incriminating evidence showing them that he's actually a résistant. We could plant such evidence in his house and then send an anonymous note to the Gestapo. They are likely to act quickly – and decisively."

"What sort of evidence are you thinking of?" asked André.

"How about multiple ID cards in different names but all with his personal details?" suggested Marie-Claire. "I can arrange to have that done if we can find out his details." She watched with interest to see how André or Françoise would react to her offer, but neither gave any indication that she was already doing forgeries for each of them separately.

André then asked, "Why don't we make it appear to the Gestapo that he is a real danger? I can get hold of plans of the Pittié Barracks where the soldiers live."

"Why would that be seen as dangerous?" asked Françoise.

"On its own it wouldn't be, but if we were to put the plans in his house along with a chart of the barrack sentry times and some explosives and detonators I suspect your deputy headmaster will never be seen again."

"Nice – the Gestapo won't like that," said Marie-Claire. "But first we must warn our friends at school not to say anything incriminating in front of him. I'll have a word with Gerhard."

André added, "And don't forget your headmaster, Stephane."

Françoise looked shocked. "What are you two saying? Are you telling me Monsieur Garnier and Monsieur Thibault are part of this group – that they are secret résistants?"

"I knew Gerhard was," said Marie-Claire, "but Monsieur Thibault? Come on André, own up."

"Stephane likes to keep a low profile, but from what you've just told us it's essential he knows about Monsieur Lefevre."

Françoise shook her head. "The things you learn when you're least expecting to."

André laughed. "They obviously kept that well hidden. But to get back to implicating Lefevre. I can get the plans and maybe even a small amount of explosive. I also know someone who can log the sentry timings. Marie, you said you'll look after the fake ID cards. You can ask Stephane to help you get the deputy's details – he knows you can be trusted. And also see if you can get a copy of his handwriting so you can transcribe the notes about the sentry timings in his handwriting."

"How about planting some foreign money," said Françoise. "I think I can get hold of some British notes. We don't need many. Just enough to show he's working for them."

"Good idea," agreed André. "It looks as if we have a workable plan here, but I think we should keep the plan to ourselves. There's no need to involve anyone else." He turned to Françoise. "Thank you for joining our group. I think it would be a good idea if you meet the others. We have an informal meeting in the Café du Monde on Thursday evenings. It's primarily a social event and it would be a good time to meet them. Do you know it?"

"Yes I do and I'll be there," answered Françoise.

Marie-Claire made sure she got to school early on Monday. She took Monsieur Garnier aside the moment he appeared and whispered, "Don't react to what I'm going to tell you, but our deputy head is in fact a Gestapo informant."

He gulped, "Are you joking?" When she shook her head he continued, "Oh my God! Here – in the school." He looked thoughtful. "Now you mention it, I've noticed he always seems to be starting politically sensitive conversations and now I see why. I don't think we've said anything compromising, do you?"

"No. I don't think we've given him any reason to report us." At this point the headmaster arrived and as he took off his coat Marie-Claire turned to him. "Monsieur Thibault, can I see you for a moment please on a personal matter?"

"Of course. Let's go to my office."

She followed him into his office and closed the door behind her. "I have some critical information for you. Over the weekend I learned that our deputy head is a Gestapo informant."

"Are you serious? How reliable is your source?"

"Completely reliable."

"It would explain some of my misgivings. Recently I've been worried about some of the things he says and frankly I regret having appointed him. Unfortunately I can't dismiss him."

"No. You mustn't do that. It could draw the attention of the Gestapo and could compromise my source."

"Ok, so what can we do? We can't live with this hanging over everything we say."

"Well, André and I have a plan but I need some details which hopefully you can obtain."

Monsieur Thibault nodded. "André has told me in the past that I can trust you unreservedly. So what do you need?"

She replied that she needed an example of Monsieur Lefevre's handwriting and also all the details that appear on his ID card.

Monsieur Thibault's response was simple. "Come and see me on Friday morning."

When Marie-Claire came down for breakfast on Thursday morning she found Madame Favier on her own, buzzing with excitement. She explained that during the night the RAF had dropped thousands of copies of the most recent edition of *Le Courrier de l'Air*, the British newspaper printed in French for the people of France. She passed a copy to Marie-Claire folded up in a napkin. "Take it up to your room to read it. It's great news."

Marie-Claire ate her breakfast rapidly so she could go upstairs. After reading the paper she threw it in the fire as she knew being caught with a copy was punishable by a prison sentence. The paper was dated the day before, 18 March, and the headline stated that a law passed by the US Congress would make it impossible for Hitler to win the war. Although it sounded like good news she didn't quite understand how an American law could affect Hitler.

With Monsieur Lefevre listening in on conversations she could not even mention the RAF newspaper during school hours. She hoped someone might be able to explain the significance on Thursday evening. As Françoise was now a member of the group, they went to the Café du Monde together. When they arrived everyone was talking excitedly about the newspaper. The Café was empty except for the group, which meant they felt they could talk openly.

After Françoise was introduced Marie-Claire asked, "Can someone explain to me how an American law can make it impossible for Hitler to win? Surely no law can stop that man – he doesn't respect laws or treaties."

"You're right, Hitler doesn't," agreed Gerhard. "But the exciting point about this law is that it allows the US President to authorize the supply of war materials to Britain, while still maintaining American neutrality. The President can do so if he deems doing so is 'vital to the defence of the United States'. It means Britain will now get airplanes, munitions, guns and ships from America and America can produce such things faster and more effectively than Germany. I find this news so encouraging."

"When we decided to start our resistance group," commented Bernard, "I was quite sceptical as I couldn't see how Germany could be defeated. But this news has now made me feel that the Allies can and will win – Vivre la France Libre!"

André had been listening in silence. "Yes, this news is really inspiring. It may well take a long time but when the Allies finally invade Europe to drive out the Germans even little resistance groups like ours could have a major impact. We could attack German supply lines, cut power and communications or even derail the trains they use for moving troops around. We need to find a way to obtain the equipment and training to do that kind of sabotage. However that mustn't stop us undertaking simple acts of sabotage right now to make the lives of our German occupiers more difficult."

At that point a group of strangers entered the Café so the discussion moved to less sensitive topics. At the end of the evening André offered to walk Marie-Claire back to her boarding house. After they left the Café he passed her a list his friend had produced of the sentry times at the barracks. "He's even documented their smoking habits and the best time to infiltrate the barracks. Talking of documents, have you been able to get the other things you need?"

"Yes. I should be able to produce everything this weekend. Françoise and I will come to your house on Monday evening to discuss how we go about planting the evidence."

Chapter 40

After school on Friday Marie-Claire and Françoise cycled out to the Deferre's farm. When they arrived Madame Deferre greeted Marie-Claire with genuine warmth. "It's so nice to see you. You can always see this as your second home. Rémi and I were just talking about your cousin. Have you heard from her?"

"No, but I wouldn't expect to for a long time."

"Well I can tell you that we haven't had any news either and that's good. I'm sure we would have heard from down the line if there had been a problem."

"Thank you. That's such a relief."

Before the evening meal Françoise had a quiet word with Marie-Claire. "Papa has given me these three blank ID cards. I assume that'll be enough for our purposes."

"Yes, three cards in different names but with identical personal details should show the Gestapo that Monsieur Lefevre is not being straight with them."

On Saturday morning Marie-Claire spent her time working on the ID cards and the note detailing the sentry patrols at the Pittié Barracks. On Friday Monsieur Thibault had given her a document handwritten by Monsieur Lefevre and she was pleased to see he had a distinctive writing style which she could easily reproduce consistently. She began with the note detailing the sentry patrols.

She had intended to use a different writing style for the ID cards but after finishing the patrol note she changed her mind. She realized it would more incriminating to have the ID cards also written in his hand. For each card she invented an address in a different town in the Occupied Zone. She felt the absence of photographs on the cards was not a problem as having cards filled in but without pictures would actually be more incriminating. It would show that Monsieur Lefevre was actively intending to deceive the Germans, not work for them.

On Monday evening Marie-Claire and Françoise met André at his house. André explained that he could not get actual explosives but that he had been able to obtain some dynamite detonator fuses which would be just as incriminating. He put them on the kitchen table. Françoise put some British money down on the table and Marie-Claire added the fake ID cards and the list of sentry patrols.

"This should be more than sufficient to convince the Germans that their supposed informant is in fact a dangerous résistant," said Marie-Claire. "Now we just have to work out how are we going to plant this evidence?"

"I think I know what we can do," said Françoise. "Apparently Monsieur Lefevre is a devout Catholic and attends a Bible study class every Wednesday at the Cathedral. I checked and the class meets from seven to nine in the evening."

André smiled. "Perfect. I know a German hating locksmith friend who will be more than willing to open the door to your deputy's house while he's away studying his Bible. During that time we can plant the evidence."

"You said 'we'. Are you wanting Marie and I there to help plant the evidence?" asked Françoise.

"No. I want you two to stand outside in the street and act as lookouts while my friend and I stash the items in the house. I'll give you a whistle and if anything awkward happens, such as Lefevre coming home early, you can blow on the whistle and call out as if you're calling for a dog."

"I like the idea of the whistle," said Marie-Claire. "But what do you mean by 'stash? We have to make sure he won't find the evidence himself but the Gestapo will."

"I know," said André. "Houses like his all have attics and I was thinking of putting the items up there."

"But how will the Gestapo know to look there?"

He laughed. "In the anonymous note we send them we'll tell them where to look. Marie, I assume you can write such a note."

"Gladly. We need to plant this evidence as soon as possible."

"I agree," said André. "The sooner the better, before he betrays any more people. I suggest we all meet here Wednesday at six."

When Marie-Claire and Françoise arrived at André's house on Wednesday evening Marie-showed the others the note she had written for the Gestapo.

Nabil Lefevre will blow up Pittié
Barracks Friday bomb in his attic

"That should get their attention," said André.

"We need to leave soon," said Marie-Claire. "When will your locksmith friend get here?"

"He'll meet me at the house," replied André. "He wants to keep his identity hidden."

André put the incriminating evidence in a small bag and they set out. When they reached a position where they could see Monsieur Lefevre's house they stopped and pretended to be having a friendly chat. André faced the house so he could see when Monsieur Lefevre left to go to the Bible class. The girls stood with their backs to the house so if Monsieur Lefevre looked at them he would not recognize them.

Shortly before seven Monsieur Lefevre came out of his house, locked the door and set out towards the Cathedral. When André started to walk towards the house Marie-Claire pulled him back. "Wait a moment until we're sure he's gone."

After a few minutes they felt it was safe. André walked over to the house and went down the side to the back door, leaving the girls to keep watch.

Françoise was puzzled. "Where is the locksmith friend?"

"I'm beginning to think there isn't one. I suspect André didn't want to admit he could break in himself."

They stood quietly for a few minutes before Marie-Claire realized that being quiet could look suspicious. "We need to act naturally," she said to Françoise. "Tell me a joke so we can be seen to be laughing."

Françoise's joke was so hopelessly bad that it had the desired effect of making Marie-Claire laugh. "If we do another stake out like this, I must remember to bring some cigarettes."

"But why? You don't smoke."

"I just need to light it and appear to be smoking. It provides a reason for just standing around talking."

About twenty minutes later André reappeared and whispered, "All done. Time to post the note and go to the Café du Monde for a drink before going home."

"I don't think it would be a good idea to use the post," said Marie-Claire. "I've heard that the postmen often destroy letters addressed to the Gestapo. The Gestapo have a drop off box specifically for denunciation notes just outside their offices at L'Hotel de Paris. Isn't it sad that so many people want to betray their neighbours."

"Dirty traitors," muttered André. "You two go on to the Café and I'll drop the note off at L'Hotel de Paris on my way there."

At school the following day Marie-Claire found it difficult to act normally when she saw Monsieur Lefevre in the staff room talking about a train crash that had happened in Bordeaux. It disturbed her to hear him insist that it was most likely the work of some anarchist résistants. Although she would have liked to say something, she knew it would not be wise. Instead she turned away and went to her classroom.

At mid-morning break Marie-Claire whispered to Françoise, "I'm surprised they haven't taken the note seriously."

Françoise shrugged, "I know. I thought they would have. I suppose they might be waiting for him at his house."

"Let's hope so. We'll see tomorrow."

When Marie-Claire turned up for school on Friday morning Monsieur Thibault called her into his office before classes began. "I thought you might want to know that Monsieur Lefevre will no longer be working here. The official reason is that he was taken ill and felt he should resign."

"You said the 'official reason'. Is that the real reason?"

"It's the reason I will be giving to the others. What I can tell you is I've heard that our Gestapo informant deputy headmaster was arrested last night for being a dangerous résistant. So dangerous, in fact, that he wasn't even interrogated here in Nevers but was immediately taken to Fresnes Prison. I don't want to know how this came about but I can't say I'm upset." He paused before asking, "Should I perhaps be congratulating you and André?"

Marie-Claire smiled back. "I couldn't possibly comment, but thank you for letting me know."

During the mid-morning break Françoise had a quiet chat with Marie-Claire. "Monsieur Thibault said that our deputy head has gone due to illness, but surely that can't be the truth."

"No it isn't," replied Marie-Claire. "The truth is he was arrested last night and taken directly to Fresnes Prison for interrogation. I suspect his insistence that he knows nothing won't go down well given that the timings of the patrols around the barracks are all written in his handwriting." With a smile she added, "One of the best days we've had in a while."

Her feeling this was a good day was reinforced when Madame Favier told her that the two Germans had moved out. "What's even better is they don't know when or even if other officers will move in. It means that right now I'm being paid to keep the rooms empty and we don't have any Germans in the house."

On Saturday morning Marie-Claire went to André's house to tell him about Monsieur Lefevre's arrest. He smiled broadly and said he particularly enjoyed the irony of having the Germans arrest their own man. "I think this calls for a little celebration. I'm away this week on a work job but I'll be back next Saturday. I was thinking it's my turn to invite you for lunch. So, are you willing to come here and risk my cooking?"

"Of course. And I've a nice Côtes du Rhône which needs drinking."

When she arrived at André's house the following Saturday she was amazed at the smells coming from the kitchen. "What have you cooked? It smells delicious."

"I did some work this week for a farmer friend. He used to keep pigs but the Germans kept requisitioning all the best animals and he resents feeding the Germans. He found out that the local German army chefs don't like dealing with rabbit meat so he decided to stop breeding pigs and he's now raising rabbits. I built him some rabbit hutches and in partial payment he gave me a large rabbit. So I've made 'Lapin a la Cocotte'."

"I'm impressed. Do you do much cooking?"

"Not really. This recipe is one Nicole taught me." He paused, "I still find it hard to believe she's gone – I miss her so much."

Marie-Claire wished she could console him. "Of course you do. I still miss my husband every day. I'm not sure the feeling of loss will ever go away."

André pulled a handkerchief out of his pocket and dabbed at his eyes. "I suspect you're right, but I didn't ask you here to discuss the past. We need to look forward."

"Do you have plans for what we'll do next?"

"Not really. Derailing a train is much more complicated than I thought and I'm still bothered by Bernard's comment that derailing a train could kill the French train drivers. Bernard has given me some railway manuals and although they are boring to read, I think there could be some useful information in them which we could use. Hopefully we might be able to create some havoc without killing anybody. It will, however, require detailed planning."

It was late afternoon when Marie-Claire said goodbye. She complemented André on the delicious meal before walking back to her boarding house. She enjoyed André's company and felt they had a special bond because they had both lost the love of their life.

Towards the end of April when Marie-Claire and Françoise met for their Sunday walk in Parc Roger Salengro they heard a band playing in Le Kiosque de Nevers and wandered over to listen. As they approached the bandstand they stopped and stared in disgust. The bandstand was covered in red banners emblazoned with swastikas. The band wore German uniforms and most of the crowd were German officers in dress uniform.

"Not more of these loathsome swastikas, they're already all over the town," moaned Françoise. "And there are so many Germans here. Even our parks are no longer refuges from these damn German invaders."

Marie-Claire agreed. "Now we know who's making the music I don't want to hear any more of it. I hope they won't be doing this every Sunday."

An elderly Frenchman who was passing by had obviously overheard Marie-Claire's comment. "Excuse me mademoiselle, I could not help but hear what you said. You'll be pleased to learn they won't be doing the same again for another year. Today, the 20th of April, is Hitler's birthday and they are obliged to celebrate it. I, however, am not obliged to do so and I won't celebrate the birth of that man – his death, yes, but certainly not his birth." He mimed spitting on the ground and wandered off.

"Well that man's certainly not a supporter of the Führer," commented Françoise. "Now we know what the music is all about, let's go somewhere where we can't hear it."

As they walked away Marie-Claire looked back and was shocked to see two German soldiers grab the elderly man and march him away. "Do you think he was overheard criticizing Hitler?"

"I don't know," replied Françoise. "Let's get out of here quickly in case they saw us talking to him."

The two girls hurried away and didn't say anything until they were out of the park. "This is no way to live," complained Françoise.

"You're right. We need to up our game and become more proactive. We need to fight harder and more directly against the Germans if we're ever going to be free."

Chapter 41

The following week André arranged a meeting of the group at his house to discuss ideas for sabotage. Marie-Claire was amazed at the suggestions they were coming up with. She liked the proposal to set fire to the Gestapo offices but feared the Germans might retaliate. She thought some of the ideas were quite promising such as contaminating food that was being shipped to Germany, blowing up fuel dumps and sabotaging German vehicles.

After a while the stream of new ideas tailed off. "Thank you," said André. "I think some of your suggestions can be done without special equipment and I'll start planning our first actions. If anybody knows a trustworthy mechanic, let me know."

"I know of someone," said Odile. "I'll make a discreet enquiry."

On Thursday everyone at the Café du Monde was talking about a leaflet the RAF had dropped all over the town. It was dated the 1st of May, International Labour Day, and was a message from the Workers of Coventry in England to the Workers of France. "Look," said Gerhard. "It says that in spite of bomb damage in Coventry, the English workers are still working night and day to produce the armaments needed to defeat the Germans and liberate France."

"Yes," said André. "It's reassuring to know that France has not been forgotten. It makes me feel our efforts against the Germans will be worthwhile even if they are small."

The following Wednesday when Marie-Claire went to André's house for their regular planning meeting he was keen to tell her about a sabotage activity he had successfully completed. Over the weekend, with Bernard's assistance, he and some of the group had been able to sabotage a food train heading to Germany. They had put rats into the freight cars and sprayed wheat sacks with kerosene. They had even smeared excrement onto meat carcasses. When he told her what they'd done to the meat she grimaced and said how pleased she was he had not asked her to join them.

Marie-Claire was puzzled by the air of tension she felt when she entered the school staff room on Monday. Everyone was looking upset and talking in low voices. She went over to Gerhard and Françoise who were sitting together and asked, "What's happened? Why is everyone looking so upset?"

"Haven't you heard?" asked Gerhard.

"Heard what?"

"During the night the Gestapo, with the help of the local police, rounded up and arrested many Jewish men. They also arrested some résistants. They've been taken to Nevers Prison. No one's allowed to see them and we can't even ask after them."

"Apparently," added Françoise, "asking if a certain person has been arrested puts that person in danger if they haven't yet been arrested. And it also endangers the person who is asking."

"How many have been arrested?" asked Marie-Claire.

"We're not sure," replied Gerhard, "but from what I've heard, at least thirty. And I know some of them."

Marie-Claire had a vivid recollection of the terrifying time in Paris when she and Emile had heard Madame and Monsieur Coutreau being arrested. It sent a shiver down her spine. She turned to Gerhard. "Did you say they arrested some résistants?"

"Yes. People in another group who collect and redistribute the RAF newspaper, *Le Courrier de l'Air*, were betrayed by one of their members. It makes me wonder who we can trust."

That evening Marie-Claire, Françoise and Gerhard went to see André to discuss if there was anything they could do. André had already heard about the arrests from Jerome. "He came to see me," said André, "to explain that he was involved but had no choice. He said if he had refused to make the arrests he would have been arrested himself and he would no longer have been able to help us fight the Germans. But I can assure you he was extremely upset."

"I can well believe that," said Françoise.

"Apparently the round-up was not as successful as the Gestapo had wanted," said André. "For some inexplicable reason some of the people were not at the addresses Jerome had been given. He didn't admit to anything but I think he was able to warn some people to disappear ahead of the arrests."

"I hope he was successful in warning people," said Gerhard. "How awful to have to arrest someone you know."

"It's one thing to be upset about this," said André, "but as a resistance group we have to ask ourselves if there's any way we can free these people."

"Are you being serious André?" asked Françoise. "They're in prison, so what can we possibly do?"

André looked quite dejected. "I don't know. But we know some of the people. We can't just abandon them. We have to try and find a way to do something. I just feel so helpless."

A couple of weeks later as Marie-Claire was getting ready to go to the Café du Monde Madame Favier knocked on her door. "That German who wants art classes is here. Do I tell him you're in?"

Although Marie-Claire wanted to say no because she was expecting Françoise to arrive any minute, she told Madame Favier it was fine and that she'd be right down. She knew that Otto wouldn't have called if it wasn't important.

When she came downstairs she found Otto standing in the hall. "I've done the sketching exercises you set for me last time."

"That's good. Are you wanting another lesson?"

"Yes please, if that's convenient Mademoiselle Bruneau."

"Would Saturday work for you Corporal Voigt?"

"Saturday is fine. Shall we say two o'clock in the same bistro?"

Marie-Claire agreed and Otto turned and left. *What critical news has he got now? Perhaps the name of another informant?*

Madame Favier came out of her room. "Is everything alright?"

"Oh yes. He's not a bad artist and pays for his lessons. Talking of Germans, any news on the replacements for the two officers?"

"Yes. I was told yesterday that no officers will be moving in after all and they no longer need my rooms."

"I guess that means you can have French people here again."

"Yes. But we still need to be vigilant," said Madame Favier. "Too many French people have become informants."

At that point Françoise arrived. "I saw a German soldier leaving the house. Have the replacement officers moved in?"

"No. It was that German translator wanting another art lesson."

"Are you still doing that?"

"Yes. I don't feel I can refuse."

When Marie-Claire and Françoise arrived at the Café du Monde, they found the group discussing an article from the front page of the *Le Petit Parisien*. The article reported that 5,000 Jews, mostly foreign, had been arrested and sent by train to various concentration camps and that these so-called *undesirables* would be put to work building the camps.

"I found the article very distressing," said Marie-Claire. "The Germans are using these people as slaves. That can't be right."

Gerhard shook his head. "No, it's not right. Hitler views Jews and other *undesirables*, as the paper put it, as non-people and treats them as slaves – literally slaves."

"If he sees Jews as slaves, does that mean the people arrested here in Nevers will become Hitler's slaves as well?"

"Quite possibly," said André with a glum expression. "I keep wondering if there's some way we can free them but I can't think of anything."

"Neither can I," said Tomas. "If they weren't in prison we could perhaps do something, but while they're behind bars there's not much we can do."

On Saturday it was raining heavily and Marie-Claire did not really want to venture out in such bad weather, but she had no idea how to contact Otto to postpone the art lesson even if she wanted to. And anyway, if he had important information she needed to hear it. *I dread to think what he might tell me this time.*

Wrapped up well in her raincoat and with her sketch books in a waterproof bag, she hurried through the rain to the Bistro d'Anjou. She arrived well ahead of the time she was due to meet Otto. At the Bistro she was upset to see a group of rowdy German soldiers drinking inside. Rather than sit inside and attract unwanted attention she sat outside under the awning with a warming drink.

As she sat there she heard the unmistakeable thump, thump, thump of hob-nailed boots. She looked up and saw a platoon of German soldiers marching up the street. She got out her sketch pad and did three quick sketches, soldiers approaching, soldiers in front of her and soldiers marching away. After they'd gone she looked at all three sketches and decided that the last one could be turned into a picture which expressed her feelings.

The main aspect of the new picture, the one which she wanted to have dominate and define the image, was the big, heavy, dark boots of the receding German soldiers. The soldiers had been leaning forward against the wind with their bodies covered in massive rain capes. They appeared to have no heads, just beetle-like helmets on top of their capes. As a finishing touch, she added slanting lines representing the pelting rain, emphasizing the overbearingly dismal sense of the scene.

When the picture was finished she realized she had just drawn an allegory of life as she now knew it. The freedom to travel around her France – *trampled!* The freedom to talk freely – *trampled!* Even the freedom to live and love – *trampled!* All trampled by the oppressive nature of the German occupation of her country.

Sitting back and looking at the final picture she did something she seldom did – she dated it – *Nevers 1941.*

This was not a picture to show to Otto. *He's a light in the darkness. Maybe just a small light, but still a light and I don't want to do anything which might extinguish it.*

It was almost time for her meeting with Otto so she went back inside and found a suitable table for the art lesson. Soon a rather wet Otto arrived and took off his soaking raincoat. As he sat down he commented, "What a terrible day. I see you've finished your drink Marie. Would you like another?"

While they waited for the drinks to arrive he took out his sketches and showed them to her. She was impressed and felt he had the potential to be a really good artist. Teaching him reminded her of the art classes she used to run in her apartment in Paris before the German occupation. *A different time and a different life.*

After an hour Otto said it was time for him to be heading back. She set him some more exercises and they tidied up their art materials and went outside. Although the awning provided a measure of cover from the weather, the rising wind meant no one was now sitting outside. Otto turned to Marie-Claire. "I thought it would be good if we establish a pattern of lessons, so that if in the future I need to tell you something it doesn't look out of the ordinary."

Marie-Claire relaxed. "A good idea. I must say you worried me on Thursday when you asked for a lesson. I feared you might have some critical information as you did last time."

"No. I have nothing critical to tell you. I just thought we should set the pattern." He paused. "But you might be interested to know that your deputy headmaster was arrested. The Gestapo discovered he was actually working for the resistance." He suddenly changed his tone as two people walked by. "And thank you for your comments on my sketches. I look forward to our next art lesson Mademoiselle Bruneau."

"So do I Corporal Voigt."

He smiled, pulled his raincoat around him and walked away.

And I came out in this pelting rain just to set a pattern? At least Otto confirmed Monsieur Lefevre was arrested and I suppose I did draw a powerful picture, even if it is of these damn Germans.

As she hurried home through the rain a car stopped beside her and a voice she knew well called out to her to get in. "Thank you Jerome. This rain is really heavy."

"I was coming to see you anyway. Ingrid has told me that one of her German clients let slip that the Jewish prisoners will be shipped out in freight cars next Saturday night."

"Are you sure? André hasn't said anything about that."

"The soldier works in L'Hotel de Paris and was drunk at the time so I think it's probably true."

"If that's the case, please drive me straight to André's house."

270

Chapter 42

Jerome stopped the car outside André's house and Marie-Claire dashed through the pouring rain to the front door and knocked. Fortunately André was in, but he looked very concerned when he saw the police car. "What's happened? Why is Jerome here?"

"Don't worry. He's given me some important information and I asked him to drive me here so I could tell you." She waved to Jerome who drove off. "The Jewish and resistance prisoners arrested recently are to be moved out of the jail next Saturday."

"You don't mean they're being freed, do you?"

"No. They're to be transferred to Paris by train."

"And I thought you had good news," said André gloomily.

"It is good news. Tomas was right when he said we couldn't do anything while they were behind bars, but perhaps we can do something while they're being moved."

"But what? Attack the trucks taking them to the station? Hold up the train? Come on Marie, there's nothing we can do."

"Think of it. No one would expect us to hold up the train. That would be a crazy idea – which means it might just work."

"You're serious aren't you?" André looked thoughtful for a moment. "My God. It's so stupid, the Germans are unlikely to have taken precautions against it. You might be on to something. Let's get the group together here tomorrow morning and see what the others think. I'll go and talk to Bernard now." He looked out of the window. "It's still raining hard. I was going to suggest you could go around and tell the others to come here tomorrow but I can't ask you to do that in this weather."

"André – it's just rain. I don't mind getting completely soaked if it means we can perhaps free those prisoners."

On Sunday morning Marie-Claire was the first to arrive at André's house. "I talked to everyone and they should all be coming. Odile asked me if she could bring Robert with her and I agreed."

"Who's Robert? And why did you agree?"

"You asked if anyone knew a mechanic. Robert owns and runs the Gaudin Garage and could be useful."

"What? That garage does lots of work for the Germans. I don't see how we can trust him."

"I can assure you we can. He's Suzette's father and Odile says he'll never forgive the Germans for what happened to his daughter."

"I see what you mean. You were right to have agreed. He could certainly be very useful."

When everyone had arrived André explained the reason for the meeting. "We've learned the prisoners will be moved by train next Saturday and I think it gives us an opportunity to free them."

"So we form a wild west posse and hold up the train, do we?" laughed Tomas. "Come on André. Is that your big idea? Really?"

"Basically, yes. I'll let Bernard explain."

"When André came to see me yesterday I checked the train details. The prisoners will be transported out of Nevers by a train which is scheduled to leave at eleven on Saturday night. It's final destination is Paris. Apparently the prisoners will then be taken to the Drancy concentration camp."

"Isn't Drancy that terrible place the Germans use as a transit prison before transporting people to German and Polish concentration camps?" asked Gerhard.

"Yes it is," confirmed Bernard. "That's why we need to stop the train and get these people off."

"I don't see how we can stop a high speed train on the main line to Paris," said Robert.

Bernard smiled. "If that was the situation I would agree, but it isn't. This train is going up the slow single track line to Clamecy where more prisoners will be picked up."

"And you are suggesting that somewhere along that line we stop the train, free the prisoners and then let the train continue. Is that the idea?" asked Odile.

"In essence, yes," replied André.

"But how are we going to stop the train?" asked Gerhard.

"By blocking the line so the train has to stop," replied Bernard. "Blockages quite often occur on rural lines. It would have to be something which can be cleared away – but not quickly. We can free the prisoners while the blockage is being cleared."

"Could we cut down a tree to block the line?" asked Tomas.

Bernard shook his head. "It's important that whatever we do looks like an accident. Cutting down a tree would be an obvious sign of an attack and the guards would know that."

"Guards! You didn't say anything about guards," exclaimed Françoise. "Are you actually suggesting we hold up an armed train at night? Have you forgotten we have no guns and no training?"

"Actually, it's not as impossible as it sounds," replied Bernard. "According to the information I have, when the train leaves Nevers it will have eight wagons. At this stage there'll only be two guards, one officer and one soldier, both in the first wagon. The last wagon will have our prisoners and the middle ones will be empty for more prisoners being collected further down the line. If we can block the line with something which the guards can help clear, then while they're doing that we can free the prisoners."

"If the blockage is to appear as an accident could it be done where a road crosses the railway line?" asked Marie-Claire.

"Yes," replied Bernard. "Have you got an idea?"

"Perhaps a truck could appear to have broken down spilling its load onto the track."

"Not a truck," said Robert. "It would be too easy to identify afterwards and also just because it breaks down doesn't mean it would spill its load."

Françoise clapped her hands together. "I've got it. A cart loaded with large stones could appear to have lost a wheel as it crossed the track and spilled its load onto the crossing. This would block the line but the stones could be cleared away by the soldiers and the cart driver."

"If the cart driver is a woman then the soldiers are even more likely to help clear the blockage," suggested Tomas.

"What do you think, Bernard?" asked André. "Is this realistic?"

"That sort of accident is not unheard of and it could appear quite plausible."

"Hold on. How do we stop the train from ploughing straight into the pile of stones?" asked Françoise.

"We warn the approaching train by using petards and a red lantern," replied Bernard. "It's a standard procedure."

"What's a petard?" asked Madame Favier.

"It's a small explosive like a firecracker that's placed on the track and goes off when the engine crushes it. The loud bang warns the engine driver that there is a problem up ahead and the red lantern tells him to stop the train," explained Bernard. "We use them all the time to warn trains of a problem on the line."

André turned to Bernard. "Where can we get some?"

"At unmanned crossings there is an emergency box containing petards and a red lantern."

"What do you mean by an 'unmanned crossing'?"

"At most places where a road crosses the track without a bridge, the train company has built a house and the occupant has the job of lowering a barrier across the road when a train is approaching. At an unmanned crossing there's no house and no barrier. Unfortunately, most crossings on this line are manned. Only a few are not and we have to use an unmanned crossing so no one sees what we're doing and reports it. If they did, the train would be stopped long before it reached our blockage."

"So which crossing can we use?" asked Françoise.

"There are a couple of unmanned crossings near Poisson."

"Before we go any further," said André, "we've got to decide if we actually want to proceed. It could be very dangerous."

"Yes, it is dangerous. But it's our only hope of releasing the prisoners," stated Marie-Claire. "I say yes."

Although Gerhard and Madame Favier did not feel they were up to being actively involved, they offered to help behind the scenes. All of the others volunteered without hesitation.

André smiled. "Although we have the outline of a plan, there are some important details which need to be resolved. Françoise, you suggested an old cart. Was that just an idea?"

"No. There's an old oxcart in one of the barns at my parent's farm. They'll be glad to get rid of it. The only problem is how to transport it."

"I can do that," said Robert. "If you're free this afternoon we can collect it in one of my covered trucks."

"Fine, but where do we get an obliging ox?" asked Gerhard.

Marie-Claire laughed. "We don't need a real ox."

"If this is an oxcart laden with stones, won't the guards ask where the ox is?"

"We'll tell them it was unhitched and put into one of the adjoining fields," said Marie-Claire. "Which means, Bernard, the unmanned crossing you select must have some woods and fields nearby to hide the non-existent ox."

"There is a problem you don't seem to have considered," said Madame Favier. "Some of the prisoners may recognize you. How do we trust they won't accidentally reveal that you're the ones who freed them."

"Balaclavas and silence," replied Tomas. "If we all wear black balaclavas and keep totally quiet they won't recognize us."

"I like knitting," said Madame Favier, "so if anyone needs a black balaclava just let me know and I'll make it. It'll be my contribution to this operation."

"We can't be quiet," said Bernard. "It'll be dark when we free the prisoners and it won't be anywhere they're familiar with. If we don't talk to them how will they know where they are?"

"I have a friend who can print some small maps of the area," said Gerhard. "As you release the prisoners you could just hand them a map and that way you won't need to speak to them."

"Excellent," exclaimed André. "This is looking good and I think we have enough to get on with. I'll leave the maps to you Gerhard. Robert, you and Françoise are going to the Deferre farm to collect and store the old oxcart. Angélique, you're knitting balaclavas. Finally, if you're free this afternoon Bernard, I suggest you, me and Marie check out a suitable crossing point. If there are no further questions let's meet up again on Wednesday evening to finalize our plans."

275

There was a definite murmur of excitement as the meeting broke up. Bernard and Marie-Claire stayed behind and after a quick lunch set off with André in search of a suitable railway crossing. Bernard gave André directions. "I suggest we go quite far north, past Poiseux to Poisson. There are some unmanned crossings in that area."

In Poisson André turned off the main road and headed east. Within a kilometre they found what they were looking for – an unmanned crossing. The road crossed the railway track and there were no houses nearby. André stopped the van and they got out to look more closely at the crossing and surrounding area.

"What do you think?" asked Bernard.

"While it meets the criteria of being unmanned," said André, "I don't like the road being straight in both directions. It means it would be difficult to hide our vehicles. I'm not keen."

"Neither am I," said Marie-Claire. "We need some woods nearby to hide the non-existent ox and there are none here."

"Ok, we're agreed this crossing is not suitable," said André. "Bernard, did you say there was another crossing nearby?"

"Yes, turn around and at the fork in the road we just passed drive south."

When André stopped at the next railway crossing he smiled. "I may be mistaken but this looks perfect."

"I couldn't have designed this better," said Marie-Claire. "Look, we've got an unmanned crossing where a track crosses the railway between two parallel roads. And there's a farm track leading away in another direction. There are no houses nearby and there are woods all around. André you mentioned hiding the vehicles. Effectively you've got five roads to choose from and none of them are straight."

"Better still," said Bernard, "it'll give the prisoners five alternative routes to escape down. And there's plenty of options to hide your non-existent ox Marie. As I expected, there's an emergency box near the crossing. It should have petards and a lantern. This crossing makes the whole plan viable."

Marie-Claire nodded. "If you've both seen enough, we should

get out of here quickly. We don't want someone seeing us here as they may remember us if they're questioned after the hold-up."

On the drive back to Nevers André pointed out that they hadn't decided who would be the driver of the oxcart. "It can't be you Bernard, as the engine drivers would recognize you."

"Actually, I can't be directly involved on the night," said Bernard. "The Germans will expect me to be at the station."

"It's obvious," said Marie-Claire. "It has to be me."

"No," said André forcefully. "I can't let you take such a risk."

"André. Have you forgotten that this whole train hold-up idea was mine? Also Tomas pointed out that the driver should be a woman so the soldiers are forced to help remove the stones."

André remained quiet. Finally Bernard broke the silence. "I have to agree with Marie. She is much more likely to convince the soldiers that it was an accident, especially if she's dressed as a young girl."

"I'm glad you agree," said Marie-Claire. "There are two things I'll need. I don't want to endanger all of us if I'm caught so I'll need false ID papers that put me living somewhere else, such as Dijon."

Bernard smiled. "If I recall correctly that's how we first met, in the station when you had a problem with your false ID card."

She laughed. "So we did. That's a long time ago."

"You said you needed two things. What's the second?"

"I'll need a disguise of some sort. I'll need a blonde wig to hide my dark hair but I can't go and openly buy one."

"No need," said Bernard. "My sister had one and she left it behind when she moved to Paris. I'll bring it on Wednesday."

"I don't like you being the oxcart driver," said André, "but I suppose it is the best idea. All we need now is a big pile of stones."

On Wednesday Marie-Claire arrived at André's house before the others as she wanted to talk to him about something which had been worrying her. "André, this train hold-up on Saturday. Are you going to be alright that day?"

He looked at her. "You're not the only person who has asked me. It should have been our wedding day – Nicole and I. The

277

thirty-first of May was supposed to be a day of celebration." He paused and wiped his eyes. "I'll be ok, and taking action against the Germans that day is probably the best thing for me. Nicole knew some of the people we'll be freeing and would certainly have approved of what we're doing."

He stood at the window, looking out. "Thank you for asking. Only you and I know how hard it is for you to talk of weddings."

The members of the group arrived soon after and there was genuine excitement when André told them that they had found a perfect place for the hold-up.

"I would like to suggest a slight change to the plan," said Robert. "I know where there's a stack of large logs which we could use instead of stones. Logs would be better than stones because stones can be picked up by one person. Large logs require two people to move them which is why the cart driver couldn't have cleared the blockage."

"Are you suggesting we steal the logs?" questioned Gerhard.

"No. I'm sure the owner of the logs will gladly loan them to the cause. After the train has passed through, we can collect them up and return them."

"Why do you think he'd be willing to help us that way?" asked Françoise. "And can we trust him?"

Robert smiled. "He can be trusted and I'm sure he'll help – one of the prisoners we will be freeing is a relation of his."

On Friday night Marie-Claire found it difficult to sleep. She kept going over and over the plan in her head, trying to make sure she had thought of everything. She knew if she wasn't able to act convincingly the German soldiers guarding the train would suspect something. If they did, she had no doubt she would be arrested, if not shot on the spot.

Chapter 43

On Saturday Marie-Claire spent most of the day going over the details of the plan. She knew she had to make her actions appear genuine and she rehearsed all sorts of scenarios so she would have a ready answer to any questions she might be asked.

I won't admit I understand German as it could be a tactical advantage. Come to think of it, even Otto doesn't know I now have a good working knowledge of German.

She went to André's house in the late afternoon with her clothes for that evening in a bag. She would be the only one not in black. Françoise had lent her a pair of farm worker's dungarees and she had chosen a simple blouse and lightweight jacket. When she had said she would be cold without a warm coat André had replied, "Remember that you, as the girl driving the oxcart, would not have expected to be out so late so you wouldn't have taken a warm coat. Also being seen to be cold could help make your story look genuine."

When everyone had arrived André went over the plan for a final time. Marie-Claire was to stop the train and persuade the German guards to help move the logs. The men were to open the last wagon and help the prisoners out. Odile was to hand out the maps to the freed prisoners. Françoise's job was to be the lookout and blow a whistle if she saw the soldiers moving towards the last wagon before all the prisoners had been freed. When all of the prisoners had been freed André was to blow the all clear on a wooden whistle which made an owl-like sound.

At half past nine they set out. Robert took Françoise and Tomas in his truck loaded with the old oxcart. Marie-Claire and Odile went with André. Jerome had given them details of German checkpoints for that night and they were able to use back roads and rural tracks to avoid them. It took them almost an hour to reach the crossing and when they arrived they saw Robert's friend,

Leon, was already there with a load of large logs. Each log was too heavy for a man to be able to pick up, let alone a girl, but light enough for two men to move.

They had been told by Bernard that the prisoner train was the only train scheduled to use the line that night so they were able to set up the apparent accident immediately. Françoise and Marie-Claire walked down the track towards Nevers to apply the petards to the rail tracks. When they returned they saw that the men had unloaded the oxcart from Robert's truck and manoeuvred it onto the crossing. Robert and Tomas broke off one of the wheels and Leon tipped his load of logs onto the crossing. The three vehicles were then driven away down separate roads and hidden.

Marie-Claire sat down beside the tracks. There was nothing she could do now except wait. Just before midnight she heard the railway tracks begin to sing, indicating that the train was approaching. She removed the overcoat she had borrowed and put on the long blonde wig. The others all pulled on their balaclavas and took up their positions in the woods alongside the track.

With trembling hands Marie-Claire lit the red lantern and was amazed at how much light it gave. Shivering now with fear as well as cold, she walked down the tracks towards the approaching train. She knew the success of the whole venture depended on what she did next.

She heard the petards explode, followed by the screech of the engine applying its brakes. She held up the red lantern. Against all wartime regulations, the engine driver turned on the large bright spotlight at the front of the engine. It almost blinded her so she turned her head away to shield her eyes. The engine came to a stop almost exactly where she was standing. The engine driver shouted down. "What's wrong? Why do we need to stop?"

Marie-Claire walked closer to the engine and shouted up. "My cart broke down on the crossing a few hours ago. A wheel came off and the load of logs has fallen onto the track. I can't move them – they're too heavy for me. I felt I couldn't leave as a train could crash into them. I saw the emergency box and found the firecrackers and lantern. Did I do the right thing?"

The driver shouted down. "Absolutely. Thank you for doing that. You prevented a serious accident."

"Warum haben vir aufgehört?" shouted a rough German voice.

Marie-Claire had not expected the two soldiers to appear so quickly. Although she knew the German officer was demanding to know why the train had stopped, she just acted frightened and shouted at the driver in French. "What is this man saying? I don't understand German. What are these two soldiers doing here?"

The driver shouted down to the German officer in German. "She doesn't speak German. She said she was driving her cart when it broke down on the crossing. Look ahead along the line. You can see the cart and its load. It needs to be cleared before we can proceed."

The German shouted back. "Well you two in the engine, get down and clear it."

Marie-Claire was not sure if the driver guessed what might be happening when he shouted back. "I can't leave the engine. It's against regulations. And I have a bad back. I certainly couldn't lift those logs. You and the other soldier will need to clear the logs."

The officer barked back. "No! Your engine stoker and the girl will have to do it."

He grabbed Marie-Claire by the arm and started marching her towards the logs while gesturing to the stoker to follow them.

The other German asked, "What shall I do, sir?"

"Stay with the engine Krause," came the reply.

They had only taken a few steps towards the cart when the officer turned back and shouted up to the driver. "Something's wrong. Where's the horse that pulled this cart? Ask her."

Again Marie-Claire gave no indication that she understood what he was saying. When the driver translated the question she replied, "The Germans stole all our horses."

"I don't think our German officer will like that reply," said the driver. "So, if not a horse, what was pulling the cart?"

"My ox," Marie-Claire shouted back.

When the driver translated her reply the officer let go of her arm, stood back and pointed his pistol at her. "I see no ox. Ask her why there's no ox here," he shouted in a threatening voice. When the driver translated Marie-Claire replied that she had unhitched the ox and put him in a field as she wasn't sure the train would stop and didn't want the train to kill her ox.

The German officer seemed satisfied with the answer, lowered his pistol, grabbed Marie-Claire's arm again and pushed her towards the logs. *I'm glad I thought of the invisible ox in a field. It appears to have worked. But I've got to get that Krause soldier away from the train and over here lifting logs.*

As the officer stood watching Marie-Claire and the stoker attempted to lift one of the logs. Whereas the stoker was able to pick up one end Marie-Claire was completely unable to lift such a weight. She didn't need to pretend, she just couldn't pick it up.

The officer began shouting at her in German, telling her to try harder, his voice rapidly becoming more and more belligerent. Marie-Claire decided she had to take a risk. She turned to him, pointed to the logs and shook her head. She spoke to him in French. "I'm not strong enough. I can't pick up such a weight." *Will he understand what I'm trying to tell him, or will he threaten me with his gun again. At least all this delay should give André and the others more time to free the prisoners.*

The officer looked at her with contempt written all over his face. He then yelled, "Krause! Get over here and help. We need to clear the logs away and this stupid girl is too weak to do anything."

When Krause appeared the officer waved his gun at Marie-Claire, motioning her to get out of the way. She stood back and watched. She looked towards the train and was again momentarily blinded by the bright light on the engine. Initially she was frustrated at not being able to see but then she realized how fortuitous the bright light was. If the officer or Krause or even the stoker looked back towards the train, they would not be able to see anything beyond the light either.

The two Germans now had their backs to her and although she would have liked to slip away, she knew she must not. So instead she just stayed at the crossing, shaking with cold. And with fear.

Krause and the stoker were clearing the logs faster than she expected and she began to worry as she had not heard André's owl whistle. She watched with rising concern as they heaved the last log away and started dragging the cart off the rails. Still no signal from André.

With the crossing now cleared of logs, the officer raised his gun and motioned to Marie-Claire that she should walk back towards the engine. *Oh no! It's too soon – I haven't heard the signal that all of the prisoners have been freed. I've got to do something to stall the Germans.* She did the only thing she could think of and pretended to trip. She fell and let out a yell of pain as she landed on the gravel of the railway line.

Neither German made any move to help but the stoker immediately knelt down beside her. "Are you alright? That was a nasty fall. Do you need help getting up?"

"I'm not sure," replied Marie-Claire. "Just give me a moment to catch my breath." *Come on André blow the all clear, I can't keep stalling.*

The German officer gestured impatiently and the stoker helped Marie-Claire to her feet. *Oh no – what can I do now?* At that point she heard the sound of an owl hooting. It sounded quite close. *Thank heavens.* She turned to the stoker, "Thank you for helping me. I think I'm ok. I just tripped."

They continued walking back towards the train. As the stoker climbed back into the engine, the officer shouted up to the driver in German. "I think I'll arrest the girl for being out after curfew and put her with the other prisoners from Nevers."

Marie-Claire felt her heart rate soar. *When he finds the prisoners have gone, he'll certainly shoot me.*

Chapter 44

The German officer turned to the other soldier. "Take this girl to the prison wagon."

"Wait," the engine driver shouted down to the officer. "You could be making a big mistake if you do that. I'll have to make a report of the blockage and I'll be praising this young girl for preventing a major crash. If she had left the logs and gone home before curfew there could have been a serious accident which could have derailed the train and possibly killed all of us. I'm not sure arresting a young girl who saved your life will look good on that report. You should be thanking her, not arresting her."

"Very well then," the officer said with a snarl. "I'll let her go."

A lifeline! The driver must be one of Bernard's people.

The driver shouted down to Marie-Claire in French. "Can you get home on your own?"

"Yes I can. I know the area. And thank you."

"What are you talking about?" shouted the officer in German.

"She says she can get home on her own. We've lost a lot of time. You two should get back on the train so we can get going before another train crashes into the back of us."

Marie-Claire smiled to herself as she knew the driver was lying about the possibility of there being another train. *He's obviously said that in order to get the Germans back on the train quickly. I wonder if he's guessed what has happened.*

The officer looked again at Marie-Claire with a steely glare. After what seemed a very long time he lowered his gun and turned to Krause. "Get back in the wagon and we can get going."

Marie-Claire watched as the two Germans climbed back into the wagon. The train slowly began moving forward and was soon out of sight. Realizing she was now safe, tears of relief started to flow and she sank to her knees in the rough grass at the side of the track. *Has this worked? Did everyone get out? Where is André?*

Just then she heard André calling her name. As she struggled to her feet he appeared and gave her a crushing hug. "I was so concerned when I saw you fall. And when he threatened to arrest you I almost shouted out. I feared he might just shoot you out of spite as the train pulled away. I could never have forgiven myself if they'd shot you. Are you sure you're ok?"

"I'm fine. Shaken but fine. And you – are you ok? Did it work?"

"It worked perfectly – we freed all the prisoners. They've all gone in different directions and they know it's up to them now."

"Do they know it was us? Do they know who we are? Could they identify us if they are caught?"

"No. Nobody revealed their identity, even when they saw someone they knew."

"Good. Knowing everyone escaped makes it all worthwhile."

"What you did was amazing. You made it look so genuine."

"Genuine? I can assure you I was genuinely frightened when he kept pointing the gun at me."

"I'm so proud of you but I'll never let you do something so dangerous again. It was wrong of me to ask."

"You didn't ask. If you recall I said it had to be me. I did it for the prisoners and to fight back against our German oppressors."

In the background she heard two vehicles approaching. Instinctively she turned to run but André stopped her. "It's just Leon and Robert coming to take away the evidence. We've got to clear up and get out of here before the alarm is raised."

"What are they going to do with the old cart? Françoise said her father didn't want it back, and anyway it could put him in danger if it was found on his farm."

"All taken care of," replied André. "Robert plans to dump it in the field of a farmer who he knows is a Nazi collaborator."

The journey back was uneventful and she and Odile were able to slip in the backdoor of the boarding house without being seen.

Marie-Claire slept late on Sunday. When she woke it was already almost midday. She lay in bed feeling elated about the success of the previous night's mission. She could scarcely believe what she had achieved. *Emile would have been proud of me. How different I am now from the scared girl in Paris who didn't want to get involved when he first started his resistance group.*

She looked at her watch and realized she had to hurry as she had arranged to meet Françoise in the park to make sure everyone else had also returned safely. She quickly washed and dressed and hurried down the stairs. As she reached the bottom of the staircase Madame Favier beckoned her to come into her apartment. When she went in Madame Favier flung her arms around her.

Marie-Claire was taken aback. "What's this for?"

"Odile has already left," said Madame Favier, "but she told me last night's mission had been a great success and that you were incredibly brave."

"It was quite terrifying but it went according to plan."

"You should be very proud of yourself."

"It was a team effort but thank you. Please excuse me right now. I'm supposed to meet Françoise to check that she got back safely and if I'm late she may worry that I've been captured."

When Marie-Claire reached their meeting place in Parc Salengro Françoise was already there. They spoke almost in unison, "Thank heavens." Marie-Claire hugged her friend tightly for a moment. "I'm so glad you got back safely as well."

"We had an easy drive back and Robert dropped me and Tomas off at the bakery. I slept upstairs in a spare room and I have to say it was so nice to wake to the smell of fresh bread and have it for breakfast straight from the oven. I could get used to that."

"Lucky you."

"And you too. Tomas was baking special pastries for a German officer and look – he's given me some for us."

"Those look delicious. Let's find a quiet bench away from people where we can enjoy these and talk about last night."

On Monday Gerhard asked if he could walk Marie-Claire home from school. As they left the school he said, "Let's not take the main road back. I'm fed up seeing those damn German banners and all the soldiers in the streets. Let's take the back roads."

As they walked through the deserted back streets, he spoke in a hushed tone. "I'm hearing whispers about the prisoners escaping."

"What have you heard?"

"Some of the prisoners you freed are people I know and I've heard they've managed to get messages back to their families. So far I haven't heard of anyone being recaptured."

"That's great news," said Marie-Claire.

They stopped outside her house. "It was an exceptionally brave thing you did on Saturday," said Gerhard. "There are many people who, although they'll never know who you are, will forever be in your debt. You really are a remarkable young woman." He kissed her on the cheek, then turned and walked away.

During the following two weeks Marie-Claire was kept busy in the evenings amending ID cards. André had told her that many of the freed prisoners were still in hiding and needed their ID cards amended before they could get out of the area safely. She knew it was important to make the amendments perfectly as there was no point in freeing these people only to have them recaptured.

On Wednesday morning as Marie-Claire returned an envelope of amended ID cards Madame Favier whispered, "I've had an urgent message from André. He'd like to see you this morning."

Marie-Claire cycled over to André's house and found him dressed in his work clothes. "If you're working why did you want to see me?"

"I've had a message from my friend Fabrice in Maubuisson," replied André. "He said he wants me to do some carpentry for him and I'd like you to come with me."

"Why?" asked Marie-Claire, puzzled.

"Because he doesn't really need anything done. It's a 'come and see me' message about resistance activities, and as my deputy I think it's about time you met some of my contacts in other groups in case something happens to me."

"Don't talk like that André."

"Hey look. It can happen, and with Nicole gone who would miss me anyway?"

She was tempted to say 'I would', but instead she hesitated and replied, "We all would."

"I suppose, but there's something else. On the way I'd like to stop in Urzy. I've been told the Germans have taken over some fields of a farm near Urzy and are using them for training."

"And why is this of interest?"

"My source told me the soldiers are practising with new machine-guns. And they've been going there every day."

"Sounds like somewhere to stay away from," commented Marie-Claire. "So why do you want us to go there?"

André smiled. "Well that area is criss-crossed with lots of little rivers and the German trucks need to cross several small bridges to get to the field they're using, The bridges are wooden structures originally designed for farm carts pulled by horses, or oxen. They weren't designed for heavy army trucks."

"Are you suggesting we could weaken a causeway so the trucks fall into the river? Is that the idea?"

"Exactly. My source also told me that they don't guard the area at night. The trucks carrying the soldiers just turn up in the morning and leave in the late afternoon. So I thought you and I might drive out that way now before going on to see Fabrice."

"What? And be seen exploring the area while they're firing live ammunition?"

"No. Not quite that. We can just drive by slowly to verify that the information I've been given is correct."

"Well, we said we'd lie low for a while after the train hold-up, but reconnoitering should be ok."

"I'd hoped you'd say that as I've already prepared a picnic to take with us."

On the way to Urzy they passed many small farms and she noticed that nearly all of the workers were either women or older men. "Conscription certainly removed most of the workforce."

"Yes," said André, "and now they're held as POWs in German camps or being used as slaves. It's so depressing."

As they neared the hamlet they heard the unmistakeable sound of machine-gun fire. "That sounds faster than the guns I've heard in the past," commented André. "They must be using the new guns. I wonder why they're doing that here."

As they drove slowly along the road it was easy to see the tracks made across the fields by the heavy German trucks. When they stopped by the church in Urzy they could still hear the tat-tat-tat of the machine-guns. "Although it seemed like a good idea," said Marie-Claire, "I don't think we should do this."

"You sounded keen before. So what's changed your mind?"

"The causeways you're talking about all appear to be on the farm. So let's assume we're successful and a German truck breaks a causeway pitching a truck load of soldiers into the river. Unless we can make it look like an accident, the first person they'll blame is the farmer and if they think he's responsible they'll shoot him."

"I agree," said André. "This idea is a non-starter."

"I certainly think so," said Marie-Claire. "I don't want to be responsible for the death of any innocent people. Let's leave."

André started up the van and drove to Maubuisson, a picturesque little village. He parked the van in the middle of the village and turned to Marie-Claire. "Fabrice isn't expecting us for another hour. I've stopped here because there's a nice bench near the river where we can have our lunch."

Marie-Claire thought he had a strange look on his face and didn't respond immediately. He looked at her and smiled. "Did you train as a mind reader? Before you ask, yes, Nicole and I often picnicked here and I haven't been here since I lost her."

"Are you sure you want to do this?"

He nodded, walked over and stood by the river. She followed and they sat on the bench, eating their lunch and watching the river birds. Out of respect for what André might be thinking Marie-Claire kept quiet. Eventually André broke the silence. He asked if she was still enjoying teaching the children at the school and they chatted companionably about her work.

When they had finished their lunch they packed up their picnic things and drove to Fabrice's house. It was a typical French farmhouse, set back from the road with a small garden at the front and a large barn to the side.

André knocked on the door and a middle-aged man answered. He looked from André to Marie-Claire and back again. "Hello, André. Who is this? I thought you'd be coming on your own."

"Fabrice, this is Marie. She was a friend of Nicole."

Fabrice looked slightly embarrassed. "Pleased to meet you Marie." He looked intently at Marie-Claire. Finally, without saying anything, he just stared at André who smiled. "Don't worry, Fabrice. You can trust Marie with anything. She's part of our organization – in fact, she's actually my deputy."

Fabrice looked visibly relieved. "Ok then. Come in. I wanted you to come here because there's someone staying here I think you should meet."

Fabrice ushered them into the living room, went into the kitchen and returned with four cups. "The kettle always takes a long time to boil. While I'm waiting I'll go upstairs and reassure my friend that he can come down and meet you."

When Fabrice left the room Marie-Claire whispered, "Are you sure this is a good idea?"

"We'll see in a moment, but I've known Fabrice for a long time and I trust him," replied André.

Fabrice entered the room followed by a non-descript middle-aged man. As soon as the man saw Marie-Claire a startled look of recognition crossed his face. Marie-Claire was immediately worried. *This man looks as if he thinks he knows me but I don't recognize him. Who is he?*

Fabrice started the introductions, "This is André who I told you about and this is —"

"Oh I know who this lady is," interrupted the man. "But what I want to know is – what is she doing here?"

Chapter 45

Marie-Claire was alarmed that this stranger seemed to recognize her, and both André and Fabrice looked worried. Her immediate thought was that the man had perhaps seen her going into L'Hotel de Paris in Nevers and therefore might regard her as a German spy or collaborator.

However his next words puzzled her even more. "How did you get here so quickly? And what are you even doing here? I wasn't told anybody else was working in this area."

"I don't understand," said Marie-Claire. "I've never seen you before. Who are you?"

"Come on, Anna. There's no need to play this silly game."

Marie-Claire's heart skipped a beat. "Did you just call me Anna?"

"Yes. It is your name, isn't it? I know we rarely spoke to each other but I never forget a face."

Marie-Claire could hardly believe what he had just called her – Anna. *Could this mean what I want it to mean?* She turned to Fabrice. "What do you know about this man?"

Fabrice hesitated. "He introduced himself as a British agent – part of the SOE, the Special Operations Executive. But listening to your conversation, I'm beginning to wonder if that is true."

"I think we can resolve this quite easily," said Marie-Claire, turning back to the unnamed man. "You claim to never forget a face. So where did you see me and when was that? Think carefully before you answer, your life may depend on it."

The man was beginning to look distinctly uncomfortable. "I saw you in England at the SOE agent self-defence training base and that was about four weeks ago."

Even if Anna had been caught, she would never have revealed that she wanted to train as an agent. This must mean she made it to England. Oh, I could hug this man for what he has just said.

While she was wondering how much to say about Anna, André stood up and positioned himself between her and the agent. Marie-Claire motioned to him to sit down. "Don't worry André. I now believe this man is what he says he is."

"How can you believe him? He says he saw you in England at a time when I know you were here in France."

Marie-Claire smiled. "This man says he never forgets a face and I believe he's probably right. It's just the face he remembers is that of my cousin, Anna, who looks very much like me and went to England to train as an agent."

André sat down. "You never told me you had a cousin."

"You're right, and I wouldn't have told you if it hadn't become necessary right now in order to vouch for this man, whose name I still don't know."

"Call me Sparks. That's my operational name."

"Pleased to meet you Sparks. But let me stress – you, André and Fabrice must never ever reveal to anyone what I've just told you about me and Anna. Understood?"

After they all agreed Marie-Claire turned to Fabrice. "Even a slow kettle will have boiled by now and I don't know about you but I could certainly do with that drink now please."

André went with Fabrice into the kitchen leaving Marie-Claire and Sparks alone. She whispered to him. "You haven't been in the field long have you?"

"No. This is my first assignment."

"Well let me pass on a piece of advice. Never indicate in public that you know someone unless you receive an acknowledging signal from them. After the blunder you just made I had to tell André and Fabrice about my cousin, something I had no intention of ever doing."

"I'm sorry. Point taken. Have you been an agent for long?"

She laughed. "You don't expect me to answer that do you?"

He blushed slightly before laughing. "No, I suppose not. Second lesson – don't ask."

It was her turn to laugh. "Not quite. Asking can be very useful, especially if you already know the answer."

When André and Fabrice returned with a jug of coffee Fabrice asked, "Has Sparks been telling you why he's here?"

"No, but I'm keen to hear."

Sparks explained that his role as an SOE agent was to help local resistance groups. "We've been taught how to train people in sabotage and we can also arrange for the delivery of the necessary equipment – guns, ammunition, explosives, whatever you need."

"Delivery? How can you deliver guns and explosives?" asked André.

"In a canister dropped by parachute. We aim to start doing that within weeks. My first task is to make contact with local resistance groups and determine their needs. Just let me know what you want and I'll see what I can do."

"Although having access to guns and ammunition is probably a good idea," said André, "killing Germans can result in serious reprisals, so at the moment we want to focus on equipment and training for sabotage."

"That's exactly why I and my fellow agents are being sent to France," said Sparks. "Not to do the sabotage but to train the local people, such as yourselves, how to do it. And I've heard there's one group in this area which has already shown what can be successfully done without specialist equipment."

"Really? What have they done?" asked Fabrice.

"Apparently they held up a prisoner train at night and freed the prisoners with no injuries or loss of life."

Marie-Claire was surprised that news of their action had spread so far and she tried not to react.

"Really?" responded André. "I heard something about that and thought it was just a fanciful rumour. So you're saying it did actually happen."

"Oh yes, but they did something we would not encourage. Apparently they used a young girl to hold up the train. Apart from the danger, it's inadvisable to trust young people."

Young girl? I like that but I doubt my students would think of me as young.

"Thanks for the advice. I'll keep that in mind," replied André, keeping a straight face. "So, how do we arrange this training and when can you do it? Also, how do we contact you?"

"Contact will only be via Fabrice here, and it will be early July before we can arrange an equipment drop and begin training."

For the rest of the afternoon they discussed the different types of sabotage for which Sparks could provide training and equipment. André said he couldn't decide immediately what his group would require but he thought it would probably be explosives as he wasn't keen on killing Germans. "We've seen that killing a German, or even brawling with one, can result in execution. I assume you know about Jacques Bonsergent."

Sparks shook his head. "No. What happened to him?"

"What the Germans did shows their attitude towards the French people. On 23 December the Germans plastered posters all around Paris proclaiming that Jacques Bonsergent had been shot that day by firing squad for '*an act of violence against a member of the German army*'. And his act of violence? He merely *pushed* a German during a scuffle, he didn't *kill* a German."

"Are you serious?" asked Sparks.

"Oh yes. I saw one of the posters. And that's why we want to concentrate on sabotaging equipment, not killing soldiers."

Sparks smiled, "You may still want small arms training at some point. When the Allies land in France to fight the Germans and liberate France, resistance groups such as yours could be critically important."

"Does that mean there are plans for the Allies to land in France soon?" asked Marie-Claire.

Sparks shook his head. "I don't know and even if I did I couldn't tell you. All I can say is the Allies are working towards it and it will happen. Germany will be defeated and France will be free again. Of that we can all be assured."

On the drive home André chatted excitedly about the day's events. "When we left Urzy I thought today was going to be a wasted journey, but making contact with Sparks and the British network has made it all worthwhile. He could be invaluable."

"I agree," said Marie-Claire. "As a group we kept saying we

couldn't do much without training and equipment but it looks as if Sparks can supply us with both."

On Thursday evening when Marie-Claire arrived at the Café du Monde, Françoise was already there. "Marie, I'm going to the farm this weekend. Would you like to join me?"

"Yes, I'd love to. It's been a while since I saw your parents."

"Papa is going to pick me up on Friday so why don't you come to my apartment around six."

When Marie-Claire arrived at the apartment on Friday Monsieur Deferre appeared pleased to see her. "I'm glad you're coming to the farm this weekend. I was going to ask Françoise if you were free. We have some ID cards which need amending."

"I'm more than happy to help. I assume Sarah's inks are still at the farm?"

"Yes they are."

At the farm Marie-Claire was greeted warmly by Madame Deferre. "It's great to see you Marie."

"Monsieur Deferre said you need some ID cards amended. Are these people here at the farm?"

"No, there's no one here right now, although for some reason it's been very busy recently. However, there's a Jewish family who need to leave the area and they need their ID cards amended as soon as possible. Talking of ID cards, I suppose you still have no word about your cousin."

"Actually I do," said Marie-Claire. "I have great news. She made it back to England and has been accepted into the agent training program."

"Oh that's so good to hear." With a smile Madame Deferre added, "And I won't ask how you know. Now come and have some supper."

Marie-Claire followed her into the kitchen. She always enjoyed Madame Deferre's generous farm cooking, especially given the meagre rationed portions she usually had during the week.

On Sunday afternoon Monsieur Deferre drove Françoise and Marie-Claire back to Nevers. They had just reached the outskirts of the town when they were stopped at a German checkpoint. "Let me do the talking," said Monsieur Deferre.

"Cards please," demanded the German officer. "Where have you been and where are you going?"

As the cards were handed over Monsieur Deferre explained he was driving his daughter and her friend back to Nevers. "Why?" was the abrupt response from the officer. Marie-Claire found his tone quite aggressive.

"Because they live in Nevers and were visiting us for the weekend."

"You said 'us'. Who is us?"

"My wife and I."

"Why are you not living in Nevers?"

"My wife and I have a farm in the country."

He handed back the cards. "Have you seen any strangers around the farm?"

"No. Nobody."

"Are you sure? We are searching for some prisoners who recently escaped from a train."

"Really? What should we do if we see someone?" asked Monsieur Deferre.

"Telephone L'Hotel de Paris in Nevers."

The officer looked again at Françoise and Marie-Claire. He then pulled out his pistol and pointed it directly at Marie-Claire.

"You! Get out of the van with your hands up."

Chapter 46

Slowly Marie-Claire got out of the van and put her hands in the air. *Is he going to shoot me? What can I do?* Motioning with his pistol the soldier indicated she should move away from the vehicle. She looked closely at him, trying to recall if she had seen him before. *Although he mentioned the escaped prisoners, he's certainly not the officer on the train. That German did not speak French. I don't think I've seen this officer before, so why has he singled me out? What does he want?*

While still pointing the pistol at her, he reassured her in a hushed tone. "Don't be afraid. I'm Lieutenant Graf and I remember seeing you at L'Hotel de Paris. So tell me. Are the other two in the van telling the truth? What do you know about them?"

Oh, so he thinks I'm an informant does he?

"Françoise Deferre is a teacher at a school in Never and the man is her father. I have no reason to suspect they're involved in anything suspicious, but if I do find out anything I'll follow the proper procedures."

"Good. I apologize for pointing a pistol at you but I thought it was better that way so they don't suspect you work for us." In a louder voice he then barked at her, "Get back in the van."

Marie-Claire climbed back into the van and the officer waved his arm for the barrier to be lifted. He looked at Monsieur Deferre through the driver's window. "You can go but be careful – the escaped prisoners are dangerous."

Once the van had moved on down the road Marie-Claire relaxed and chuckled. Françoise, who was sitting in the front, turned around. "How can you laugh about that? I was almost sick at the sight of him walking you away at gunpoint."

"It was scary but I surprised myself at how well I coped."

"What did he want?"

"You know I had to do a portrait of a Gestapo Colonel?"

"Yes. But what has that got to do with what just happened?"

"Apparently this officer saw me when I was taken to the Gestapo HQ in L'Hotel de Paris prior to sketching the Colonel. He's drawn the conclusion that I'm an undercover informant and wanted to know what I knew about you two."

"I like his style," said Monsieur Deferre.

"Well I didn't," responded Marie-Claire. "I don't think I'll ever become accustomed to a German pointing a loaded firearm at me."

Monsieur Deferre laughed. "What I meant was that by forcing you out and away at gunpoint he was trying to make sure he didn't blow your cover."

Marie-Claire thought for a moment. "You know what – this officer may have just created a cover story for me. If he thinks I'm an informant that could be very useful in the future."

"Did he say anything about the train?" asked Françoise.

Marie-Claire glared at her. "No nothing. Why would he? Anyway, we don't know anything. He just wanted to know about you two."

Françoise's eyes and face showed she knew she'd made a mistake mentioning the train in front of her father. She mouthed back a silent 'sorry' and turned back to face the front.

"The officer said that some prisoners escaped from a train," commented Monsieur Deferre. "I've heard rumours about it. Did that actually happen? If it did, that would explain the number of people we've had down our escape line recently." He paused. "I'm not going to ask any questions, but I'm sure whoever was involved in such an operation showed incredible courage."

Françoise smiled at her father. "I'm sure they did Papa. I'm sure they did."

On Tuesday morning everyone in the school staff room was discussing the news that on Sunday Hitler's armies had unexpectedly invaded Russia. Marie-Claire had read about the invasion in *Le Petit Parisien* the previous evening and was not surprised. She recalled Emile saying that Hitler made it clear in *Mein Kampf* that invading Russia was always part of his plan.

As Marie-Claire and Françoise left the school that afternoon, they talked about the news. "If the Germans are focused on fighting Russia," said Françoise, "maybe this would be a good time to look at our options for sabotage."

"I wonder what André thinks. Let's go and ask him."

When they walked into the kitchen at André's house they saw that the table was covered in newspapers.

"I collected as many different newspapers as I could to try and get a clear picture of what is actually happening," said André. "I even listened to the French program on the BBC and everything points to this attack on Russia as being the largest military operation ever. Apparently Hitler has thrown literally millions of soldiers into the battle. Although I like the fact Germany is now focusing on Russia, I'm not sure it will actually be good for us."

"Surely if millions of German soldiers are now fighting Russia, there should be fewer soldiers left here in France and that must be good for us," said Françoise, "and give us more opportunities for sabotage."

"In some respects I agree, but at this point we don't want to hinder them leaving. So we need to consider carefully what sort of sabotage we should do." He paused and sighed. "And it could mean there's now another problem. So far in this war the French communists haven't been fighting the Germans. They've been taking their orders from Moscow and have been working against their fellow French countrymen for their own political agenda. But all that's going to change."

"Are you thinking the communists will now be fighting against the Germans?" asked Marie-Claire.

"Yes, and that could be disastrous for us."

"Surely not," said Françoise. "They'll be résistants like us."

"Résistants – yes. Like us – no. They have a different agenda from us and want to turn France into a communist state like Russia. They don't care if killing Germans means French people get shot in reprisal. We may end up fighting against the communists as well as against the Germans which means we may need the guns and ammunition Sparks can supply after all."

Françoise looked surprised. "Guns? Ammunition? Sparks? What are you talking about?"

Marie-Claire looked at André. "You're the leader. You tell her."

"We have been in contact with a British agent from the SOE – the Special Operations Executive. He and other agents have been parachuted into France to help resistance groups and supply them with the necessary equipment and training for sabotage."

"Why haven't you told us?" asked Françoise. "And who is Sparks?"

"Sparks is the name of the agent, and I haven't told the group yet because we've only just met him and he won't be able to start training us until early July."

She asked, "Is that why you wanted the group to wait before doing any more sabotage?"

"Partly, yes. However I have a plan which doesn't need to involve everybody. It's really a one person job but could be very effective. I was inspired when I thought about Sparks. Well, not the agent but the name he uses – Sparks."

"Am I missing something here?" asked Françoise.

"Sparks is the nickname often given to electricians because if they make a mistake and short circuit the wiring the result is a shower of sparks."

"What are you planning to short circuit?" asked Marie-Claire.

"I remembered an experiment we did in school with a length of string soaked in brine laid across bare electric wires."

Marie-Claire remembered her electrician father talking about the issue of short circuits on the major power lines leading to the Maginot Line. "That's brilliant, André. Brilliant and easy."

"Ok, you two," said Françoise. "I'm completely lost."

"Let me explain," said Marie-Claire, "and André will correct me if I'm wrong. I think he plans to throw a length of rope over a high voltage power line. The rope will have been soaked in salt water and, lying across the power lines, it'll cause a short circuit."

"You've got it," said André. "It should result in a major short circuit which will blow the main fuses and probably destroy the transformers."

"Are you being serious André?" asked Françoise. "How could you throw a rope over the lines?"

"If I attach a wooden ball to one end of the rope I should be able to throw it over the power lines so that the rope lies across the lines. If a wet rope touches two or more of the lines at the same time then – bang. A big bang. All I've got to do now is determine which power line I sabotage. I don't want to disrupt the electricity for French people, just the Germans."

Françoise chuckled. "I may not have guessed what you wanted to do, but I think I know where you can do this. How about a factory making parts for German machine-guns?"

"You say that as if you know of one locally," said André.

"There's one close to Urzy. It's only a small factory but they manufacture some of the internal workings. A friend of a friend works there on the machine lathes."

"A machine-gun factory," said Marie-Claire. "Near Urzy?" She and André smiled and nodded at each other.

"That sounds perfect," said André. "We can drive up that way on Saturday and check out where I can hit the power lines to have the greatest impact. I've got some carpentry to do for the Germans on Saturday morning but my afternoon is free."

Marie-Claire was still thinking about André's plan. "Surely a wet rope would be too heavy to throw over the power lines. And even if you could do it, the wires would short circuit immediately which could be dangerous for you standing beneath the wires."

"I won't throw a wet rope," replied André. "Ahead of time I'll soak the rope in brine and dry it. I'll throw the dry rope over the lines and leave it there. The next time it rains the rope will get wet and the salty wet rope will act as a good conductor and short circuit the lines."

"I'm confused," said Françoise. "Why dry the rope if the effect only happens when it's wet?"

"Delay," replied André. "One of the things Sparks stressed is that if we don't want to be caught we must never wait around to see if our sabotage works. He said that wherever possible we should use a delay fuse of some sort. So I'll throw the rope over in

301

dry weather when rain is forecast. By the time it rains and the lines short circuit I'll be long gone."

"That's a perfect delay fuse," said Marie-Claire.

"That's what I thought," said André. "So on Saturday afternoon let's drive out to find this factory and its power lines."

On Saturday morning Marie-Claire had just finished her breakfast and gone back up to her room when Madame Favier knocked on her bedroom door. "That German soldier who keeps calling here for art lessons is here again asking to speak to you."

Marie-Claire was surprised. Otto had never called early in the morning and never on a Saturday. Her heart sank as she realized he must have a very good reason for doing so today. She hurried downstairs. "Good morning Corporal Voigt. Have you come about another art lesson?"

"Yes. My schedule is free for this afternoon and I'm keen for you to see what I've done. Is it possible for us to have a lesson today?"

Marie-Claire wanted to say 'no' but felt she really had no choice. She couldn't tell him that she had planned to be out in the afternoon scouting around for a sabotage location with her résistant friends. "Yes. I can do that. May I suggest the usual place and time?"

"Thank you Mademoiselle Bruneau. That would be fine. I look forward to it."

As he walked away, she went back upstairs and grabbed her coat. She walked quickly to André's house to tell him she could not go with him that afternoon. When she knocked on his door and got no reply she remembered that he had said he would be working for the Germans in the morning. She was about to write him a note when he opened the door. "I thought we said this afternoon Marie. You've just caught me on my way out. Is something wrong?"

"Not exactly," said Marie-Claire. "Something important has come up and I can't make it this afternoon." She waited to see how he would react.

"That's not a problem," said André. "After all it doesn't take three people to find some power lines. Why don't you come by later and I'll tell you how Françoise and I got on."

Marie-Claire's meeting with Otto that afternoon followed the pattern of the previous 'art classes'. She was, however, so anxious to hear what he had to tell her that she found it hard to concentrate. After the lesson they walked a short distance away from the Bistro.

Otto looked around before speaking in a hushed tone. "You may wish to tell anybody who might be interested that the German soldiers have been told that anybody, including résistants and foreign agents, found fighting against the Germans in the Occupied Zone can be shot on the spot rather than be treated as prisoners of war."

Marie-Claire made no comment and Otto continued.

"More importantly, though, I thought you might know some people who might want to be aware that a round-up of more Jews is planned for tonight at around three o'clock." He looked intently at her, "For some reason they will be transported directly to Dijon during the night – and by truck rather than by train."

She looked back at him with wide eyes. "I'm sure I have no idea what you mean." She paused then smiled, "Thank you for telling me, Otto. I'm sure Greta would have approved of what you're doing."

He bowed slightly. "I think about her every day." He then turned away and walked off, leaving Marie-Claire wondering what she should do about the two warnings he had just given her.

Chapter 47

As soon as Otto was out of sight Marie-Claire headed straight to André's house, hoping he would be back. She knocked on his door and he answered almost immediately. "Come in Marie, I've got great news," he said excitedly. "We not only found the power lines to the factory but also the perfect place to sabotage them. There's a wooded area where the power lines are basically out of sight unless you are walking through the woods looking up. It means I can throw the ropes over the lines without them being seen."

He looked at her. "Marie, you don't seem to have been listening to what I've just said. What's the matter?"

"André, something critically important has come up. There's to be another round-up of Jews tonight at three o'clock – that's less than twelve hours from now."

"A round-up? Tonight? How do you know?"

"I can't tell you my source, but I have complete faith in them."

"Are you really sure you can trust this person?" asked André. "Could this be a trap?"

"I trust this person completely and I don't think it's a trap. This is the person who warned us about the deputy headmaster being a German collaborator and informant."

"Well I have to admit that was certainly right," said André.

"My source didn't just warn me about the round-up. I was also told rather pointedly that the prisoners would be taken to Dijon tonight by truck – not by train. André, if you have any Jewish friends still living in Nevers you should warn them at once."

"My Jewish friends all left Nevers after the last round-up."

At this point there was a loud knock on André's front door. "I'm not expecting anybody," said André. "Quick, go into the kitchen out of sight."

From inside the kitchen she could hear André answer the door and invite the caller in. He shouted to her. "It's ok. It's Jerome."

When she came out of the kitchen Jerome greeted her with a warm smile. "I can't stay long. I just came to give you a heads-up. I don't know what it is but something big is planned for tonight – all our police leave has been cancelled and we have to be at the station for two o'clock in the morning."

"I think we know why," said André. "It looks like another round-up of Jews. I assume the Germans weren't happy about Jews escaping from the prison train a few weeks ago."

Jerome sighed. "Now that I know what's planned for tonight I need to start warning people. But I don't see how I can warn enough people in time. I don't suppose there's some way to delay the Germans and give more people a chance to get away."

"We'll see what we can do," said André.

After he showed Jerome out he came back into the living room and slumped into a chair. "I know I told him we'd see what we can do – but what can we do?"

"Could we delay the round-up by sabotaging the trucks?" asked Marie-Claire. "That could give the Jews more time to get away."

André sat up. "You may have something there Marie. Robert told me the German trucks are kept in a large parking area on the edge of town and it's not well guarded. He'll be able to tell us if there's something we can do tonight to sabotage the trucks."

"If you think it's possible," said Marie-Claire, "then the first thing we need to do is to get everybody over here now. You take your van and get Robert and Odile. I'll get Françoise and I'll tell Tomas as I pass the bakery."

André jumped up. "Ok. See you back here soon."

When Marie-Claire got back with Françoise everybody else was already there except, for Odile who could not be reached.

"Why have you called us here so urgently?" asked Tomas.

"We've just heard that the Germans are planning another round-up of Jews for tonight," said André.

"Tonight!" exclaimed Tomas. "How can we do anything to help tonight? Surely that's impossible."

"I know it's very short notice," said André, "but if we could delay the round-up it would give more time to warn the Jews and more time for them to hide. If we can't do anything tonight it will be too late as the people they arrest are to be taken away in trucks immediately. There will be no opportunity to free them later."

"But what can we do at such short notice?" asked Tomas.

"Marie suggested we could at least delay the operation if we were able to sabotage the trucks. Robert, you've looked at the German truck park. Is sabotage an option?"

"Yes it is," said Robert. "I checked it out recently and they just do a ten minute patrol every half hour."

"If the trucks are unguarded for twenty minutes at a time that should give us time to do something," said André.

"Could we slash the tyres?" asked Marie-Claire.

"You could try slashing them but I wish you luck," replied Robert. "Truck tyres are thick and designed to take punishment. You can slash a car tyre but not a truck tyre. You can, though, put nails against the tyres so they puncture the tyre the moment the truck moves. That's easy, quick and quiet, but after the first truck is disabled they'll check before moving any more trucks. It would be much more effective, although slightly slower, to let the air out of the front tyres."

"But surely all they need to do is pump the tyres back up again," said Marie-Claire.

"Yes, if that's all you've done," said Robert, "but it won't be possible to pump them up again if you've smeared the inside of the valve with quick setting plaster of Paris. That's really destructive because the inner tube is then useless."

"We can do that easily," said André. "And what about contaminating the fuel? I've heard it can be quite destructive if you pour in things like bleach or vinegar or even molasses."

"Yes. They would slowly ruin the engine," said Robert, "but for tonight, forget about pouring liquids into the fuel tanks. It's too slow and you won't be able to carry enough liquid to be effective. Instead the best option is to put rice into the fuel tanks. Very soon after they drive the trucks away the rice will be sucked into the fuel lines, blocking the filters and bringing the trucks to a halt. They wouldn't be able to continue without repairs."

"Thank you Robert," said André. "These options only require things that we can get right now and that we can carry easily." He took a deep breath. "I know it's a lot to ask of you at such short notice and it will be difficult and dangerous, so if anyone doesn't want to join in I can understand. Does anyone want to withdraw?"

When they all shook their heads, André continued. "I'm thinking we could have two teams doing the sabotage. Me and Françoise as one team with Tomas and Robert as the other and Marie as the lookout. Marie, you'll have the wooden owl whistle I used when we released the prisoners."

"That's fine. I'll blow two hoots as a warning and three hoots will be the all clear."

"Now, I've got nails and plaster but I don't have any rice. Does anyone have some they can spare?" asked André.

"I've got some back at my apartment," said Françoise, "but I'm sure it won't be enough."

"I have rice at the bakery," said Tomas, "so I'll go and get that."

"Before you go," said André, "let me remind everyone. We need to wear dark clothes and balaclavas. So I suggest you all go back home right now, put your dark clothes in a bag and meet back here as soon as possible. Remember to come in by the back door. We don't want my neighbours wondering what we're doing. I think we need to be at the truck park around midnight which should give us about an hour to get the job done."

Marie-Claire was the first to get back to André's house. She slipped in the back door and found him in the kitchen. "I can see you've been busy," she said, looking at the table where he'd laid out packets of sabotage materials – packets of nails, packets of plaster of Paris and little bottles of water. Marie-Claire added a packet of rice which Madame Favier had given her. The others soon arrived and added their contributions. Robert went over the sabotage instructions again and André then shared out the packets between the saboteurs.

"We'll leave in two groups," said André, "and meet at the bend in the road on the south side of the truck park. At that point there are bushes to hide in and there's a good view of the guard house."

Everyone changed into their dark clothes and just before eleven o'clock they set out. Robert, Françoise and Tomas left first, followed a few minutes later by André and Marie-Claire. When André and Marie-Claire arrived at the truck park just before midnight they were pleased to find the others had all got there without incident and were hiding in the bushes.

"It looks as if there's only a dozen trucks," said André, "so if we work quickly we should be able to disable all of them. Marie, this looks like an ideal position for you. From here you can see the guard house clearly and warn us the moment anybody steps outside. If we hear a warning we'll stop and hide until you blow the all clear signal."

When Robert began moving towards the park André whispered, "We can't start yet. We need to wait here until we see the patrol. We don't know if they're inside the guard house right now or walking around."

A few minutes later two soldiers came into view, smoking and chatting in German. Marie-Claire could just make out what they were saying. "Only an hour to go before the others come to collect the trucks."

"When are they taking the trucks out?"

"If I know them, not before they've had a drink."

"André." whispered Marie-Claire. "Did you hear that? We've just got an hour before more soldiers arrive."

"Yes, I heard." He turned to the others. "When those two go into the guard house we need to work quickly."

They watched in silence as one of the guards opened the guard house door. For some reason they didn't go straight in but stood chatting in the open doorway, silhouetted against the light from inside. Marie-Claire found the wait frustrating. *Come on you two. Go in and close the door. What are you waiting for?* Eventually the guards threw their cigarette ends on the ground, went into the guard house and closed the door.

"Let's go," whispered André, and the group dashed across the road and approached the first pair of trucks.

With the whistle at the ready in her hand Marie-Claire kept her eyes on the guard house door. Suddenly the door opened and she immediately blew the two hoot danger signal. One of the soldiers stood in the doorway. *I'm sure it's too soon for them to go out on patrol. Has he heard something?* The soldier then emptied what looked like a coffee pot, shook the pot, went back inside and closed the door. She felt so relieved she almost forgot to blow the all clear signal.

About fifteen minutes later the door opened again and she immediately blew the danger signal. She could not see where her friends were. *This is more nerve wracking than actually sabotaging the trucks.*

The soldiers set out on their patrol and she knew it would be about ten minutes before she could blow the all clear. It felt like the longest ten minutes she had ever experienced but finally the two soldiers came back into view. This time they went straight back into the guard house. She blew a strong all clear signal and kept her eyes firmly focused on the guard house door.

With nothing to do but keep looking at the door, ready to blow the whistle, time seemed to pass slowly for Marie-Claire. She was beginning to wonder if it was getting close to their one o'clock cut-off time when she heard the unmistakeable sound of vehicles approaching the truck park. *That must be the soldiers coming to collect the trucks.* She quickly blew the danger signal.

She scanned the truck park but could see no sign of her friends. She waited and with a sickening feeling watched two German jeeps pull up outside the guard house. The guard house door opened and the soldiers all stood outside chatting. The open door cast a bright light across the truck park. Desperately she looked around but still couldn't see any sign of her friends. *Where are they? If we don't leave soon we could all be caught.*

She was about to blow the danger signal again when she heard a rustle in the bushes behind her and felt a hand on her shoulder.

Chapter 48

Marie-Claire froze in panic. *Have the Germans discovered me? Have they caught the others?* She felt a warm breath on the back of her neck. Then a voice whispered in her ear. "I'm back."

She spun around and with a huge sense of relief she saw it was André. "Thank goodness you're safe," she whispered. "I was so worried about you."

"Everything worked perfectly. I'll tell you more later, but right now let's get out of here."

"Where are the others?"

"They're already making their own way back. The moment the Germans realize the trucks have been sabotaged they will raise the alarm and search the area. It's essential for everyone to get away as quickly as possible. That includes us – so let's get going."

André led Marie-Claire through deserted back streets and tiny lanes she hadn't known were there and they reached his house without encountering any patrols. "I thought the others were making their own way here. So where are they?" asked Marie-Claire when they were inside. "I thought they'd be here by now."

"They've all gone back to their own homes. It's safer that way in case any of us were being followed. I've asked everybody to meet here at ten o'clock tomorrow, but right now we should get some sleep. You take my bed and I'll sleep on the sofa."

As they were having breakfast the next day there was a knock on André's front door. He turned to Marie-Claire. "I wasn't expecting anyone this early. Wait here while I see who it is."

Marie-Claire heard André open the front door and then greet Jerome loudly. Realizing it was safe she immediately joined them. "Have you got any news?" she asked.

"I don't know how you did it," said Jerome, "but the round-up last night was called off at the last minute. It's been rescheduled for this coming Friday night. The Germans don't seem to realize that will give time for everybody to be warned and I suspect it means there won't be many Jews left in town by then. Hopefully even those who may not want to leave will see that they really have no choice."

"Thanks for letting us know Jerome," said André. "I won't say what we did but it's good to know it was worthwhile."

"It certainly was, and I thought you'd want to know. But right now I'd better be going back on patrol."

"I think we can clock that one up as a success," said André after Jerome left. "I'm sure the others will be pleased to hear the effect we had."

By ten o'clock everyone had arrived except for Tomas. "Does anyone know if he got back safely?" asked André.

The others all shook their heads. "I hope he's not been captured," said Marie-Claire. "I'll go to the bakery and check."

As she was about to leave Tomas appeared with a bag of freshly baked buns. "I'm sorry I'm late. I was just waiting for these to come out of the oven."

As André poured out coffee he thanked everyone for their efforts. "I think we can regard last night as a stunning success. Jerome came by earlier this morning and told us that the round-up had been called off at the last minute. He didn't know why but I think we all do. No trucks – no round-up."

Everyone smiled at the news and raised their cups in a toast to their success.

Tuesday the first of July was the last day of term and the children were sent outside to play sports while the teachers tidied the classrooms. Marie-Claire had just started tidying up the art room when Monsieur Thibault called her into his office.

"As you know, when you came to us in October it was to fill an unexpected vacancy. I hope you've enjoyed your time with us."

"I've been very happy here Monsieur Thibault."

"I've called you in here to tell you that there will have to be some changes next year."

Marie-Claire tried hard not to show her disappointment. *I hadn't thought this would happen. What am I going to do now? How can I find another job?*

Monsieur Thibault continued. "Paper's in very short supply and I'm having trouble obtaining any for next term. You may have very little for the children to draw on. You'll have to be even more creative in your teaching methods."

"So you haven't asked me into your office to fire me?"

"Of course not. You've been a wonderful addition to the staff. I certainly don't want to lose you."

At that moment the sound of a car outside caught his attention and he turned to look out of the window. "Oh no, what's this?"

Marie-Claire looked out and gasped. A German staff car was parked across the school entrance. *Have they found out I was involved in the truck sabotage? Are they coming to arrest me?* As she watched the driver jumped out and opened the back door. A Gestapo officer stepped out and the two Germans walked towards the school. She didn't know what to think as she recognized both Otto and the Colonel she had sketched.

She watched anxiously as Monsieur Thibault left his office and greeted the Germans at the school door.

"Is Mademoiselle Bruneau available?" asked Otto in French. "The Colonel would like to speak to her."

The headmaster beckoned to Marie-Claire and she walked over and stood beside him. The Colonel bowed slightly as she appeared and Otto explained. "I was driving Colonel Zeigler to a meeting and when we passed the school I mentioned that this is where you work. He asked me to stop as he said he had been thinking of asking you to do another portrait."

She breathed a sigh of relief. "Of course I can do that, Corporal Voigt. In fact this is the last day of the school term so I can do another portrait of the Colonel any day this week."

Otto smiled at her before translating. She kept a straight face as she listened to the exchange in German between Otto and the Colonel. "The portrait he wants is not of himself," Otto explained, "but of his wife who will be in Nevers on Thursday morning."

"Tell him it would be an honour to do her portrait. What time on Thursday would be convenient?" She had already heard the Colonel tell Otto ten o'clock but knew she had to ask in order to maintain the pretence that she did not understand German.

Otto answered directly and added that he would collect her in the car. The Colonel spoke again to Otto in German and Otto seemed rather surprised. He turned to Monsieur Thibault. "Colonel Zeigler hopes it wouldn't be too inconvenient but he would like to see the art class and what the children have been drawing."

Monsieur Thibault agreed and escorted the Colonel to the art class, followed by Marie-Claire and Otto. When they reached the classroom the Colonel examined the children's work and looked up with a puzzled expression. Marie-Claire wondered if any of the pictures the children had drawn could be interpreted as incriminating. She thought of the picture Philippe had drawn of dead Germans piled in a heap.

The Colonel spoke to Otto who translated. "The Colonel says he's impressed with the children's work but notices all the pictures are small. He asks if this is a teaching method."

She shook her head. "No. We are just short of paper."

When the Colonel was told the answer he frowned and Otto translated his response. "Colonel Zeigler is not pleased to hear this. He said he'll arrange for a supply of suitable paper to be delivered to the school for the children's artwork. He said the children should be given every opportunity possible to learn from such a gifted artist as you."

Marie-Claire blushed slightly. "Please thank the Colonel not only for the paper but also for his kind words."

"I will," said Otto. "The Colonel said he'd like to stay longer but he has to leave now. I'll collect you on Thursday morning."

Marie-Claire smiled at Otto. "I look forward to it."

When Otto arrived on Thursday morning he was on his own and Marie-Claire felt able to talk freely. "The extra paper the Colonel is sending will be so useful. I certainly wasn't expecting him to make such an offer."

Otto smiled. "Actually, the Colonel is not a bad man. He's one of the easiest people to deal with, unlike his wife. Be careful what you say in front of her. Whereas the Colonel is a gentleman, she is an ardent outspoken Nazi of the worst kind."

Marie-Claire did not know how to reply so she just nodded.

It was not long before they arrived at the L'Hotel De Paris. "Am I to do the sketch in the Hotel?"

"Yes, we'll be back in his office."

As Marie-Claire followed Otto through the office space she was aware there were more local French people at desks conversing with German staff than the last time she was here. She was shocked at how many French people appeared to be willing to inform on their fellow countrymen. As she walked by she tried to study their faces discreetly so she could identify them later. There was one man in particular whose face she was sure she'd seen before but could not remember where. As she passed he looked up and stared at her, which she found disturbing. *I wonder if he recognizes me and thinks I'm also an informant.*

Just as Otto was about to knock on the Colonel's door, he came out, saw Marie-Claire and greeted her in a warm and friendly manner. He then ushered her into his office and introduced her to his wife. Frau Zeigler had a sharp face with eyes which did not convey any warmth and a look which expressed disdain and superiority. Marie-Claire took an instant dislike to her but knew she'd have to hide her feelings. *This is going to be a challenging portrait.*

The Colonel left the office and through Otto Marie-Claire discussed suitable poses with Frau Zeigler. Eventually they agreed on a pose which Frau Zeigler was happy with. Marie-Claire did not dare point out that her sitter's facial expression was cold and would not look flattering in the portrait. Fortunately the Colonel appeared at that point and his sour-faced wife smiled at him. "Ask her to hold that look," Marie-Claire said quickly to Otto. On a separate piece of paper she did a quick sketch before Frau Zeigler changed her expression. It turned out this was a good idea as very soon the cold disdainful look returned.

It took Marie-Claire just over an hour to complete the portrait. Frau Zeigler looked at it in silence for a disconcerting length of time. She then turned to Otto. "Tell this artist this is the best portrait anyone has done of me. It captures me in a way no one else ever has."

At that point the Colonel came back into the office and Frau Zeigler showed him the portrait. He admired it and asked Otto to thank Marie-Claire. He opened his desk and pulled out an envelope. When he went to pass it to Marie-Claire his wife rebuked him severely. "You're not going to pay this French woman are you? I like the portrait she did but that's no reason to pay her. Are you forgetting that we Germans are in charge of France and they'll do what we tell them when we tell them. They should be thankful we haven't sent all of them to work in German factories. So put that envelope away."

The Colonel nodded and put the envelope in his pocket. Marie-Claire gave no indication that she had understood Frau Zeigler's words and Otto did not translate.

When Frau Zeigler looked rather pointedly at her watch, Otto said, "I think we should leave now." As they walked out through the office space Marie-Claire kept glancing at the various people sitting at desks, hoping for another look at the man she thought she recognized but he was no longer there.

As they were about to leave the Hotel a Gestapo soldier came running after them. "Corporal Voigt," he called out. "Colonel Zeigler wants to speak to you in his office right now."

"Wait here," Otto said to Marie-Claire.

Standing here on my own in the foyer of the Gestapo HQ is not what I want. Anyone who sees me will assume I'm an informant.

A few minutes later Otto returned and handed her an envelope. "Put this in your bag." Once they were safely outside he explained. "The Colonel insisted I give you the envelope. His wife did not want him to pay you but the Colonel felt you should be paid. And he asked me to tell you how much he appreciated your work – and your tact in dealing with his wife. As I said before, Colonel Zeigler is a gentleman."

315

"So how did he end up married to such a woman?"

"From what I understand, she is very well connected within the Nazi hierarchy and it was made clear to him that marrying her would be good for his career and rejecting her would not."

Marie-Claire smiled. "I hope he thinks it was worth it."

Otto laughed, "I don't think he really had much choice." He looked around. "If you wait here, I'll arrange for a car to take you back home."

"Don't worry, Otto, it's a nice day and I'll enjoy the walk."

"You might as well make the most of the good weather. Apparently we are in for a major storm tonight with heavy rain, thunder and lightning."

"I didn't think it was going to be that bad," said Marie-Claire.

"The forecast I was looking at is an operational one compiled by the German air force to let them know if they can stand down – the British don't attack during storms. The air force forecast is not circulated to the public."

"Well, if you trust that forecast then perhaps I should as well," said Marie-Claire. "And please, let me know when you want another art lesson."

"Of course. Our art lessons can be most helpful – for both of us," he said with a twinkle in his eye. He smiled and bowed slightly before turning around and walking back into the Hotel.

Heavy rain tonight? With thunder and lightning? The weather is perfect for André's plans to sabotage the power lines. I know he's out this afternoon but I hope he turns up at the Café tonight so I can tell him.

That evening the Café du Monde was a bustling hive of activity when Marie-Claire arrived. When André finished his game of dominoes she suggested discreetly that they go outside to talk.

André was the first to speak. "What's so important?"

"The weather. The forecast for later tonight is that there'll be heavy rain. I was thinking balls, ropes and electricity."

"I know it's due to be cloudy, but I didn't think a storm was expected. What makes you think it is?"

"Today I was in L'Hotel de Paris doing another portrait."

"What? You were in the Gestapo headquarters again?"

"Yes, and as I walked through I overheard a discussion about the air force weather forecast for tonight. Apparently they will be standing down their fighter pilots because the British never attack during thunderstorms. From our point of view tonight is perfect. The Germans will probably blame any electrical outages on the lightning, which means once they think they've fixed the problem and turn the power back on it'll short out again."

André looked at his watch. "If I set off right now I can get back before curfew."

"Do you need help?"

"No. It's best I go alone. I don't need help, and if I'm seen I'm the only one they'll catch. And if I'm stopped at a checkpoint and it's just me with my work tools it will be easier to claim I was out doing a job."

"If you're sure. I'll go back in and you can get going." She paused before adding in a softer voice, "Be careful, please. We don't want to lose you."

He smiled at her with a warmth she'd not seen in his face before. "Don't worry, I'll be careful. I'll call by at Angélique's in the morning."

She stood and watched as he walked away.

I hope he doesn't do anything stupid. I don't know what I'd do if he doesn't come back.

Chapter 49

Marie-Claire had a restless night worrying about André. With the heavy rain that night she had no doubt the sabotage would have worked successfully as long as André had been able to throw the ropes over the power lines. But that was not what was worrying her. She was concerned he might not have been able to return before curfew. She was also concerned that someone might have seen him.

There's no way he could have thrown the ropes and looked out for danger at the same time. How stupid of me not to think of that. I should have insisted on going with him. We must make it a rule that nobody goes on a sabotage mission alone.

At breakfast she sat quietly, trying to make herself eat something even though she didn't feel hungry. She realized she must be looking worried when Madame Favier asked what was troubling her. "You've hardly eaten anything and you've been staring out of the window most of the time."

"I had a bad night," replied Marie-Claire. "The thunder and lightning kept me awake." After a pause she added, "André said he'd call by this morning. Have you seen him?"

Before Madame Favier could answer there was a loud knock on the front door. Marie-Claire stood up promptly. "That might be him now. I'll answer it."

When she opened the door and saw André standing there she wanted to fling her arms around him but stopped herself. "I see you're smiling. Does that mean you were successful?"

"Yes. I got two ropes over the lines and I got back before curfew. It hadn't started raining when I left, but with last night's heavy rain it should have worked. Hopefully the short circuit will have blown out the transformer at the machine-gun factory. That should put the factory out of commission for a month or so. It's not that easy to replace a large transformer."

"Well done," said Marie-Claire, "but you should not have been doing it on your own. Françoise or I should have gone with you to act as a lookout."

"I agree. When I got there I felt a bit exposed but I'm pretty sure nobody saw me or the van. Perhaps we should make it a rule – when we do any sabotage we must always have a lookout person."

"I think that's important. But to get back to last night, I'll tell Françoise when I see her next week. I'm sure her friend who knows someone at the factory will be able to tell us if it worked."

"Aren't you going to the farm with her today? Last night she mentioned going there for a few days."

"No. Not this time. I have some things to do this weekend."

"Talking of things to do, I must get going. I've got some more jobs to do for the Germans today."

As she walked back into the house Marie-Claire thought about her weekend. The reason she had decided not to go to the farm was she knew that on Sunday she would not be good company – it would have been Emile's twenty-fifth birthday. Françoise did not know about him and she wanted to keep it that way.

On Sunday Marie-Claire sat at breakfast thinking of Emile and feeling utterly dejected. As soon as she saw her Madame Favier asked Marie-Claire what was upsetting her. Through quivering lips Marie-Claire lied. "I've had some bad news."

Madame Favier put her arms around Marie-Claire and gave her a warm hug. Although Marie-Claire knew the hug was done with the best of intentions, it deepened her feeling of loss as it reminded her of the way her mother used to hug her.

"I won't ask," said Madame Favier, "but if you want to talk, you know I'm always here for you."

"Thank you. I appreciate that."

After breakfast Marie-Claire went for a walk in the park. Tears came to her eyes as she recalled how different life had been on Emile's birthday just a year ago. They had had a long walk along the Seine followed by a special lunch. She thought about the surprise she'd arranged – the evening concert listening to Edith

Piaf, his favourite singer. She sat on a bench staring at nothing in particular as she tried to come to terms with the dramatic changes that had occurred since that blissful day.

When a passing couple stopped to ask if she was alright Marie-Claire realized her distress was too evident and she hurried back home. She spent the rest of the afternoon in her room, going over and over in her head memories of Emile – and her mother – and all the others she had lost.

She was aroused from her thoughts by a knock on her door. Madame Favier came in. "André is downstairs in the living room. He said he wants to talk to you. I can see you're still very upset. Shall I tell him you're not well?"

"No, No. I'll come down."

Madame Favier put an arm around Marie-Claire's shoulders. "I hate seeing you so upset. I'll be in the kitchen. Come and see me if you need anything."

When she entered the living room Marie-Claire saw that André was bubbling with excitement. He started speaking the moment she entered the room. "Fabrice has contacted me. He wants you and me to go to his house tonight for something important."

He stopped abruptly and looked closely at her. "Marie. What's wrong? You look as if you've been crying? And here I am babbling on about Fabrice. I'm sorry. What's wrong?"

She looked at him and burst into a flood of tears. "Today would have been my husband's twenty-fifth birthday," she whispered. "And you're the only person I can tell. You're the only person who knows about him."

André pulled a handkerchief out of his pocket and passed it to her. "I'm so sorry. Forget about tonight. I can go on my own."

"No, I'll come with you. I've spent too much of today moping about and lamenting what could have been. I miss Emile so much, but listening to you talking about Fabrice and resistance makes me even more conscious of the reason he was risking his life. He was trying to protect not just me but all of us from the Nazi tyranny."

As she dried her eyes André spoke softly. "Don't answer if you don't want to, but it sounds as if he was an important résistant."

"Yes, he was. More so than I knew at the time. And that's why the Gestapo killed him – and were looking for me. But he's gone and I have to accept it."

More tears ran down her cheeks. André waited a minute before speaking. "To quote a close friend of mine, he's not entirely gone. Looking at you right now, I can see he lives on in your memory. Cherish that."

Through her tears she smiled at him. "I'm surprised you remember me saying that to you."

"I often think of Nicole and those words you said. And I also know we must not let the Germans ruin our lives through what they did to her and your husband. If we do, then they have won."

She wiped the tears from her face. "You're right. Perhaps the best way to remember and honour them is to live life and vow to continue their fight."

She sat in silence for a while and then added, "We can't live in the past. We need to live for now and the future." She took a deep breath and asked, "Why do you think Fabrice wants to see us?"

"Well, I remember what Sparks said about supplying us with equipment and, given that the moon is almost full and the weather is forecast to be clear, I think Sparks may have arranged a canister drop for tonight."

"I thought Sparks said it would be a few weeks before he could arrange such a delivery."

"He did, and it has been almost three weeks since we met him. So it seems the most likely reason."

"Well that changes everything. If you're right I can't go skulking around fields at night in this dress. If you wait here I'll go upstairs and get my dark clothes. Then we'll both go to Maubuisson and see if you're right."

"But Marie, I doubt he'll expect you to be part of the parachute party. It could be very dangerous if the Germans see the parachute and come after us."

She frowned. "And don't you think it was dangerous when I flagged down the prison train?"

"Yes, but that was different."

321

"You're right it was different. Standing right in front of two German soldiers with a gun pointed directly at me was much more dangerous than it would be running away across a field in the dark. I'm a full member of our group and I'll take the same risks as everyone else."

"I was just thinking —"

"André. I do not shy away from danger. My husband didn't and neither do I."

It was early evening when André and Marie-Claire arrived at Fabrice's house. It was obvious that Fabrice was very excited. "Tonight. It'll happen tonight at around two in the morning. Isn't it fantastic. We'll be able to do so much."

André held up his hands. "Slow down Fabrice. Exactly what is supposed to happen tonight? Is it a canister drop?"

"Yes. Yes it is. Sparks says the RAF have confirmed the drop."

"So where is Sparks?" asked André.

"With his radio operator in case there's any change of plan."

"What is the plan?" asked André.

Fabrice explained that in one of the large fields north of the village they were to stand with three lanterns positioned in the shape of a large capital L. "We will light the lanterns at two o'clock as a beacon for the RAF plane and extinguish them the moment we see the parachute."

"Did Sparks say how many canisters are being dropped?" asked Marie-Claire.

A male voice answered from the kitchen. "Just one this time." As Sparks entered the living room he greeted André and Marie-Claire. "Good to see both of you were able to make it. We need all the help we can get when the canister lands so we can hide the contents quickly."

"What exactly will be in the canister?" asked André.

"I've been told we'll have a few Sten sub-machine guns with ammunition, a spare radio and lots of plastic explosive, detonators, grenades and caltrops."

"What's a caltrop?" asked Marie-Claire.

"It's an ancient device the Romans used against horses and we now use against military trucks," explained Sparks. "Basically it's made of four sharp spikes such that no matter how it lands on the ground one spike is always pointing upward. Throw them on the ground and they puncture the tyres of moving vehicles."

Marie-Claire looked at André with a slight smile. "I'm sure that could be very useful."

He kept a straight face as he responded. "Yes. I suppose it could be, if we need to stop some German trucks sometime." He turned to Sparks. "However as we discussed, our main interest is in the explosives."

"Once the canister has landed, where are we going to hide the contents?" asked Marie-Claire.

"That's my responsibility," said Fabrice. "Many members of my resistance group will be there and we will share out the contents so that each person is only hiding a few items."

André looked puzzled. "Fabrice, if you've already arranged for your group to be ready to unload and hide the contents, why did you want us to come here today?"

"Actually, it was my idea," said Sparks. "Any activity using things like explosives needs very specific training. I was impressed with you and Marie when we met last month and as some of the supplies are for your group, I thought you two should be trained along with Fabrice's group. You can then pass on the training to your group."

Fabrice nodded. "And I don't want my people resenting you using equipment from this canister when you've apparently had nothing to do with the canister drop. That's another reason we wanted you to be here tonight."

"I have to leave in a few days," said Sparks. "So I'd like to start the training tomorrow. Can you come back tomorrow morning?"

André looked at Marie-Claire who nodded. "Yes, tomorrow is fine," replied André. "But I'm not keen on driving back tonight after curfew, especially if we just need to drive back again in the morning. It's probably best if we stay here tonight after the drop."

"That's fine," said Sparks, "you two can have my room."

Marie-Claire was horrified. *Oh my God. Does Sparks think André and I are a couple. How do I get out of this?*

"No, no, Sparks," said André. "The floor's fine. Fabrice can give us some blankets and —"

"André's right," interrupted Marie-Claire. "We're used to sleeping on the floor. So just give us some blankets and some pillows and we'll be fine."

"If you're sure," responded Fabrice, "I can do that when we get back. But right now, I know I could do with a drink."

As they all walked through to the kitchen Marie-Claire whispered to André. "Thank you for intervening and suggesting the floor." He smiled and whispered back, "Sparks obviously doesn't understand our relationship."

Just after one in the morning Fabrice led Sparks, André and Marie-Claire out through Maubuisson towards the field to be used for the drop. Sparks carried a small bag of tools he said might be needed to open the canister, the other three carried the lanterns. There were no clouds in the sky and the almost full moon provided enough light for them to see easily. They walked in silence past the other houses in the village.

They hadn't gone more than three hundred metres when Marie-Claire tapped Fabrice on the shoulder and whispered, "Do the Germans do any curfew patrols in this area?"

He whispered back, "Sometimes. Why do you ask?"

"Because I think I can hear a motorcycle approaching."

Chapter 50

Fabrice motioned to everyone to follow him and they all hid behind a small outbuilding. As Marie-Claire peered around a corner of the building a German motorcycle with side-car came into view. The soldier in the side-car was shining a torch back and forth, obviously looking to see if there were any people around violating the curfew. She quickly drew back and everyone huddled behind the building, listening intently. The motorcycle did not stop. Marie-Claire heard it drive slowly through the village and from the decreasing sound of the engine it appeared the Germans were driving away from the direction of the field.

"A patrol? Just as we're expecting a canister drop," said Sparks. "I don't like coincidences. Are you sure you can trust all of your men Fabrice?"

"As much as one can trust anyone, yes."

The group crept out from behind the outbuilding and continued their journey in silence. As they walked down muddy farm tracks and climbed over stiles Marie-Claire was pleased she had insisted on changing into practical clothes.

After half an hour Fabrice opened a farm gate and whispered, "We're here. This is the landing field. I chose it because there are no roads nearby. Even if that German patrol comes back when the plane flies over, they couldn't drive to this field and we would have time to hide."

Seven figures emerged from out of the shadow of a nearby tree and walked over to Fabrice. One of the men spoke directly to him. "We're all here. The trenches you wanted us to dig in the woods are ready."

In the semi-darkness a voice asked Marie-Claire. "Do you enjoy danger?"

She turned around and recognized Leon, the man who had brought the logs for the train hold-up. "No, but any form of resistance inevitably involves some kind of danger. André didn't tell me you were part of Fabrice's group."

"Out here we're a fairly close farming community and we —"

"Shush," interrupted Marie-Claire. "I hear a motor. Could it be the German motorcycle coming back?"

"No. I recognize that sound," said Sparks. "It's our plane. Fabrice, you go down the field and light your lantern. We'll stay here and light ours. I'll watch out for the identification signal."

The group dispersed across the field as the sound grew louder. Marie-Claire quickly lit her lantern and shone the light upwards as directed by Sparks. She was just able to make out the dark shape of a plane in the sky. A short burst of white flashes came from the plane and Sparks flashed back what she deduced must have been a coded reply as the plane immediately flew down close over the field. As it roared overhead another dark shape appeared beneath the plane and started plummeting rapidly towards the ground.

Marie-Claire was fascinated at how quickly the parachute opened up and slowed the descent. She could just make out the shape of a long cigar-like tube dangling below it. She was so absorbed in watching that she forgot to extinguish the lantern she was holding and had to be reminded to do so by Sparks. By the time she had put out the lantern and looked back up the parachute and canister and plane had all disappeared from her view.

At first she felt it was almost as if nothing had happened. Then she saw dark figures running to the centre of the field. She ran after them and reached the canister just as Sparks opened it. One of Fabrice's men had already detached the parachute and was running towards the woods with the silk in his arms. "What's he doing with it?" she asked.

"He'll bury it in the woods," replied Fabrice.

"As I mentioned earlier," said Sparks, "I want some of the caltrops, detonators and explosives for tomorrow. Everything else needs to be taken away and hidden." Fabrice's men pulled the items out of the canister and disappeared off into the darkness.

"What happens to the canister?" asked Marie-Claire.

Sparks answered quickly with one word, "Watch."

Now it was empty Sparks tapped the canister in various places with his rubber hammer and it fell apart into smaller pieces. "We bury these in the woods in trenches Fabrice's men dug earlier."

Fabrice, Sparks and André picked up the pieces and ran with them to the woods. Marie-Claire was left standing alone in the field. Surprisingly soon the men returned. "Did all that really happen?" she asked. "It's must be less than ten minutes since the plane appeared."

"You're right," said Fabrice. "But right now, we need to gather up the supplies for tomorrow and get home quickly and quietly."

When Marie-Claire had said she would happily sleep on the floor in Fabrice's farmhouse she had not taken into account the nature of the floor. At André's house the floor was made of wooden floorboards. In Fabrice's house the floor was made of cold hard stone. After an hour of trying to find a way of using the blanket as both a cover and a makeshift mattress Marie-Claire gave up and curled up in Fabrice's armchair. She slept fitfully and was glad when morning came.

André had spent all night on the floor and when he woke he whispered to Marie-Claire, "I'm cold and sore. Next time we should bring a stack of our own blankets."

However, there was an advantage to being on a farm. Like the Deferres, Fabrice had been able to hide some of his produce from the Germans and breakfast included bacon and butter, items which were rarely available in shops. André devoured his meal as if he hadn't eaten for a month.

Sparks looked up as Marie-Claire tried to stifle a yawn. "I hope you slept well. This morning I want to explain how to use the detonators and explosives, and I don't want anyone dozing off."

After breakfast André and Marie-Claire accompanied Fabrice to the big barn where Sparks had already laid out some of the equipment delivered in the canister the previous night. They were soon joined by Leon and two others from Fabrice's group.

"When I did my training in Scotland," said Sparks, "we set off actual explosions. For obvious reasons we can't do that here, so you'll need to listen carefully as you'll never have a chance to experiment or practise. The first time you use these it will be for real. Fortunately, the Germans are not yet aware that resistance groups such as yourselves have access to such explosives, so your potential targets are unlikely to be heavily guarded."

When Sparks asked if anyone had any experience with explosives, Yves, one of Fabrice's group, said he'd used some dynamite before the war when building roads.

"I'm glad you said that," remarked Sparks, "because sabotage is completely different. When doing things like mining or building roads, you stay nearby behind some protective barrier. In sabotage our protective barrier is time. We don't stick around. We lay our charges, set a time fuse and run away as far and as fast as possible, never to return to the scene."

"With dynamite," said Yves, "we used rope fuse. I didn't see any last night or here so how do we get the time delay?"

Sparks smiled. "We don't use rope fuse. It sparks and fizzles which means it can be seen or heard by the enemy. Instead we use this time fuse." He held up a small metal tube which looked like a fat pencil. "Unfortunately, we don't have as many as I hoped we would so I won't demonstrate it working. Unlike rope fuse, there is no light and no sound and it works perfectly in the rain, which is a great advantage for sabotage."

He proceeded to explain that if the closed off end of the device was crushed with the heel of a boot or a pair of pliers it would start a chemical reaction. "The open end of the device is then pushed into the plastic explosive. The chemical reaction will continue and after a set number of minutes a detonation cap in the device is released. This sets off the plastic explosive."

"How do you adjust the time?" asked Marie-Claire.

"See this little tag," said Sparks, holding up the pencil detonator. "It has two purposes. If it's a black tag you have ten minutes after crushing it. If it's red you have thirty minutes and if it's white you have two hours. Nothing in between. I'd always advise using at least the thirty minute if not the two hour fuse."

"What's the second use?" asked Yves.

"Once you've pushed the detonator into the plastic, it serves as a safety check. If the delay aspect has failed the detonator inside will have been released pinning this tag tightly in the tube. If that happens, and you can usually hear a click, do not pull the tag out. If you do it will be the last thing you do as the plastic will explode immediately. There's also a little inspection hole. If you can't see through it you must not pull out the tag."

"Why is it called plastic explosive?" asked Leon.

"It's called plastic because it can be moulded and shaped easily like plasticine. It's perfectly safe and you can cut off as much as you need with a knife."

He went on to describe how much would be needed for different situations and how best to place it.

At the end of the training session, André took five of each of the ten minute, thirty minute and two hour detonators and a big block of plastic explosive. "Fabrice, I'm so glad you suggested we come to help with the canister drop. I have a target in mind and this should do the job perfectly."

"Good luck and be careful you follow my instructions exactly," said Sparks. "We don't want to lose either of you." He handed André a bag of caltrops. "Don't forget your tyre bursters."

André thanked Sparks and he and Marie-Claire set off back to Nevers. Once they were in the van Marie-Claire asked, "What target do you have in mind? I didn't know we had one."

André smiled. "We don't. At least not yet. I just thought it would be better if we had our own supply in Nevers in case we identify a target and need to act quickly."

On Wednesday evening Françoise arrived at Marie-Claire's lodgings in a jubilant mood. When she said that apparently André's rope trick had caused havoc Marie-Claire suggested they cycle over immediately to tell him. At André's house Françoise waited until they were inside and the door was closed before exclaiming, "It worked! Your rope trick worked."

André looked pleased. "How do you know?"

"Earlier today I met my friend who knows someone who works

329

at the factory. She'd been told that last Thursday around midnight there was an almighty bang at the factory and all the machines stopped and the lights went out. She said it's going to take at least two months to get a replacement transformer and fix all the damaged equipment. I found it hard not to show my excitement."

André clenched his fists and punched the air. "Fantastic. I wasn't absolutely sure it would work. Taking that factory out of action will seriously impact the production of the new machine-guns. Great!"

In his excitement he leant forward and kissed Françoise on both cheeks. Marie-Claire felt unexpectedly jealous. *He has never kissed me, but I suppose we have a different relationship. Although I'm not exactly sure what that relationship is.*

André smiled like a kid in a candy store. "Yes, yes, yes. In the bigger scheme of things blowing out one transformer may not be much, but if all the resistance groups did something, no matter how small, it would have a serious impact on the Germans. I have some cognac laid aside. I think your news calls for a little celebration before we begin our next operation."

After they raised their glasses to the overwhelming success of the rope trick, Françoise asked, "Next operation? You sound as if you have one in mind. Do you?"

"Yes – but I can't tell you much. Gerhard contacted me earlier today saying he has a plan which is really exciting and asked me to arrange a group meeting for tomorrow evening. I assume you two can be here tomorrow?"

"Of course," said Marie-Claire.

Chapter 51

The following evening when Marie-Claire and Françoise arrived at André's house, Gerhard, Odile, Robert and Tomas were already there. In an excited voice Gerhard explained. "A friend has told me that the Germans have taken over a farm near Saint-Benin-d'Azy. The farm has a large outbuilding where the Germans are storing fuel – barrels and barrels of petrol – and you all know how scarce petrol is."

"Are you suggesting we steal the fuel?" asked Françoise.

"Well, that is an option," said Gerhard, "but I had a more interesting suggestion. I was thinking we could set fire to the depot and destroy the fuel."

"Burn it – or blow it up?" asked Marie-Claire, looking at André.

André smiled back before answering. "Blow it up. We now have explosives and blowing it up would be much more effective."

"Explosives? When did we get explosives?" asked Robert.

"Just this last weekend," answered André with a big grin. "The RAF delivered some to a local resistance group. Marie and I were there and we've been allocated enough to create serious havoc. I don't know what the rest of you feel, but I think blowing up a German fuel dump would be a perfect use of our explosives."

There was a buzz of excited conversation as everyone discussed the options having explosives would give them.

"Obviously an attack on a fuel dump requires careful planning," said Gerhard. "But we're not under the same time pressure which we had when we released the prisoners or disabled the trucks."

Robert looked concerned. "Blowing it up is one thing, but how can we get away without being caught? We would need to be close by in order to set off the explosives. I can't see this being practical. It sounds a bit like a suicide mission."

"The RAF didn't just supply us with plastic explosive," said Marie-Claire. "British scientists have come up with some ingenious time fuses. They're small, silent and work chemically. We would have a two hour window between setting the explosives and having them go off. That should be more than sufficient time to get back to Nevers before all hell breaks loose."

"That sounds better," said Robert. "I can live with that – literally. André, how soon do you think we can do this?"

"At the moment I don't know, and won't until we've done our reconnaissance. We don't know the place, and we will need to determine the layout, how they guard the place, how they store the barrels, how we approach it, how we get away and things like that. With this being our first explosives operation we need time to plan in detail exactly what we're doing. So let's find out more about this place before we decide on a date."

"I've never handled explosives," said Françoise.

"Marie and I have received training," said Andre, "and I suggest on Saturday we train the rest of you in how the use them."

Marie-Claire was impressed by everyone's willingness to get involved in the project. Everybody turned up for the training session on Saturday. When it was over Tomas said he travelled the road by the dump frequently and would take notes of anything happening at the farm as he drove by. Robert offered to go there on his motorcycle at night and record the pattern and details of the night guard patrols around the dump. He reported back that the guarding was unbelievably lax with just one fifteen minute patrol of two soldiers every hour on the hour.

Marie-Claire and Françoise cycled the road a few times, passing the farm slowly and looking for anything which could be useful. When they returned from one such trip they stopped at André's house to tell him what they had discovered. "It appears they certainly don't understand safety," said Marie-Claire. "Can you believe they're allowed to smoke in a fuel dump? We've seen them lighting up very close to the storage buildings and then throwing empty packets and cigarette ends on the ground."

"Stupid idiots," said André, "but that could be to our advantage. When the dump explodes they're likely to blame the smokers."

In the first week of August Marie-Claire got an urgent message from André saying everyone should meet at his house on Tuesday evening. When everyone had arrived he explained, "Tomas saw a large shipment of oil barrels being delivered to the farm. I think we should act now so we destroy as much as possible. Robert, are the guards still on a once an hour pattern?"

"I did another all night check last week and it was still the same. Two soldiers for fifteen minutes every hour on the hour."

"Good," replied André. "Today is Tuesday. I'd like to suggest we go tomorrow. The moon should be almost full which will give us enough light to work by. If it's too cloudy tomorrow we can go on Thursday. Excluding you, Gerhard, can everyone do that?"

When everyone agreed, André went through the basic plan. Robert, Odile, Tomas, André and Françoise would be handling the explosives, with Marie-Claire acting as lookout. He then pointed out that since the whole operation would take place well after curfew and a considerable distance from Nevers, they needed to determine how to get there and back. "I'll take my van but I don't have room for everyone. Besides we shouldn't all travel together. If the van were to be stopped, we would all be arrested."

"I'll take my motorcycle," said Robert.

Marie-Claire looked over at Françoise and made a rotating motion with her hands. When Françoise nodded Marie-Claire proposed that she and Françoise go on their bicycles. "As you know, Françoise and I have cycled that way many times. If we set off a bit earlier we can cycle and meet you there. And you must admit – our bicycles are much quieter than a van or a motorcycle. We can also hide easily if we hear a vehicle approaching."

After a lively discussion about the safety of the girls travelling by bicycle Marie-Claire's suggestion was accepted. "Very well," said André. "Robert you're on your motorcycle, so Tomas and Odile you'll come with me. We'll all meet up at the farm track just off the main road about half a kilometre from the fuel dump."

Early the following evening Marie-Claire packed a warm jacket and her black balaclava in her bicycle bag along with a scarf, a torch, a penknife and her fake ID card. She cycled to Françoise's apartment and they both set off to the fuel dump which was about 18 kilometres away. They reached the meeting point first and by half past eleven everyone else had arrived.

André went over their roles again. "We have two teams. Odile you're with Tomas, and Françoise you're with me. Robert, you'll work with both teams and select the positions for the explosives. Marie, you'll be watching the road and the farmhouse. Remember – a double owl whistle is a warning, a triple is the all clear."

"Timing is everything," he continued. "Please check your watches. I make it eleven forty-five. The guards should start their patrols at midnight and get back at a quarter past. Once they go into the farmhouse we go into the barn and place the explosives. We leave the fuel dump by a quarter to one at the latest which means we have at most a thirty minute window to achieve our objective and get back here. We must all prime the two hour fuses at exactly twelve thirty so they all go off at two thirty."

Walking quietly, they set out for the fuel dump and hid in some bushes from where they could see the buildings. At exactly midnight three guards came out and began their patrol. André whispered to Robert, "I thought you said there were only two."

"There were only two last week."

"Oh great. Let's hope they've not changed their timing as well."

The guards reappeared almost twenty minutes later and sauntered lazily back into the house. André peered nervously at his watch and signalled everyone to move off to their assigned tasks.

Owl whistle at the ready Marie-Claire stood where she could see both the road and the farmhouse. *This is more stressful than actually placing explosives. Everyone's life depends on me warning them if anything happens.*

Just after a quarter to one the five saboteurs emerged from the barns. They hurried over to where Marie-Claire was standing. No one spoke but André held up his thumbs to indicate success. They hurried quietly back to the vehicles. Robert got on his motorcycle and whispered, "So that we don't have two engines starting up at the same time, I'll go right now. See you tomorrow evening."

334

Before André had time to answer Robert drove off. It was then that Françoise let out a soft moan. "I don't believe it. My front tyre has a flat. I can't cycle back like this. I have a puncture kit but —"

"There isn't enough time," interrupted André looking at his watch. "The guards will be out again soon and fixing your tyre will take too long. But somehow we've got to get you out of here."

"André, put Françoise's bike in your van," whispered Marie-Claire, "and all four of you get in. I'll cycle back on my own."

"I can't let you cycle back alone," objected André.

"André. We have no choice. Françoise can't cycle and there isn't room in your van for five people and two bikes. So just do it. You've got to drive off before the guards reappear. They mustn't hear the sound of your van or we'll all get caught. Now go! I can easily hide in the woods at the roadside if necessary."

He reluctantly agreed, loaded Françoise's bike into the van and after Tomas, Odile and Françoise climbed in, he drove off.

Now all alone in the dark Marie-Claire shivered nervously. *What was that stupid thing I said about facing danger?*

Wanting to get away from the fuel dump as fast as possible, she climbed onto her bike and began pedalling frantically towards Nevers. After about ten minutes she heard a vehicle approaching from behind. She stopped abruptly and quickly dismounted with the intention of hiding both the bike and herself in the bushes at the side of the road. However, the vehicle approached so rapidly she did not have time to hide and was still on the side of the road when it drove past her at speed.

Her heart started racing when she saw it was an open-topped German army staff car with swastikas fluttering in the wind.

As she watched the car disappearing down the road she breathed a sigh of relief and felt she was safe.

But that feeling vanished when she realized the car had stopped and was now reversing back towards her.

Chapter 52

Because the German staff car continued to reverse in her direction Marie-Claire was certain she had been seen and there was no point in trying to hide. When the car had passed her she had seen that there was an officer sitting in the back seat but had not been able to see if he was army or Gestapo. She realized that once the fuel dump exploded only a few kilometres away, it probably wouldn't make much difference what kind of German was in the car. Being out after curfew would be the least of the charges she'd face.

For a moment she felt that the situation was completely hopeless and that she had no way to save herself. But then she recalled Emile telling her, 'Never give up, even if the situation seems hopeless.' *If I'm going to survive I need to act quickly. I need to have an acceptable reason for being out after curfew.*

She reached into her bag and pulled out her penknife. She plunged it forcibly into her front tyre, twisted it slightly to expand the hole, pulled it out and dropped it in the ditch at the side of the road along with her black balaclava. She pulled out her colourful headscarf and tied it around her head to hide her hair.

As the car continued to approach, she decided the best course of action was to take the initiative and not wait for the Germans to ask questions. When the car stopped alongside her she immediately began speaking rapidly in German. "Thank you for stopping. I'm so tired pushing my bike. My front tyre burst and I'm so far from home and I'm really scared out here on my own."

When she paused for breath, the officer in the back seat spoke in a pleasant tone. "I'm sorry to hear that. Do you have far to go?"

In the bright moonlight she could see from the man's uniform that he was Army, not Gestapo, and that the braiding on his hat indicated he was a very senior officer. She decided to take a risk and ask for help. "I'm staying in Nevers and it's many kilometres from here. I don't suppose you could help me and give me —"

"Give you a lift?" interrupted the officer. "Of course I can. I'm going that way on my way to Bourges and I can't leave a damsel in distress." He gave instructions to the driver to strap her bicycle to the rack at the back of the car. He then leant over and opened the car door. Marie-Claire stared in disbelief.

Is he actually expecting me to get in with him? I thought I'd be sitting up front with the driver. Surely an important German officer would not want me, a young French woman, sitting next to him – not unless he is expecting something from me in return.

She stood transfixed, not knowing what to do. The officer patted the seat next to him. "Fräulein. Please. Get in." *I suppose if it's this or arrest and torture, I really have no choice!* With a feeling of dread she climbed in and closed the door behind her. "Thank you," she said, trying not to let her fear show in her voice. "I'm so tired from pushing this bike, it's good to sit down."

The officer introduced himself, "I'm General Haas and I'm pleased to be able to help. And you are?"

Remembering the false ID card she was carrying, Marie-Claire responded, "Fräulein Bouchard." *I'll have to destroy that card in case he remembers the name Bouchard.* She almost missed hearing him ask, "How long have you been pushing the bike?"

"My tyre burst more than three hours ago. I waited, hoping someone might come along but no one did so I decided I had to push it home. I'm so thankful that you stopped."

At that point the driver got back in and the car moved off. To her relief the wind in the back seat made further conversation difficult and she didn't need to answer any more questions. She sat with her head down, tense and frightened by what might happen next. But to her relief the General made no move. *Perhaps he really is just a gentleman wanting to help a damsel in distress.*

She felt the car slow down and she looked up. To her horror she realized they were approaching a German checkpoint on the outskirts of Nevers. *Perhaps he was always planning to hand me in.* As they reached the checkpoint she held her breath and gripped her bag so tightly her knuckles went white. But the car was waved through without being stopped and with a salute. She regained her composure and directed the driver to a part of the town near the river, well away from her boarding house. "If you can stop here, I'm just up this narrow alley on Rue des Ratoires."

When the General suggested his driver could help her by taking her bike up to her house, she declined, "I can manage thank you. You've already done a lot for me. More than you can imagine and I'm truly thankful General Haas."

As the car drove away she waved and began pushing her bike into the alleyway. Once she was out of sight of the road she leant her bike against the wall. She collapsed to the ground shaking uncontrollably with relief at having escaped from what had seemed a hopeless situation. After several minutes she realized she wasn't yet safe. She staggered to her feet. *Right now I must get home avoiding the curfew patrols while pushing this damn bike.*

She had never felt so relieved to reach the boarding house. As she pushed her bike into the garden shed she heard the sound of footsteps behind her. She turned around rapidly but in the darkness she could not see anyone. Then she heard a whisper, "Thank goodness you're safe," and recognized André's voice.

"What are you doing here?" she whispered back.

"I couldn't go home until I knew you were back safely. I should never have let you cycle back on your own. I'd never have forgiven myself if anything had happened to you. I'll never ever let you do that again."

Shaking, she collapsed into his arms and he held her close.

"What's the matter? Did something happen?"

She looked up at him, not knowing whether to laugh or cry. "I got a lift back from a German General."

"This is no time for joking," he remonstrated.

"I'm not joking. I got a lift back to Nevers from General Haas in his army staff car – with swastikas fluttering in the wind."

André stepped back and stared at her in disbelief. "Are you serious? A German General?"

They went into the house and Marie-Claire began to relax as she recounted her adventure. He complemented her on puncturing her tyre. "I'm not sure I would have been so quick thinking."

"It's amazing what you can think of when your life depends on it. But I'm concerned that when the General hears about the destroyed fuel dump he will report giving a girl a lift after curfew on the same road as the dump just a few kilometres away. The police and Gestapo might then begin looking for bicycles like mine with a burst tyre. Coming to think of it, we must tell Françoise to fix her tyre immediately."

"And get you a new tyre."

"Unfortunately my bike is quite distinctive and there's no way to disguise it. The General's driver strapped it to the car and may well remember it. I'll have to hide it for a while."

"I know you probably don't want to lose your bike but it sounds as if it's too dangerous to keep. I think we need to destroy it in case the Gestapo find it and arrest you."

"But I use my bike – I can't do without it. And you know how hard they are to come by."

André looked thoughtful. "I have a spare bike you can have. It was Nicole's and I haven't had the heart to part with it until now."

She could see the thought of parting with Nicole's bike was distressing him. "You don't need to do that. I can buy another."

"And advertise to the world that you suddenly need another bike? No. They could be looking for anyone buying a new bike. This is the best thing to do. And she would have approved. In the morning I'll get her bike from my shed and put it in my van. I'll bring it here and swap the bikes. I can then dispose of your old one before anyone comes looking. But right now, if you're going to be ok, I think I should head home."

With a lump in her throat she responded, "I'll be fine – and if you're sure about the bike, I'd appreciate it."

"I am sure. I can't risk losing you as well."

The next day André arrived to swap the bikes and told her that people were talking about a major fire at a fuel dump. "It worked," he said gleefully. "And nobody is suggesting it was sabotage. They're blaming the soldiers for smoking, but I think we should keep our heads down for a while. I still find it hard to believe you were driven back to Nevers by a German General."

"It's something people would talk about so we can't tell anyone, not even Françoise. I'll just say I got back safely."

Marie-Claire's nerves were on edge for the next few days and she tensed every time she saw a German soldier. So for several days she tried to avoid going into town as the streets were always full of soldiers. Instead she spent most of her time in her room sketching. When Madame Favier told her that people were no longer talking about the fire, she felt that probably no one was looking for her and life could go back to normal.

The following Wednesday Madame Favier came into the dining room as Marie-Claire was eating her breakfast. "Your artist soldier friend is here. He wants to speak to you."

Marie-Claire got up and went to the front door where Otto was waiting for her. He spoke before she even had time to greet him. "If you're available Mademoiselle Bruneau, I would like another art lesson. I've been trying to draw buildings and I've been struggling with perspective."

"Of course. When would you like to have a lesson?"

"I was hoping Friday."

"Friday is fine. Shall we say at the bistro at the usual time?"

"Thank you Mademoiselle Bruneau. I'll see you there." Otto turned and walked away.

Marie-Claire returned to her breakfast wondering why Otto really wanted a lesson. *He has never asked to have a lesson on a week day before. And he seemed very anxious – he didn't even smile. The reason for this lesson must be very serious.*

When Marie-Claire arrived at the bistro on Friday afternoon Otto was already there with his drawings spread out on a table. She could see that he really had been trying to draw some of the buildings around Nevers and had been having trouble with perspective. She spent the next hour explaining in detail how to draw perspectives and wondering what he wanted to tell her.

As they were putting their art materials away Marie-Claire said, "For your next lesson I want you to draw the cathedral from many different angles both outside and inside."

When Otto didn't comment, she sensed something was amiss but knew she couldn't ask while they were still inside the Bistro.

After the lesson he guided her to a seat at the edge of the covered area outside where no one could hear them. "Marie. I have some news I wish I didn't need to tell you."

Although immediately worried she tried not to show any fear. *Has someone found out that I was involved in the fuel dump explosion? Is Otto going to warn me that the Gestapo suspect sabotage and are questioning people?*

"What's wrong Otto?"

"I am being posted back to Paris."

Marie-Claire was stunned by his news. All she could manage in response was a weak, "When?"

"Tomorrow."

She was surprised to find herself feeling sad that he was leaving. *He's a German, supposedly an enemy. And yet I'll miss him – he's become a friend. A little light in the darkness.*

"So soon? I'm going to miss you Otto. And I don't mean because of the things you've told me. I'll miss you as a friend. I've enjoyed teaching you. And you've shown me something I'll never forget. You've shown me our enemy is not the German people. It's Hitler and his Nazi thugs. You've also shown me that there are Germans who hate Hitler as much as we do."

"You're right, some do. But I'm sorry to say, too many enjoy the fight. I should know – I'm on the inside. I have a simple warning – be wary of trusting anyone."

They sat in silence for a moment. He looked her in the eyes. "This is the last time we'll meet. I'm going to miss you Marie. Please be careful. The Nazis took away my Greta and I don't want them to take you as well."

As he got up to leave Marie-Claire could see a tear in his eye.

She knew she must not show or ever tell anyone about the emotion she was feeling. *It's utterly stupid but somehow, without Otto around, I feel more vulnerable.*

341

Chapter 53

When Marie-Claire returned to her boarding house after her meeting with Otto she found a simple message from André.

I have cooked Lapin a la Cocotte

She smiled at the note. She didn't believe he'd cook for her without telling her ahead of time. *I think he's just asking me to go over to see him right now.*

When she reached his house he apologized. "I haven't actually done any cooking."

She laughed, "I thought as much."

"It's just that Fabrice has said he wants some work done and you know what that means."

"Yes, so it's a good thing I brought a warm jacket and a toothbrush. So let's go – and don't forget the blankets."

At Maubuisson Fabrice greeted them with enthusiasm. "Sparks has been away for a while and has just returned. As well as wanting to do some more training he said he has some important information for us. It's to do with the BBC. Do you listen to the French program on the BBC?"

Marie-Claire knew that it was a serious offence to be caught listening to the BBC so she kept quiet. André shrugged his shoulders. "Not really. Should I?"

"I'll let Sparks tell you. He's out in the barn."

As Marie-Claire walked into the barn she felt almost sick at the smell inside. Sparks looked up from the bench he was working at. "I hope you like rats Marie. We've got quite a few to process here."

The meaning behind his words became evident when she looked at the bench. There were piles of dead rats and Sparks was cheerfully slicing one open and removing its guts. "Fabrice and I are making bombs. Rat bombs."

"What's a rat bomb?" asked André.

342

"See here," replied Sparks. "I'll replace this rat's guts with some gunpowder mixed with plastic explosive and I'll then sew it back up so it looks normal. You can toss these rat bombs onto piles of coal and when they are then shovelled into a fire or boiler – bang. Very effective. Some of my colleagues have suggested dropping them from bridges onto train engines."

Marie-Claire tried to hide the disgust she was feeling. "Is that why you wanted us to come here? To make rat bombs?"

Sparks laughed. "No. Not just to teach you how to make these. I want you to listen to the French program on the BBC. It's on in the evening and now includes something which will be very useful."

After they finished their evening meal Sparks turned on the radio, tuned it to the BBC French program and they all listened. They heard an announcement asking them to 'Please listen to some personal messages'. Then a series of seemingly unconnected sentences and phrases were read out. Although Marie-Claire could not understand why they were listening to a selection of inane and ridiculous phrases, she kept quiet until the short program ended.

"Is this supposed to be comedy?" she asked. "What's funny about 'The lease is renewed' or 'The bishop is going bald'. What am I missing?"

Sparks smiled. "These are coded messages from SOE headquarters in London to various resistance groups. But it's not like any ordinary code – it can't be broken because the words and phrases have no intrinsic meaning."

"How is it coded," asked André, "if the words and phrases have no meaning?"

"Let's pretend I'm waiting for a canister drop. I don't know on which night the RAF will fly over. But if I listen to the BBC and hear a particular phrase, such as 'The lease is renewed', this message let's me know my canister drop is on for that night."

"But won't the Germans catch on when the same phrase always means a canister will be dropped?" asked Marie-Claire.

"That's the beauty of this system. The phrase used is different every time. You heard them say 'The bishop is going bald'. Personally I don't know what that phrase means, it has nothing to do with me. But it may tell some other resistance group to blow up a bridge tonight. The phrase is a trigger not a code."

"How would that group know what it means?" asked André.

"The phrase is created by the group and the SOE agent in that area transmits it to London which means only that group and London know it has any significance. And if on any evening there aren't enough genuine messages, then SOE will include some random phrases with no meaning at all just to confuse the Germans. Each phrase is unique."

At the end of the evening when André and Fabrice were in the kitchen cleaning up after the meal, Sparks again suggested to Marie-Claire that he sleep on the couch so that she and André could have his room upstairs for the night.

"No thanks. We're fine down here on the floor."

He looked puzzled. "Really? But aren't you a couple?"

Marie-Claire shook her head while blushing slightly. "No. We are friends and we work together but we're not anything more than that."

Am I speaking from my head or my heart? Sparks is right that André and I are close. Have our losses brought us so close that we are becoming a couple? Nicole is gone. Emile is gone. If we become closer would it be all that wrong?

Sparks was still speaking. "I'm sorry if I've embarrassed you. I'll not mention it again."

On the following day Sparks taught Marie-Claire and André how to make rat bombs. When they left to go back to Nevers they decided not to take any with them, primarily because of the smell.

"If we find we could use some," said André, "we know how to make them. And I'll tune into the BBC each evening. It should make amusing listening."

On the last Wednesday of August André turned up at Marie-Claire's boarding house in the early evening. "I've been asked to join a special mission being organized by Fabrice and Sparks."

"What will you be doing?" asked Marie-Claire, "or are you not allowed to tell me?"

"Actually, I'd tell you if I knew but I don't. All I know is it's something to do with an RAF mission. I'll be gone for two perhaps three days as we don't know on which day the weather will be suitable for the RAF planes."

"Does that mean you'll be listening for one of those silly messages on the BBC?"

"Yes. I shouldn't tell anyone – but you're not anyone. If you hear 'Cinema seats cost eighteen francs' you'll know we're going on our mission that night."

"When is this mission? When do you leave?"

"Actually I'm driving to Maubuisson right now. I'll be back on Friday. Or Saturday at the latest."

His announcement came as a surprise. "Take care, André. And let me know the moment you get back. Promise me you will."

"Of course I will."

He went back to his van and Marie-Claire watched him drive away. *I hope he'll be alright. I told Sparks that we're not a couple but I feel so worried for him it almost feels as if we are.*

That night she listened to the 'Personal Messages' on the BBC French program. When she was at Fabrice's house she had not noticed that each message was repeated but tonight her attention was more focused. Amongst other messages she heard twice that 'Honesty is rare' and that 'The canteen supervisor is rude'. But by the end of the short program she had not heard 'Cinema seats cost eighteen francs'.

Not tonight then. Perhaps tomorrow night.

She had a fitful sleep and found herself feeling at a loss throughout the following day. She tried reading, sketching and going for a walk in the park, but nothing she did took her mind off her concerns about André.

After her evening meal she turned on her radio in time for the BBC French program. She was not in the least bit interested to know that 'Our ancestors used candles' or that 'Chapter five comes after chapter four'. However she gasped slightly when she heard the phrase 'Cinema seats cost eighteen francs'. She now realized

345

why all messages were repeated. The first time all it did was get her attention. The repeat confirmed that she had heard the phrase correctly.

What are you doing André? Please be careful and come back tomorrow. Please.

On Friday morning she went into town to do some shopping. However the sight of German soldiers was a constant reminder of the risks André was facing. She abandoned her shopping trip and returned to the boarding house. In the afternoon she tried painting but soon realized all she was really doing was waiting for Madame Favier to knock on her door to tell her André was downstairs.

It was well past five o'clock before there was a knock at her door. Marie-Claire jumped out of her chair, tipping it over in her excitement to open the door. When she saw it was Madame Favier standing in the hall she asked in an anxious voice, "Is he here?"

"Is who here? Do you mean your German artist?"

"No. I thought you might have come to tell me André is here."

"No. Nobody's here. I just came up to ask if you wanted to go to the cinema with Odile and me tonight."

"Thanks for asking but not tonight. I'm expecting André to call so I'll stay in. But thank you."

Why am I so upset? He didn't say he'd definitely be back on Friday. He said it could be Saturday. Tomorrow. He'll be back tomorrow.

On Saturday Marie-Claire didn't go shopping. She didn't sit reading. She tried painting but she just could not concentrate. She only nibbled at her lunch and she ate almost nothing in the evening.

The words of the important warning published just the week before in *Le Petit Parisien* kept going through her mind. The German administration had stated that all prisoners in jails would now be considered hostages who could be shot in the event that any German soldiers were killed by French people. *Has André been caught? Is he now a hostage?*

By bedtime when he still hadn't called, her stomach was in knots. She was almost sick with worry and couldn't sleep. Half way through the night she had to turn over her tear-drenched pillow. *This can't be happening again. I can't add André to the list of people I've lost. How did I not see my feelings for him growing to this point?*

On Sunday morning she woke to the sound of someone knocking on her door. She jumped out of bed, flung on her dressing gown and pulled the door open. She was disappointed to see it was Françoise, not André. "What are you doing here?"

"That's not much of a welcome," said Françoise. "Last Sunday we arranged that today we'd go out for the day and I just came by to pick you up. Why aren't you ready? You look awful. You look as if you've been crying all night. What's wrong Marie?"

"It's André," she said, and started crying again. "He went on a sabotage mission on Wednesday and should have been back on Friday."

Françoise put her arms around her friend. Marie-Claire sobbed, "He said Saturday at the latest and he's still not back. I can't go through another loss. Not again – not again."

Chapter 54

Françoise closed the bedroom door and guided her weeping friend to a chair. She knelt down beside her. "You can trust me with whatever you want to say."

Through her tears Marie-Claire found it hard to speak. "Before, before I came to Nevers, the Gestapo —" She paused and tried to wipe her eyes. "A long time ago you asked me why I came here and I've never told you. I've never told you what the Gestapo did."

She paused again. *How much do I tell her?*

"The Gestapo ripped my life apart. They killed my friends – Simone, Hannah and Katia. And they also shot my mother – I saw them do it."

Françoise gasped in shock as Marie-Claire struggled to continue. "And then they murdered —"

At the sound of a knock on her door she stopped and held her breath as Françoise went to the door and opened it. André stood there looking slightly dishevelled. Marie-Claire jumped up and flung her arms around him. "Thank God you're safe. I've been worried sick. What happened?"

"We had to abort the mission and hide. I only got back this morning and came straight over. Angélique said Françoise was here and I could go straight up."

André looked at Marie-Claire's tear-stained face. "But has something happened to you? Are you alright? What's wrong?"

"When you weren't back when you said you would be I thought maybe you'd been caught – or worse."

She wrapped her arms around him again. "Oh I'm so pleased you're ok."

Françoise came over and hugged him as well. "So am I. I was worried when Marie said you were missing."

"We were nearly caught, but we escaped and had to hide for a couple of days. I wanted to send you a message to say I was ok but obviously I couldn't phone. Fabrice suggested I send you a message via the BBC 'Personal Messages' but Sparks said that wasn't possible as to do that he'd have to physically take the message to his radio operator. He also pointed out that by the time any such message would be broadcast we'd be back."

"I'm intrigued," said Françoise. "I thought BBC messages were prearranged. So how could you have sent an unexpected message that Marie would understand?"

"Knowing that Marie would be listening each evening I would have sent something that she would know came from me."

Marie-Claire smiled. "Let me guess. 'The carpenter has cooked Lapin a la Cocotte'. Am I right?"

André smiled back. "Spot on. But as we were in hiding Sparks could not contact his radio operator."

Marie-Claire became conscious of the fact she was still wearing her dressing gown and pulled it tightly around her. "Françoise is here because she and I were going out for Sunday lunch and a stroll. If you can give me a moment to freshen up and get dressed I suggest all three of us go out together."

After André left to wait downstairs Françoise asked, "Are you sure you don't want it to be just the two of you for lunch?"

"Until I thought André wasn't going to return, I didn't know exactly how strong my feelings were for him. But equally, I don't want to say or do something I may regret. He's a very close friend and I don't want to risk jeopardizing that. So let's all go and celebrate his safe return."

When Marie-Claire got back home after their day out she sat on her bed thinking about the last few days. She was unsure about her relationship with André, especially after her emotional display that morning. Although she now realized the strength of her feelings for him, she didn't want André to think she was trying to replace Nicole, so she decided not to say anything to him.

The following day was the first day of the new school term. Marie-Claire was perturbed to find that some of the paper Colonel Zeigler had donated was missing. She went to the secretary's office. "Madame Segal. What's happened to the art paper?"

"I decided you wouldn't need all of it so I've allocated some of it to the other classes. I didn't think you would mind considering it came from the Germans."

Marie-Claire was annoyed but decided she should just accept the decision. "I see. Well I suppose there is a general shortage but please don't take any more of it. It was given specifically for the art lessons." She left the office before saying anything she might regret and went to the staff room.

There she found all the other teachers chatting about the holidays and their plans for the new term. She was delighted to hear that Gerhard had been appointed as deputy head. Monsieur Thibault made a short speech welcoming everyone back and explaining that there would be fewer pupils this term as many Jewish families had moved away. Remembering the round-ups during the summer Marie-Claire was not surprised, but was sad as some of her most promising pupils would be missing. She enjoyed being back teaching and was pleased to find that the children seemed as happy to see her as she was to see them.

When she came back from school on Tuesday she was surprised to find André sitting in his van outside the boarding house. He got out of the van to talk to her. "Are you free tomorrow? Fabrice wants me to do some work for him. You know what that means and I thought you might want to come along."

"That's slightly awkward. I've arranged to meet Françoise."

"Why don't we all go to see Fabrice? It'll just be a day trip and I was going to suggest it was time Françoise met him and Sparks. Do you think she'd mind a change of plan?"

"If you want, we can go and ask her right now."

Far from being disappointed at the change of plan, Françoise was excited at the prospect of meeting Fabrice and Sparks and agreed enthusiastically.

As they drove to Maubuisson the next day André explained to Françoise that Sparks was not just an agent but that he was actually a British army officer trained in sabotage and guerrilla fighting techniques and sent over by the British to train French resistance workers.

"If Sparks is actually a British army officer, isn't that incredibly dangerous for him?" asked Françoise. "What if he's caught?"

"Apparently the agents are British army officers in the hope that if they're caught they'll be treated as prisoners of war rather than shot as spies."

"Does that work?" asked Marie-Claire.

"Knowing the Gestapo, I doubt it," answered André. "But I suppose it's at least worth trying."

When they arrived in Maubuisson Fabrice looked pointedly at Françoise and asked, "Who is this?" in a very unwelcoming tone. "I wasn't expecting you to bring someone new with you."

"This is our friend Françoise Deferre. She is a critical member of our group and has been involved in planning all of our missions. There's nothing you might tell me that she should not hear."

As Fabrice ushered them into his living room he said, "It's not what I might say that's bothering me. Sparks is here and wants to talk to you about a plan and he's very security conscious."

"And so are we Fabrice," said Marie-Claire. "I can assure you we trust Françoise completely otherwise we would not have brought her here with us today."

Sparks stepped out from behind the kitchen door and asked, "Françoise Deferre? Are you related to Rémi Deferre?"

"Rémi is my father. Do you know him?"

"Indirectly yes. Which means I have no problem including you in these discussions."

"Does my father know about you then?" asked Françoise.

"Probably not, and it's best we keep it that way. But to get to the reason I asked André to come here, it looks as if we may have an interesting sabotage target in a joint operation with the RAF. There's an important metalworking factory in Bourges which is making armaments for the Germans and the British want to destroy it, or at least have it destroyed."

"What has that got to do with us?" asked Marie-Claire. "If the

British want to destroy it, then why don't they just bomb it?"

"It's not that straightforward," said Sparks. "Back in the last century the factory owner built residential accommodation for the workers close to the factory and people still live there. Bombing is not accurate enough to be sure of only hitting the factory. It would most likely destroy some of the nearby houses and kill many of the French residents."

"I can understand the problem," said André. "The papers would make a big thing about how this shows the British do not care about killing French people. But you've obviously got some idea how to counter this. So what's your plan?"

Sparks smiled. "The idea is that we sabotage the factory from the inside, blowing up the most important machines."

"So where does the RAF come into this?" asked Françoise.

"Sabotage on this scale could bring severe German reprisals. So the idea is to have RAF bombers fly over a minute or so before the sabotage explosions go off. They won't drop bombs but hopefully the Germans will blame the RAF and not the French resistance."

"Nice idea," said André, "but it would require intricate planning and precise timing and I don't see how we would be able to guarantee the timing."

"That's where it becomes more interesting," said Fabrice. "The factory manager is also the owner of the factory. Sparks wants to go to him and ask for permission to blow up the factory. If we get the permission we will have the manager arrange it so we can enter the factory at night and place our charges timed to go off as the planes pass overhead."

"You're going to ask the factory owner for permission!" exclaimed Marie-Claire. "Permission to blow up his factory? And what would make him agree? Are you going to bribe him?"

"No," answered Sparks. "I'll use logic and appeal to his conscience and personal safety. I will tell him in no uncertain terms that his factory will be destroyed one way or another. I will point out that if he does not agree to the sabotage approach then the RAF will bomb the factory anyway and some bombs are likely to hit the nearby houses. I'll also point out that when the local

352

people are told that he could have prevented the deaths of the local residents, they may take a dim view of his decision. And that could put his life in jeopardy."

"So basically, you're going to blackmail the factory owner. Is that right?" asked André.

"I'd prefer to say I'll be appealing to his sense of patriotic duty," said Sparks, "but if necessary, I'll use blackmail."

"What has this got to do with us?" asked Marie-Claire.

"Before I talk to the manager I need to know that Fabrice can arrange a completely reliable and efficient sabotage team and you and André were his first choice to be the core of the team."

André looked in turn at Marie-Claire and Françoise both of whom smiled back and nodded their heads. "If you want us, Fabrice, we'd all be happy to join your team."

"I hoped you'd say that," said Fabrice.

André turned to Sparks. "When are you going to see this factory manager?"

"Now that I know you're with us, I'll go this afternoon. Can you three come back on Saturday?"

André looked at Marie-Claire and Françoise, both of whom agreed. "We'll all be back on Saturday morning," said André. "Is there something else we can do right now?"

"Yes," said Sparks. "I suggest we spend the rest of this morning doing some more explosives training – you can never have too much."

On Saturday morning André collected Marie-Claire and Françoise in his van. On the way to Maubuisson he expressed his scepticism. "I hope this isn't a waste of time. Although I have faith in Sparks I just don't see how he can pull it off. The notion a factory owner would voluntarily agree to having his factory destroyed sounds utterly ridiculous."

"I know what you mean," said Françoise. "In one sense it's a great idea, but I also think it's far too optimistic."

"I think you've both forgotten there are two aspects to this plan," said Marie-Claire. "Our part, sabotaging the factory from the inside, can only happen if Sparks can persuade the manager that this approach minimizes French casualties. If he can't do that then we're no longer involved and the RAF will actually bomb the factory. But if he can, the brilliant part of the whole plan is to have the RAF pretend to bomb the factory so that the Germans don't blame the resistance. That's so absurd it might just work."

"I had forgotten the alternative is a real RAF bombing raid," said Françoise.

"In war, thinking outside of the box is how you win," said Marie-Claire. "The Germans tend to be noted for taking a logical approach and this is so illogical they might just fall for the ruse. And if they think the RAF bombed the factory they'll have no reason to suspect our involvement."

"Yes," agreed André, "but the whole thing still relies on the unlikely premise that Sparks can persuade the manager."

When they arrived in Maubuisson Fabrice greeted them enthusiastically. "Come in, come in. You know where the kitchen is. Make yourselves some drinks while I get Sparks. He's out in the barn with Sebastien."

As they went into the house André asked Fabrice, "Who is Sebastien? Can we talk in front of him?"

"I forgot. You haven't met him," replied Fabrice. "Sebastien is part of my resistance group but he couldn't join us last week. He'll be the one going into the Bourges factory next week as a supposed employee."

"Into the factory?" asked Marie-Claire incredulously. "Are you saying Sparks was successful?"

Chapter 55

As Marie-Claire, André and Françoise walked into Fabrice's kitchen to prepare their drinks Marie-Claire turned to the others, "Am I understanding Fabrice correctly? Has a factory owner really been persuaded by a British soldier to allow the resistance to destroy his factory, his business, his livelihood?"

"Unbelievable," said André. "I want to know how he did it."

As they carried their drinks through to the living room, Fabrice came into the house accompanied by Sparks and Sebastien. After Fabrice introduced Sebastien, everyone looked at Sparks.

"I know you all doubted I could do it, but I was able to persuade the owner, Monsieur Soulier, to help us blow up his factory. Right from the start he let me explain what I was proposing without objecting or interrupting. However, when I was finished he said that he could not trust a word I had said because I could be a Gestapo agent assessing his loyalty to the Nazis."

"How did you change his mind?" asked André.

"When I told him I was a British officer he laughed and asked me to prove it. André, I remembered how you wanted to have the BBC send a message to Marie and I asked Monsieur Soulier to create a silly phrase. I said if I got the BBC to broadcast his phrase in the French program that was something the Germans couldn't do and it would prove my credentials. He laughed again, looked around the room, stared at his coat rack and asked me to have the BBC broadcast the phrase 'She wants a coat hanger'."

"I heard that on the BBC a few nights ago," said Marie-Claire.

"You're right Marie. It's something the SOE hadn't thought of doing but it worked and we'll use BBC personal messages that way again in the future. Hearing his silly phrase on the BBC must have persuaded him because when I went back to see him yesterday he was extremely helpful. Apparently he hates the Nazis but was forced into producing shells for the German guns."

"Could being helpful just be a cover?" asked Marie-Claire. "Could he actually be setting a trap to catch us?"

"Possible but unlikely," said Sparks. "I'm very confident he is genuinely anti-Nazi. But to get back to the plan. Sebastien will become a temporary employee and the foreman, who also hates the Nazis, will give him a floor plan of the factory and show him where to place the explosives to maximize the destruction."

"Can we trust the foreman?" asked Françoise.

"I think so," answered Sparks. "He's Monsieur Soulier's son."

"I'm impressed," said André. "So when are you and the RAF planning this combined attack?"

"We need Sebastien to be there for two weeks and the plan needs to merge with the RAF bombing campaign. This operation is pencilled in for Friday 26 September, with Saturday as a fall back in case of bad weather. That gives Sebastien time to learn what he needs to know and quit his job a week before the attack."

"Won't it look suspicious if he quits?" asked Marie-Claire.

"You're right," replied Sebastien, "as a new employee I would be number one suspect. But I won't actually quit – I'll be dismissed on health grounds. You see, I will develop a tuberculosis cough during the second week. It will be so bad that the other employees won't want me around. You know – coughing all the time and spitting blood so no one wants to come near me. Monsieur Soulier will dismiss me. And a week later – bang."

"How about the factory guards?" asked Françoise.

"Not a problem," answered Sparks. "It's a family business and they're both relations of Monsieur Soulier. In fact the plan is that they'll be opening the factory gate for us."

"Sparks, this whole thing is your idea and you're in charge," said André. "So what is your detailed plan?"

Sparks shook his head. "Actually the role of an SOE agent is not to conduct sabotage but rather to train people how to do it. You know – give a hungry man a fish or teach him how to fish. I'm the contact with London and the RAF and I've laid the groundwork with Monsieur Soulier. But from now on someone else needs to be the mission leader. Treat me as a consultant, not a leader."

"André, that's why I asked you to be part of this mission," said Fabrice. "Seeing how you took control last weekend and saved the lot of us, I think you should be the leader."

Sparks agreed. "I was impressed how quickly you adapted to the changing situation and that's what's needed on this mission."

André took a deep breath before responding. "Ok, if you're sure, I'll do it. Sparks, when does Sebastien start at the factory?"

"Monday. He'll meet Monsieur Soulier on Monday."

"Under what name? He certainly can't go as Sebastien."

"I referred to him as Frédéric Voisin."

André turned to Sebastien. "Is that what is on your fake ID?"

"No. On that card I have the name —"

"I don't need to know," interrupted André. "We'll be changing it to Frédéric Voisin. Have you got that card with you?"

"No. It's back at my house. But how can you change it so quickly? I'll need it tomorrow when I go to Bourges."

"Don't worry about that. You just go and get it and I'll bring it back tomorrow with your new name. I know someone who is a magician when it comes to amending cards."

After Sebastien had gone André asked Fabrice, "Can we trust Sebastien, and can he do the job properly?"

"Yes to both questions, Before the war he was an apprentice engineer which is why we chose him to go into the factory."

"And where will he be staying in Bourges?"

"He has a cousin there," answered Fabrice. "Talking of cousins, my cousin Clément lives in the area. He has a large farmhouse and a big barn which we could use as our base."

"Excellent. Does Clément know anything about the plan?"

"No. I wasn't going to tell him anything until we were sure we'd be doing this. He won't be a problem though. We're very close and he's told me before he'll do anything to help fight the Germans."

"That's good. This operation is taking shape," said André. "When Sebastien returns we'll head back to Nevers and I'll bring his ID card back tomorrow in the name of Frédéric Voisin. In the mean time, Sparks, could you work out how to blow some holes in the factory roof to make it look as if it had been bombed."

"I won't be able to do that properly until Sebastien reports back here at the end of his first week in the factory," said Sparks. "I suggest we all meet here again next Saturday. I'd advise against having a large number of people involved." He turned to Fabrice. "How many people have you got for this?"

Fabrice thought for a moment. "I can rely on four. Julien and Raoul who you met when we did our first training session. And Leon who you met last weekend. And obviously Sebastien. So along with the four of us here that makes eight."

"Not Sebastien," said Sparks. "He'll need to be going around pointing out to the others where to place the explosives. André, do you have anyone else in your team who could join us?"

"We have a mechanic who I trust completely, and I know will take every opportunity to fight back against the Germans."

"That's perfect," said Sparks. "Let's all meet here next Saturday to finalize all the plans. This is one of the first time-coordinated missions with the RAF and I want to make sure it's a success."

When Sebastien returned with his ID card, André, Marie-Claire and Françoise said their goodbyes and set off back to Nevers.

Buttermilk worked its magic without any problem and Marie-Claire found it easy to amend Sebastien's ID card. When she was finished she took it over to André's house. "Here's Sebastien's card, or should I say Frédéric's card? As you know I wasn't entirely convinced this whole blow up the factory plan would actually come to fruition but amending this card has made it feel real."

"You'll be pleased to know I spoke to Robert and he's fully behind the plan. He thinks he'll be able to provide a truck to take us there which is much better than going in my van. Do you want to come with me tomorrow?"

"I'd like to but I'm going to a concert in Parc Salengro with Françoise. A local French group are playing and I want to support them. I hate German bands playing in our park bandstand as if it was theirs. They've been doing it all summer and it annoys me."

"Can you let Françoise know that I'll come by your houses and pick you two up shortly after breakfast on Saturday. Let's hope Sebastien is able to gather the information we need."

When the Nevers group arrived in Maubuisson on Saturday morning they found the atmosphere in Fabrice's living room was almost electric with excitement. Sebastien had returned with comprehensive layouts of the factory and detailed information on the critical machines to be destroyed.

Sparks had devised a plan for the destruction of the factory. "We'll use four teams, three on machines and one on structural damage. The factory foreman identified six critical machines and they will be our targets. He has also indicated on the layout the most vulnerable points to hit to collapse the building structure."

André turned to Sebastien. "Well done. How did the other workers accept you?"

"I had no problem at all. The foreman introduced me as a maintenance apprentice which provided a reason for me to be shown the inner workings of each machine. Oddly enough I think he's actually looking forward to us destroying the factory. He really hates being forced to work for the Germans and doesn't believe the family will ever regain control of the factory again."

"I'm still slightly concerned," said Marie-Claire. "How do we know the factory owner is not pretending to be on our side only to have the Germans waiting in the factory when we turn up?"

"You're right to be concerned Marie," replied Sparks. "Double agents and traitors are always our biggest problem. But I did make it very clear to Monsieur Soulier that in fighting the Germans we're fighting an enemy who has no scruples, so we would have no scruples in dealing with those who betray us."

Marie-Claire was about to question his approach but then she remembered what the Gestapo did to Katia, Hannah, Emile and her mother. So she merely nodded and stared at the floor. *What I'm going to do won't bring them back but it might help save other people's loved ones. It's not so much revenge for their deaths as it is fighting back.*

The following weekend Robert drove Marie-Claire, André and Françoise to Maubuisson. There they met up with Fabrice's group, Julien, Raoul, Leon and Sebastien. Marie-Claire was again

359

impressed with the way Sparks conducted the training session. "Were you a teacher before becoming an agent?"

Sparks smiled. "No. I was a philosophy student but I was aiming to become a teacher. Why do you ask?"

"Your explanations were so clear. I'm feeling more confident we can pull this off."

"That's good. Being confident is essential, especially when handling explosives. Not overly confident but equally, not unsure. I've been watching you and you'll do just fine." Marie-Claire felt reassured. *I'm sure he wouldn't have said that unless he meant it.*

When Sparks asked Robert if he could make false licence plates for the trucks she was puzzled. "Why do we need false plates?"

"Clément's farm is a few kilometres from the factory," said Sparks, "and you will need to drive part of the way. If someone sees the real licence plates the trucks could be tracked back to us."

During lunch Marie-Claire asked Sebastien about his supposed tuberculosis. "When we first started planning this, you said something about spitting blood. How did you do that?"

"Sparks taught me to cough into a handkerchief which was already stained red and make sure everyone saw me do it."

Marie-Claire had an immediate flashback to Katia rejecting a German officer's advances in Paris. "Most people are frightened of catching TB so I'm sure coughing like that would put them off."

"When Monsieur Soulier dismissed me yesterday on the basis of my ill health, he made sure other people heard him so there was no doubt as to why I had to leave."

After lunch André went over the plans again so everyone was familiar with their individual roles. Sparks said he would cut the plastic explosive up into the required portions that afternoon. "I think we should take them to Bourges tomorrow. It's best they are transported separately from the group."

"I'd suggest Monday instead," said André. "We can go in my van and I'll load it with tools and plumbing gear. That way, if we're stopped it'll look like we're working. To the untrained eye, the explosives look like plumbing sealant and the pencil detonators can be mixed in with pipe fittings."

For Marie-Claire the following week seemed to pass very slowly. As a distraction she and André went to the cinema on Wednesday evening and although the film was a boring romance it passed the time. When they came out of the cinema André took her arm and they walked slowly back to her house, chatting about the film. They stood outside saying goodbye for longer than normal and for a moment she thought he might kiss her – but he made no move.

After he left she went up to her room feeling confused. *It's probably a good thing he didn't kiss me. I don't know how I would have reacted, and starting a relationship now could compromise the mission. Perhaps after we get back. I don't know – somehow it doesn't feel quite right.*

At lunch time on Friday Marie-Claire and Françoise went for a short walk together. "It hardly seems like three weeks since Sparks first suggested this crazy idea," said Françoise.

"I know what you mean," agreed Marie-Claire. "And yet here we are, today, going to Bourges to blow up a factory. Which reminds me, André asked me to tell you to bring a warm jacket, a toothbrush and some spare clothes. If the RAF can't fly tonight, he said we'll have to stay at the farm in case they can fly tomorrow."

"Let's hope we go tonight," said Françoise. "I've had my fill of sleeping on hard floors."

At half past five Madame Favier knocked on Marie-Claire's door. "André's here but he's got a truck. Has he changed his van?"

"No. Robert is taking us in his truck for a special outing. If there are any delays, I may not be back until Sunday."

"Good luck, and let me know when you're back."

Marie-Claire picked up her bag and went out to the truck. "I'm ready so let's pick up Françoise and get going."

On the drive to Bourges nobody spoke. Everyone seemed preoccupied with their own thoughts. Marie-Claire wondered what Emile would have thought of her being a résistante using explosives to blow up a French factory requisitioned by the Germans. *I'm sure he would have encouraged me. I know he would have gladly joined in. I miss you Emile. I'm continuing your fight without you but I wish you were here beside me.*

At the Clément farm they found that Fabrice's group had already arrived and there was a general hubbub of conversation. André called for silence so he could tell them the final details. "The RAF planes are due to fly over at two in the morning. If we're on for tonight we'll need to activate the two hour fuses at midnight. And here's the bit you've been waiting for. The magic phrase is 'The shop is closed'. If we hear that on the BBC it's go for tonight."

When Clément turned on his radio everyone fell silent as the announcement came over the air waves – 'This is Radio London. Please listen to some personal messages'. During the repeats of the messages, some of the group chuckled at the silly phrases.

However everyone fell silent when they heard the critical message – 'The shop is closed'. When they heard the repeat there was general shouting of 'yes' and 'tonight' and 'let's go'.

Their combined voices almost completely drowned out the next message but Marie-Claire heard just enough of it to yell at the top of her voice, "Quiet – I need to hear this message."

Everyone stopped talking and listened to the repeat of the message Marie-Claire had only partially heard. This time she heard all of it – 'Pascal wants champagne in a broken teacup'.

She gasped and whispered softly, "Oh my God. There's only one person in the world who would use those words – and I thought he was killed by the Germans. It can't be him – can it?"

She felt as if the world was spinning and her legs buckled under her as she slumped to the floor.

Chapter 56

André and Françoise rushed over to where Marie-Claire was sitting on the floor looking dazed and mumbling to herself, "It can't be him. It can't be."

They knelt down beside her. "What's wrong?" asked André. "What did that message mean?"

"It means he's alive – but he can't be," replied Marie-Claire.

André turned to the others who had now gathered around Marie-Claire. "Please, give Marie some room. Something has obviously upset her and you're not helping by crowding around. Can we give her some room, please."

As Fabrice ushered the other saboteurs into the kitchen he said to André, "Remember we have to leave soon." He then closed the door, leaving André and Françoise alone with Marie-Claire.

André turned back to Marie-Claire. "Do you mean who I think you mean?"

"Yes. But he can't be alive – he was murdered."

"I'm not understanding," said Françoise. "Who was murdered?"

Marie-Claire turned to her, "I think that message means my husband is still alive."

"You never told me you were married," exclaimed Françoise.

"I had to keep my past life secret as the Gestapo were looking for me even before they killed Emile."

"Is Emile your husband's name?" asked André.

"Yes," replied Marie-Claire. She looked at him anxiously. "Where's Sparks? I need to have the BBC broadcast a reply. Where's Sparks?"

"We'll see him tomorrow when we get back to Maubuisson," said André. "But Marie, what makes you think Emile had anything to do with that message?"

"I know Emile is certainly involved but I don't understand how. I thought they had killed him. I was there at the time."

"Marie you're not making much sense," said Françoise sympathetically. "We want to help, so please tell us why you're so sure your husband is involved."

"Emile was planning to write a detective novel using the pen name Pascal. We both used to laugh at the title he was going to give his book. But the war came and he never wrote the book. He was going to call it *'Champagne in a Broken Teacup'*. Now do you understand?"

"I see what you mean," said Françoise thoughtfully. "The wording in that BBC message was too unusual to be a coincidence. But why did you think Emile was dead?"

"I was told that the Gestapo stormed into the bookshop where he worked, sprayed the inside with heavy machine-gun fire and then set the shop on fire. I was on my way to see Emile and as I approached I heard the machine-guns and when I saw the shop the firemen were just standing around watching it burn."

"Oh how awful." Françoise put her arm around Marie-Claire. "And you were actually there!"

"Yes, and there was nothing I could do. If the Gestapo had come a few minutes later I would have been in the bookshop when they machine-gunned it. As I watched the building burn some of Emile's resistance group saw me and fearing for my safety they dragged me away. They suspected the group had been betrayed so after they took me to a safe house they drove away immediately saying they had to disappear."

"When was this?" asked André.

"Almost exactly a year ago."

"Seeing your husband murdered – I don't know how you coped," said Françoise. "I don't think I could have."

"When you have no choice, you just have to carry on. With the Gestapo looking for me I changed my name, my status and my life, and I came to Nevers as Mademoiselle Marie Bruneau."

"I understand now why you've never spoken about your past."

"If Emile's alive, this is amazing news Marie," said André, reaching out and taking her hand. "That message must be him trying to contact you."

"It would be the only way he could. After the bookshop attack I disappeared immediately. I had to cut off all ties with my past. I couldn't even go home to collect anything – no clothes, nothing. As the Gestapo were looking for me as well, I just disappeared without trace. It didn't matter to me that Emile would not be able to find me as I was convinced he was dead. But after hearing that message tonight I think he's alive and has used the BBC to broadcast that message in the hope that I might be listening. That's why I've got to get Sparks to respond. But don't tell anyone what I have just told you about me and Emile – our lives depend on that."

They both nodded.

Fabrice came back into the room and approached them. "I don't want or need to know what has upset you Marie. I've spoken to Clément and he says you can stay here while we go to the factory. We can pick you up on the way back."

"I'm not upset," said Marie-Claire. "I just wasn't expecting to hear that message tonight. But don't worry, it was good news so I'm ready to go to the factory with everyone else."

As she stood up André looked at Fabrice. "Marie was just surprised but I'm completely confident she can play her part tonight without any problem. You can trust me on that."

André called the others back into the living room. "You all heard the message 'The shop is closed' which means we're on for tonight. If you wondered why Marie was so affected by the champagne message it was just that it was unexpected. It was very good news so there is no need for you to be concerned. But to get back to us, Robert, can you and Leon please attach the fake licence plates to the trucks. While you're doing that I'll distribute the supplies and then we'll be ready to go."

Each of the four teams were issued with two lumps of explosive wrapped in paper, four two hour detonators, a small flashlight and a pair of pliers to be used for priming the detonators.

"Won't a flashlight be seen if we turn it on?" asked Raoul.

"Not when you're inside the factory," replied Sebastien. "They run a night shift on Tuesday and Wednesday evenings so the factory is permanently blacked out. And, as Sparks taught us, you'll need the flashlight to check the detonators after you've pushed them into the explosives."

When Robert and Leon returned André went through a final briefing. "In order that the explosions all go off just after the planes fly overhead all of the detonators must be activated at midnight. Squeeze the detonator tubes with your pliers at that time. They all have a two hour delay, so don't wait until you push them into the explosive. That way all of the explosions should go off within a minute or two of each other, just after the planes fly over at two in the morning. For each lump of explosive use two detonators, just in case one of them fails."

Twenty minutes later the first of the two trucks left the farm with Robert, André, Marie-Claire and Françoise. Clément had given Robert directions to an alley close to the factory where they could park and not be visible from the main road.

On the way Marie-Claire couldn't stop thinking about the champagne message. *Can Emile really be alive? What message can I send back to him? And how will we be able to find each other? I certainly can't ask the BBC to broadcast my location, and resistance groups don't share the names of their people.*

She was still thinking about Emile when she felt the truck stop. "Is this a checkpoint?" she asked nervously.

"No," replied André. "We've arrived in the alley."

It wasn't long before the dark shape of Leon's truck appeared in the alley and he parked behind Robert. All nine saboteurs descended from the vehicles and Sebastien gave directions to the factory gate. At two minute intervals they set off in groups of three. It was now well after curfew so they made their way through the streets slowly and cautiously, flitting from shadow to shadow.

When they reached the factory they stood silently in the shadow of a large tree on the other side of the street from the factory gate. On the far side of the road Marie-Claire was able to see the fence surrounding the factory complex. She looked left and right and in the darkness was just able to make out that this side of the road consisted of a long row of terraced houses. She understood completely why a bombing raid on the factory could easily result in some bombs missing the target and hitting the houses. Given that the factory would be destroyed one way or another, she felt they were not just sabotaging the production of German munitions but also preventing the deaths of many French people.

She was still thinking about the lives they were potentially saving when she saw a ghostly figure emerge from the shadow of the factory building, unlock the gate and motion for the group to come inside. He locked the gate behind them and led them quickly into the factory.

Once they were all inside he turned on a small light and another man joined him and addressed them all. "Welcome to our factory. I'm Gil and this is my brother Marc. Our uncle, who owns this factory, has told us that you wish to sabotage our factory to prevent us making shells for the Germans. It is our sincere hope that you succeed."

The saboteurs exchanged looks of surprise at this statement.

Gil continued. "If there's any way we can help just ask me or my brother." He stopped for a moment then holding up his arms he cheered them on with a resounding, "Vive la France Libre".

I know Sparks had persuaded them to allow the sabotage, but I never expected them to be so keen for us to do it.

André thanked Gil, looked at his watch and then spoke to the saboteurs. "It's ten minutes to midnight. The planes should fly over at exactly two o'clock, so in ten minutes we need to activate all of the detonators. I suggest we all wait here until then to be sure we all do it at the same time. We can then concentrate on placing the explosives exactly where they need to go. We should be able to complete placing the explosives within half an hour. When you're finished come back here and wait."

"How can we help?" asked Marc.

"Sebastien should know the machines, but in case he has a problem why don't you help him direct the teams. And remember, for your own safety, you and your brother must both be outside, away from the factory building, at least ten minutes before two this morning."

André kept looking at his watch and at exactly midnight told everyone to activate their detonators. Marie-Claire took the pliers from her bag and activated both of her detonators by crushing the closed off ends.

Sebastien took André and Marie-Claire to the 50 ton press they were to destroy. He showed them where to put the explosive before going off to direct another team to their target.

Marie-Claire held the flashlight as André carefully unwrapped one of the packets of explosive and moulded it around the main thruster of the machine. The foreman had told Sebastien that destroying that part would mean the press could not be repaired.

"Pass me a detonator," whispered André.

She passed one to him and watched André carefully push the open end into the plastic. As she passed him the second detonator she recalled the less than reassuring words Sparks had used during training, 'If you get it wrong, don't worry – you'll never know. The explosion will kill you immediately'.

With both detonators safely inserted into the plastic explosive, André stood up, "One done, one to go."

Sebastien then guided them to a large metal lathe. Again André carefully unwrapped the lump of explosive and moulded it around the critical part of the machine. He asked Marie-Claire to pass him a detonator. Just as he was pushing it gently into the explosive she heard a quiet click.

She realized at once that the detonator delay fuse had just failed and it was ready to blow. The safety strip which André was about to pull out was now the only thing preventing an immediate, massive explosion.

Chapter 57

With her heart racing Marie-Claire whispered urgently to André, "Stop! Don't move!"

"Why not?" asked André as he held his hands still.

"Didn't you hear that click?" she asked in a shaky voice.

"What click?" asked André, still in the same frozen position.

"The one Sparks told us to listen out for. Do not touch the safety strip – if you do the plastic will explode. Instead pull the detonator tube back out right now – carefully and steadily."

She held her breath as she watched him pull the tube back out of the plastic explosive. She breathed a sigh of relief when he passed it to her. She shone the flashlight into the inspection hole and sure enough she saw it was now blocked with the firing pin. "This detonator has failed and would have fired the moment you pulled out the safety strip."

André took a few deep breaths. "Thank God you were listening. I see why Sparks recommended we do this in teams of two. Let's start again. Can you pass me another detonator please."

André again followed the procedure for inserting the detonator, pushing the open end carefully into the explosive. Using the flashlight he then checked that the inspection hole was clear before pulling out the safety strip. He stood up slowly and stepped back from the lathe. "We didn't have any faulty ones when we blew up the fuel dump. Perhaps we were just lucky."

"Let's hope our luck continues. Sparks said the SOE agents spend weeks training with active detonators and actual explosives. All we've had is just a lecture. This type of sabotage is so nerve racking. If it works, we all deserve medals."

"What do you mean 'if'? We've set enough explosives to blow this factory sky high. With eight targets, even if one or two fail the result will be spectacular." With a smile he added, "The Germans will think that RAF bombing has become much more accurate."

By half past midnight all four teams had finished. In one of the strangest speeches Marie-Claire had ever heard, Marc thanked them for arranging to demolish his family's heritage. He finished with a heartfelt 'Vive la France Libre' which they all repeated. His brother then turned out all the lights and let them out through the factory gate. In their separate groups they made their way back towards the alley where the vehicles were parked.

As Marie-Claire, André and Françoise approached the alley they found the other saboteurs hiding behind a building. "There's a group of German soldiers standing talking at the entrance to the alley," whispered Robert. "If they've seen our trucks, it's a good thing we changed the licence plates."

"Yes," agreed Leon. "If they seize the trucks they won't be able to trace them back to us. But where am I going to get another truck, let alone a petrol truck?"

"If they were going to seize them then they wouldn't be just standing around chatting," said André. "Stay here all of you. I'll creep up and see what they're talking about."

Why do I keep falling for strong courageous men? Emile would have done exactly what André's going to do, in spite of the danger.

Ten minutes later André returned. "It doesn't look like it's a security patrol. They've all got large rucksacks which are on the ground at the moment. I think they're on night exercises." He looked at his watch. "It's almost five to one right now. I suspect they'll march off at one. I'll go back and see when they move away. The rest of you, stay where you are and keep out of sight."

"Shall I come with you?" asked Leon.

Marie-Claire looked around at the others and no one said anything. "If anyone goes with you I think it should be me," she whispered. "If they see two men that will look suspicious – but a man and a woman? Out late at night together? We can just pretend we're a couple."

André agreed, and he and Marie-Claire crept towards the alley entrance, keeping in the shadows. They stopped about thirty metres away and lay down in some long grass from where they were just able to see the soldiers.

At one o'clock the sergeant gave an order and the soldiers picked up their rucksacks and rifles and formed up as a platoon. They then marched off towards the town centre, their hobnailed boots making a distinctive sound in the still night air.

André and Marie-Claire waited until they could no longer hear the sound of the boots. They then stood up and began walking back to the others. "Why did you volunteer to come with me?" asked André. "You've got Emile to think of now."

"As I said back there, it was best you were accompanied by a woman and I didn't see Françoise volunteering, so I did. And Emile's never really been out of my thoughts."

"You were there for me when I lost Nicole and that has brought me very close to you. So please know, I'll do everything I can to help you find Emile."

For a short moment they hugged, then stepped back, smiled at each other and continued walking towards the others.

"The soldiers have gone," said André as he and Marie-Claire reached the group. "We can go now."

When they reached Clément's farm and climbed out of the trucks there was a sudden babble of voices as everyone relaxed from the tension they had been under. Despite the late hour no one was sleepy. They sat around chatting about the experience and frequently looking at their watches in anticipation of hearing the RAF bombers.

At five to two Fabrice suggested they all go outside to listen. They stood silently in the still night air. A few minutes later Marie-Claire heard the sound of a plane. The noise grew as it became evident there was more than one plane. Soon the sound became almost unbearable as five low-flying RAF twin-engined bombers roared overhead.

As the sound of the planes disappeared Robert asked, "Do you hear what I hear?"

"I hear explosions," said Marie-Claire as she looked west towards Bourges. "Look. You can see flashes. Isn't it amazing that those little lumps of plastic can produce such a reaction."

At that point the sky above Bourges lit up for a moment in a blaze of light. "Wow," exclaimed Leon, "That must have been more than one going off at the same time. I don't think they'll be making many shells for German guns tomorrow."

"I'm not exactly sure what you guys have done," said Clément, "but if you've hit Mr Hitler I think it calls for a celebration drink. Let's go inside. I have some champagne which I've been keeping for a suitable occasion and this certainly qualifies. But I'll put it in glasses not broken teacups."

As he poured out the champagne they discussed when to drive back to Maubuisson. "If we go now," said Fabrice, "they won't have had time to suspect resistance activity. It's likely they'll still think it was the RAF."

"Yes," said André, "but two trucks heading away from Bourges, during curfew, just after some explosions? It could attract attention. No. I suggest we wait until curfew lifts and leave at six. That'll give those who want to sleep about three hours."

Some of the group tried to sleep curled up in chairs or lying on the floor, but Marie-Claire was too wound up to sleep. She went through to the kitchen to make herself a drink and was joined by André and Françoise.

"Have you thought of what kind of message you want Sparks to send?" asked Françoise. "It's got to be something Emile would know comes from you. Can you think of some odd phrase only he would recognize?"

"He wasn't the only one thinking of writing a novel," replied Marie-Claire. "I was planning a fantasy story with the title *'Oranges Are Just Sunburnt Lemons'*."

"Did Emile know that?" asked Françoise. "Because if he did that's a perfect phrase."

"Yes, we joked about it and my pen name was to be Hortense."

"The phrase is good," said André, "but is there some way you can tell him where you are? Did you ever visit Nevers together?"

"No," replied Marie-Claire. "But you've just reminded me. When Belgian refugees were fleeing the Germans he read in the *Le Petit Parisien* that they were being sent to Nevers. When he asked me if I'd ever been to Nevers and I said no, he told me he'd been there as a child. He said the only thing I'd find interesting to do in Nevers was to sketch the cathedral. He might remember."

"I think I have it," said André. "I think I know what your message should be. How does this sound? 'While sketching the cathedral Hortense said oranges are just sunburnt lemons'. There are many cathedrals in France but only he would know which one he'd told Hortense she'd find interesting to sketch."

Marie-Claire thought for a moment before agreeing. "You're right. It tells him everything, but no one else could decode it. Thank you André. That's brilliant. Let's hope he remembers."

When they arrived back in Maubuisson on Saturday Sparks was anxious to hear all the news. He seemed genuinely thrilled when he was told that everything went according to plan. "I'll send a message back to London to report on the success of the mission."

Marie-Claire took Sparks aside. "I have a message I'd like you to ask the BBC to broadcast in the 'Personal Messages' section."

"You have?" asked Sparks. "May I ask why?"

"One of the messages broadcast last night was from another resistance group specifically to me and I've got to reply."

"I always thought there was more to you than you've let on. So what's your message? I'll write it out to make sure I get it right."

When he was finished writing it down, he folded the paper up and asked Fabrice if he had any mayonnaise. Marie-Claire was puzzled and asked why he wanted mayonnaise.

Sparks laughed. "It's a trick I learned from another resistance group. Apparently the Germans won't look inside a mayonnaise sandwich for fear of making a mess of their hands and uniforms. So that's where this piece of paper will be hiding. I'll ask SOE to have the BBC broadcast your message."

Back in Nevers, Marie-Claire slept most of Saturday and spent Sunday trying to read and sketch. She found it hard to concentrate as her thoughts kept coming back to the news that Emile was still alive. *Emile, you can be proud of me. When I think back to last year and my trepidation at just carrying a book to one of the members of your resistance group, I can see how much I've changed. It's so wonderful to know you're alive, but how are we going to find each other?*

She tuned into the BBC French program on Sunday evening but there was no mention of oranges and lemons. Monday was the same. However on Tuesday evening she heard the French voice say 'While sketching the cathedral Hortense said oranges are just sunburnt lemons'. When the message was repeated, it sounded even sweeter to her ears. She turned off the radio and danced a little jig around her bedroom.

Thank you Sparks. Emile – wherever you are – did you hear that message? Do you remember telling me about the cathedral in Nevers? Please, please remember.

On Wednesday morning, still feeling ecstatic at hearing her message the night before, Marie-Claire pulled her bicycle out of the shed and rode to André's house. When he opened the door he immediately smiled, "I heard it Marie. You must be so excited."

"Unbelievably so."

"I thought you would be," said André as they walked through to the kitchen. "And I've some news for you. I've heard from Fabrice. Our operation was a great success and it appears that everyone thinks it was the RAF bombs. No one suspects sabotage."

"I've not seen anything about it in the papers," said Marie-Claire. "Have you?"

"No, but then the national papers generally don't report successes against the Germans, they only report Nazi successes. I suspect this paper will be more likely to report it," he said pointing to a scrappy looking news-sheet.

"What's that?" asked Marie-Claire.

"It's the September issue of *Défense de la France*, an underground resistance newspaper printed in Paris."

Marie-Claire almost jumped out of her chair. "But of course that's how he did it. Thank you André. You've solved it."

Chapter 58

André looked at Marie-Claire with a puzzled expression. "I'm glad I've solved something, but can you give me a clue as to what I've solved?"

"I've always assumed that when the Gestapo machine-gunned Emile's bookshop he would have been in the shop. His friends, the ones who saved me that day, said they had been talking to him in the shop literally just a minute before. They told me he was killed and I had no reason to doubt them. But what you've just said has reminded me that he ran a printing press in the shop basement. He could have just gone down the stairs to the basement when the Gestapo burst in. He never took me downstairs but he once told me that there was a service door in the basement through which they had brought in the printing equipment. Until now I had completely forgotten that the shop had a basement and that he could have escaped that way. My God, why didn't I think of that before?"

"If his friends who had just been talking to him told you he was killed you would have had no reason to doubt them. I'm sure —"

André did not complete his sentence as there was a knock on his front door. He went to answer the door and came back into the kitchen with Bernard. "Hello Marie. I'm pleased you're here. I have a question for the two of you. How would you like to blow up a German munitions train?"

"Oh, that's a hard one to answer," said André as his face burst into a broad grin. "Tell me more."

"In just over two weeks the local garrison will be shipping most of their munitions back to Germany to move them to the Eastern front. I know because we've been told to supply the necessary wagons and a locomotive."

"I think I can speak for our resistance group when I say – we would. However, I'll need to consult with our explosives expert as

I recall him saying blowing up trains is quite difficult. I think you should meet him. Are you free on Saturday?"

"I'm on nights on Saturday so yes, I'm free most of the day."

"I'll check if he's available on Saturday and let you know. If he is I'll pick you up first thing in the morning and the three of us will go to see him."

Saturday morning brought heavy rain, but that did not dampen the spirits of Marie-Claire, Bernard and André as they drove to Maubuisson. André explained to Bernard that his explosives man was in fact a British agent called Sparks who had been trained by the SOE in Britain. "He will know the best way to demolish your munitions train."

"Don't call it *my* munitions train," said Bernard indignantly. "It's a train filled with *German* munitions."

"But if you're supplying the locomotive and we blow it up, how will your engine driver survive?" asked Marie-Claire.

"I don't mind if he doesn't," said Bernard. "I have a couple of workers in our roster who have made it clear they are Nazi sympathizers, and oddly enough they will both be scheduled to be driving that train. You have complete freedom to blast it to bits."

In Maubuisson, after Bernard was introduced, Sparks looked at the three visitors. "Fabrice told me you were coming here today and I'm suspecting you've come to discuss some kind of plan."

Sparks listened with interest as André and Bernard told him about the munitions train and their idea of blowing it up. However, he disagreed with their plan. "Blowing it up is not the way to do it. For a munitions train the best thing is to set it on fire so the munitions do the exploding. Bernard, what kind of wagons will be used for this train?"

"Standard small box wagons."

"Made of what? Metal or wood?" asked Sparks.

"Wood," answered Bernard. "I think I see where you're going. The ammunition will all be in wooden boxes in the wagons. So how do we set it on fire? I don't want it to explode in the station which is in the middle of town."

"Agreed. My plan would be to slow the train down in a rural area and hit it with Molotov cocktails. If you can use the same group as you had in Bourges that would mean at least ten hits which should be enough to start a good blaze."

"Are you saying we don't use any explosives?" asked André.

"Correct. Explosives would stop the train which would enable guards to get off the train and attack you. But they can't get off a moving train so after throwing the petrol bombs all you'll need to do is lie down and avoid their bullets."

"Is that all?" asked Marie-Claire sarcastically. "Just lie down and avoid the bullets."

"It's better than it sounds because if there are any guards they won't be expecting you and in the dark they won't know you're there until they see the flames. By the time they react the train will have moved away."

"Assuming we go ahead with this," said Fabrice, "is there anything special we need to know about these petrol bombs? I've never used one before."

"Yes there is," replied Sparks. "You should use standard wine bottles, and before filling them score them so they crack and break easily. Half fill each bottle with petrol and top it up with kerosene and then add some baking soda."

"Baking soda?" queried Marie-Claire. "What does that do?"

"Baking soda and the kerosene make the mixture sticky so the flaming liquid sticks to the sides of the wagon."

"SOE training again?" asked Fabrice.

Sparks laughed. "Yes. We had fun making and testing those. But to get back to this operation. André. I assume you'll be in charge again?"

"I suppose so," said André. "I'll ask my group if they want to be involved and Fabrice you ask your group. Bernard, if I remember correctly you said the date for the train is two weeks from today, which would be Saturday, the 18th of October."

"Yes. It's scheduled to leave around eight-thirty in the evening."

"That's good," said Sparks. "So I suggest the full team meets here next Saturday for some training. In the meantime you need to start collecting wine bottles, petrol and kerosene. I suggest you collect as many bottles as possible so next week you can practice throwing them. It's not as easy as it sounds."

"And I'll work out how to send the train onto the slow single line track," said Bernard. "That would give you a much better chance of hitting it."

On Monday, during the school lunch break, Marie-Claire asked Françoise if she would like to help destroy a train carrying German munitions by throwing Molotov cocktails at it. In response, Françoise laughed, "You need to ask? Of course I would."

"There's a training session this weekend. Will you be able to make it?"

"I had been thinking of going to the farm this weekend, but a training session throwing flaming bottles sounds much more exciting. Will we be using petrol in the bottles when we practice?"

"Sparks didn't say, and I doubt it given the shortage of petrol," answered Marie-Claire. "But I suspect we might be practising with actual flaming rags."

"Will Odile want to join us, do you think? She wasn't involved in the Bourges operation."

"I bet she will," said Marie-Claire. "I'll go to the bookshop after school and ask her. I haven't spoken to her for a while."

When Marie-Claire explained to Odile that they intended to destroy a German munitions train Odile was keen to be involved.

"We're going for a training session this Saturday in Maubuisson so we'll pick you up on the way. Given what we'll be doing, wear some old clothes. It could get messy."

"This sounds exciting. See you Saturday."

The weather was warm on Wednesday morning and Marie-Claire decided she'd walk to see André rather than cycle there. Although she was sure André had given her the bike without regret, she always felt slightly awkward riding Nicole's bicycle to his house. When she arrived Marie-Claire found him covered in sawdust.

"Sorry, am I disturbing you?"

"Not at all. I've been making some furniture and I could do with a break now."

While they drank their coffee substitute, André told her that Bernard had mentioned that the schedule for the munitions train might be changed. "I'm busy with this piece of furniture. Could you go and check with him? That would save me a trip."

After they had finished their drinks Marie-Claire walked to the station, enjoying the warmth of the sun. It reminded her of walking around Paris with Emile. *Please Emile, let me know where you are. I want to see you again so much.*

As she arrived at the station Marie-Claire saw Bernard standing on the platform. She waved and he immediately came over to her. "Hello Marie. What brings you here?"

"André sent me to ask about that train."

He looked over her shoulder. "Just a moment. I think one of my drivers wants to speak to me. Wait here."

Marie-Claire turned around to see who he meant and instantly recognized the person as the informant she'd seen in L'Hotel de Paris. *That's why I thought I knew him – he's a railway worker. I wonder if Bernard realizes this man is actually a Gestapo informant?*

Chapter 59

The man Bernard was talking to looked straight at Marie-Claire and acknowledged her with a small nod of his head. Her heart skipped a beat. *I think he's recognized me from the Gestapo HQ.*

A few moments later the man walked off and Bernard came back to talk to Marie-Claire. "My driver seemed to know you."

"I don't actually know him but I've seen him before. How much do you know about him?"

"He was posted here a few months ago. He's one of the men who appears to be a Nazi sympathizer and I don't trust him at all."

"You're wise not to trust him. I know for a fact he's actually a Gestapo informant."

"I won't ask how you know, but thank you. That's made my decision much easier. He'll definitely be one of the drivers on the munitions train."

"Is the munitions train still scheduled for eight-thirty at night on the eighteenth?"

"Yes. There's been no change. And I've got two bits of good news. I've not been asked to supply any wagons for soldiers or guards so it looks as if you won't have any trouble that way. And secondly it's going on the slow line towards Clamecy to pick up even more munitions. Apparently fighting Russia on the Eastern front is using more shells than the Germans planned for."

"Clamecy?" asked Marie-Claire with a smile. "Wasn't that where the prisoner train was heading – the one that lost all its prisoners?"

Bernard laughed. "Yes, and after this fireball operation the Germans are going to think it's a very dangerous line."

Marie-Claire smiled, thanked him and walked back to André's house. "I saw Bernard and things are better than we could have hoped for. The train is going to Clamecy which means it's on the slow single rail line. You remember the one?"

"Of course I do. How could I forget the danger you were in when you stopped the train and faced the soldiers. I should never have let you do that."

"André. Just because I'm a woman doesn't mean I'm any less courageous or determined. Have you forgotten – I volunteered to be the oxcart driver. It was far better that the driver was a woman. It was dangerous and frightening, but then so is everything we do. We won't rid France of these loathsome Germans by always choosing the safe path."

André looked at her for a moment before responding. "I wish some of the men I know had as much fire in them as you do. But to get back to what you were saying, that's great news about the train. If it's going slowly it will make it much easier to hit."

"And I've got some even better news – the train is not being guarded. No soldiers, no guards."

"That's excellent news," responded André with a smile. "It means we can select the best position to attack without worrying about anyone firing at us. That aspect had been concerning me."

"Is Robert picking us up on Saturday?"

"Yes. You, me, Françoise and Odile. We'll be making a full day of it. I know Fabrice runs a farm but I don't like imposing too much on his hospitality, so I'll see if Tomas can supply us with some extra bread."

"In these days of rationing it's good to have a friend like Tomas. Do you want me to ask him? I pass his shop on the way home."

When Tomas heard that she was looking to feed ten to twelve hungry résistants, he readily agreed. "Fortunately right now I have been asked to bake for the Germans and I should have enough extra flour to bake some loaves for you. I'll take them to André early on Saturday morning. It will be my contribution as I can't go with you. What will you be doing?"

"Learning how to destroy a German munitions train."

"I'd like to be doing that with you, but I can't leave here until I find a replacement apprentice. My assistant, Jacob, had to escape to the Unoccupied Zone after his parents were arrested. Take care Marie. We don't want to lose you."

381

With all the loaves Tomas had provided, the inside of Robert's truck had a delicious smell of bread as the group drove to Maubuisson on Saturday morning. For the practice session André had been able to collect lots of empty bottles and had made some wooden crates in which to carry them. "We'll need these on the night. We don't want to be driving with loose bottles of petrol rattling around in the back of the truck."

"Have you ever thrown a petrol bomb?" Odile asked André.

"No, but we all may have by the end of today. I think Sparks wants us to practice not just throwing bottles but also getting over the fear of throwing a bottle with a flaming rag attached."

"I think the main thing to remember," said Françoise, "is throw it – don't drop it!"

"Oh thanks," said Odile. "You're making me wonder if I should have agreed to be part of this operation."

"Odile," said Robert from the front of the truck, "as you throw each bottle, think of Suzette."

"Is Suzette still in Toulouse?" asked Marie-Claire.

"Yes," replied Robert. "Ever since she was attacked she's been staying with my sister who lives just outside Toulouse in the Unoccupied Zone. The sight of a German soldier was terrifying her. I wouldn't mind if destroying the train killed some Germans."

Marie-Claire did not comment. She was sure, that like her, both André and Bernard had kept silent about their part in removing the drunken German who had attacked Nicole. *Each bottle I throw at the train will be for them and for my Parisien friends. Emile, I'd love to tell you what I've been doing. I gave you a clue as to where I am. Please contact me, please.*

At Fabrice's farm Sparks had prepared a full training session. The first thing he asked each person to do was throw a particular stone as far as they could. After everyone had thrown the stone in turn he explained the purpose.

"This stone is about the weight of a wine bottle filled with petrol. I wanted to see how far you could throw it. The last thing you want is a petrol bomb not reaching its destination. From what I've seen, I think we should have five teams. Four will throw proper Molotov cocktails with flaming bottles. The other team will throw top up bottles."

"What's the difference?" asked Fabrice.

"Lighting and throwing a flaming bottle takes longer than you'd think and hence the first four teams will only be able to throw at most two flaming bottles each before the train has passed. This should be enough to cause the wagons to catch fire. A little further down the railway line, perhaps sixty metres or so, the other team will mount a second attack. The people in this team will just throw petrol-filled bottles at the already burning wagons. These bottles won't have burning rags – they'll just add more fuel to the burning wagons. That team should be able to throw more bottles since they don't have the delay of having to ignite the rags."

"The train should be burning well after that," said Robert.

"I think it should be burning very well," said Sparks. "But remember, the moment the train has passed you must get out of there as fast as possible taking everything with you. Do not hang around to see if the munitions explode."

"You said four teams throwing flaming bottles and one top up team. Are you suggesting two people per team?" asked André.

"Yes I am," said Sparks. "Attacking a moving train is not like throwing a petrol bomb at a building. You'll only have very few seconds in which to throw the bottles. That means you can't ignite the petrol soaked rags with matches – it could take too long. The four flame throwing teams will each have two people. One to throw the bottle and one to hold a burning wicker torch. The thrower holds the bottle over the torch to light the rags, throws the bottle at the train and then does the same with the second bottle."

Sparks turned to André. "Have you decided on your teams?"

"Yes I have," replied André. "Considering how far people were able to throw the stone, I think the flame throwers will be Robert supported by Odile, Leon supported by Françoise, Sebastien supported by Fabrice, and myself supported by Marie. The other team, the top up bottle throwers, will be Julien and Raoul."

Sparks gave Julien and Raoul instructions on how to prepare the bottles. Before filling each bottle they scratched the outside to provide rapid breakage points. They then filled each bottle with a petrol, kerosene and baking soda mixture and closed it off with a normal wine cork.

While they were doing that Sparks taught the flame throwing group how to stand with the torch holder to the side of the thrower so they could light the fuse rags quickly. He then brought over several water-filled bottles to which he had attached a kerosene soaked rag. The teams then practiced lighting the rags and throwing the bottles.

When André and Marie-Claire had used all their bottles, Marie-Claire put out her torch. "Sparks was right," commented André. "Throwing a bottle with a burning rag attached is not easy."

"I'm glad you're doing the throwing rather than me," said Marie-Claire. "Holding that flaming torch while you lit the fuses was bad enough."

At that moment, Robert let out a yell. Marie-Claire looked over and saw that Robert's sleeve had caught fire while he was trying to light a bottle fuse. He was waving his arm around in a frantic attempt to put out the flames.

Instinctively Marie-Claire ran over to him, ripping off her jacket and wrapping it around his arm to smother the flames.

Sparks came dashing over. "That's my fault. I should have checked what you were wearing. When you're working with petrol bombs you must never wear loose clothing. You're fortunate Robert. You've had a lucky escape due to Marie's quick action."

Robert looked at her. "Thank you for your quick thinking. I'm sorry about your jacket. I'll get you another. It's the least I can do."

"Don't worry, Robert. It wasn't even mine in the beginning. It's just an old one which was given to me by a friend when I needed one." *Actually it was Rosa at Chantal's who gave it to me but I can't tell anyone that, not even André or Françoise. She gave it to me to help me and now I've used it to help Robert.*

"Seeing how easily this accident happened," said Sparks, "I would suggest that on the night you take along an old blanket which you can use to smother flames if there's another accident. You can't pour water onto burning petrol, it spreads the flames."

"Noted," said André. "I have an old blanket which can do the job and I'll make sure we take it with us."

By mid-afternoon Sparks felt they had all had enough training. "The only thing left to do now," he said, "is to pick the spot."

André said he thought he knew a suitable spot but it needed to be checked out. He arranged with Fabrice and Sparks that he would come back to Maubuisson the following day so the three of them could drive out and look for the best location.

Marie-Claire was pleased he had not suggested she go with him. She was aware that the following day, Sunday 12 October, was exactly one year since she left her life in Paris and she was planning a quiet day on her own. On the drive back to Nevers she remained deep in thought.

My life has changed so much in just one year. Back then I wasn't even sure I wanted to live, what with Maman and Emile gone – or so I thought. I know Maman can never come back – but Emile? I hope he will still like the person I've become. I've certainly grown in confidence, but surely that's not a bad thing.

Her thoughts were interrupted by Françoise reminding her that the French band were playing in the Park again on Sunday. Although Marie-Claire had thought she would prefer to be on her own on this Sunday, she realized that spending time with Françoise would help take her mind off her losses. "I'd like to hear that band again. It will be nice to hear French songs played by a French band and escape from the reality of the German occupation – even if only for a short while."

"That reminds me of something I overheard. This lady was talking to her friend and said 'We live in troubled times but I would much rather be reading about them in a book instead of living through them'."

Marie-Claire smiled. "I agree with what she said. But you have to admit it's exciting to be doing something. Although I must say I never thought I'd become an arsonist attacking a German munitions train."

Chapter 60

When Marie-Claire arrived at the Café du Monde on Thursday evening there was an air of excitement in the room. As she sat down next to Françoise she saw André look directly at Bernard and tilt his head slightly as if he was asking a question. Bernard nodded and smiled and Marie-Claire took this to mean the attack on the train was on for Saturday. Robert then asked André if it would be convenient for him to collect everybody around six on Saturday. André glanced at Marie-Claire and Françoise before answering. "Yes, Robert. That would be fine."

Now that the evenings had closed in and it was dark by the time they left the Café, the men would not allow the girls to walk home alone for fear of them being accosted by German soldiers. André walked back with Marie-Claire and on the way he suggested that she and Françoise come to his house on Saturday afternoon to have a meal before Robert picked them up. "I know where I can get another rabbit to cook."

"That sounds good. By the way do you have a bucket which could be used for water?"

"Why do you want a bucket of water?"

"It'll be somewhere for us to put out the torches when we've finished using them."

"Well thought of Marie," replied André. "I'll put a bucket and bottles of water in the van along with the old blanket Sparks suggested. How are you feeling about Saturday?"

"Both excited and terrified. I just hope Sparks knew what he was talking about when he said this should work."

"I'm sure he does. I had a long chat with him when I saw him and Fabrice on Wednesday. He's changed a lot since the first time we met him and seems more confident in what he's doing. Apparently he has been working with many resistance groups all across this part of France – very successfully by all accounts."

When Marie-Claire and Françoise arrived at André's house on Saturday afternoon there was a delicious smell of cooking throughout the house. During the meal Françoise complemented him on his cooking. "André this is delicious."

She turned to Marie-Claire. "I can see why you thought if André had to send you a cryptic message it would be about cooking rabbit."

"I'm glad you like it," said André. "It's one of the few dishes I can cook and I thought we needed something substantial tonight. I wouldn't advise you to try any of my other efforts."

Shortly after six Robert arrived with Odile. "We didn't meet any checkpoints but I'm concerned about our drive to Maubuisson."

"I've had a word with Jerome," said André, "He's told me where all the planned checkpoints are for tonight and I've worked out a route that should avoid them all."

"Well done," said Robert. "That makes me feel a lot safer."

At Fabrice's farmhouse they found the rest of the group were already there, drinking large mugs of hot chocolate. "What a treat," exclaimed Françoise. "How did you arrange this?"

Fabrice put his finger to his lips. "That's my secret."

Marie-Claire smiled as she realized it was probably a black market transaction – something one never discussed openly.

After finishing their drinks the girls changed out of their skirts into their dark trousers. André did a quick inspection to make sure no one was wearing loose clothing which could catch fire. Afterwards, the crates of petrol bombs and torches were loaded into the trucks along with the bags of the girl's clothing.

The trucks left Maubuisson soon after seven o'clock. Marie-Claire was relieved that Jerome's information had been accurate and they didn't encounter any checkpoints. They reached their destination just before eight o'clock. The sun had already set and there was no moon that night, so they needed their flashlights to find their way around.

The place Sparks, André and Fabrice had chosen was near Sichamps where a small back road ran close to the railway track. It was a long way from any main road and there were no manned crossings nearby.

"This location means there will be a considerable delay before anyone can raise the alarm after the attack," said André, "which will give us more time to get away. With any luck we will be back home before the alarm is raised, and well before curfew."

The four flame throwing teams positioned themselves a safe distance apart. They each had their own wicker torch, two petrol bombs with fuse rags attached and a small bottle of petrol with which to soak the rags to make them easier to light.

The top up team walked further down the railway line carrying their crates of bottle bombs. After walking about fifty metres they left the rail lines and took up a suitable position on the railway embankment.

Marie-Claire sat down beside the track so she would be able to hear the railway lines whine which would indicate that the train was approaching. Just before nine she shouted, "I hear it," and scrambled back to her position on the embankment.

The four flame throwing teams then poured a little petrol onto the wicker torches and the rags attached to the bottles. Standing well back from the bottles André lit the torch Marie-Claire was holding. He then went to the other three teams to light their torches and returned to his position beside Marie-Claire. He picked up his two bottles, holding one in each hand well away from the torch.

The sound of the train grew louder and louder and it wasn't long before the small white sidelight of the engine came into view.

Robert was the first to throw, but threw his bottle too soon. Marie-Claire saw the flaming bottle land inside the engine compartment setting it ablaze. Horrified, she heard the two people in the engine compartment yell out in pain as their clothes caught fire. She reminded herself that they were both Gestapo informants who were willing to send others to their deaths.

Leon and then Sebastien were the next to throw and their bottles broke easily against the wagons. The sticky petrol, kerosene and baking soda mixture immediately burst into flame as it slowly trickled down the sides of the wooden wagons.

André lit the fuse rag of his first bottle from Marie-Claire's flaming torch and hurled the bottle in the direction of the train. He did not look to see what happened to it, but concentrated on lighting the fuse of the second bottle and throwing it before the end of the train passed him.

Marie-Claire then doused her torch in the bucket of water before looking down the line at the train. She was just in time to see the top up bottles being thrown against the now burning wagons and almost explode into fire-balls. It looked to her as if all of the wagons were now on fire, but the train did not seem to be moving as fast as it had been.

"André," she yelled, "The train appears to be slowing down. We've got to get out of here."

He immediately called out to the others to get back to the trucks as quickly as possible. Going back to the trucks was not easy as the railway track was now covered in broken glass and small fires where flaming petrol had dripped off the wagons.

"If the engine drivers have slowed the train down – it may be the last thing they do," panted Robert as he ran back. "It appears my first bottle landed in the engine compartment and the drivers may not survive the flames."

"And if the boxes in the train catch fire and the munitions start exploding, we may not survive either unless we get out of here right now," added Leon as they all clambered back into the trucks.

They hadn't gone more than a couple of kilometres when they heard a loud explosion which was soon followed by several others.

"I hope there was no one nearby who has been injured by the explosions," said Robert.

"One of the reasons we chose that location," said André, "was that we calculated that the train would not be near any villages or towns when it began to explode. But those explosions were so loud the Germans are bound to have heard them and will come to investigate. We won't do any more sabotage for a while."

They got back to Nevers just before curfew. Marie-Claire went up to her room and lay down on her bed. *I vowed to fight back and that was certainly effective. Emile would be proud of me.*

Late on Wednesday afternoon she went to visit André. He looked very worried as he pointed to the newspaper on his kitchen table. "Have you seen the latest issue of *Le Petit Parisien?*"

"No," replied Marie-Claire. "Why? What's happened?"

"We are in serious danger. Look at the notice and lead articles."

Marie-Claire leant over the table and read the notice and the articles. The paper was reporting that on the 20th of October two résistants, supposedly under orders from London or Moscow, had assassinated Lt Colonel Hotz, head of the German military police in Nantes. As a consequence 50 hostages had been shot in reprisal.

"Look at what they're going to do," said André. "They say they'll keep executing hostages until the two résistants are found. The mayor of Nantes is pleading with the people to tell the authorities the names of the assassins to avoid further executions."

"I doubt executions will work. Shooting hostages is more likely to harden resistance."

"I would agree if that was all they were doing, but it's not. They're offering a 15 million franc reward for information."

"Buying betrayal?" Marie-Claire shook her head. "I suppose there are people who could be tempted by such a large sum."

"Unfortunately, yes. This kind of resistance and assassination is exactly the kind of problem I said would happen back in June when Hitler invaded Russia. It appears the assassins are communists. I told you the French communists wouldn't care if their actions resulted in French people being executed as hostages. And that's exactly what's happened."

"How will this affect us? Nantes is nowhere near Nevers."

"You're right, it's not. But the Germans have mounted a major countrywide effort to find the two résistants. Jerome came by earlier today to warn me that we must not do any kind of resistance activity until this calms down."

"I didn't think we had anything planned," said Marie-Claire.

"No we don't, but he also said we mustn't help any escapers and no one must attempt to cross the Demarcation Line except at the official crossings. He told me that in their attempt to find the résistants the Germans are patrolling the whole line and will shoot on sight anybody they see trying to cross illegally. This means no one can risk going across rivers or through the forests – even during the darkest nights."

"Do you have any escapers in your line right now?"

"I'm not aware of any, but I'm concerned that such a large reward, 15 million francs, may tempt some people to betray us. We mustn't do anything to attract attention. I'm not sure Fabrice will have heard and I think I should warn him. I only learned about the Demarcation Line patrols through Jerome this afternoon. I'll drive to Maubuisson now and tell him. Can I drop you off on my way?"

Marie-Claire immediately thought of the Deferre's escape line and realized that she must warn Françoise. "I was going to see Françoise so perhaps you could drop me off at her house, please."

When Marie-Claire told Françoise about the Demarcation Line patrols, Françoise was very concerned that her parents might not know about the new danger they were facing. "I don't know if they have anyone passing through their escape line at the moment, but in case they have they need to know about the extra patrols immediately. I can't wait until Friday when I normally see Papa. I guess the only thing I can do is cycle out to the farm this evening."

She looked at her watch. "The sun won't set for a while so I should be able to get there before it's dark but I can't get back again tonight. Marie, if I'm not at school tomorrow, can you tell Monsieur Thibault that I had a family emergency and might not be in for the rest of the week?"

"Of course I can."

On Monday Françoise was back at school and no one asked why she had been absent. During the break she and Marie-Claire went outside to talk. "Fortunately there was no one staying with my parents but they wanted me to thank you for the warning."

"It seems so wrong," said Marie-Claire, "that captured airmen are sent to a POW camp but those who help them escape are shot."

"My mother put it succinctly," said Françoise, "when she

pointed out that it takes more courage to do clandestine laundry for an escaper than it does to be a soldier with a machine gun."

"I suppose so. I had never thought about it that way. But I'm glad you were able to warn them." She sighed, "I still haven't heard any more from Emile and it's been a month since his message."

"Have faith Marie," said Françoise. "He will find you."

When Marie-Claire came back from school on Tuesday afternoon, Madame Favier stopped her as she was about to go upstairs. "I have a parcel for you."

"A parcel? For me?" asked Marie-Claire. "I'm not expecting anything. Did it come in the post?"

"No. A young girl brought it. She didn't give me her name. She just asked me to pass it on to you. Wait here and I'll get it."

Madame Favier returned with a box covered in brown paper. It was addressed simply to M B at the boarding house address. Marie-Claire carried the box up to her room and studied it carefully before opening it. As she held it up for inspection she heard a small sloshing sound and put it down carefully but quickly. *What on earth can this be? I hope it's safe to open.*

She cautiously tore off the wrapping paper and opened the cardboard box. It appeared to be filled with crumpled paper. She carefully pulled out the paper, piece by piece, and then stopped and stared at the contents – one small bottle of champagne and one broken teacup missing its handle.

She saw there was an envelope underneath the bottle which she quickly grabbed and opened. Inside was a simple note.

> We'll drink a toast together on Anna's birthday

Marie-Claire read and re-read the note. *Emile – you've found me. My God! I can't believe this. You'll be here on Anna's birthday – that's in four days time!*

By now her heart was racing, her breathing was erratic and she began trembling – not with fear but with excitement. *Four days time! Just four days time! I can't keep this to myself. I've got to tell someone. I'll go and see Françoise – right now.*

She picked up the note, put it in her pocket and hurried downstairs. She dashed out of the house and ran to the bicycle shed, her heart pounding with excitement.

She was about to open the door of the shed when she heard footsteps behind her and then felt a hand on her shoulder. A German voice spoke in a commanding manner.

"Stop right there – Frau Marie-Claire Blanchet!"

She froze. *Who knows my real name? How have they found me? Was Emile's parcel a trap?*

Not knowing how to react she spun around to face the man.

"Otto! What on earth are you doing here? I thought you were in Paris. And why have you called me by that name?"

"I've come to warn you that the Gestapo have found out who you really are."

"How?" gasped Marie-Claire.

"They've been looking for Emile Blanchet and while they were doing that they discovered that you are his wife – Madame Marie-Claire Blanchet. Tomorrow morning you will be arrested and questioned about him, and because they believe you are part of his resistance group you will never be released. They will most likely torture you for information and probably execute you."

He put his hands on her shoulders and looked directly into her eyes. "To put it bluntly, you've got to leave Nevers before tomorrow morning. In fact you've got to leave the Occupied Zone before tomorrow morning – and you can never come back!"

Chapter 61

Marie-Claire looked at Otto in total disbelief. *No, I can't leave now – not when Emile has just found me. No, no, no!*

"Otto, I can't go now. I have to stay – just a few days."

"No Marie. If you want to survive you have to go by tomorrow morning. I assume you've heard about the shooting in Nantes?"

"Yes, I read about it in the newspaper. But what's that got to do with me?"

"If you read about it in the newspaper you'll be aware of the 15 million franc reward that was offered for information. Although it didn't help catch the assassins it resulted in a lot of greedy people betraying their resistance groups in the hope of financial gain. A French traitor in Troyes betrayed the group he was in. His list of members in his group including someone known as Tarik – your husband's resistance identity."

That name brought back painful memories of the first time she'd heard her Emile referred to as Tarik – the day the Gestapo attacked his bookshop and shot her mother.

"Someone in the Gestapo office remembered the name," Otto continued. "They then dug out the file on Tarik and handed it to Colonel Zeigler."

"Colonel Zeigler!" exclaimed Marie-Claire in surprise.

"Yes. This morning the Colonel called me into his office and showed me two photographs in the file, one of a man – Tarik, and one of a woman – you. He said 'We may not know where to find Tarik, but I think we know exactly where to find this lady, his wife'. I didn't know what to say. The Colonel then told me he felt so many people had seen him with you in Nevers that he had no choice but to come here tomorrow morning to personally arrest and interrogate you."

"Tomorrow!" gasped Marie-Claire. "The Colonel will be here tomorrow to arrest me?"

"Yes – tomorrow morning. The Colonel then gave me a surprising order. He told me I must go to Nevers immediately to prepare everything for his arrival tomorrow. He then looked me straight in the eye, handed me an envelope and said 'It contains some money for your expenses and I'm sure you'll know what to do with it.' I immediately left his office and came straight here."

He paused, then handed her an envelope. "Having looked inside I'm sure the Colonel wants me to give this to you."

She looked inside and was stunned by what she saw. Along with money the envelope contained an Ausweis pass for a female to cross the Demarcation Line at Moulins the following day, Wednesday, 29 October 1941. It was signed by the Colonel but the space for the holder's name had been left blank.

She studied it carefully then looked back at Otto. "It looks genuine. Is this for real?"

"It's absolutely genuine. As you can see he's left the name blank and I'm sure with your skills you can fill it in with whatever name you intend to use tomorrow. Let me put it this way – I don't think the Colonel wants to find you here tomorrow when he comes to arrest you."

"I'm lost for words Otto. The Colonel is risking his position, even his life, by doing this. Why?"

"You've met him and his wife and, as you and I discussed before, it appears he got his position more by marriage than by promotion. Fundamentally, he does not approve of the inhumane organization the Gestapo has become. He's being posted back to Germany at the end of this month – to an unknown fate. He's actually a good man at heart, Marie, and it's obvious he doesn't think you should be arrested and interrogated."

Marie-Claire was overwhelmed by the enormity of what Otto had just told her. "If you get a chance tomorrow please let him know how grateful I am, both for the warning and this pass. But please don't put either of you in danger by doing so. Will you be posted back to Germany as well?"

"As far as I know I'll be staying in Paris. Perhaps our paths will cross again, Marie, but hopefully at a time when I don't need to be wearing this loathsome German army uniform. Take care and may your God go with you."

Before she could respond, he turned around and walked swiftly away. *What do I do now? How can I leave just when Emile has found me? There must be some way I can stay until he gets here. But how?*

She put the envelope securely in her pocket, wheeled her bicycle out of the shed and in a mental haze cycled to see Françoise.

Françoise took one look at Marie-Claire and asked. "What's happened?"

Marie-Claire hardly knew where to begin. "When I got back to my boarding house there was a parcel for me. In it was a bottle of champagne, a broken teacup and a note." She took a deep breath. "It means Emile has found me. Françoise – he's found me!"

"That's wonderful news Marie," said Françoise giving her a big hug. "So when are you going to see him?"

Marie-Claire handed her Emile's note. Françoise read it, then asked. "Who is Anna? When's her birthday?"

"My cousin. You knew her as Mieke and then Aletta. Her birthday's on Saturday. Just four days away."

"That means you'll see him in four days time. So why aren't you looking happier?"

"Because I won't be here," answered Marie-Claire, her voice breaking with emotion.

"What do you mean you won't be here?" asked Françoise.

Marie-Claire broke down and her eyes filled with tears. "I've just been told the Gestapo intend to arrest me tomorrow and that I have to leave Nevers before tomorrow morning – it means I won't be here when Emile gets here."

She started sobbing loudly.

"Who told you this? Jerome? How would he know?"

"It wasn't Jerome. It was Otto."

"Who is Otto? You've never mentioned anyone called Otto."

Marie-Claire wiped her eyes. "Actually I have, but not by name. He's the German translator I was giving art lessons to."

"Marie, if I'm going to help you, you need to tell me the truth. Is Otto more than just a translator and an art student?"

"He works for the Gestapo, but he's not part of the Gestapo. I've known him for over a year, long before I came to Nevers, and he's strongly anti-Nazi. The Gestapo murdered his fiancée. She was Jewish and they shot her right in front of him – so he hates the Nazis just as much as we do. Every time we had an art lesson it was because he wanted to pass me some information. How do you think I knew about our deputy headmaster? Or the planned round-up of Jews?"

"You kept that quiet," said Françoise. "But I thought you told me he'd left Nevers and gone to Paris."

"He did, but he came back this afternoon just to warn me that I'll be arrested tomorrow."

"But why do they want to arrest you? Have they found out about our resistance activities?"

"No. They've been searching for Emile because he ran an active resistance group and they've discovered I'm his wife. Apparently they want to interrogate me because they think that I will know where he is."

"Oh, so it's nothing to do with our activities."

"No. I don't think they suspect any of us. Otto just said if I want to avoid being arrested I had to cross into the Unoccupied Zone at Moulins tomorrow morning."

"Cross the Line? Openly at Moulins? Are you mad?" asked Françoise. "You need an official Ausweis for that."

Marie-Claire reached in her bag and pulled out the envelope Otto had given her. "You may find it hard to believe but Otto brought this for me. Look at this. Look who's signed it."

She passed the signed Ausweis to Françoise who stared at it. "This is unbelievable." She examined it closely. "This certainly looks genuine. So what are you planning to do?"

"I don't know," said Marie-Claire. "Emile is going to be here in four days. If I leave now he may not be able to find me and I may never see him again. But the Ausweis is my only chance to escape and it's only valid for tomorrow."

"Marie. You have no choice. If you stay in Nevers you'll be arrested and then it's certain you'll never see Emile again. But if you follow Otto's suggestion and escape via Moulins then you'll still be alive and free and Emile can find you again. Only this time André and I can help him find you. There really is no choice. You've got to leave."

The logic of what Françoise said convinced Marie-Claire. She sighed deeply. "Ok, so I leave. But where can I go when I've crossed the Line? I don't know anyone in that part of France."

"You may not, but I do," said Françoise. "I know of a safe house in the unoccupied part of Moulins. Once you cross the bridge and the Demarcation Line it's off to the right in Rue de la Madeleine – about 300 metres or so from the crossing point."

Marie-Claire was about to comment on the coincidence that as a child she had lived at Place de la Madeleine in Paris when she realized she had never told Françoise that she had lived in Paris. Instead she just memorized the address and the password required to gain entry. "Do you think André would drive me to Moulins tomorrow morning? Can I even ask him?"

"Of course you can. I know he'd do anything to help you. We all will. Did you come here on your bicycle?"

"Yes."

"Then we'll cycle to his house right now. Come on. There's no time to waste. He'll know the best way to handle this whole situation."

Chapter 62

André took one look at Marie-Claire's distraught face then put an arm around her shoulder, guided her gently to the sofa and sat down beside her. "Marie. What's wrong? Have you had bad news about Emile? Has something happened to him?"

She rested her head on his shoulder and burst into tears. "I've just got a message from him – he'll be here Saturday – but I won't be – I can't be – I've got to go away."

"Marie, you're not making much sense. It's wonderful news that he's found you. So why are you saying you've got to go away?"

Marie-Claire struggled to answer as she continued sobbing so André turned to Françoise. "Do you know what she's talking about?"

"I'm not sure," answered Françoise. "She told me that the Gestapo are going to arrest her tomorrow and she has to leave before they do."

"I'm sorry but that makes no sense at all," said André. "The Gestapo do not give advance warning before they arrest people. Something's wrong here. So what's happened?"

Marie-Claire sat up and wiped her eyes. "I'll tell you what's happened. Today when I got back from school there was a parcel for me. It contained a bottle of champagne and a broken teacup. So you know who that must be from. It means Emile understood the message we sent on the BBC. There was also a note."

She pulled the note out of her jacket pocket and handed it to André. "Anna is my cousin and her birthday is on Saturday. It means that Emile expects to be in Nevers at my boarding house on Saturday."

"That's great news Marie," said André, "but why are you saying the Gestapo are going to arrest you tomorrow?"

"You know that at times I've had some critical information and I've not told you where it came from. Well it came from a translator who worked in L'Hotel de Paris, the Gestapo office. He's someone I knew before I came to Nevers and he's now based in the Gestapo offices in Paris. He came here as a friend to warn me that in trying to find Emile the Gestapo have discovered who I really am and intend to arrest me tomorrow."

André seemed sceptical. "Can you trust this person? I mean how would a translator have access to such information and how could he take time off to come and tell you? There must be more to this Marie."

"There is. He didn't take time off. You could say he was sent to warn me. Sent unofficially by the man who intends to arrest me tomorrow – Colonel Zeigler."

"Isn't he the colonel you did a portrait of?" asked André. "Now I really don't believe this story. What makes you think it's true?"

Marie-Claire reached in her bag, pulled out the envelope, extracted the Ausweis and handed it to André. "My contact gave me this. Look who has signed this Ausweis allowing me to cross the Demarcation Line at Moulins tomorrow."

André looked utterly stunned. Marie-Claire continued. "Look – the place for my name is blank so I can put in whatever name I choose to use."

"This changes everything," said André. "Of course Emile will be disappointed that you are not here on Saturday but we can take care of that. He would be much more disappointed to learn you've been arrested and possibly shot. So yes, we need to get you out of here tomorrow morning."

André paused before continuing. "You can obviously produce a convincing fake ID, but I suggest you also adopt a disguise in case the checkpoint guards are looking for you."

"What kind of disguise?" asked Marie-Claire.

"I was thinking of how Sebastien acted in the Bourges factory. He pretended to have TB. Perhaps you could do the same. You know coughing and spitting up blood."

"You could even cough up a bit of blood over your documents," suggested Françoise. "Do that as you pass them to the guards and they won't want to touch them."

"I'll need to go home to get my inks to amend my ID card and fill in this Ausweis," said Marie-Claire. "But more importantly, how am I going to get to the crossing point in Moulins and where am I going to get blood? Enough blood to cover my documents and spit some out?"

"That's not a problem," said Françoise. "I'll fetch Dr Macon. He is completely trustworthy as he often helps my parents if one of their 'friends' is injured. I'm sure he will help with blood and teach you how to cough convincingly. And while I'm getting him André can take you back to your boarding house to get your inks – and any other items you don't want the Gestapo to find."

"And as for getting to Moulins, we'll drive you there tomorrow morning," said André. "So let's all get going."

At her boarding house Marie-Claire picked up a large bag and put in it all her inks, spare ID cards and everything from the secret compartments including the money Colonel Zeigler had given her for the portraits. She added a change of clothes and the drawing she'd done of Emile. She also put in all her pencils, sketch books and the sketches she'd done, including the one she'd done of the German soldiers in the rain.

While she was packing her bag André picked up the broken teacup which was beside the bottle of champagne. "Is this the teacup? I see it's missing its handle."

"Yes that's the one which was in the box. I guess Emile must have broken the handle off before he packed it. We would have drunk the champagne out of it together. But that's not going to happen now." She sighed as she put the champagne bottle and the teacup in her bag. *I'm not leaving those behind for the Gestapo. If Emile and I can't drink it together on Saturday, then at least he can drink it with André and Françoise.*

As André helped her downstairs with the bag Madame Favier came out of her room. "Is everything alright Marie? You look as if you've been crying."

I can't tell her the truth. "I've had some news about someone I know in Troyes and I need to go and see them. André is helping me – I may be some time."

Madame Favier took a deep breath. "Did you say 'I may be some time'? I've heard that phrase before and I know what it means. Was it something to do with the box?"

André replied before Marie-Claire could say anything. "Angélique, we're in a bit of a rush. I'll come by on Friday and tell you more then."

Marie-Claire hugged Madame Favier and whispered in her ear, "Thank you for everything, Angélique. May God look after you."

She then turned around and walked quickly out to André's van before she started crying again.

As André drove Marie-Claire back to his house he asked, "Do you know what false name you're going to use this time?"

Marie-Claire thought for a moment. "Baissade, Michelle Baissade. She was my governess when I was young. She looked after me then and hopefully her spirit will do so again."

"Let's hope it does. Now listen. When you get through the checkpoint you'll need a safe house. I know of one on Rue Colombeau. After you go through the checkpoint it's on a side street to your left, less than 200 metres away."

Marie-Claire did not mention that Françoise had already given her directions to a different safe house. Instead she just thanked André and memorized the address and the password. *It's always good to have an alternative.*

Back at André's house Marie-Claire realized she didn't have any buttermilk with which to alter her ID card. "André, while I'm filling in the details on the Ausweis can you please rush down to Tomas and ask him for some buttermilk. I don't need much, just half a cup will do."

"I have some proper milk if you want some in your coffee."

"You won't believe why I want it, so please just get it."

While he was gone she entered her new name in the Ausweis, being careful to replicate the handwriting already used on the document. By the time she had finished André had returned with a small bottle of buttermilk. She applied it to her ID card and was soon able to insert her new name – Michelle Baissade.

She had just finished all her documents when Françoise arrived with Dr Macon. Without explaining the reasons, Marie-Claire asked him if he would be able to teach her how to cough as if she had TB. "I know it sounds ridiculous but I also need to be able to cough up blood so I can spit it out."

"Usually I'm asked to cure such coughs not create them, but I'm sure you have a good reason. And yes I can teach you. Am I right in assuming this is urgent?" asked Dr Macon.

"Yes. It is. I need to learn this evening."

"Coughing convincingly is not that difficult but you don't want to cough so much you lacerate your throat. If you were to do that you could get a serious infection. Instead, I think we should put some blood in a small bottle and you can then put it in your mouth just before you need to spit it out."

"Fine," said Marie-Claire, "but where am I going to get blood?"

Dr Macon smiled. "You've got plenty in your own body. We could take some out as if you were donating blood for a transfusion."

"Ok, but perhaps you should teach me how to cough first."

How ironic. Emile suffered from TB when he was a child and here I am learning how to pretend I have TB so I can escape from Nevers just days before he is due to meet me here.

While Dr Macon taught Marie-Claire how to cough as if she had severe TB, André and Françoise discussed other aspects of her disguise. They decided her clothes should have some blood splatters and her face and hands should be dirty. And as for her hair, it should be dirty and dishevelled.

"And you should also darken around your eyes. It will make you look really sick," added Dr Macon as he prepared to draw blood from Marie-Claire's arm. He soon collected enough to fill three small bottles.

"I think there's nothing more I can do Marie. I wish you well, which seems an odd thing to say having spent all this time showing you how to appear to be seriously ill."

"Thank you Dr Macon. Your help is greatly appreciated," replied Marie-Claire as she sat back on the sofa feeling rather groggy and tired.

After Dr Macon left Marie-Claire asked André to hand her the bag she had brought from the boarding house. She rummaged inside and pulled out the broken teacup and bottle of champagne. "Drink this with Emile when you find him on Saturday."

She then pulled out the sketch she had drawn of Emile. "Please, André, look after this. I daren't take it with me in case I'm searched at the checkpoint. I don't need to provide them with a picture of the man they're looking for!"

André took it and after looking at it for almost a minute spoke softly. "I'll keep it safe for you for when you return. I'll hold on to it as safely as the drawing you did of my Nicole. We're going to miss you Marie. More than you realize."

He put the drawing down and stood up. As he walked through to the kitchen Marie-Claire saw his eyes were filling with tears. "And I'll miss all of you," she replied.

Françoise picked up the drawing. "It's good we know what Emile looks like. I was wondering how we could identify him. I'll stay with Madame Favier on Saturday so we can look after him when he appears. We'll find a way of keeping him safe."

Françoise sat down beside Marie-Claire and put her arms around her. Marie-Claire leant against her friend and soon fell asleep.

At five o'clock the next morning André gently woke Marie-Claire. "It's time to get ready and go."

He had prepared some porridge for breakfast and he brought her a bowl. "You'll need all the strength you can muster today."

After breakfast they dirtied Marie-Claire's face, hands and hair. They then splattered her clothes with some blood. Remembering what Katia had shown her in the cafe, Marie-Claire stained her handkerchiefs with blood.

"Marie," said André, "I suggest you hide this little bottle of blood in a handkerchief so that just before the checkpoint you can discretely fill your mouth from it. You can then spit blood all over your documents just before you hand them over."

"And remember to apologize as you do so," added Françoise.

Although said and done with the best of intentions, their words and actions saddened Marie-Claire. She knew the reality was she was once again being forced to leave everything and everybody behind and set out into the unknown – alone – again.

Oh Emile – so near and yet so far. My friends will look after you, my dear. I know they will. They will tell you why I had to leave, and they will help find a way to bring us together.

She took a last look around André's room, picked up her bag and strode resolutely to the door. "If I have to do this, if I have to leave, then let's go."

Although the roads were relatively empty the drive south to Moulins took nearly an hour. It was seven o'clock before they arrived at Pont Régemortes, the long bridge across the Allier River. This side was the Occupied Zone, the other side was the Unoccupied Zone – relative freedom.

André parked the van up a side street and he, Françoise and Marie-Claire got out. Before setting out towards the bridge Marie-Claire took off her left shoe, put a one centime coin in her sock under her heel, put the shoe back on and stood up. "Ouch." *Thank you Emile. You were right – with this coin in my shoe I won't forget to limp.*

When the three of them reached the bridge Marie-Claire's heart fell. The checkpoint was almost 300 metres away to the west, at the far end of the very long flat bridge. There was no way she could cross quickly. She knew if she was supposed to be ill she would have to walk slowly, and with the coin in her shoe she couldn't do otherwise.

She turned to her friends. "This is as far as you should go. We mustn't let the guards see I have anybody with me."

She wanted to hug André to thank him for being such a good and close friend, even after he knew Emile was alive. She wanted to hug Françoise to say thanks for being – well for being the rock that had helped her rebuild her life after Paris.

But she didn't hug either of them.

She knew if she was genuinely suffering from TB they would

not have wanted to hug her. So, reluctantly, she had to keep her distance in case anyone saw them. Her emotions must have shown on her face as André said softly, "Don't worry Marie. We will find a way. I just want to say – I just —"

He turned away, tears streaming down his face.

Françoise put her hand on Marie-Claire's arm. "This is one of the hardest things I've ever done, but it's not the end. You will survive, and it's not goodbye. We will see each other again, I know we will."

"You're right," replied Marie-Claire, stifling her desire to hug Françoise. "It's not goodbye." In a soft voice she added, "Please, look after André."

Marie-Claire noticed Françoise's lip was quivering as she replied, "Of course I will."

"Thank you. And now I have to go – alone."

Without saying anything else Marie-Claire turned west and started hobbling along the bridge towards the checkpoint. After about twenty paces she stopped, looked back, and saw her two friends holding on to each other. She was not sure who was supporting who. She turned back towards the checkpoint, feeling even more alone.

Chapter 63

To Marie-Claire the walk across the bridge seemed to be taking an eternity. She desperately wanted to turn back. Halfway across she paused, but knew that turning back wasn't an option. Instead she resumed the slow painful walk, each step taking her away from the life she'd built over the last year and into the unknown.

I will survive. I will not give up. On Saturday when Emile meets my friends he will understand and he won't give up either. This is just a temporary set back. That's all.

As she approached the checkpoint she saw a large sign with the German words 'HALT – Demarkationslinie'. Its use of German annoyed Marie-Claire. *This is France and here we speak French. These words are obviously intended as a cruel reminder that the Germans now control our country.*

She was pleased to see that there were a growing number of people queuing to have their cards checked by the guards. *A crowd could be good – the guards may want to push me through quickly.*

While the man in front of her was having his documents examined by the guard she faked a protracted bout of coughing. As she did so she pulled out the handkerchief which hid the bottle of blood and surreptitiously transferred some from the bottle into her mouth. It tasted metallic and her instinct was to immediately spit it out. With difficulty she kept it in her mouth, trying not to gag.

Then it was her turn. The guard shouted at her in French in a harsh voice. "Cards. Show me your cards."

With shaking hands she rummaged in her bag for her ID card and Ausweis. She had made sure the Ausweis would be on the top.

As she pulled out the cards to pass them to the guard she began to cough violently. In doing so she leant over as if the coughing was hurting her and spat a fine spray of blood onto the cards. "Pardon, pardon, Monsieur," she blurted out as she held out the now blood-covered cards to the guard.

He had stepped back while she was coughing. He eyed the cards with fear and disgust written all over his face and did not take them from her. He peered at the top card – the Ausweis. "Your name. What is your name?"

"Michelle," she stuttered, "Michelle Baissade." She coughed again, spitting the last of the blood in her mouth onto the roadway.

"Where are you going?" demanded the guard.

Between coughs she answered. "My priest said – I need to – go to Lourdes."

She doubled up in a prolonged coughing fit. "He said – only God – could cure me."

She became concerned when a second guard approached. They spoke in German and she gave no indication she understood. "What's holding you up, Gunter? Oh my God. I can see why you don't want to touch those cards. What has she got? Is it TB?"

"I think so. Advanced stage – she's coughing up blood. She said she's heading to Lourdes, probably to seek a miracle."

"It will take more than a miracle to heal this wreck. I see she's got an Ausweis." Without getting too close, he leant over and peered at the Ausweis. "It looks valid."

"It's properly dated and signed," said Gunter. "I saw that clearly before she coughed up all over it."

The second guard looked closely at Marie-Claire who was shaking and beginning to cough again. She noticed that the other people waiting to cross were backing away from her and she also noticed that the queue behind her was now quite long, with people looking at her impatiently.

"Gunter. We don't want her hanging around here. She's so sick she won't even make it to Lourdes."

"So, do I let her pass or send her back?"

Marie-Claire was horrified by his question and started coughing to hide her reaction. She wished she had more blood to spit out.

"We don't want sick people on our side of the Line. If she dies on our side we'll have to fill out all those damn papers. So let her through. She can die over there."

Gunter laughed, shrugged his shoulders, turned to Marie-Claire

408

and barked at her in French. "Move. Get going. You're through. Get out of here."

Hiding her feeling of elation, she slowly turned west and started hobbling towards freedom.

She continued coughing and spluttering as she limped away. She was soon far enough away from the checkpoint that the guards would no longer be able to see her amongst the crowd waiting to cross over in the other direction to their jobs in Moulins.

She came to a road junction and had to decide between the two safe houses. She was exhausted from coughing and the pain in her foot from the centime coin was becoming excruciating so she decided to head towards the closest, the one André had told her about on Rue Colombeau.

She had not gone far in that direction when someone stepped in front of her, "Halt! Fräulein! Papers please."

She started to panic but then realized she knew the voice. She looked up at the man in front of her. "This time I really want to know what you're doing here Otto. Aren't I supposed to be arrested in Nevers, not Moulins?"

"I thought you would be coming this way and I've been waiting and looking out for you. Your disguise is so good I almost missed you. To make this look normal show me your papers."

He recoiled slightly as she pulled the bloodied cards from her bag. "Your coughing and cards are very convincing. I can see why they didn't hold you back."

"Are you arresting me? And if so why did you wait until now that I'm across the Line?"

"I'm not arresting you, and I don't have long. It would have been ironic to have you go through all this trauma to escape the Nazis only to be arrested by the French police."

"What do you mean?"

"Acting on information from the Gestapo, the French police will be raiding a safe house this morning and I wanted to warn you in case you were heading to it. I'm glad I came as you appear to be going in the direction of that very house."

"Where is this safe house that I should avoid?"

She gasped and swallowed hard when he replied, "Rue Colombeau. Apparently they intend to raid it this morning."

"Is that the only raid they're planning?"

"Yes. It's the only one."

"Otto, thank you for coming all this way to warn me. You've saved my life yet again. But why? Why are you willing to risk everything for me?"

"I lost Greta to the Nazis, and I didn't want to lose another friend if there was anything I could do about it. That's why I came looking for you. Make use of your life Marie – please keep fighting – you will win in the end. Now I must leave you. I've got to get back to Nevers to meet our Colonel at ten o'clock."

Before she could say another word he turned away and disappeared into the crowd heading towards the bridge.

Rue Colombeau! I would have been caught if I'd gone there. I know I'm in the Unoccupied Zone but I've been told the Vichy government is basically a Nazi puppet and the French police hand their prisoners over to the Gestapo. How ironic that I've been saved by a German, yet again. Thank you Otto – may your God go with you.

She turned around and began heading towards the safe house that Françoise had told her about. *Further away, but safer.*

After just a few steps she stopped and rebuked herself. *Marie-Claire, you have information which could save lives. The people at that safe house are risking their lives in the fight against the Nazis. How would you feel if someone could have saved you and your friends but instead turned away to save their own skin. Even though you don't know the people on Rue Colombeau you cannot abandon them. Think of the Deferres, think of André's line. Otto risked his life to save yours – you now need to risk yours to save the people in that safe house.*

She turned around and headed towards the safe house on Rue Colombeau as quickly as her hobbling gait could carry her.

At the safe house she knocked on the door. Not once but three times as André had told her to do. An older woman answered, took one look at Marie-Claire and tried to shut the door in her face, but

Marie-Claire stuck her foot in the doorway. She quickly spoke the first part of the password. "Has Genevieve gone to Toulouse?"

The woman looked surprised and responded with the correct second phrase. "Amandine went to Marseille last week."

When Marie-Claire replied with the third phrase, "Pity, I had a message from Alix," the lady opened the door and let Marie-Claire in. The moment the door was closed Marie-Claire spoke rapidly. "You've got to leave immediately. The French police will be raiding this house this morning."

The lady looked Marie-Claire up and down with obvious disapproval and asked, "And how would you know this?"

"Don't waste your time questioning me. I told you, the police will be here very soon and you need to leave."

"Wait here," said the lady as she turned and went into a back room. She only partially shut the door and Marie-Claire was able to hear her talking to someone. "There's a strange woman here claiming that the French police will be here soon to raid this house. She knew the passwords but I'm not sure we can trust her."

"What does she look like?"

"She's not old but she looks very sick. I hate asking you to check her out, Eugene, as you're the one who's supposed to be hiding here. Normally I would ask Justin, but with him away I wonder if you could talk to her and see what you think."

"Alright, I'll talk to her but come back with me. You can watch her reactions."

When the door opened and the man came into the room, Marie-Claire's heart almost stopped. She stared, unable to say anything.

The man looked at Marie-Claire with a look of complete amazement. "Is that you? Is that really you?"

Before Marie-Claire could answer, the lady interjected, "Eugene, do you know this woman?"

"Know her? Of course I do – she's my wife."

Marie-Claire limped over to Emile and took his hand in hers. "I can hardly believe it's really you. Until I heard your radio message on the BBC I thought you were dead, killed in the bookshop."

He squeezed her hand tightly. "No. I'm very much alive. I escaped from the bookshop. But what's happened to you? You look seriously ill."

"Don't worry. I know I look awful but there's nothing wrong with me. It's a disguise so I could escape."

"Escape? Escape from what?" asked Emile.

"I'll explain later but right now we've got to leave. The police are on their way."

Emile turned to the lady. "If my wife says we've got to leave then I'm going with her right now. Stay if you want, but you've been warned." He dashed upstairs and returned with a small bag. He then opened the front door, peered up and down the street and whispered, "All clear." He took Marie-Claire's hand and they headed out into the street.

The lady of the house had obviously changed her mind and decided to take Marie-Claire's warning seriously. "I've got to find Justin and warn him. Take care Eugene." She grabbed her coat and bag, closed the door behind her and hurried off up the street.

Emile and Marie-Claire headed off in the opposite direction. They had just turned off Rue Colombeau into Rue du Chambon when three police cars came roaring down Rue Colombeau in the direction of the safe house. Emile grabbed Marie-Claire's arm and pulled her quickly into a tight embrace. After the cars passed they both breathed a sigh of relief.

Marie-Claire rested her head against his shoulder. "I've often dreamt of having you hold me again, but not in circumstances like this. That was close. I'm so glad I reached the house in time."

"So am I. It's wonderful to see you and there's so much to talk about, but right now we need to get well away from here. We need to hurry but you're limping. Can you go any faster?"

Marie-Claire laughed and took off her shoe. She took out the one centime coin and put her shoe back on. "It's a trick my wonderful husband taught me last year before he disappeared," she said as they set off again, walking quickly.

"You're the one who disappeared," replied Emile. "You can tell me about that later but right now I sense you're walking very purposefully – do you know of somewhere safe we can go?"

"Françoise told me of a safe house on Rue de la Madeleine."

"Did you say Rue de la Madeleine? Really? Are you confusing it with Place de la Madeleine where your mother lived in Paris?"

"No. It's on Rue de la Madeleine. A strange coincidence isn't it? Perhaps Maman is still looking after me. Françoise gave me the details. The house is not far from here."

"Who is this Françoise person? Can we trust her?"

"Absolutely. She's one of my résistante friends in Nevers. But you've just reminded me – she and André will be expecting to see you on Saturday to tell you I had to escape. They'll be very worried when you don't turn up."

"So you got my package?"

"Yes. And your message about drinking a toast on Anna's birthday. But what can we do to let my friends know we're safe and together? They'll be worried if you're not there on Saturday."

"Are you saying they know about the champagne and the broken teacup?"

"Yes, they heard your BBC message and they know about you. Actually, André helped me devise my reply to your message. Last night as I was preparing to escape he even commented on the teacup you sent in the parcel – the one that is missing its handle."

Emile smiled at his wife. "Then I know exactly how we can tell your friends that we are together. We'll send them a teacup with its broken handle obviously glued back on."

"That's perfect," said Marie-Claire. "We'll do that as soon as we get somewhere safe." She looked at her husband, put her arms around him and held him tightly. "And wherever we end up, I'm never ever going to let you go."

413

AUTHOR'S NOTES

MY NEVERS CONNECTION

This picture of German soldiers exercising in Nevers was drawn in 1941 by my French aunt, Marie-Thérèse Pellissier, when she was an art teacher in a school in Nevers. When not teaching or drawing she spent time forging documents for the resistance and sometimes blowing up fuel dumps. On one such occasion she was given a ride back to Nevers from a German General. One day she received warning of her imminent arrest. After being coached that night by her doctor, she escaped the following day across the Demarcation Line to the Free Zone of France. At the checkpoint she pretended to be a seriously ill TB patient spitting blood all over her documents as she handed them to the guards. Not surprisingly, she was waved through without inspection.

REFERENCE MATERIAL

The following items were used during the research phase.

BOOKS

Anderson, Janice; *World War II Witness Accounts*; 2009

Bailey, Roderick; *Forgotten Voices of the Secret War;* 2009 (Recorded words from active SOE agents and handlers)

British War Office; *Home Guard Manual*; 1941

Brooks, T.W.; *British Propaganda to France 1940-1944 (Annexe One – Evidence);* 2007

Buckmaster, Maurice; *They Fought Alone*; 1958

Cobb, Richard; *French and Germans, Germans and French;* 1983

Darman, Peter (Ed); *World War II – A Day by Day History*; 2007

Eparvier, Jean; *A Paris Sous La Botte Des Nazis;* November 1944 (Photographs taken during the occupation)

Foot, M.R.D. & Langley, J.M.; *MI9 – Escape and Evasion*; 1979

Foot, M.R.D.; *SOE in France*; 1976

Grose, Peter; *A Good Place to Hide*; 2014

Halls, Monty; *Escaping Hitler*; 2017

Hilberg, Raul; *The Destruction of the European Jews;* 2003

Hitler, Adolf; *Mein Kampf*; (Ford translation and Murphy Translation); 1924

Kaminsky, Sarah; *Adolfo Kaminsky – A Forger's Life*; 2016

Lewis, Damien; *Churchill's Secret Warriors;* 2014

Lucas, Laddie (Ed); *Voices in the Air, 1939-1945*; 2003 *(Words from those who were there)*

Macintyre, Ben; *Agent Zigzag*; 2007

Mortimer, Gavin; *World War II In Secret – The Hidden Conflict 1939-1945*; 2015

Sebba, Anne; *Les Parisiennes – How the Women of Paris Lived, Loved and Died in the 1940's;* 2016

Sergis, Anie; *Education in France during World War II*; 1991 (PhD Thesis at Loyola University Chicago)

Special Operations Executive; (Facsimile of SOE training documents) published as *Secret Agent's Pocket Manual 1939-1945*

Verneret, Hubert; *Teenage Resistance Fighter*; 2017 (Translated from *Que Faisiez-vous au Temps Chaud?* 1972)

NEWSPAPERS

NOTE: Dates cover period examined, not publication life

Défense de la France; resistance underground newspaper; 10 Sept 1941

Le Courrier de l'Air; British news sheet dropped over France by Royal Air Force (issues of 18 March 1941 and July 1941)

La Croix; French daily newspaper; 1940

Le Matin; French daily newspaper; 1939-1941

L'Oeuvre; French daily newspaper; 1940-1941

Le Petit Parisien; major French daily newspaper; 1936-1941

FILMS

Odette; (1950); (True story of secret agent Odette Sansom with a bit piece starring Colonel Maurice Buckmaster, the actual person in charge of the French section of SOE)

School For Danger OR *Now It Can Be Told*; (1947) (UK Office of Information); starring people who were SOE agents.

OTHER ITEMS

Armistice Agreement Between The German High Command Of The Armed Forces And French Plenipotentiaries; June 22, 1940

BBC – Page 3 of Personal Messages Broadcast to the French resistance the evening of 5 June 1944 - the day before D-Day

Nuremberg Trial Proceedings, Volume 6; Forty-Second Day 1946 (Presentation of German documents relating to hostages*)*

Photocopy of British leaflet in French dropped on Nevers (courtesy of Royal Air Force Museum)

Photocopy of British leaflet in French from *Workers of Coventry to the Workers of France – May 1 1941* (courtesy of the Resistance Museum of Nevers)

Photographs of Nevers taken by a German soldier 1940 including Rue de Calvaire (https://www.vintag.es/2022/04/france-1940s.html)

Recording of De Gaulle's Speech to the French June 22, 1940 (recorded by BBC)

Text of General de Gaulle's 3 critical resistance inspiring BBC broadcasts of 18, 19 & 22 June 1940

Titre I – Signaux, Règlement Général De Sécurité; Société Nationale des Chemins de Fer Français; 1941 (*Signal regulations for French trains 1941*)

Printed in Great Britain
by Amazon

63338173R00241